GUILTY IN MISSISSIPPI

PERCY LYNCHARD

GUILTY IN MISSISSIPPI

PERCY LYNCHARD

To my wife, Vanessa. Raised in the hills of Mississippi,
she took a chance on an old Delta boy like me.
Without her I would be nothing.

CHAPTER 1

The Mississippi Delta, that flat and fertile floodplain created by the Mississippi River eons ago that lies between Memphis, Tennessee and Vicksburg, Mississippi, is severed in half vertically, by U.S Highway 61. The same highway whose bars and juke joints gave birth to the blues. As the highway meanders through fields of cotton, soybeans, corn and occasionally rice on its way to Baton Rouge, Louisiana and beyond, it connects the Delta towns of Cleveland and Shaw, Mississippi. Somewhere in between the two towns, Trunkline Road, a paved county road, runs east off of Highway 61 past a spattering of small farm houses, barns and sheds mixed into the fields of cotton across the landscape, until it plays out into gravel about four miles later, cutting through the heart of what is locally known as Interstate Woods, a community so named for the Interstate Logging Company that had cleared the timber from it many years back. About a half mile from its paved ending, a small farmhouse sat on a lengthy private drive in the middle of a cotton field, the home to the Strawberry family, one of the many farm families who make their living from the rich soil of the Delta. The farm was probably no larger than 200 acres, most unlike those conjured up in the minds and movies of Hollywood, but certainly tiny in comparison to some Delta farms. The house sat on the banks of Porter's Bayou with cotton fields on three sides and a large tract of bottomland hardwoods behind it. The closest neighbor was a quarter mile away, with the closest town of any size being Shaw, still some 8 miles in the distance.

The weather in August in Mississippi can be as brutal as February in Minnesota but on opposite ends of the spectrum. While Minnesotans avoid the outdoors in February so as to steer clear of the frigid temperatures, those in Mississippi do likewise in August to escape the searing heat and humidity that hits a crescendo at that time of year. The air, filled with the mixed smell of honeysuckle, bitterweed and defoliate, becomes still most of the time allowing the heat and its cohort, humidity, to settle over the countryside like a thick wool blanket, making breathing difficult, sapping a person's energy and almost completely prohibiting any outside activity. The old adage exchanged among the citizenry, "if you think it's hot now, wait 'til August" was more of a warning than mere passing conversation. Even the nighttime brought little relief because, though the temperature fell a few degrees, the mosquitoes were then active, having hidden from the heat themselves during the day. They came in swarms like a biblical plague from the irrigation ditches and bayous, feasting on blood drawn from any exposed skin. And so it was on that night in August of 1969, that everyone huddled in their homes, desperately trying to sidestep the sting of summer, whether derived from the heat or the mosquitoes, at least those who didn't have to be out and about by necessity, and were totally unaware of the danger about to descend upon their community.

Linda, the eldest of the two Strawberry children stood before the mirror on her dresser brushing her hair in preparation for bed, dressed only in blue bikini panties, her long brown hair falling below her shoulders before it curled back up on its end. She was proud of herself and the way she looked which made her even more eager to begin her senior year of high school which seemed to her would never arrive, but in reality, was only three weeks away. This would be her year—the year she would be the proverbial belle of the ball in anything that mattered to her. Things that meant everything to high school girls, like cheerleading, beauty review and even class officer elections, all lay ahead and would be hers for the taking. She had already discovered the effect she had on boys and was slowly, but surely mastering the art of being a first-class tease. The boys and the rest of the world was hers for the taking.

In the front yard of the Strawberry house, alone in the darkness, a man was watching. He had been there since just before her family had left, backing into the high cotton to conceal himself as they passed him on the long gravel driveway. He sweated and swatted the mosquitos, but otherwise remained motionless, intently watching the home. He had seen her turn off the television in the front room and watched the light in one of the back rooms come on, her bedroom that she shared with her sister, and he knew from past times that he had watched, that she was readying for bed. He had been patient those other times watching the house and tonight was no different. He had little to do and all night to do it. Those other times he had watched as she and her sister had gone through this same routine while talking or arguing about different things. He knew which bed was hers and which belonged to the sibling. He knew which room of the small frame house was the bedroom of the parents and how they generally went to bed just before the girls. There was no need for the occupants to pull any curtains as no one could see as far off the road as the house was situated and he had capitalized on that. He had their routine down to a fine art and most importantly, tonight he knew she was alone. But tonight, would be different. The urges that had infatuated him in the past had reached a crescendo and could no longer be ignored but had to be fulfilled. He was force driven by his rage and desires and had yielded his will to them.

He entered the home by simply walking through the front door. It wasn't locked because no one in this rural community had ever seen the need to do so. He slowly and methodically shut the door behind him, and proceeded toward the back of the house. He was an apex predator on the hunt and was enjoying the feeling. He smelled the scent of perfume and bath powder as he got closer to her bedroom and was excited by it, and he heard her softly singing to herself. He smiled to himself when he saw a single stocking lying on the floor in the hall near the bathroom. Then, after he bent down to pick it up and had felt its silkiness, he became aroused.

It can only be speculated as to whether she saw him before he grabbed her around the throat. Maybe seconds before the attack she had seen him in the mirror as she brushed her hair, but that was mere speculation. She may have heard him shuffle from the front of the house to her bedroom and thought simply that the family was back. It will never be known.

What is known is that she was strangled to death by one of her own stockings from behind. She had been raped after her death on her sister's bed, her underwear torn from her. She had not put up much of a struggle as the only visible wounds were from strangulation—bruising about the neck and ruptured blood vessels within each eye. Her painted nails were unbroken and no skin from the perpetrator was found underneath. As for the rape, there was trauma to the genitals, but little blood because the act was postmortem. There was semen both in the body as well as on the bed. He had walked in, strangled and raped her, then left. Nothing appeared to be missing from the house and nothing in the bedroom was in disarray except some makeup and toiletries found near her dresser.

When the man had finished, he drew up his pants and sat on the bed next to his victim, still panting from the sexual act. He looked at her eyes which were wide open, staring into eternity, and then gently ran the back of his hand across the side of her face. Even in her grotesque state she was beautiful to him and he wished in his mind he could linger longer with her. When he had sufficiently recuperated, he stood, patted her naked derriere, and as quietly as he had entered the home, he left it, the hot and humid Delta night swallowing him.

@ @ @ @ @ @

Dewitt and Estelle Strawberry, parents to their two gorgeous teenage daughters, had taken the youngest one with them to the East Bolivar County Hospital to visit a relative who had been admitted the previous day with heart palpitations, leaving Linda at home alone for no other reason than she "just wasn't feeling good". At 17 it seemed she was never feeling good when it came time for family functions, a disease that seemed to afflict most adolescents at that time in their lives. It had become much more of a hassle to argue and have her join them unwillingly these days than to just let her be. She had been this way for the past few months and her parents had thrown their hands in the air and surrendered. By 9:30 that night they began the twenty-minute ride back home from the hospital.

"Daddy, I'm thirsty, can we stop for a coke?" asked Carolyn, the youngest daughter.

"I wish you had gotten one back at the hospital," her father replied. "Had plenty time there."

"But, I didn't want to leave Aunt Ruth's room."

"Ok, ok. We'll stop at the Pic-a-Bit, but just a coke—nothing else."

People blame themselves too often when tragedy occurs, in a self-made effort to erase the past. Some wonder if things would have turned out differently if they had called upon a troubled friend or relative the day that person committed suicide. Others bemoan the route they took when they are involved in a terrible automobile accident. For the Strawberry family, they wished they had insisted that Linda go with them that night. Despite her resistance and foul mood, she would still be alive if only they had insisted. Though that may have been the case, unbeknownst to them, their stop at the local convenience store for a soda after leaving the hospital may well have given the perpetrator just the right amount of time to act, then slip silently away. If not for the stop, they may have actually arrived in time to see and identify the man who would single-handily destroy their world and send panic throughout the community. Speculation, though, accomplished little.

CHAPTER 2

Only a few short years prior to the Strawberry murder, Tyrone Braid sat in the hall outside the parole hearing room in the administration building of the Mississippi State Penitentiary at Parchman, Mississippi, the notorious plantation prison known throughout the South and beyond simply as Parchman Farm. It had deservedly earned its reputation for generations as a brutal institution for its policy of hard work by the prisoners in the agricultural fields, cruel and pitiless punishment toward its inmates by the free world guards and the trusted inmates who also served as guards, and for its desolate location in the midst of the Mississippi Delta where temperatures were extreme in both summer and winter, the only two seasons that Mississippi seemed to experience. At just 20 years of age, Tyrone had spent the better part of the last 18 months as inmate number MS32256 where he had been housed at the First Offender's Camp along with approximately 75 other inmates, the vast majority of which, like Tyrone, were black.

As he sat handcuffed and shackled to a wooden bench that ran along the cinder block walls of the building, he watched the hustle and bustle of clerical activity among the free world employees, enjoyed the air conditioning of the building (something he had not had the opportunity to do since he was admitted there a year and a half ago) and said a silent prayer under his breath that the scheduled parole hearing that he was about to endure would prove successful for him. This was his first chance at parole and, like most inmates, was well aware that parole didn't come easily, particularly on your first attempt, but he had no choice but to be optimistic. To think otherwise would do nothing but increase the pangs of depression that had haunted him on a daily basis since his arrival there.

He shifted his body on the hard bench in an effort to get more comfortable and caused the cuffs and chains to grate against the bench, leaving a scuff mark on its heavy wood, one of many marks from previous inmates bound there before him. His mind wandered back to his admission there, a short time ago by most sentences, and he pondered the circumstances that had gotten him to this point.

He had been in high school not long before his legal troubles began, a star running back for the all-black McEvans High School football team in Shaw, Mississippi. That seemed like a lifetime ago to him now, a place and time where he was a Friday night hero and a Saturday celebrity among the black population there. However, he was a big fish in a very small lake, so when his senior year had ended, he had been put out into the world as a high school graduate with no chance at any further education in a society where his kind had nothing but common labor to look forward to as a career. Even that wasn't easy to find.

Tyrone's father had abandoned him, the oldest of the three children, along with the rest of the family, his mother, brother and sister, when he was 13. If anyone knew why he left, they never said. His mother had been ill with cancer for the better part of a year before he left, and the disease was spreading. Maybe his father had grown tired of caring for her or maybe he had grown tired of a life that was hard enough without the additional burden of a sickly wife and three young children. Who knew, really? One day he was just gone and never returned or contacted them. His mother fought hard, but in the end, the cancer won out as it almost always seems to do, and she passed away on Tyrone's 15th birthday.

Tyrone and his siblings, Darcel, the youngest, and John lived with their paternal grandparents for much of the time until Tyrone had graduated, at which time he and his siblings returned to the former home of their parents where they had grown up before their mother's death and lived there alone with the help of their Uncle Lonnie and a few other distant family members. There they remained together until Tyrone entered Parchman Farm which was devastating, not only because Tyrone lost his freedom, but because his two younger siblings depended on him for support, both financial and moral.

A permanent job of any kind had eluded Tyrone, though he looked hard and was not afraid to work. He did odd jobs around the Delta for anyone who needed plumbing, carpentry, painting, landscaping or, of course, agricultural work. It was the landscaping work that brought him to the employ of the Courtney family, white residents of Shaw who often needed yard work on the grounds of their brick home, a home that to Tyrone was a mansion, but to most, was a typical, working class home to any number of white families in the area. Mrs. Virginia Courtney was approaching her 40s but looked like she had just finished her junior year at Ole Miss and was ready to begin her senior year there with the rest of the Kappa Deltas. With brown hair and green eyes atop a shapely frame, she was surely the fantasy of many, and that included Tyrone. The shorts and halter top that she often wore didn't help matters for him.

"Tyrone, if you will finish trimming the hedges along the carport and put all of the tools you used back in the shed, I think that will be all for today," Mrs. Courtney told him. "I'm going to go ahead and pay you now, because I've got to get ready for something I have this evening," she told him as she handed him two dollars.

"Thank you, ma'am. I'll get in touch with you next week about cuttin' the grass for you," he responded.

"That'll be fine," she said as she turned to go back in the house. He watched her leave and marveled at her shape. At his age, it didn't take much to stir the hormones or make the testosterone rise.

Tyrone had returned to his work and was putting tools away when he heard the unmistakable sound of water running in the bathroom within the home. His mind reeled with thoughts of the pale-skinned beauty soaking in a bubble filled tub, and he gave in to the urge to have a look through the window. He slowly raised his head to the level of the small window, which had no curtain or shade because it looked into the brushy backyard of the Courtney's, out of the vision of any neighbor or passerby. Sure enough, there she was, totally nude with her back to him as she prepared her bath. He lingered a millisecond too long and was enthralled in her nakedness when she turned around and was face to face with him.

When Tyrone was subsequently arrested, he was scared and concerned, but had no idea of the gravity of the situation. He knew some guys who had been charged as a "Peeping Tom" before as juveniles and they merely had to appear for a good tongue lashing in court. What he didn't know or didn't consider, was that the charge was a felony in Mississippi, he was black and the victim was white. The fact that it was Mississippi in 1966 was the final factor that sealed his doom. He never had a chance. The charge was not reduced to a misdemeanor, though that was common, and the star running back found himself Parchman bound in a matter of a few short months.

An overweight, white, free world guard, sweating profusely, approached Tyrone as he continued to ride the bench outside the hearing room. He was friendly, but gruff with his orders.

"Let's go, Braid. It's your turn to be denied parole," he told him as he unlocked the cuffs from the bench, but left his hands shackled.
"Yes sir, boss, but I'm more optimistic than you," he returned.
"Just tryin' not to get your hopes up, boy," the guard grunted back.

As Tyrone entered the room, he was met by five stern looking white men sitting behind a table in front of a single chair, none wearing a coat, but all five with white shirts and thin dark ties of various colors. He was ordered to sit in the chair and for the first time since he had been transported earlier that morning, his hands were then freed. He rubbed his wrists in an effort to restore the circulation in his hands left that way by the tightness of the handcuffs and because he was nervous as well.

A reel to reel tape recorder sat on the table in front of the men and the middle board member turned it on and started the reels to turning, a continual red light showing from the machine. A large woman sat on the end of the long table with a small spiral tablet and pen, obviously skilled in shorthand dictation.

"The record will reflect that we are proceeding in the parole hearing of Tyrone Braid, inmate number MS32256 at the administration building of the state penitentiary at Parchman, Mississippi on this the 15th day of May, 1968. All board members are present as is the inmate," Member 3 and obviously the chairman, dictated mechanically, something he had undoubtedly done hundreds of times. He was meticulous with the introduction to the point of being mechanical.

Thereafter, each member was introduced to Tyrone and the requisite facts of his conviction, sentence and conduct reports were placed into the record. Shortly, the hearing turned into a question and answer session with the board members asking the questions and Tyrone providing the answers.

"I see from your conduct record that you were involved in an altercation with another inmate the week of your arrival here that resulted in injuries to both of you. Do you remember that incident and want to elaborate on it?" the chairman asked.

"Yes, sir, I remember it well. Another inmate came at me in the chow line and took the cornbread from my plate. I tried to get it back and he hit me, so we fought," Tyrone responded.

"Do you regret that action?" the chairman inquired.

"No, sir, I don't," Tyrone responded, obviously causing a discomfort to all. "I mean, I hate it happened, but if I hadn't fought him, I'd a been his boy for the rest of my sentence. His and everybody else's."

Though the answer had originally raised the eyebrows of the entire board, most seemed satisfied with his explanation.

"What can you say positive about your stay here, Braid?" Member 1 asked, a ridiculous question to pose to someone who had just spent the last 18 months in the most vicious and violent institution in the United States.

"I don't know, sir. I was hoping when I got out of high school that I didn't have to go to Vietnam, so I guess I got my wish," he said with a grin, looking at his feet and shuffling them.

The entire board, except for the uptight Member 1, erupted into uncontrollable laughter as did Tyrone. Member 1 simply tightened his lips and looked at Tyrone with disdain. When the laughter stopped and order was returned, the chairman asked Member 1 if he had any other questions, to which he replied, "I don't think I need to know any more."

"What are your plans, Inmate Braid, upon your release from here?" posed Member 4.

"I plan to go back home which is here in Sunflower County over near Shaw. I lived with my younger brother and sister and they need me."

"What about employment, do you have any ideas?"

"Yes, sir. My uncle has a farm and a store and I might be able to work for him."

"I see you're alone today, did none of your folks want to be here for you?" asked Member 5.

"My father left when I was 13 and my mother is dead. I didn't know anyone else could come, so I really didn't let anybody know," he said.

"I'd like to know if you have any regrets," Member 2 stated.

"Yes, I do, sir. I think about it every day and wish I could take back what I did, but I can't. I've asked God for forgiveness and I'm straight with him," he said, exposing the strict religious upbringing he had experienced at the Pilgrim's Rest MB Church. "I sent a letter apologizin' to Mrs. Courtney more than a year ago. I'd tell her to her face if I could. She a nice lady."

The banter went on for the better part of thirty minutes before the board tired of the questions and told him they would consider his parole and let him know in due course. The same sweaty guard was summoned and after cuffing him again, Tyrone was returned to the barracks at the First Offender's Camp just in time for the noon meal of hamburger patties, veggies and cornbread, all grown and produced from within the penitentiary.

Riding back to his camp in the prison station wagon, he sat cuffed in the back seat and watched as they passed the fields of cotton, vegetables and soybeans. He saw the endless rows and the many prisoners working them, knowing he would be joining them in a short time, just as any other day. The heat and humidity at that time of day had to be a matching one hundred degrees and percent, respectively. Just another day on Parchman Farm.

He wanted to hear some good news terribly, of course, but had no way to gauge the board. All except for Member 1, of obviously. He was certain that pious jackass didn't want him to go anywhere and probably would have extended his sentence if he could. To put it simply, he was a young black man who had been forced into the frightening and terrifying world of incarceration, didn't know what to expect from day to day and only had his dreams of freedom to keep him going. He had been sodomized by other inmates on more than one occasion since he had "broken in to Parchman" as the locals called a prisoner's arrival at the penitentiary, been worked like a slave and been abused by guards, both trusty and free world, on a daily basis. Parchman was a horrendous and traumatic experience for anyone, much less a young man and Tyrone desperately wanted to get out and put it all behind him.

When he returned to the camp and was eating with the rest of the inmates, Big James, a lifer who had to be at least 60 years old, and looked all of 75 because of what prison life does to a man, began a conversation with him. Big James had been at Parchman Farm for at least 30 years, stood 6' 4" and weighed no less that 285 pounds. He had befriended Tyrone from the time he first entered the prison gates. Big James was assigned to the first offender's camp as a trusty guard, and his size and demeanor demanded respect from everyone except the highest ranked free world guards.

"What yo chances Tyrone, any way to know? He asked.

"Don't have a clue. I know one of 'em was against me, but ain't got no idea 'bout the rest," Tyrone responded.

"Odds say your first time ain't gonna turn out good," Big James told him. "I'll say a prayer, but don't get too excited."

Sometime that afternoon, another trusty guard summoned Tyrone from the field and his job of picking butterbeans to see the camp boss. Upon his arrival, he was informed with little fanfare that the board had approved his parole! He would be out of Parchman within the next 30 days, barring some unforeseen calamity, and would almost immediately be transferred from the First Offender's Camp to the Pre-Release Center to begin his transition from incarceration to the free world.

Tyrone openly wept for the first time since he arrived at the penitentiary. Any other time he would have suffered harassment and bullying from the other inmates and even the guards, but after receiving this news, there was no problem. He was looked upon as somewhat of a celebrity once again and nobody would bother him. Even convicted felons understood his joy and simply envied him. He dropped to his knees in front of the boss's desk and somehow through the tears thanked God for answering his prayers.

Big James came over and congratulated him on his good fortune. Free world people would have probably hugged each other, but in the presence of other inmates, to do so would have signaled weakness, so they merely shook hands.

"I'm happy for you," he told Tyrone, and then gave him an ominous warning: "You remember this though, boy. It don't take much to be guilty in Mississippi. Since you is black, you halfway there. You watch yo step every day, you hear? And don't you never come back here."

Tyrone thanked his friend for the advice, then threw his hands into the air.

"Thank you, Jesus, thank you! I promise you, I'll never come back to this place," he prayed aloud. "My nightmare is over!". Only the good Lord knew for certain.

CHAPTER 3

While Tyrone was enthusiastically counting down the days to his release from prison, in adjoining Bolivar County at the same time, another young man, only slightly older, was sitting in the reception area outside the office of the District Attorney for the 11th Circuit District of Mississippi. Like Tyrone, he had visions of a better life ahead and was eagerly hoping for it to begin sooner than later. Paul Lane shuffled nervously in his chair watching the secretary perform her daily rituals of answering the phone, taking messages and shuffling papers. He had scored an interview with the DA for a job as an investigator and was keeping his fingers crossed that he could be impressive enough today to land it. The air-conditioned room with the smell of cheap perfume from the secretary mingled with the smell of mimeograph ink kept him at attention. He muttered a silent prayer as he waited.

Like Tyrone, he was the product of the Mississippi Delta and had spent nearly his entire life there. He had been born there, lived there, educated there and worked there, but that was where the similarities between he and Tyrone would end.

Unlike Tyrone, Paul was white, and though he certainly wasn't born with a silver spoon shoved into his mouth, his parents could by no means be considered poor. Paul had had the luxury of completing high school and then moving on to obtain a bachelor's degree from Delta State College there in his hometown of Cleveland. Though he had to work part-time to get it done, he finished his degree and was accepted into the Ole Miss School of Law, something that wasn't remotely possible for the likes of Tyrone.

The phone buzzed on the secretary's desk and she immediately answered it. Looking toward Paul as she hung up the phone, she smiled and told him, "Mr. Fall will see you now. Last door on the right. The office at the end of the hall."

"Thank you, ma'am," Paul said as he returned the smile. He stood, straightened his tie, brushed back the front of his dark brown hair with the palm of his hand, took a deep breath and headed down the hall.

The office was filled with the usual government supplied furnishings: walnut desk with a green-shaded banker's lamp on the right side, credenza crammed with numerous law books and two wooden chairs in front of the desk. Framed prints of ducks hung on the walls along with the requisite diplomas and certificates of admissions to the various state and federal courts. A large wooden replica of the official seal of the State of Mississippi commanded one's attention taking up nearly one wall.

"Hello Paul, I'm Landon Fall," he said as he stood from his high back chair and extended his hand. "I'm glad you could make it."

You're glad? I wouldn't have missed this opportunity if they were burying my brother today, Paul thought to himself.

"It's an honor, sir," Paul returned as the two shook hands and tried to size the other up.

"Have a seat and can I get you anything to drink?" Landon inquired.

"Not a thing, sir", Paul responded, though his mouth was dry as the Sahara. They exchanged pleasantries for a few minutes and then got down to the purpose of the meeting.

"I want to talk about the elephant in the room, Paul. Tell me why a young lawyer with a reputable practice in a growing county like DeSoto is interested in a job with me as an investigator. You have to be making more money now than this job pays."

He gets straight to the point Paul thought.

"Two reasons, Mr. Fall. First, this is home to me. It's where I grew up and as you know, it's hard to get the Delta out of you once you experience it. Second, I hate the practice of law. I can't complain about the money, but the stress and the cost of overhead take the fun out of it. I'm burned out after a little more than two years."

"I knew your folks were from here, met your Momma and Daddy as well as your grandparents on the campaign trail," Landon said. "Think a lot of all of them."

There's a politician's line if I ever heard one, Paul thought. Next, I guess he'll tell me he kissed me once when I was a baby.

"Thank you, sir, I appreciate that," Paul schmoozed.

"I take it your practice involved some criminal work?"

"Yes, sir, mostly court appointed, but some retained cases. More misdemeanors than felonies, but some of both."

"Tell me a little about yourself, Paul."

He hardly knew where to start with such a broad question, but he did his best. He had married while in law school, a mistake from the beginning. Trying to juggle the responsibilities of a marriage and the demands of getting through law school proved too much for his wife, a petite sorority girl from Ole Miss. While he toiled in the law library over torts, contracts and civil procedure, she waited at home for him until the wee hours of the morning sometimes, dreaming of the days when their biggest and most difficult decision was whether to go to her sorority sponsored formal ball in the state capitol or to his fraternity's "Old South" formal in Memphis when they were tragically scheduled on the same day. She longed for the days of flirting, dancing and partying with her sorority sisters and all the new pledges, and she had heard just about enough of how Professor Cochran and Dean Williams were determined to cut the class down to a smaller size by flunking students, particularly him, so that it would not unleash too many lawyers into the field and flood the market. One night he had come home to an empty apartment and a note, basically telling him she had found someone else and had left for good. His thought at the time was at least they didn't have children to fight over in the future and he thanked

God for that. If nothing else, the breakup caused him to bury himself in his studies even more.

He had lived in the Delta all of his life, save the almost three years he spent in the hills after law school, and knew everybody that *was* somebody and many more that weren't. He went to church with them, had gone to school and college with them, worked with them and celebrated life with them. He had been employed by a local power company reading the meters of the customers each and every month during college, so he knew where most people lived in not only Bolivar County, but consequently in adjoining Sunflower County as well. He understood the local politics and knew who were the movers and shakers in the county and who were the wannabes. Uniquely, that included the members of the black community as well as the white, having been smart enough to straddle the line between the races as much as possible, a remarkable feat in itself for anyone in Mississippi. He didn't get into to all the specifics of his past, just hit the high spots.

"Let me ask you this, Paul. How you feel about niggers?" Landon asked. The question caught Paul off guard and he hesitated with his answer. It wasn't that the DA referred to the black people as "niggers" that shocked him. That was the custom in the South, some using that term and honestly never thinking that it was insolent. It was the subject of race itself and why it was important here. Sensing the awkwardness, Landon followed up his question.

"What I mean Paul, is this: I need to know if you're one of those that think the white man owes the niggers something for the past, sort of toting what I call a white man's burden. Are you one of those who hates niggers and is "out to get" all of them because they're black? Or maybe you're out here to change the world and make the niggers equal to us overnight. Either way, I need to know," he said.

Paul was well aware that Mississippi had famously earned its reputation for racial unrest in the decades of the 40s, 50s and especially the 60s. He understood that segregation was the norm and no one questioned it. Like other states in the South, there were separate entrances to restaurants, separate waiting rooms in doctor's offices, separate bathrooms and drinking fountains for whites and colored people, all designated clearly by sign. If not actually designated by sign, it was no secret to anyone that the separation of the races was expected by all and to question it, or God forbid, challenge It, was to subject one to not only social outcast for the whites, but physical assault for the blacks. Sometimes the physical assaults were meted out to the "nigger loving" whites. There was the South, but then there was Mississippi.

Paul straightened himself in the chair in front of the DA's desk, nervously straightened his tie and looked down toward the desk.

"I can tell you this with a straight face, Mr. Fall: I was raised in the Mississippi Delta one generation from a sharecropper. I went to an all-white public school and never even thought about dating outside my race. My grandfather was a member of the Ku Klux Klan right here in Bolivar County, but if the Klan was still active here, the thought that I should join or support it would never cross my mind. I believe everyone should be given a fair shake in life regardless of their color, but I don't believe anyone should be given opportunities over anyone else because of the past. I try to treat everyone alike until they give me reason to do otherwise. Having said that, I want to be honest and say that I believe forced integration is wrong. If the races wanted to mix, you wouldn't see separate churches. I personally disagree with the Supreme Court's finding that "separate can never be equal", but since that's the law, I accept it. I know I'm rambling, but I'm trying desperately to be honest," he said almost apologetically. "I'm sure I would think differently if I was black, but truth is what it is," Paul replied. "I've got black friends that I grew up with and they are as welcome in my house as anyone. Do we go out together to parties or anything else? No. That's just not the way it's done. Maybe I can say it best by telling you about an incident that happened to me when I was eighteen years old and had a dramatic impact on me and thoughts about racism." And with that, he began to tell the story to Landon Fall.

At the age of 18 he worked in the summer of 1958 at a filling station owned by his Uncle Hugh, a Pure Oil station located in the small town of Boyle along Highway 61 in the middle of the Mississippi Delta. Hugh was a big man, standing 6'3" and weighing nearly three hundred pounds. He had coal black hair and his face was scarred from the numerous bar fights and automobile accidents in which he had been involved in his checkered past.

One afternoon a Cadillac bearing Illinois plates pulled up to the gas pumps and the driver, a black man of probably 40 years of age, requested a dollar's worth of gas, just a little over four gallons at the time. Paul was about to pump the gas when his uncle interceded.

"Don't pump a damn thing for that bastard," his uncle yelled out from the office inside the station.

"Do what?" Paul asked.

"He ain't gettin' nothing here but a hard time. You hear me, Yankee nigger?" his uncle called out.

"Is they a problem, sir?" asked the man, getting out of his car.

"Not unless you push it, boy. Best thing you can do is get your black ass back under the wheel and you and your whore get the hell outta here," Hugh said, now only feet from him, having come outside and standing near the pump island.

Only then did Paul notice that the occupant of the front seat on the passenger side was a blonde white woman of similar age. Interracial couples in the 1950s in the Magnolia State were as common as royal flushes are in Las Vegas today.

"I believe I know my rights, sir," the black man stated.

"Good. Let me show you mine," Hugh told him as he swung at the man who had no clue what was coming. Hugh's right fist landed solidly on the left jaw of the black man sending him to the ground and causing him to lose the keys to the Cadillac as they went flying toward the highway.

"Don't you ever tell me what your rights are, you nigger bastard. Your rights are what I damn well say they are," Hugh yelled at the man on the ground as he began to kick him in the ribs, stomach and in the face. The man balled up into a fetal position in an effort to defend himself from the blows. He was bruised and bloody from the pounding he was taking and cut from the concrete pavement on which he was writhing in order to shield himself. Blood streamed from his face and scalp into his eyes, momentarily making it difficult to see.

"Please don't kill me, sir! Please God, don't kill me!" the black man cried out. His cries for mercy were almost drowned out by the screams of the woman from inside the car who was obviously terrified, but dared not get out to help. Hugh landed kick after kick from his work boots onto the black man and when he tired from the beating, he ordered the man to his feet which, surprisingly, he was able to do.

"Get me those car keys, Paul," Hugh yelled. Paul obliged and retrieved the keys and gave them to his uncle. Hugh opened the trunk to the vehicle, pushed aside some luggage and yelled at the man.
"Get yo' ass in here now, boy!"
"Please sir, it's so hot in there," the man pleaded.

A slap across his face by Hugh's large left hand was his answer and the man crawled inside. When he was in, Hugh slammed the trunk shut and walked around to the passenger side of the car and leaned his head inside facing the terrified white woman who had fled then to the driver's side of the front bench seat.

"Now you get under that wheel, turn this sumbitch around and don't you stop 'til you get to Memphis across the Tennessee line. You understand me, bitch?" Hugh growled as he tossed her the keys.

She never said a word, but she took the keys, cranked the car and did as she was told. She was last seen heading north toward Memphis as she was ordered. Had the woman opted to report the assault to the local authorities, she would have found that Hugh was one of the part time sheriff's deputies in the county and her attempt at pressing any charges would have been an exercise in futility.

The incident had stuck in Paul's memory and shaken him to the core that day, but really, it was business as usual in Mississippi at the time. Though that may have seemed like a significant event to an impressionable teenager, it was just another day in the South at that time and most especially, Mississippi. He felt compassion for the woman as well as the black man, but in doing so he felt like a traitor to the Mississippi way of life, a tough burden for a young white boy in those days.

When he had finished, Landon looked him up and down as he sat in the chair in front of him and knew what he saw. Here was a young man who had been baptized in the culture of Mississippi, particularly the Delta, but time had watered down the anger and the prejudice that was instilled in him from birth. With each generation, that prejudice became less and less apparent, but like some radioactive material, it would never, ever completely disappear. That was okay to the DA, though. With the help of federal authorities, black voting strength was growing more and more with each election, and he needed someone on his staff who at least could be perceived as an ally to the blacks. He didn't need a true bigot or a home-grown freedom rider. He needed something in between and this kid just might be what he was trying to find.

The two carried on their discussion and interview for the better part of an hour, talking law, hunting and football, the only subjects most lawyers knew anything about, with the possible exception of golf. Finally, Landon stood to his feet, extended his hand once again and told him, "Again Paul, I'm glad you came down to talk to me. I have to be honest, I have two more applicants to interview and I'll make a decision shortly thereafter, hopefully within the next week to ten days."

"Thanks, so much Mr. Fall," Paul responded.

Paul had the 90-mile drive back to DeSoto County to think about the interview and its possibilities, along with anything else for that matter. He thought it had gone well and though he had no idea who the other applicants were that the DA had agreed to interview, or more importantly, what or who their connections might be, but he felt good about his chances at securing the job. His biggest concern was what his prospective employer thought about his response to the racial issue. Had he come across like a Yankee liberal? Did Landon perceive him as a racist? It was hard to know, but he had been truthful, so what the heck? He would know in due course. Highway 61 seemed to stretch for miles before him and he found himself engrossed in the cotton fields, single family houses and farms that lined that mythical stretch of road from Cleveland to DeSoto County, near the Memphis city limits.

The times and traditions would never allow Tyrone Braid and Paul Lane to know or understand what was going on in their respective worlds at this time and place. One was keeping his fingers crossed that he would be hired for a suit and tie job paying upwards of $20,000 per year. The other was counting the days until his release from prison and hoped to find a job paying fifty cents an hour. Unbeknownst to both, in a very short time fate would intervene and their worlds would collide, for better or for worse.

CHAPTER 4

In 1969, Paul Lane was without a doubt what anyone in Mississippi would call a "good ole boy". He could easily pass the good ole boy test, that being: "Would he come and bail you out of jail in the middle of the night if you got into trouble?" That was the test. That was all it took. There was little doubt in the minds of those that knew him that he would do so without reservation. In the South, what more could you ask from a friend, anyway? He was unpretentious, Mississippi Delta born and educated, his undergraduate degree coming from Delta State College in Cleveland, the heart of the Delta by location, and friendly as a politician in late October. Though he was born and raised in Bolivar County, he had moved from there shortly after he finished law school at Ole Miss and practiced law up in the hills of DeSoto County for three years before growing tired of the practice of law and yearning to return to his roots in the Delta. Like 90% of all lawyers, he hated the practice of law and was intent on getting out of it as soon as the opportunity presented itself. The other 10% of the lawyers simply lied and proclaimed to love it. Maybe that 10% just couldn't leave the money or the prestige of being a lawyer behind since in 1969 lawyers were *actually* respected. There were no cheesy wreck-running advertisements dominating billboards and airwaves. It had taken him only three years to want out, so when he learned that the District Attorney in Cleveland, Mississippi was offering the job of investigator for the 11th Circuit District that included Bolivar County, he eagerly accepted the much lower paying job, handed off his clients to his worst enemy, and cut a trail back home to Cleveland. Though less money, there was something to be said for a guaranteed paycheck, health insurance and state retirement, not to mention ever having to listen to another crying woman, and usually her mother as well, whose husband had traded up and left her and the kids for a younger model.

Paul took up residence in a rented house, approximately halfway between Cleveland and Shaw. It consisted of two bedrooms, a single bath, den, kitchen and open carport and was leased to him by a man who lived next door, but still about a half a mile from Paul. When he first rented to him, the man had remarked about how he might like having a policeman living next to him, a comment that stuck in Paul's craw forever. Though he didn't like practicing law, under no condition did he want to be referred to as a common policeman. His ego simply wouldn't allow that. Yet and still, he was what he was and in his current employment he was certainly more of a law enforcement officer than he was a lawyer.

He enjoyed what he was doing, but was unprepared for what he would face in August of that year. That month alone would cause him to examine his beliefs in the legal system, the relationship between blacks and whites in Mississippi at the time and would frustrate him more than he had ever been in his life.

@ @ @ @ @ @

CHAPTER 5

Sheriff L.B. Williams knew the community of Interstate well. When you ran for office in Mississippi at that time, people expected you to go door to door and ask them personally for their vote. If your opponent asked and you didn't, you were out. All the political signs, advertisements and flyers in the world could not substitute for old fashioned glad handing. He had made those rounds no less than 3 times and been elected to a four-year term each time. He not only knew the community, but he knew the people, too. He was vaguely familiar with the Strawberry family and shocked as anyone as to the brutality of the crime that had been described to him by the dispatcher at the office. He had not bothered to dress in his usual uniform because of the lateness of the hour, just pulled on some civilian clothes and grabbed his badge and service revolver. As he sped to the scene with lights flashing and sirens blaring from his squad car, he wondered almost aloud which "nigger" should he talk with first in the investigation. It was a nigger without question. Niggers always craved white women, anyway. Such was the beginning of a murder investigation in Mississippi in 1969, and most of the community would agree.

Word of the murder spread through the small community of Interstate as rapidly as rumors of infidelity did. In the coffee shops and businesses of nearby Cleveland and Shaw, it dominated the conversation. On the farms throughout the Delta, tractor drivers and other laborers spent their breaks and lunchtime leaning against farm implements or under equipment sheds repeating the story they had heard from someone, often claiming to know something that wasn't being told to the general public but to which they were privy because they knew the sheriff or someone in his department. Almost always it was nowhere near the truth, but was sworn to be nonetheless. The sheriff had a suspect in custody one said, a stranger to the area who had been picked up hitchhiking on Highway 61 with bloody clothes. Another knew for certain that a former black farmhand of Dewitt Strawberry had lusted for his daughter until he could no longer control himself and was now on the run with the sheriff and his men close behind. It wouldn't be long they all said and he'd be caught. Just a matter of time. Probably the most absurd rumor was that she had been decapitated by the intruder and he had left, taking her head with him.

The fact of the matter was that there was little evidence for the sheriff to move on. The hot August weather with little to no rain for the past 2 weeks meant no footprints around the house. The gumbo mud around the home as well as the fields and the edges of the gravel road were dried brick-hard yielding nothing by way of tracks. There was no forced entry because of the unlocked door of the home from which evidence could be collected and accordingly, whether or not the victim knew the assailant was nothing more than mere speculation. There appeared to be no fingerprints lifted other than those who regularly came in contact with the home, so it was assumed he wore gloves. As everyone in the general vicinity were indoors that night because of the heat and mosquitoes, nobody saw anyone or anything out of the ordinary. The lack of houses in the area decreased the likelihood of any witnesses even further. Yet and still, it could not be ignored that pure evil had invaded their lives, done the devil's work and vanished just as quick as it had come, hopefully for good or at least until captured. The sheriff had talked with Paul Lane at the scene and one of the deputies had photographed the bedroom as he had been instructed.

At the Sandpit Store, the closest country store to the scene of the crime, the locals who gathered after work the following day to throw back a few beers and snack on hot sausages and pig's feet had a message for the culprit—venture onto their property and they would quickly respond with a shotgun blast to his head. Some even boasted that they wish he *would* come to their house with his wicked intentions so that they could bring him to justice Southern style, but deep inside they were concerned about leaving their wives and children home alone. In the darkness, objects that were so passive in the day took on the form of danger. The movement of a stray dog took the form of a crouching man making his way across the yard and bushes hidden in the shadows became a foreboding figure of someone watching the home. The women and children were terrified. The most heinous of all nightmares had come true and no one was sure who would be next until he was caught and hopefully, that would be soon.

@ @ @ @ @ @ @

Nothing can be more emotionally crushing to someone than the loss of a child. The Strawberry family was learning that the hard way. Dewitt had gone through all the emotions of shock and disbelief, sadness and now anger. the kind of anger that consumes a person and permeates his sense of reason. Everyone was a suspect to him until he convinced himself otherwise and he couldn't hold a conversation with his best friends without vowing to extract blood from the guilty party one drop at a time. Estelle on the other hand had drawn into a shell like a frightened turtle. She refused to see friends before the funeral and rarely spoke even to her husband and that consisted of regrets through tears for leaving her child alone that night. The younger child, Carolyn, handled her grief even differently than her parents. She needed to be surrounded by friends and talk about what had happened. She didn't want them to leave but to stay with her so she would not be alone. Members of her Sunday School class were of immense help to her by visiting her in shifts so that someone was always there with her, bringing food and snacks when they came as did other church members.

What the Sunday School class had done for Carolyn was nothing compared to what the local pastor at their church did. For the past two years W.D. Kirksey had pastored the small but growing Interstate Baptist Church that sat in the middle of the community of Interstate and garnered its members from the nearby farms and houses as well as from the towns of Cleveland and Shaw alike. With a record high membership of 128, Kirksey was responsible, along with the Holy Spirit, for the recent growth to that figure. He was charismatic, intelligent and had come to the church by way of Gunnison Baptist Church where he had served the previous six years before the Lord called him to Interstate. He was the heir apparent to the leadership of a church that served as the social and spiritual hub of the area and as such, was looked upon with great admiration by the residents. He accepted that role with great relish and worked hard to keep their faith and their trust in him, as well as the Lord.

The morning following the murder, the pastor had located the Strawberry family at the home of fellow church members, Glenn and Jean Davidson where they had stayed overnight as suggested by the sheriff, in order to get away from the house and the murder scene within. He visited them there, prayed with them and assured them the best he could that the night was always darkest just before the dawn. Linda was called home by her heavenly father and was this very moment in the loving arms of Jesus, free from any further wickedness of this world. Though his words rang true, the realities of the night before continued to hang over them like a pending squall line. Accordingly, the pastor continued his best efforts to console the family. He organized a food drive for them during their period of mourning, a practice that was observed throughout the South anytime a death occurred. Church members and neighbors arrived almost continually bearing platters of fried chicken, baked hams, vegetables, breads and desserts the likes of which could only be found in the casino buffets of Las Vegas. It was no wonder that obesity ran rampant in the South. Every occasion in life seemed to call for eating. If you're ill, someone would bring food; if someone within the family was hospitalized, the family back home was flooded with platters of food. As it was repeated with a religious fervor every time someone passed away, most apparently believed that it worked. Grief was an illness obviously treated through the stomach.

Pastor Kirksey volunteered to consult with the sheriff and his deputies concerning the progression of the investigation and keep the family informed. Though there was little media with which to be bothered other than the local newspapers and possibly the local CBS television affiliate in nearby Greenwood, he offered his assistance in dealing with them, a gesture that was met with great appreciation by the bereaved family. No one looked forward to dealing with the media who traditionally had the habit of seeking the sensational rather than the truthful. Someone with the preacher's speaking ability and education would surely be helpful in handling those jackals and they felt better for it. Finally, he prayed with them before leaving and called upon the Almighty to not only bring the sinner to justice but carry the family through these troubled times. He left them much better than he had found them earlier that morning.

@ @ @ @ @ @ @

The young girl's body was transported to the funeral home in Cleveland in preparation for burial. Sheriff Williams didn't need an autopsy if he could have gotten one in the first place, the state crime lab being overwhelmed with cases from across Mississippi.

"Hell, anybody could see she had been strangled and raped. Don't need a doctor to tell that," he had said. The gathering of evidence from an autopsy was only given a passing thought.

The mortician at the Thweatt-King Funeral Home noticed immediately that she wore no jewelry, but dismissed it because he understood she was preparing for bed at the time of the murder. However, he was surprised when her father inquired over the telephone that morning about the opal ring she wore on her right hand, a birthday gift from him and her mother. The sheriff confirmed that she had no jewelry on when he examined the body at the scene. Either it was somewhere at the house or her attacker had taken it. A thorough search of the house later revealed nothing.

Sheriff Williams had worked through the night and was in desperate need of sleep, yawning as he drove. Nevertheless, he had a stop to make before heading home for that much-needed rest. He headed southeast from the crime scene to Braid's Grocery, a small country store located just across the county line in Sunflower County. Other than the Sandpit Grocery it was the only store within a five-mile radius of Interstate and had been founded by and operated by the Braid family for years. Much like the Sandpit, it had a couple of gas pumps, sold beer and soda, deli meats, snacks and a few canned goods but little else. Unlike the Sandpit Store that was owned by an Italian family, Braid's Grocery was black owned and operated, something as uncommon as Republicans in Bolivar County, Mississippi.

Lonnie Braid, college educated and an astute businessman in his own right, was a consummate gentleman. He had inherited farmland from his father, who had done well himself, built a store and managed to make a good living from both. Others in his family were not quite as prosperous or fortunate. Williams knew Lonnie's nephew, Tyrone, 21 years old, had been convicted three years earlier and sent to the penitentiary for four years for being a "Peeping Tom", an offense that, though a felony in Mississippi, one that he knew would result in probation almost always, particularly if the offender was white. However, Tyrone Braid had the misfortune of not only being black in the 60s, but also of looking into the window of a white woman for whom he worked during the day as a yard boy. Along with that, thought the sheriff, when he had played football at the all-black McEvans High School in Shaw where he was a star running back, his popularity there had clouded his judgment to the extent that he had once introduced himself to a couple of cheerleaders from the all-white Shaw High School while the girls were working at a bake sale for a school fund raiser in town. His actions had created quite the stir within the county when one of the girls told her father that he had hit on her, a lie that may have cost him his life had his Uncle Lonnie not intervened and given his word that Tyrone would never approach his daughter or any other white girl again. Still, the memory of that incident had weighed heavily in the mind of the judge when he sentenced Tyrone on the "Peeping Tom" charge years later, persuading him that the "uppity nigger" should go to the penitentiary.

He immediately came to the mind of Sheriff Williams because of his past transgressions and the proximity of his residence to the victim, a distance of no less than five or six miles. He was black, so that made him the perfect suspect in the sheriff's mind. Out of courtesy, he called Sheriff Holder in Sunflower County who agreed to meet him and discuss the case and Braid's possible involvement. They met at Braid's Grocery and over a Nehi orange soda they discussed the matter while sitting in the Sunflower County Sheriff's car with the air conditioner blowing on its highest setting. Holder agreed with his colleague's analysis of the Braid suspect entirely. Shortly, they left together to go over to the house where Tyrone Braid was currently staying, approximately a mile away, each following in his own car.

CHAPTER 6

Wayne Milton, 38 years of age, lived with his parents on Interstate Road some two miles from the Strawberry residence. They really weren't his parents, but just a kindly couple who had taken him in following the death of his mother who had died giving birth to him. His real father was unknown. He had no education whatsoever and accordingly was totally illiterate. Because he had an IQ of only 55, the State of Mississippi wouldn't permit him to attend the public schools in the state and there was no "special education" for him short of institutionalized education at the Ellisville State School in South Mississippi nearly 300 miles away. Consequently, he was kept at home and performed menial chores around the house and neighborhood if anyone needed him. It wasn't unusual to see him walking the roads and highways of the county on his way to Cleveland or Shaw and back toward home at any hour of the day or night. He generally hitchhiked if he was fortunate enough to have a familiar face going in his direction. At this he was quite successful, as everyone in the community knew him and often gave him a lift unless they were in a great hurry to get where they were going.

His stature was of medium height and weight and his lineage was no doubt Irish which accounted for his red face and hair. He had a peculiar habit of rubbing his hands together and subsequently crossing his arms into a self-hug which caused his face to contort into a lip curling sneer that made anyone unfamiliar with him uncomfortable. He was always dressed in khakis, both shirt and pants, and was normally never without a straw hat, his only defense against the Mississippi sun in the summertime. To a stranger, he was odd and most kept their distance from him for that reason. To those that knew him, he was just

Wayne and certainly no one to fear. He never stayed in one place very long during the day, but was back home sometime in the night, each and every night. His passion was walking the roads of the community, talking to anyone who would take the time to talk to him and when he wasn't talking, he was listening, evidenced by his habit of standing on the road at the end of driveways to the various homes and watching for its occupants in order to engage them in conversation, all the while listening to them through the screen doors and windows of their homes, open by necessity because of the summer heat and lack of air conditioning. He learned a lot by listening, such as who was having financial problems, who was having marital problems, who drank too much, who didn't like their neighbors and what children were having difficulty in school. He was probably the least educated but most knowledgeable person in the county. Life had stacked the odds against him, but he was doing the best he could with what he had and seemed happy. One advantage he did have in life at that time in history: He was white. That fact alone would prove to serve him well in the days to come.

Like most of the others in the community, Wayne was a member of the Interstate Baptist Church and was as faithful in his attendance as was the chairman of the deacons. Like all of the church members, he seemed upset and troubled by the previous night's violence in a community that had never experienced such or even dreamed of the possibility.

The Sandpit Store was open as usual that morning and the usual crowd that stopped for sausage and biscuits on their way to the fields had long cleared out by the time he got there. The temperature at 8:30 that morning had already reached 84 degrees and was climbing like a bull market to its predicted 98. Though the murder was less than twelve hours old, everyone was aware.

"I guess you heard about Linda Strawberry didn't you Wayne?" asked the lady behind the counter as she handed him change for the drink he was purchasing that morning.

"Yes'm. What they saying about it?" he asked back, opening the drink on the corner of the machine where the opener was located.

"Depends on who you ask, I guess. Everybody's got their opinion, but I ain't sure anybody knows much. Hope they catch the nigger and hang him," she said as she resumed her position on the stool she had been sitting on behind the counter.

"Yes'm, me too." Wayne had yet to make eye contact with her.

"Such a nice girl from a good family," she retorted, wiping the counter with a moist rag.

"Yes'm."

And then uncharacteristically, he was gone, obviously in a hurry to be somewhere.

"Damn fool, if the man had a brain, he'd probably take it out and play with it," she said to herself when she realized he had left.

@ @ @ @ @ @ @

As the two cars pulled into the gravel drive of the Braid house off Highway 442, a cur dog was forced to give up his spot in the shade lest he be run over. Chickens loose in the yard scattered as the uniformed men got out and approached the front porch of the wood framed house. There was a pungent smell of either an open sewage ditch or soured food in the air. Two old rockers with cushions in their cane seats sat idly by on the porch. A mirror was attached to the outside wall of the house on the porch as well. Legend had it that black folks always put such a mirror on the front porch of every home to prevent it from being haunted, reasoning that a spirit who attempted to come into the house would see his reflection and assume the house was already haunted and go away. Others thought it was merely for shaving in the morning light, so as to not waste electricity. The truth was probably somewhere in between. Before the two law officers could even knock, a young teenage black girl appeared at the screen door.

"I need to see Tyrone," Sheriff Holder asked, apparently feeling the need to begin this inquiry since these were his people. The girl had not opened the screen door to welcome them in but continued to talk through it.

"He ain't here. Ain't seen him," the young black girl said. "I thank he looking for a job in Shaw this morning." She had a dust mop in her hands and was nervously twirling it while speaking to the men.

"When's the last time you saw him?" Sheriff Williams interjected. "And don't you lie to me." These weren't his voters and he had all he could take of the pleasantries.

"I seen him last night when he got home."

"What time did he get home'

"'Bout 11 or 11:30. When I got up this morning he was gone again. I thank he said he was going to Shaw to look for a job he said before." She was taken aback by the bluntness of Sheriff Williams, but was desperately trying to be coy.

"What's he driving?"

"That old '62 Ford he got."

"What color?"

"White, but it's dirty."

"You tell him Sheriff Williams from Cleveland came looking for him. I need to talk to him and I don't want to wait for two or three days to do it. You tell him he needs to call me to meet me today, you hear. I'm gonna call his parole officer if I don't hear from him. You tell him that," Sheriff Williams threatened.

"I sure will."

And with that, the two sheriff's cars left the drive, one heading toward Cleveland for a nap, the other heading toward Indianola, the county seat of Sunflower County, to the office. Had they searched the house, they would have found Tyrone in the closet with the water heater, praying to God that they wouldn't find him. He had told the young black girl, Darcel, one of his siblings, to tell them he wasn't there when he had seen the cars pull up. Her explanation of his whereabouts was understandable since another sibling that also lived there, John Braid, had borrowed his car to *actually* go look for a job in Shaw earlier that morning. There was no reason to believe he was there without his car. He hadn't counted on her volunteering information about the time of his coming home the night before and that bothered him. Bothered him a lot. He needed to be alone to think about his next move—whether to call Sheriff Williams like he had said to do or take a chance on his parole officer looking for him as well. Either way there was going to be trouble. How in the hell did they find out so soon and zero-in on him, he wondered almost aloud to himself?

"Ain't never caught a break," he said. "Probably ain't never goin' to, either."

CHAPTER 7

"I'm sorry, but he cannot come to the phone now. Please consider the family's privacy in this difficult time," Mrs. Davidson said to the caller. This was the third time the caller had tried to make contact with the Strawberry family.

"Would you ask him to call Jed at the *Bolivar Commercial* if he doesn't mind," the caller responded.

"I'll pass the message along to him," she said, "but I can't make any promises as to when that will be. If you'd like, I can refer you to Reverend W.D. Kirksey who is assisting the family. That's about all I can do. Please don't call again." The bereaved couple sat at the table in the kitchen where Mrs. Davidson had answered the call and just shook their heads.

After giving him the pastor's telephone number, she hung up the phone, even though the caller persisted in asking more questions. And with that, the onslaught of the press began for the family. Their daughter wasn't even in the ground yet and people were wanting to know such mundane information as, "Do you believe there is adequate law enforcement for the county?" or better yet, "How is her sister handling Linda's death?" How do you think she is handling the death, dumbass? She's heartbroken, shocked and terrified as everyone is. And no, there isn't adequate law enforcement in the county and won't be until every home has their own personal sheriff's deputy. Give me a break.

Later in the day there would be calls from the *Delta Democrat Times* newspaper in Greenville, the Memphis based *Commercial Appeal* as well as *WABG*, Channel 6, the local CBS affiliate in Greenwood. One by one they were all referred to Pastor Kirksey as the family's point of contact. Fortunately, at least for the immediate time being, they didn't call back.

Kirksey was in his element as he fielded the calls on behalf of the Strawberry family, mainly from his study in the back of the church. He reveled in the spotlight of talking to the papers concerning a member of his flock and the events of last night. It stroked his ego and put him in the spotlight of the biggest news story to hit the county in years.

"They are staying with some church members and friends for the time being until they are able to move forward with the services for their daughter," he told them all. "They are safely in the care of loved ones and the Almighty and are going forward with their lives as they know their daughter would want them to do. Plans for a funeral service have not been finalized at this time." That was his statement to the press.

When questioned about specifics of the crime, he refused comment which again was fortunate as he knew absolutely nothing other than what everyone else knew: That a young girl in her prime had been raped and strangled in her own bedroom. That was it. Nothing else. Nada. Though he acted as if he was playing his cards close to his chest in an effort to tease the public into believing there was more, he knew better. Even when the television cameras showed up later that evening at his office and interviewed him with the multiple books and Bible references in his office as the backdrop, with its bright lights and beautiful reporter, all he could say was that the family was doing well under the circumstances and everyone should remember them in their prayers. He added further that he would be happy to share more information when it came to him and was permitted to be disclosed, but his transparent ignorance screamed that he had nothing else. His fifteen minutes of fame lasted a full ten seconds on the 5 o'clock news and didn't even make the 10 o'clock edition. Instead, pictures of the Strawberry home surrounded by yellow police tape cut him out of it.

@ @ @ @ @ @ @

Mrs. Mullen, Wayne's mother, was worried about him. He had come home shortly before lunch today and had not ventured out the rest of the day. He chose instead to remain in his bedroom with the door closed, most uncharacteristic of his daily routine. She couldn't remember the last time he had not rambled the roads in the afternoon after eating his lunch at home. Maybe if it had been storming, or freezing weather had set in during the winter, but never on days like today. The heat would never keep him in. Maybe the news of the Strawberry child was weighing on him. Though they certainly couldn't be considered friends, he knew who she was from the church services they attended together. She had been about as regular in attendance there as he was. He had mentioned Linda to her one day after a service, remarking about how pretty she was when she had been cast as Mary in the Christmas play. He also seemed to like to hear her sing on the rare occasion that she performed a solo there, seemingly hanging on every word as she sang from the choir loft of the church. His mother pushed back the idea in her mind of sitting down and chatting with him about it, choosing instead to leave him alone and see how he was tomorrow. Maybe he just had a bug and didn't feel well. No use in bringing out ghosts if they aren't dead, she thought. Then the irony of her thought hit her and she shook her head.

@ @ @ @ @ @

As darkness fell over the countryside for the first time since the murder the night before, the reality of raw fear gripped the people of the community and held them in a bear hug. Any woman who had to be out late or traveling in the dark made plans to have someone else accompany her. Hunting rifles and shotguns were loaded and propped against the doors to various rooms in their homes and calls to those living alone were made throughout the evening just to check on them. The paranoia was uncontrollable.

Back in Cleveland, Sheriff Williams had gotten up from his short, but much-needed nap and returned to his office. Checking his phone memos left for him by his receptionist, he noted some 60 plus calls from citizens and news outlets in that single day, all no doubt wanting the inside story of the crime, but he found no call at all from the still missing Tyrone Braid, solidifying in his mind that the boy had something to hide or he would have come forward. Pitching the memos back onto his secretary's desk, he walked into his small office in the courthouse, locked the door behind him and dialed the home number of Paul Lane. He had seen and spoken to Paul the night before at the crime scene, but hadn't seen or talked to him thereafter and was anxious to find any tidbit of information that was useable. He also wanted to tell him about Tyrone Braid and his theory of guilt.

When Paul Lane got the sheriff's call that night, he was going over some notes he had made at the crime scene the night before. He actually enjoyed being bothered by the sheriff this time because he had begun to lose track of his thoughts from the day's work and needed the break.

"You remember Tyrone Braid that was convicted of being a Peeping Tom a couple years ago over near Shaw?" the sheriff asked.

"I don't. Jog my memory," Paul answered.

"He got caught looking in on Virginia Courtney while she was taking a bath. She lived
on the Sunflower County line right at the Shaw city limits inside Bolivar County. Had been doing yard work for her."

"I'm drawing a blank, but what about him?" Paul asked.

"He served the bounce of two years at Parchman, then was released on parole. Still on it," the sheriff responded.

"Two years for being a peeping Tom? You just told me he was black."

"You got it. Sumbitch should a got more," the sheriff opined.

"Ok, I know where you stand, now get to the point, L.B," Paul responded, rolling his eyes.

"He lives with his sister and brother about five miles from the Strawberry's house. Three or four as the crow flies. He's the only sex offender that comes to mind in the area and his sister says he was out last night 'til almost midnight. Came home about then and left again early this morning. She don't know where he went this morning. Thought maybe he went looking for a job, but we both know that's a lie. I told her to tell him to call me but so far, no call. What you think?" asked the sheriff.

"Hard to understand why you haven't already arrested him with those facts," Paul said with all the sarcasm he could muster.

"That's what I'm saying," the sheriff returned gleefully, happy to know someone agreed with him. "Need to put out a BOLO for him."

"You gotta be kidding me L.B. I'm just joking. All you have is a lot of circumstances and no substance at all. If we arrested every black guy that lived within a five-mile radius of Interstate that came in last night at midnight and didn't call the sheriff to talk about some trouble he might be in, we'd have to lease Camp 5 at Parchman to hold all of 'em," Paul snapped. "Get real, man. We need to be sure and we need to be thorough on this one. This is not a robbery gone bad, a crime of passion where a man catches his wife cheating and shoots the boyfriend or some drunk that gets mad in a bar and kills someone over a crooked card game. Everyone, and I mean everyone, is watching this one. Let me put it into words you can understand, L.B. You could lose the next election if you don't get a conviction and it doesn't need to be some nigger that you could convict for any crime, any time in Bolivar County with a predominantly white jury. You hearing me?" Paul snapped, his frustrations beginning to show.

"All right, all right, I get the picture. But I'm still gonna talk to the boy," the sheriff stated defensively. He really resented the little piss ant, but had to deal with him nonetheless.

"Do what you gotta do, L.B. And keep me posted before you do something rash. Don't screw it up for everybody."

"You'll be the first to know. And I'll accept your apology then for doubting me."

CHAPTER 8

Tyrone Braid traced his finger around the top of the can of Old Milwaukee beer that he was nursing while sitting at a table covered in a red and white checked plastic tablecloth at P. Willie's Place, a juke joint just outside of Leland, Mississippi. He was some 20 miles away from home and in a neighboring county, giving him a false sense of security. He felt safe for the time being that he was away from the trouble back home and the reach of Sheriff Williams. He needed time to think and plan his moves from what he had done the previous night, so he had hitched a ride with a friend, a fellow felon who was heading to Greenville that day. P. Willie's Place seemed as good a place as any to kill some time during the day and following evening and give him the time he needed to think, without worrying about the sheriff or his parole officer showing up and ruining his day.

He was in a mess, no doubt. Some kind of way the sheriff had zeroed in on him as the number one suspect for what he had done the night before. How that could be was anybody's guess. He had been overly cautious and methodical he thought. Get in, get out and leave nothing behind. He had done just that he thought, but someone had to have seen him. It's always the couple making out on a rural road, the guy who happens to let his dog out at the perfect time or the deliveryman that's running late or early that sees something and tells it that gets you caught. However, for the life of him he couldn't imagine who it could be. It had to be someone, though. He hadn't been out much over twelve hours and the sheriff was in his yard looking for him. Someone had seen him.

While Tyrone sat drinking, and speculating at P. Willie's Place, closer to home his brother John, was wrapping up the day joyriding in Tyrone's white, '62 Ford. Failing to secure work that morning, he had gotten disgusted at himself and the world in general, picked up a couple of friends and spent the rest of the day and early evening, driving around and drinking beer. When they stopped at the Sandpit Store for yet another six-pack, they learned of the Strawberry murder.

"Y'all hear what them white folks was saying in the store"? John asked.

"Yeah, 'bout that killin'," one answered from the backseat. "They'll hang it on a black dude."

"Girl lived just up Trunkline Road. I'll show ya'll," John announced as he turned the car and headed east up the road.

It took less than five minutes before the trio were within a quarter mile of the long private drive that intersected Trunkline Road and led to the Strawberry home. John hit his blinker.

"Man, I know you ain't goin' down the drive to that house," the black kid in the front seat said. "We be the first ones they arrested if they see us hangin' 'round, fool."

Knowing there was a lot of truth in what the kid was saying, John immediately turned north onto an old gravel road he was about to pass and floored the old Ford. Excessive speed, gravel and alcohol rarely combine for a good outcome and this time was no different. One hundred yards off the main road the car began to fishtail. John hit the brakes, locking them and causing the car to slide sideways, turn 180 degrees and come to rest in the ditch on the west side of the road heading the opposite direction it was originally traveling. Though there was no water in the ditch, the car couldn't be driven out of the ditch because of the depth of it and was hopelessly stuck. Realizing their predicament, John and his two passengers bailed out, walked back to Trunkline Road and caught a ride with yet another friend who, as luck would have it, was just passing through about that time and wanted to see the scene of the crime from a safe distance. They all were subsequently taken to their homes, happy to escape from an automobile accident and the ensuing DWI charge that was sure to come had they lingered and been found by the cops.

Sometime during the night, a deputy sheriff on patrol in that area, turned onto that same little used gravel road to relieve himself. In so doing he spotted the car and reported it, running the plates through the sheriff's office. When it came back registered to Tyrone L. Braid, alarms went off in every head in that office. Every deputy wanted to call the sheriff and wake him up to let him know that the car of his number one suspect was found in a ditch a quarter mile from the murder scene. No one knew how long it had been there, but it appeared he had indeed been in a big hurry, lost control and was forced to abandon the car there. Who knew what treasures of evidence lay within it? He would be ecstatic and everyone wanted to be the one to bear the good news and thereby stroke his ego, but it was not to be. Paul Lane was contacted first.

"We found Tyrone Braid's car in a ditch on that gravel road just west of the Strawberry driveway, not a quarter mile from their house," the deputy told him by phone.

"Anybody got any clue when he ran it in there?" a groggy Paul asked.

"Don't know. Not but one house on that road and it's closer to the other end where it comes out on Interstate Road. Don't know if anybody's been that direction where they'd see it. Think that's a man and his family name of Vance that lives in that house. He can tell us tomorrow morning," he answered.

"Ok," Paul said. "Have it towed and impounded and we'll search it in the morning. Don't pop the corks yet, I'm still not convinced he's our man. And you and the rest of those coconuts in the department keep your hands off of it 'til in the morning. We'll go over it with a fine-toothed comb then. Maybe we'll get lucky and L.B. will be right for a change."

"Hope he is," the deputy said and then hung up.

It was just after 11 when Tyrone left with a girl from P. Willie's. He was angry, drunk, broke and scared, a terrible combination. He had spent his last dollar earlier in the evening and had begun running a tab for the remainder of his stay there, never once considering how he would pay it. However, the thought of spending the night in Leland with the girl lifted his spirits a little and between his buzz and lust, he didn't worry about it.

He had considered all his options as it pertained to his next move and had decided on a plan. Like many people he thought he could get lost in a big city among the sheer numbers away from the small-time law enforcement of the South. He was going to head to Chicago and disappear among the masses. Those rednecks looking for him here would never bother to look for him there because of the difficulty. Surely a city with a black population larger than all of those in the entire state of Mississippi would make him anonymous to the point that he could hide in plain sight, assuming he kept it clean and avoided any further legal transgressions there. Doing so would violate his parole, but what the hell? He was looking at a long stretch if they found him, anyway. What Tyrone didn't understand was that there were two cities the law always looked to when a black man disappeared for any length of time from Mississippi: Chicago and St. Louis. Sometimes Memphis, but that usually wasn't far enough away to feel comfortable. Unknowingly, he was heading for the first place they would look as soon as they realized he wasn't in Mississippi any more, and he *would* be found.

Whether it was the effect of the booze, the lust for the woman, the occupation of his mind by his legal woes or just plain intentionally done, when Tyrone left P. Willie's that night, he skipped out on his bar tab totaling $48.00 plus the tip for the waitress who had not only catered to his needs most of the afternoon and night, but who had introduced him to the girl he planned to bed in due course. Accordingly, neither the owner or the waitress was a happy camper at the close of business that night.

@ @ @ @ @ @ @

Mrs. Mullen awoke from her sleep that night to the sound of Wayne crying in his room behind a closed, and as she soon discovered, locked door. He had come out earlier only to eat the meal she had prepared just for him, although she and her husband loved it every bit as much as he did. Skillet fried chicken, fresh peas and butterbeans, sliced tomatoes and mashed potatoes. Top that off with the cornbread she cooked in a black iron skillet and you had a meal most Southern people would rather eat than the finest steak and seafood served at *Commander's Palace* in New Orleans, especially since you didn't have to contend with the uppity waiters there. As soon as he finished, he returned and took refuge behind the locked door in his bedroom. Maybe she was worrying a bit too much, but she didn't think he ate nearly as much as usual. He spoke only when spoken to and avoided eye contact almost completely. He had left out of the house about 10:00 p.m. or so, she assumed to walk around the yard or sit on the porch, something he did quite often if he was unable to sleep. She had no idea when he came back in because she had slipped back into sleep shortly thereafter. It was now almost 3 o'clock in the morning. She thought something was bothering him before and now after hearing his crying in the middle of the night she was certain.

Leaving her husband lying in the bed, she went across the hall of the small house and knocked on his door. When he didn't immediately answer she tried to go in, then finding it locked.

"Wayne," she called. "Let me in, son."

She heard him shuffling around and the bed springs squeak. Soon enough he opened the door without her calling to him again.

"What's wrong, son? I thought you were upset earlier today."

"Nothing, Momma," he replied.

"Now you don't think I believe that do you? Tell me what's got you going on like this."

She sat down on his bed and invited him to sit as well. She could count on her ears the number of times she had seen him cry, the only incident coming to mind being when he took some cookies from the church kitchen and was caught. But that had been when he was 18 years old.

"Momma, I'm scared," he confessed.

"Scared of what child?

"I don't think God will forgive me and I'll go to hell," he sobbed.

"Honey we've talked about this many times. You know there's nothing you can do the good Lord won't forgive you for if you only asked him. 'Ask and you shall receive' he says in the Bible. Nobody's perfect and 'all have sinned and come short of the glory of God' ", she quoted to him. "You just gotta pray for forgiveness whatever your sin is."

Her mind was reeling. *I wonder what he had done that makes him think he is going to hell* she wondered?

"You think Linda Strawberry is in heaven?" He queried.

"I know she is, son. You remember her walking down the church aisle and then getting baptized a week or so later? That tells you she is in heaven."

"What about the man that killed her? Is he going to heaven or hell?"

"I don't know who he is or nothing about him, but if he is like you and gave his soul to Jesus and then was baptized, God will forgive him, too and take him to heaven. That's all it takes. He just needs to ask for forgiveness for that and it will be all right," she responded.

So *that* was it. The news of the Strawberry murder had him upset. Maybe he considered Linda much more of a friend than she thought or maybe he was just confused and shocked by the whole episode. God knows everyone else was and they weren't mentally challenged like him. He had never been associated with anyone that had met such a violent and sudden death and he didn't know how to deal with the emotions he was experiencing. It certainly was understandable that he would have questions about death and the hereafter in times like this. She felt immensely sorry for him but didn't want to make a bigger deal of it than it was.

"You understand, now? You got any more questions?"

"No, Momma. I'm ok now."

He climbed into bed and under the cover as she closed the door and left. He really did feel better. He felt much better, actually, knowing that what he had done was forgivable and the fires of hell had been quenched by the Almighty. He turned on his side and quickly went to sleep.

CHAPTER 9

The car had been towed to an impound lot controlled by the county near the southern city limits of Cleveland the night before. They had covered it with a tarp and kept the enclosure locked at the gate all night with a night watchman or "rent-a-cop" as the deputies called him, watching over it. At the appointed time, Sheriff Williams, Paul Lane and a host of deputies, some doing nothing more than gawking at the proceedings, met there and began the tedious task of searching the vehicle. They immediately recovered a pair of cotton gloves, brown in color, from under the driver's seat of the car. The gloves were bagged, tagged and placed in a cardboard box in Paul's car as evidence and a note was made by him on a log book noting the date, place of finding and time as well. Unfortunately, with the exception of a great number of empty Falstaff beer cans and two full ones, nothing other than the gloves was found that might indicate a connection to the crime.

"Told you we'd find something," the sheriff cooed.

"Not sure a pair of gloves in a car belonging to a man who has never done anything but manual labor for a living really amounts to a smoking gun," Paul cut back.

"Let me get this straight. We have a convicted sex offender, living a short distance from the victim who is on the run. His car is found a quarter of a mile from the crime scene in a ditch with a pair of gloves in it. There were no fingerprints at the scene and the car is obviously wrecked because the driver was going too fast, and you don't think that's at least a little strange?" the sheriff asked.

"You forgot to mention he is black," Paul said teasingly.

"Damn right," the sheriff agreed. "The dominoes keep falling."

"I think you have at best what is called a person of interest," Paul said. "Everything, and I mean everything, is circumstantial. We have no motive, no connection between the victim and the killer and a constitutional right not to talk to you. Look, L.B., don't go jumping the gun. If word gets out that this boy is a suspect, he's likely never to make it to trial. You know how these things go. Black on white crimes are never good odds for black folks. Let's make sure on this one."

"Fine, but I'm beginning to wonder if you've gotten over that short stint as a public defender you served a while back. We'll play it your way, though, but I'm telling you, it keeps adding up. I'm going to find him and when I do, I'll break him down." And with that, the sheriff climbed into his car and headed out to parts unknown.

Paul did likewise, heading in the opposite direction, leaving the horde of deputies there.

@ @ @ @ @ @ @

Funeral services for Linda K. Strawberry were scheduled for 10.00 a.m. on Friday, two days away at the Interstate Baptist Church, Thweatt-King Funeral Home being in charge of the services. Reverend W.D. Kirksey would deliver the eulogy. The family would receive friends at the funeral home from 5:00 to 8:00 p.m. on Thursday night, foregoing the long Delta custom of bringing the body back to the house for visitation.

@ @ @ @ @ @ @

The murder was now almost three days old. The DA's office, in conjunction with the Bolivar County Sheriff's office decided it was time to hold a press conference to inform the public as much as they could as to the status of the case and it was scheduled at the courthouse in Cleveland for Wednesday afternoon at 4:00. Everyone agreed it was necessary and should be done before the funeral. It would be tricky to do because outside of the fact that a young girl was dead, there was little to tell. Nevertheless, elected officials feel the heat in such times and then proceed to put out the fire that is the hottest. This one was burning toward an inferno. People were scared and if nothing else, needed some assurances that something, anything, was being done to not only protect them, but to bring the culprit to justice so as to insure he didn't have an opportunity to do it again. Landon Fall was the elected District Attorney for the district and with the assistance of his longtime investigator, Paul Lane, would handle the matter for their office. Actually, Paul would field any questions, but it was necessary for Fall to appear as the front man and primary spokesman for political purposes. Basically speaking, if Fall wasn't reelected next year, the new DA would in all probability want his own team of investigators and assistants, thereby sending those like Paul and the others out to pasture and back to practicing law unless they had enough years in the state retirement system to take an early retirement. Therefore, it was crucial that Fall appear in the papers and on television anytime possible. Though money may be the mother's milk of politics, name recognition is the cornerstone of a political career and Landon Fall understood it completely.

Although he rarely participated in the actual trials anymore, a high-profile case like this was the exception. Fall fully intended to be the main character of the play that was unfolding at the time in his district. Besides, like every other elected official in the world, he loved the spotlight and had an ego the size of Texas that feasted on it.

@ @ @ @ @ @

At his office, just off of Court street in Cleveland, less than a block from the courthouse, Paul went over his investigation notes in preparation for the afternoon press conference. The press release that would be given out at the time of the conference was the following:

Linda Kathryn Strawberry, age 17, was discovered dead in her bedroom at her family's home in the Interstate community of Bolivar County. She had apparently been strangled by a ligature that was recovered at the scene. Evidence suggested that she had been raped after she had died. The District Attorney's Office, along with the Bolivar County Sheriff's office, is following a number of leads and attempting to talk to a number of people believed to have material knowledge of the crime. It is requested that anyone who believes they have information that may be beneficial in the investigation and prosecution of this crime is encouraged to call either the District Attorney's Office at 601-843-5862 or the Bolivar County Sheriff's Office at 601-843-4208. Our prayers and condolences go out to the family of Miss Strawberry.

And that was it. Even the most gullible press official could read between the lines and decipher that what the two offices were saying was that they didn't have anything except sympathy for the family. The questions that would come following the release of that would be brutal. So brutal Paul thought, that for a minute he contemplated calling his boss and the sheriff and asking them to delay the conference until they had something concrete and with some semblance of substance. But as quickly as it came to mind to do so, Paul dismissed it. The notice of the conference had been sent out to all media and the questions that would arise if it were postponed might be worse than those they were about to be hit with this afternoon. Never should have scheduled it in the first place, he thought. Oh well, hindsight is always 20/20, but damn, this release was more suited for release the morning after the murder, not three days later. Everything contained in it had already been made known to the public over the last couple of days. The more he pondered it, the more he dreaded attending that press conference.

@ @ @ @ @ @

The assurances Wayne received from his mother during the night had him feeling much better about his eternal future. So much so, that he gorged himself on scrambled eggs, bacon and hot biscuits that his mother prepared for him that morning and then promptly hit the door to begin his daily rituals of walking the roads. From his short driveway, he got on Interstate Road and headed south toward Trunkline Road. No reason, just someplace to go. He hadn't gone but a couple of hundred yards when he was picked up by the preacher in his blue Volkswagen Beetle headed for the church office that morning.

"I'm going to the church office, Wayne. I can take you that far," Kirksey told him.

"Yes, sir. That would be good," he replied.

"Where you going this morning?" the pastor inquired.
"Just up the road a little bit. When's that girl's funeral?" Wayne asked.
"Friday morning. That was just a terrible shame," the preacher stated. "You didn't see anyone around their house that day or night did you, my friend?"

Wayne shifted uncomfortably in his seat and looked out the window avoiding eye contact. He began rubbing his hands together nervously.

"No, sir. No, sir," he said. "You can just let me out right here at the Warren's house."

The preacher was stunned for a couple of reasons. He appeared to have struck a nerve with Wayne and made him very uncomfortable when he began quizzing him about maybe seeing someone at the Strawberry place at the time of the murder. Further, he suddenly wanted to get out of the car—and they had barely gone a half a mile.

"I thought you were going as far as the church, though?" the preacher asked.
"No, sir. Right here be fine," he said.

So, without any more questions, the pastor pulled over to the side of the road, let him out and pulled away. As he drove away, in his rearview mirror, he saw that Wayne had turned and was walking back toward his house. He wasn't sure what was up, but Wayne apparently knew something.

@ @ @ @ @ @ @

Tyrone had no idea when he rolled out of bed that morning, leaving the nude girl in the bed with him still sleeping, that his car had been wrecked, seized, towed and searched. For a few fleeting moments in the grogginess of waking up, he only knew that he was hungover, hungry and sexually satisfied. He needed to put some distance between him and this old girl and take care of the hangover and the hunger. Slipping on his clothes and shoes, he eased out the front door of the second-floor, government-subsidized apartment where she lived, went down the stairs, which he couldn't remember climbing last night, and disappeared into the streets of Leland. When he found his way to U.S. Highway 82, he headed for the first open café he could find. He needed something to drink and eat as well as a pay phone to call John to come get him.

Outside of Bennie's, a local dive that catered to black people, he bummed two dollars from a man and his wife who were going into the café under the pretext of getting gasoline for his car that was supposedly stranded on the side of the road back toward Greenville, a scam he had learned long ago, but perfected after his release from Parchman Prison. Instead of going into Bennie's, he cut back into the city streets of Leland and found a gas station that sold biscuits with assorted meats and egg in them, soft drinks and had a pay phone booth out near the street. After devouring the biscuit, egg and ham and washing them down with an *RC Cola*, he went into the phone booth and placed a call to John. The phone rang five or six times and he was about to tell the operator he would try later when someone answered.

"Hello," his sister said.

"Collect call from Tyrone Braid, will you accept the call?" the operator asked.

"I guess I will," she responded to the operator.

"Go ahead, sir."

"Darcel, where is John?" Tyrone asked.

"He still in the bed. Why you callin' here collect, Tyrone? You know we ain't got that kind of money," she stated.

"I got to get my car, Darcel, wake John up and tell him to get on the phone," he responded, avoiding the collect call issue completely. He had bigger problems than a dollar phone call and she obviously could tell by the tone of his voice. The line went quiet while she retrieved John. A minute later, he answered.

"Hello?"

"John, take my car and come and get me. I'm in Leland."

"Uh, uh, ----I can't."

"What you mean you can't?"

"I had an accident in it and had to leave it over toward Interstate last night. I can get Ray Ray to help me get it this morning, though."

"What the hell you done done with my car, man. I gotta have it now," Tyrone fumed.

"It just slid off in a ditch, man. It ain't hurt, just in a ditch. I'll get it soon as I get ahold of Ray Ray."

"Is Darcel's car at home," Tyrone asked?

"I thank, so. Why?"

"Come get me in her car. We'll get my car when I get home," he declared.

"She gone want some money for gas," John responded. "You know how she is."

"Tell her I'll take care of it," he lied. "Just get down here and get me, now. I'm in Leland at a place called Bennie's on Highway 82. Meet me in the parking lot in 30 minutes, no more or I swear 'fore God I'm gonna kick yo ass, dude," Tyrone yelled.

"I'm coming," John retorted. "Don't get yo panties in a wad."

Tyrone hung up the phone and started back toward Bennie's, thinking any moment that a city policeman, sheriff deputy or Highway Patrolman would come roaring up to him and arrest him for his transgressions, but he saw none. He heard the loud resonating blast of a train's horn as it approached an intersection, accompanied by the clunk and squeal of boxcars being towed along the tracks as it made its way through the center of Leland. Every Delta town had been built around a railroad and Leland was no different. For a fleeting moment, he considered jumping the train if he could, but then thought better of it. He killed time under the shade of a gargantuan cypress tree along Deer Creek, all the while wondering where his ride might be.

Almost an hour later, Darcel pulled up in the parking lot in her car without John and picked him up. She knew the fate of Tyrone's car with John and she wasn't about to let that happen to hers. He climbed in the front passenger seat and she pulled out of the parking lot headed back toward Bolivar County. Tyrone had mixed emotions about going back there, but he had to get some clothes and his car before heading out to Chicago.

CHAPTER 10

The preacher couldn't get the thoughts of the incident with Wayne off his mind. It dominated his thoughts and overrode every other rational notion he had during the day. He wasn't overreacting, he didn't believe. Something about discussing the murder set off alarms in Wayne's head and made him highly agitated and uncomfortable. What did he know? It ate at the preacher the rest of the day and even further. He would get to the bottom of it eventually, he thought. It may take more time than he would like, but he would know the truth about what Wayne knew, somehow, someway. He swore that to himself.

In the meantime, Wayne had headed back in the direction of home on his way to nowhere. He was visibly shaken by the preacher's questions and didn't want to talk about it to anyone, including his mother. If he went back now, she might want to talk further about it if she knew he was upset. Eventually, he passed his house and headed further north up Interstate Road toward Cleveland. As he always seemed to do, he caught a ride in the back of a pickup truck all the way to Cleveland from a distant neighbor on his way to town. Not long after arriving, he bought a hamburger from the local pool hall grill and ate it at the counter. Soon, he was lost in the everyday hustle and bustle of the largest town between Memphis and Vicksburg, yet a town that only had just over 10,000 people calling it home. He made his way through downtown and crossed the train tracks, walked toward the courthouse and settled in a shaded area where he sat and watched for the next few hours as people came and went—in the parking lot of Thweatt-King Funeral home.

@ @ @ @ @ @

When the two arrived back from Leland, John was waiting in a rocker on the front porch.

"Man, you know I hate to tell you this, but yo car's gone," He said almost fearfully.

"The hell you mean it's gone?" Tyrone shockingly asked, almost in panic mode.

"I mean it ain't there where we left it last night. Somebody musta pulled it out and took it," he speculated. "Me and Ray Ray ain't been back from there more 'n five minutes. It's gone."

Tyrone wanted badly to punch him, but things were going downhill for him fast and he couldn't get caught up in a fight at the moment. His mind was spinning. He needed to get the hell out of there and just run. It was only a matter of time before Sheriff Williams was going to come around again and arrest him. He had messed up two nights ago and somehow, someway they had come straight for him. If Sheriff Williams made good on his threat and called his parole officer, that would make it that much harder to get away. The more people looking for him, the easier it would be to find him.

"Darcel, you got to take me to Shaw," he told her. "I need to catch a Greyhound bus."

"I ain't taking you nowhere 'til you tell me why you runnin'," she replied. "I didn't ask on the way back from Leland, but now I gots to know."

"Trust me, Darcel, you don't wanna know. Just get me the hell to Shaw. I need to throw a few things together and we need to split."

He ran to his room, recovered $20 from between the mattresses of his bed, his hiding place of choice, threw all the clothes his single suitcase could hold into it and grabbed some cake from off the counter in the kitchen which he ate as he got into her car on the passenger side. He reached over and blew the horn for Darcel. When she didn't come out immediately, he blew it again. That time she appeared on the porch.

"Look, Tyrone, I just called the bus stop in Shaw. Both buses, northbound and southbound have already left. Next one leaves tomorrow, northbound at 10:00 in the morning, southbound at 11:00. Ain't no use getting in a hurry 'til in the morning," she declared. Which way was you headed, anyway," she asked?

"Damn. North," he said. "And that's all you need to know or gonna know."

Now he had to decide what to do for the night. Stay here and the sheriff or his parole officer might show up and take him in. Leaving without a car and relying on someone else to give him a ride while walking, would be almost as risky and virtually impossible as well. He didn't like his options, but without a car, he was grounded until he could get a bus ride out of there. Had he known at that very moment that a man working for P. Willie's Place was on the way to his house to collect the money for the bar tab he had skipped out on, he would have liked his options even less. He really hadn't been hard to find. The waitress who had been stiffed merely called the girl she had introduced to Tyrone last night to find him, and collect for her and the bar. The girl, not at all happy that he had left her bed without so much as a thank you, was more than willing to tell her friend that he had informed her that he lived two houses down from Braid's Grocery on Highway 442 out of Shaw. Better catch him quick, though. He had also volunteered to say he was leaving the next day for Chicago for a big job he had up there. His bravado and the beer had spilled his guts.

@ @ @ @ @ @ @

At precisely 4:00 p.m. on the steps of the Bolivar County Courthouse in Cleveland, District Attorney Landon Fall stepped up to a microphone and welcomed the press and the public to the previously scheduled news conference. He was flanked by Paul Lane, Sheriff L.B. Williams and no less than seven deputies from his department that stood behind them, solemn faced and at attention. The deputies' sole job was to portray a look of power and protection. The "Law" was ready, willing and able to catch a killer and was out in force.

The camera from Channel 6 rolled and local press writers took notes as the DA read the prepared statement that Paul had written and that had been passed out earlier to press members. Photographers snapped pictures of the expressionless group throughout the entire conference as if anyone actually changed positions or expressions. When he was through reading, the DA thanked the Sheriff and his department for the endless hours they were spending on the case, and then turned it over to Paul Lane for questions.

This was the moment that Paul had dreaded the entire day, but he swallowed hard and fielded the first question.

"Mr. Lane, can you elaborate on possible witnesses or suspects?" one asked.

Why, hell no. We don't have any witness or suspects except the black kid that the sheriff keeps trying to pin the damn thing on, Paul thought to himself.

"Not at this time, we cannot. We do not want to risk the safety of any witnesses or the dissemination of information that might tend to inhibit our investigation," he responded. Damn that was good he thought, and not a lie.

"Was there evidence of a robbery?" another asked.

"It does not appear to be so at this time. Nothing appears to have been taken from the home," he answered, remembering the missing opal ring from the girl's hand.

"How did he gain entry into the home?"

"There was no forced entry. Like many of us do, the home was left unlocked, particularly when someone is home," he said. "That's according to the homeowner." Finally, a reasonable question from the media, he thought.

"How is the family holding up?'

Ah, there it is, the question you ask to assure everyone present that you have nothing intelligent to say or ask.

"I have not spoken to them since the night of the murder. You can imagine the trauma they are going through, but I'm sure they are making the best of a bad situation".

And so, it continued for about 15 minutes. They asked the questions, he answered as best he could. Finally, the DA stepped forward and was about finished thanking everyone for their interest and reminding them to pray for the family, when Sheriff Williams stepped up and made a comment into the microphone.

"Let me say this. We have spent the better half of the day on Cleveland's east side looking for a young man we would like to question. I can assure you, we will keep up the pressure until we bring the guilty party to justice. If anyone has any information they feel may be useful, regardless of how trivial you think it may be, please contact my office. Thank you."

"Dammit!" Paul said through clenched teeth and under his breath. He thought they were doing pretty good until that jackass in a period of five seconds told everyone here that they were looking for a black suspect and short of that, had nothing whatsoever to go on. Damn him, he thought to himself! The east side of Cleveland was composed of almost 100% black residents. Now the race baiters and hate mongers would surely take the hint and the speculation would be hard to handle. Damn him!

Paul's thoughts about the sheriff's east side comment was prophetic. Brock's Café, almost directly across from the courthouse had filled up with diners from the press conference. Lawyers, insurance salesmen, bankers and local businessmen as well as farmers filled the main dining room afterwards to talk about what they had heard over hamburger steaks smothered in onions and gravy, sandwiches and breakfast food that was available all-day long. The room was abuzz with criticism for the lack of real information, information they hadn't already heard a dozen times from as many sources over the last three days. But everyone seemed agreed on one point: The sheriff had sent them a message that was received loud and clear, the man was a black man and God help him if they got to him before the sheriff did. They just needed to find out who the bastard was.

"Ten years ago, we wouldn't need no damn jury," one said.
"Who says we do now?" another chimed in.

"All we need is a good gin fan to weigh him down in the river," another laughed. "He can go skin diving with Emmitt Till. I ain't fixin' to sit back and let them niggers run wild and crazy."

These were not white trash rednecks making hollow threats they would never have the guts to back up. These were the so-called pillars of the community, respected across the board and throughout the county. When they talked, people listened, whether in matters of finance, government, education or racism. It was a scary thought and a sight to behold. God help the black man arrested for this crime because that's what it would take to save him.

As the crowd in front of the courthouse had broken up, two familiar faces went their way. Wayne Milton, who had left his perch at the funeral home only to see what the crowd forming on the courthouse lawn was all about and Reverend W.D. Kirksey who listened intently to the news conference, but who was as much concerned as to why Wayne Milton was there as anything.

@ @ @ @ @ @

Andrew Johnson, age 19, had been at The Oasis, a black-owned bar in Cleveland, for the last five and a half hours. He and some friends had met there after work with all intentions of sharing a few beers and heading home shortly thereafter. However, a group of women, out celebrating one of the group's impending marriage, had shown up about the same time, and with such a target rich environment, Andrew had decided to stay longer in hopes of scoring with one of them. He introduced himself to the group and bought them a round of drinks. He danced with each, including the bride to be, and felt a definite vibe from one of them and he centered his attention on her the remainder of the night. Sure enough, towards 10 o'clock, he persuaded her to go home with him for a while under the promise that he would bring her back when she was ready.

Andrew had graduated from Cleveland's East Side High School, Cleveland's all-black high school, a few months back where he starred in football and basketball. He had no plans or hope for college and like most other black kids in the Delta in 1969 had little else than a steady job to hopefully look forward to in the future. He had found it at Douglas & Lomason, a chrome factory on the north end of Cleveland where he worked the 3rd shift in the press room, stamping out aluminum parts for automobiles. Shortly after securing the job, he did like most teenagers that age would do and purchased a car, a used 1966 Chevy Chevelle. And, like most teenagers, Andrew had a lead foot, resulting in several traffic violations for speeding and reckless driving.

When he left with his hopeful lover from The Oasis, he had consumed no less than a dozen beers since he arrived and had no business attempting to drive.

He took the backway to his house that was located in the quaint town of Boyle, just south of Cleveland, in an effort to avoid any law enforcement and was successful until he arrived at Highway 446 and turned west toward his home. He failed to come to a complete stop at the intersection and the next thing he knew, a patrolman with the Mississippi Highway Patrol was behind him, blue lights flashing in an attempt to pull him over. Whether Andrew had decided not to get yet another ticket or was trying to impress his date is nothing but speculation. Whatever the reason, he tried to outrun the patrolman, his speed reaching in excess of one hundred miles per hour before he lost control. When the car began to swerve, Andrew fought it hard to keep it in his lane but was unsuccessful. The car skidded sideways due to the high rate of speed and crashed into an oncoming Ford station wagon driven by Allen Hughes who, with his wife and two children, were headed home themselves from visiting the children's grandparents. The two vehicles collided, with the Chevelle becoming airborne over the station wagon after doing so, landing in the opposite lane of travel behind it. All six of the people involved were either dead on impact or pronounced so on arrival at the East Bolivar County Hospital. A sample of Andrew's blood was drawn at the hospital thirty minutes after the crash and revealed an alcohol content of .23, over twice the legal limit and the amount necessary to convict a person of DWI in Mississippi. The wreckage and carnage was unlike any the law enforcement officers or emergency personnel who worked the scene had ever seen in all their years of service.

Allen Hughes had been the manager of the local John Deere dealership in Cleveland for the past twelve years. He was respected throughout the community and known by almost

everyone because of his employment in the agricultural field. He and his wife were members of the Skene Baptist Church where he was a deacon and she taught the Youth Sunday School Class. Her occupation as principal at one of the elementary schools in Cleveland made her well known to as many people as her husband. Their children, a boy and a girl, ages six and nine respectively, went to the same school. The car accident was a tragedy of massive proportions, not only because it claimed the lives of six people, but because of its senselessness. It rivaled the news of the Strawberry murder for the week.

At Brock's Café the following morning, the local crowd voiced their shock and frustration over pancakes, eggs and country ham. Part of the regular crowd that came each morning consisted of six people, plus or minus a couple on any given day, and sat at the back of the dining room at a large, round table. At that table they elected local officials, shared investment tips, discussed the latest local and world news and generally gossiped the same way men accuse women of doing.

"I know ya'll heard about Allen Hughes last night, didn't ya'll?" one asked to the group in general.

"Yes. God knows it doesn't get worse than that. A whole family wiped out. Damn good folks, too," another answered.

"Wished the son of a bitch had lived that caused it," yet another wishfully added. "We'd burn his ass. Anytime there is a senseless killing or any kind of a crime really, it's always a nigger. I knew that bastard, never been worth a damn his whole life. Don't know nothing about the girl, but if she was runnin' with him, she wasn't worth a damn either."

"Them poor kids, my wife knew them from school. One was in her class last year. Don't know which one, but she said both of them were great kids. Killed by a drunk nigger," another observed.

"One of these days folks are gonna get fed up with this crap," one responded.

Paul sat in a booth by himself, downing a short stack of pancakes and listening intently to the conversation from the nearby table about the tragic accident from yesterday. As they saw it, thought Paul, two drunk niggers trying to outrun the law had killed a family of four of the finest people around in the prime of their lives. And though, the racial epitaph aside, that was exactly what had happened, and despite the undebatable point that this was an epic tragedy, Paul surmised that the entire black race couldn't, or shouldn't be held responsible for it any more than the white race could or should have been, had Andrew Johnson been fortunate enough to have been born white. Nevertheless, the conversation in Brock's showed that to be the logic among the white people in the county at the time, and coming on the heels of the Strawberry murder which looked more and more like a black culprit, the cauldron of emotions bent on revenge was cooking on high and anything further might cause it to boil over.

Andrew Johnson was dead and couldn't be forced to pay, and that was frustrating. Somebody would have to eventually though, Paul feared. It was as simple as that. Unfortunately, Paul knew that the fuse of that racial bomb was about to burn down and Tyrone Braid may just be the one to suffer for Andrew's transgressions, if not his own.

CHAPTER 11

It was approximately 10 miles from Cleveland to the Interstate community and Wayne Milton knew every inch of the road, having walked it countless times in his life. Tonight, his luck had run out on him as far as friends go that would consider giving him a lift home. He had loitered around town following the press conference at the courthouse and it was after dark when he began the long trek home to Interstate. Except for the many buzzing mosquitoes that continuously hovered near his face, he didn't care. What else was he going to do, anyway? He had missed supper at home, so he had eaten some fried chicken and potatoes logs from a convenience store around 6:30, stood and watched the nightly crowd of sinners slip invisibly, or so they thought, into the bar at the Holiday Inn hoping to hook up with anyone other than their spouses, and finally headed toward home. Following Highway 61 south, he turned onto Jones Bayou Road. By 9:30 that night he had reached the intersection of Jones Bayou Road and Interstate Road on which he lived and was approximately 2 miles from his home.

At the intersection of the two roads sat a small brick home occupied by James Weeks, his wife and daughter, Jeanne, age, 16. He stood at the entrance to their drive for a second and noticed the lights on throughout the house, evidence that they were still up. He stood and watched, listening intensely in an effort to hear anything from within the house, the entire time rubbing his hands together like a fly before a good meal. A passing car on Jones Bayou Road flooded him with headlights and continued on as they passed quickly, neither acknowledging the other. However, what the passing car had accomplished by illuminating Wayne was to give away his presence to a rather large shepherd-mix dog that was chained in the back yard of the residence. He began barking loudly and tugging at the chain that held him, giving the impression that he would certainly maul the man who had dared stop so close to the house and invade their space. Seeing that the dog was chained and he was not in harm's way, Wayne stood his ground. He didn't want to pass up the opportunity to pick up a juicy tidbit of gossip that he might glean from eavesdropping there if at all possible. The dog continued his barking for the next few minutes until the back-porch light came on and the daughter appeared from within the house in an attempt to find the cause of the dog's behavior or at least quieten him. As she stuck her head out of the door, being careful not to open it too much, she saw Wayne standing at the end of their drive, draped in darkness. A scream that would curdle the blood of any man emitted from the frightened girl as she slammed the door, the dog increasing his barking more rapidly and with renewed vigor. The startled Wayne turned up Interstate Road, the commotion being too much for him at that point. Besides, his discovery there had dashed any hopes he had of overhearing anything from within the house.

He had only made a few steps away when James appeared, pump shotgun in hand, yelling at him to stop and threatening to shoot him if he failed to do so. Having never been confronted in this manner before, Wayne was confused and scared. He kept walking, but slowed his pace, unsure of exactly what he should do. His mind was made up for him when James fired a single round from the shotgun in his direction that fortunately didn't hit him, but was close enough that he heard the pellets hit the cotton stalks in the field on the side of the road. He had been looking back, but with the blast he wheeled and ran as fast as he could. More yelling and a second blast came shortly following the first, but Wayne had shifted into high gear and was further down the road so that the pellets from the shotgun round missed again. Feeling he would have to hide as opposed to remaining on the road to escape, Wayne dove into the cotton field, settled on a row off the road so that there was no way he could be seen if he laid down, and ran down it until he could barely breathe. Bent at the waist in an attempt to catch his breath, he heard the commotion back at the house as James's truck pulled out and roared down the road in a desperate attempt to find him. He saw the lights of a handheld spotlight as James trolled the area trying to locate him, throwing light off of either side of the road and into the fields. Wayne remained still as a cat preparing to pounce on his prey, mainly because he was exhausted but also because he was terrified. He lay face down and did his best to become part of the field, the high stalks surrounding him on all sides. Minutes evolved into an hour and only when he heard the truck pull back into the drive of the Weeks home did he move from his hiding place and start to make his way through the field and back home.

When he got home, sometime shortly after midnight, he was tired, sweaty, and itching from contact with the cotton and grass that he had come through to get there. He was lucky though; he was not hurt and very well could have been—seriously. The only casualty he had suffered was the loss of his favorite straw hat that he always wore. It had fallen off his head after the first shot in his haste to get away and he wasn't about to stop and get it then.

What Wayne wasn't around to see, was that the deputy who had been called by James Weeks to take a report of the incident, had retrieved the straw hat on the side of the road, tagged it as evidence and made a note of the time and location of its discovery and subsequently checked it in later that night to the evidence room at the sheriff's office.

@ @ @ @ @

Tyrone had kept his bags packed and waiting by the door in anticipation of the next day's bus ride. No use putting anything up just to drag it out again in the morning. Besides, he wasn't sure at this time if he was staying there tonight or heading out somewhere else before the Sheriff came looking again. The decision was pretty much moot when the navy blue '65 Cadillac with gangster whitewalls pulled into his yard. A burly black man dressed in a white suit, black shirt and without a tie got out of the vehicle and came on the front porch, knocking on the outer screen door and peering inside. Darcel answered it, and having no idea the man's presence spelled trouble, invited him in.

"I'm lookin' for Tyrone Braid," he said with authority.

"Ain't here. Ain't seen him," she replied with her stock answer. She now knew this could not be good. "He gone out of town. Don't know when he comin' back."

"Damn sure left in a hurry, didn't he? Wouldn't think anybody would leave on a trip and leave their luggage behind," he said, pointing to the suitcase at the side of the door.

Crap, he was good, she thought and she started to squirm. "That's mine. I'm leaving in the morning myself," she again lied, trying her best to be convincing.

"Let's see what you takin'," he responded. He grabbed the suitcase and popped open the buckles, causing the contents to spill forth. Nothing but men's clothes littered the floor of the front room from the suitcase.

"They look mighty big for a little girl like you. Now get outta the way and let me see what else I can find," he snorted as he brushed past the girl and started into the other rooms, opening closets as he went. The third door he opened revealed a surprised and terrified Tyrone who had no idea who this man was or what he wanted, but was certain it would end badly for him. When the man saw Tyrone crouched by the water heater, he grabbed him by his arm and front of his shirt and dragged him out, throwing him onto the dining table, head first as he did. He dragged him back off the table and into one of the chairs.

"You left outta P. Willie's without paying yo tab, motherf...., and P. Willie is PO'd," he said. "Not to mention the girl that kissed yo ass all night long bringing you drinks. She pissed, too, and I'm here to see that you pay yo bill to both of 'em."

He pulled Tyrone out of the chair and slammed him back into the table, rebounding his body face first, into yet another chair. Tyrone was stunned and as of yet had not tried to fight back. His mind was spinning from the beating he was receiving, coupled with the screams of Darcel doing her best to summon John for help. John never came.

"Look man, I was drunk when I left and just forgot,"Tyrone pleaded. "I'll pay it, man, I got the money,"he hollered in between being bounced off the table, chairs and wall.

"Damn right you will, motherf...., damn right," he said, pushing Tyrone to the floor. "$75, even," he said.

"It wasn't that much, I know,"Tyrone said. "Couldn't a been more than 20 or 30 dollars at the most—with the tip!"

"Carrying charges my man, carrying charges, he returned. "Get it now or we go again,"he said.

"*We*" go again, Tyrone thought? Hell, he didn't get to participate the first time.

"Let me go to my room. I got it,"he said, knowing full well that was a lie. He got to his feet and stumbled into his room. His body hurt all over from the thrashing and his face was bleeding, not to mention the swollen eye he had developing as he retrieved twenty dollars from his wallet on the dresser.

"Darcel, where the hell the rest of my money," he hollered toward the front of the house.

"You don't even want to think about playin' no games with me, you little bastard. Don't have no time for games and I don't play fair to start with," the man warned as Darcel came into the bedroom.

"Where my money, Darcel?" he asked again, hoping she would take the hint to get him some more money from anywhere.

"I guess John borrowed it, how much do you need?" she inquired, taking the hint.

"Fifty-five dollars," he returned.

"I'll loan it to you," she shot back. "Let me get it." She turned and headed to her bedroom, pulled a roll of bills from a shoebox in her closet and counted out the money. In doing so, she remembered the .38 caliber pistol she had in her nightstand that no one else knew about, and for a fleeting moment gave serious consideration to putting it to good use and saving the money. It's $55, she thought. A lot of money, but not enough to kill somebody over, her better judgment told her. If he comes back again, I'll blow him away. She walked back to Tyrone's room where the two were waiting and handed it to the man who counted it out on the bed. When he finished and was satisfied that he had the total amount he had demanded, he got up to leave.

"Save yourself some trouble *and* money next time and don't stiff nobody. Don't start nothin', won't be nothin'," he said as he turned to leave.

Neither Darcel or Tyrone said a word until they were certain the Cadillac had backed into the highway and was gone, presumptively back to P. Willie's Place to divide the booty. When he was gone, Darcel started in on him.

"What the hell was that all about?" Darcel screamed. Before he could answer, she started again. "And how you gon' pay me back my money?"

Tyrone had no earthly idea and although he was genuinely concerned with how to pay her back, he was just relieved that the man who found him there was neither his parole officer or the sheriff, despite the whipping he had just taken. He was certain now that he had to get out of there for the night even it meant staying under the bleachers of the high school football field for the night if nothing else. And that is just where he stayed. Darcel dropped him off there sometime shortly after dark with his clothes in tow along with forty dollars he had gotten from her.

"What you gon' do 'til in the morning, Tyrone?" she asked.

"I'll find something to entertain myself," he said. "Maybe just walk around."

Though she was furious with him, she still loved him as much as any relative and couldn't stand by and let him fend for himself. She handed him another twenty-dollar bill. He never explained to her why or where he was going and she didn't ask again.

"You don't want to know," he had told her earlier. And she had decided he was right.

CHAPTER 12

The preacher's vehicle was at the church from about an hour from the end of the courthouse news conference until around 9:30 p.m., an indication that he was preparing his Sunday sermon. He had stopped by the Davis residence to see the Strawberry family and fill them in on the facts derived from the news conference, all of which they had already learned from the Channel 6 newscast at 5 o'clock. They were all in agreement that at this point so early in the investigation, the sheriff had very little, but apparently all leads pointed toward a black man as the culprit. The family was in shock as any white family would have been, at the thought of a black man violating and murdering their daughter, as if a white man doing the same would have been preferable. Estelle didn't want to talk about it, while Dewitt raved and vowed revenge. Damn justice, he wanted an eye for an eye, and he wanted it sooner than later. After attempting to console him for a few minutes, the preacher asked the family if they would pray with him. The prayer accomplished, he excused himself and headed for the church office.

@ @ @ @ @ @ @

Paul and Landon Fall had discussed the sheriff's intentional message to the public at the previous news conference the following morning over coffee and donuts in Paul's office. Both agreed that the sheriff was playing with fire in insinuating that the murderer was a black man unless there was proof positive, which there clearly was not.

"You can't fix stupid," Landon surmised. "I've wrestled with him for the past 10 years and you just have to ignore him and his ways and do your job."

"Easy for us to do, but what about the black guy? He'll be sentenced before he's even arrested if some have their way," Paul argued.

"I know what you're saying, Paul, but I learned early in my career that I can't save the world and neither can you."

"I'm not trying to save the world, just trying to keep a kid from being killed," he responded.

"Ok," Landon said, "Let's look at it for a second and I'll be the Devil's advocate. I've got a convicted sex offender living close to the victim, . . .," he said when Paul interrupted him.

"I know the facts, boss, but I think the perpetrator knew her," Paul said.

"How can you know that with any degree of certainty? There was no forced entry to the home because nobody out there ever had any reason to lock their doors. Anyone, stranger or friend, could have just walked into the living room and caught an episode of *Bewitched* on the tv," Landon argued.

"If it wasn't someone who knew her, why was he there? If he was a stranger to the area, he passed a lot of secluded houses to get to that one," Paul returned. "And why was nothing taken if it was a stranger," he argued further, "he could have helped himself to anything in the house."

"Ok, I'll bite. Did she have a steady boyfriend that she may have jilted?" Landon shot back.

"No."

"Anyone you know of that was infatuated with her at school, work or anywhere else?"

"No."

"Any enemies we know of? Any jealous rivals? Anybody she had wronged that we may know of?"

"For Christ's sake, Landon, we're talking about a 17-year-old girl. The type enemies she would have would be the girl she beat out for cheerleader or someone she turned in for breaking line in the lunchroom. Of course, she had no enemies or rivals," Paul said getting very tired of the debate.

"All right then, I would submit that what we have is a crime committed for the thrill of it, whether she knew him or not. That would seem to point us to a sex offender like Tyrone Braid, who somewhere, somehow learned of her and maybe quietly stalked her until the opportunity arose to act. Maybe the sheriff isn't as far off base as we once thought," Landon concluded.

"I'll admit the possibility, I just don't like picking a suspect and then building a case around him, and that's what L.B. has done," Paul conceded.

"Follow the evidence, Paul, follow the evidence and let the chips fall where they may. This is not mine or your first rodeo. We'll figure it out, we always do. People are counting on us," he advised. "Start by checking into the Braid kid and see what you can find. Up to now it seems you have failed to pursue that lead simply because you want the sheriff to be wrong."

"All right, I'll keep my mind open and find him. I have to admit that it is a little suspicious as to why he hasn't come looking for his car today," Paul said.

Landon and Paul both left the office and went their separate ways. Paul did as he promised and headed out toward Interstate and the Sunflower County line in an effort to find and talk to Tyrone Braid. He lived out toward there and had been through the community before, but for some reason it seemed farther than he remembered.

The drive, though longer than expected, sure brought back memories of his growing up in the Delta. He remembered frog gigging outings that lasted all night long, spotlighting rabbits after a rain and buying beer at the age of sixteen from any number of small Chinese grocers that had stores in each town, the proprietor always giving them a "church key" opener for the cans. He thought about the time he and a friend had ventured over to Benoit, on the west side of the county near the Mississippi River one night, and sat in the street listening to good blues music coming from within an all-black bar one night. When they asked a local black patron to go inside and buy them a beer in the place, in return for them buying him one for his effort, he had refused, offering instead to take them in with him to buy it. Though terrified, they had gone inside with him, and spent the better part of the night sitting at tables made from huge wooden spools used for electrical cables on cane bottom, ladder-backed chairs, drinking beer and listening to the most authentic blues tunes they would ever hear with a few of the brothers they had never seen before or since. Only in the Mississippi Delta, he thought. The Delta was home to him and always would be.

As he passed the individual homes and farms that dotted the landscape, he could almost understand why no one out here locked their doors, at least before the Strawberry murder. It was quiet, peaceful and everyone knew everybody. They had either gone to school with their neighbors, gone to church with them or their children had done so. They didn't see the crimes committed to which he personally had a front row seat. They weren't aware of the rising rate of drug crimes, violent crimes or property crimes that he saw and lived with day in and out. He almost wished he lived there as opposed to Bright's place, but there wasn't much distance from his house to here, anyway.

Turning off of Interstate Road onto Trunkline Road where the church sat, he could see the radio tower and buildings of Trunkline Gas Company, a large natural gas compression station that was located on the eastern end of the community. He turned south when he got to the station and went about 3 miles until he intersected Highway 442. Across the highway sat Braid's Grocery so he knew he was almost at his destination. A half mile or so to the east and he saw the house that he sought. As he stepped up on the porch, he was greeted through the screen door by Darcel.

"Good morning, ma'am. I'm Paul Lane, investigator for the district attorney's office in Cleveland, and I was wondering if I could speak to Tyrone Braid?" he stated as he showed her his badge.

"He not here. Ain't seen him in a while," she returned, almost telling the truth.

"Do you know where I could find him?"

"He left here Tuesday, and I thank he said he was going to Leland, but I ain't see him since," she said. She was acutely aware that it was only nine o'clock in the morning and the bus north didn't leave until ten. She had to throw him off the track to give Tyrone time to get away from there.

"Fair enough," Paul said. "But I'd like to talk to you as well. May I come in?"

Darcel hadn't counted on this and was caught off guard. "I guess so," she said, remembering the bad experience she had with the collector from P. Willie's after she had let him inside. Paul came in and sat on the old sofa that lined the wall. Darcel continued to stand at first, but finally, nervously, sat in a chair across from him.

"When did you last see Tyrone?"

"He came in late Monday night from somewhere, I don't know where. Then he left early that morning before I got up." So far, she was telling the truth. "He said earlier he was going to Leland to look for a job." The truth train had run off its tracks.

"You're sure about that?"

"Yes, sir."

"Sure, he didn't go to Shaw?"

"Yes, sir. He said Leland. I think he was going to P. Willie's Place 'cause he heard they was lookin' for somebody to do some work on the roof of that club," she lied, hoping not only that somebody there would confirm that he had gone there, but also would again throw them off long enough for him to leave on that bus.

"You didn't tell Sheriff Williams this past Tuesday that he went to Shaw looking for a job?"

"No, sir. It was definitely Leland."

"And you haven't seen him since then? Well, what was he driving when he left?"

"He was in his car, a white '62 Ford."

"And he hasn't been back since?"

"No, sir. Not since early Tuesday morning."

Paul knew when he hit a dead end. She had taken the best route she could when being questioned: Don't know anything and don't say anything beyond what you absolutely have to say. He was wasting time with her, now. The best thing he could do was to head up to Leland and see what he could find that would corroborate her story about him. On the way back, he could also stop in Shaw and ask a few questions. He'd find him soon enough, and when he did, he'd either put his involvement to rest or go after him with a vengeance. He suspected his sister was lying for him, but there was no way to prove it.

As Paul headed toward Leland down Highway 61, it was just after 10 o'clock a.m. when he passed the tiny town of Shaw. A few minutes later and he would have passed a Greyhound bus headed in the opposite direction of him, rolling toward Memphis, St. Louis and Chicago as well as other cities north of Mississippi. Slumped down in a seat toward the back, with a cap pulled down over his eyes to shade the glare of the mid-morning sun so he could catch some sleep, was Tyrone Braid who was more relaxed at that moment than he had been in the last four days, speeding north toward a new life and leaving behind what he had done forever, or so he thought.

It didn't take Paul long to get to Leland and find the infamous P. Willie's Place that the girl had told him about. He pulled off the highway and parked near the front of the building, only two other cars being parked in the lot. The joint was yet to open as evidenced by the locked door, but Paul was undeterred and strode around the back. He wasn't there to eat, drink or carouse with the clientele, he was there for information and wasn't leaving before he talked with someone. Sure enough, the back door was wide open and he could see inside. A rather large black man in an apron was stacking cases of beer into a large upright cooler, sweating profusely in the process.

"You wouldn't happen to be P. Willie, would you?" Paul asked with a smile.

"Nope. He ain't here. Ain't seen him," the man answered without a smile. That seemed to be the stock answer for the day, Paul thought, convinced the man was lying. He introduced his name and badge to the man and questioned him further.

"You know a man named Tyrone Braid, by chance? Mid to late twenties, about 175 pounds—black dude with a small afro driving a '62 Ford?"

"Uh-huh, sure do. Who else he robbed?"

"You tell me. I'm the one looking."

"Dude came by here Tuesday afternoon, late. Drank 'til sometime that night. When he left, he skipped out on his tab. Ain't seen him since," the man reported. "You find him, tell him there's a world of hurt coming his way," he said, apparently oblivious to the successful collection effort by P. Willie's man yesterday.

"Have any idea where he went or who might know?" Paul asked.

"You can check with Lucille. She inside and waited on him that day. Stiffed her, too," he grunted as he shifted a case of beer to the back of the cooler.

"I assume we're talking figuratively about her tip," Paul said laughingly, doing his best to be friendly.

"Like I said, she inside," the man returned, either failing to get the joke or not thinking it funny.

"Thanks, man, I'll do that," Paul said as he went through the back of the place and into the bar area.

A woman was wiping down the bar and some glasses when he came in and she looked at him with suspicion.

"You, Lucille?"

"I could be, who's asking?"

"Paul Lane, investigator for the district attorney. I understand you met Tyrone Braid the other night, is that right?"

"Yeah, I met him. Treated him good for a long time before he left out of here without so much as a thank you, much less a tip."

"Have any idea where he went?"

"Said he was headin' up to Chicago for some big job. Who the hell really knows, though," she responded, purposely forgetting to tell about her friend's rendezvous with him.

"Did he say when he was leaving?"

"The next day, would a been yesterday."

"Was he traveling alone or with someone?"

"Wasn't with nobody."

"Did you see his car?"

"Told me a friend dropped him off here and I didn't see him leave. Never saw no car." That part was true, but she still didn't volunteer information about his date.

"Thank you, ma'am," Paul added and left out the back and went around front to his car.

Thinking to himself as he turned back toward Bolivar County, they still had Tyrone's car, and they knew where it had been from Tuesday night until the present. So, if he was heading to Chicago, he had to be with someone or had taken a bus. Since no one had seen anyone with him, he'd bet on the bus unless something told him otherwise. Either way, he had as much as a two-day head start on him that was going to be difficult to overcome, but he would manage someway. It was funny though, everybody thought they were safe in a big city and cut a trail to it at the first sign of trouble. Maybe the sheriff had it right about Tyrone from the start.

CHAPTER 13

Janice Galtelli was a recently divorced woman who had battled the odds and returned to her studies at Delta State College following the breakup of her marriage. With no children and having completed her sophomore year at the college before she was married, she had vowed to go back and finish her teaching degree there before any more of life's future curves prohibited it. Standing at 5'5" and weight proportionate with black hair and brown eyes, the beautiful 23-year-old, dark complexioned woman could have been a poster child for the Italian community in the county. She was as shy as she was beautiful, but her divorce had forced her to come out of her shell more than she ever had.

She was originally from Jackson, Mississippi and had no family in the Delta. Her parents themselves were divorced with problems of their own, so she didn't hear from either of them but occasionally, at best. Once her own divorce had been final, she rented a house out on the north end of Interstate Road from a lady that, like her, had recently divorced and taken a job near Clarksdale, Mississippi, thus necessitating a move to that town and the need to rent the house in Interstate to help pay the mortgage on it. Janice had moved in at the start of the summer and had taken one summer school course at Delta State in anticipation of the full load of classes she would have starting in September. She had a job at a small women's clothing boutique that started in September, but for now was unemployed by design. During the summer course, she had met a great guy who treated her with all the respect that her husband never did, and they had, on this night, been to a movie and dinner, returning around 11:00 p.m. to her house, where he kissed her goodnight under the carport.

"Goodnight, Janice. Had a great time," he said afterwards.

"You *know* I did," she answered. And then he left.

As she entered the home, she turned on the light to the room and then locked the door behind her, her capitol city upbringing showing. The exterior door was equipped with a lock that merely required the turning of the clip in the center of the knob, not as secure as a deadbolt, but at least offering resistance of some type to an intruder. She headed back to her bedroom, turning off lights as she left each room and turning them on as she entered the next. When she finally got to her bedroom, she began her nightly routine in preparation for bed, including changing into her nightgown.

On the outside, near the beginning of her short driveway, he watched in eager anticipation. He had to dive into the cotton field earlier when she had arrived with her date, surprised by the car as it made the turn off the road into the driveway, a move he had perfected. Now he was calmly watching the house again, as he had done so many times before, planning his move. He had been able to control his urges for years now, but recently, they had become too much. His appetite for this had become too much to keep at bay, and though he didn't understand it, he knew it had to be fed.

When her bedroom light had come on finally, he moved through the carport to the door and slowly turned the knob. Meeting resistance and discovering that it was locked, he drew a card from his wallet and slid it down the edge of the door between the facing, easily forcing the catch on the door to release its hold and open with little resistance. In a matter of seconds, he was inside and closed the door behind him. He quietly, but methodically, made his way to the back of the house, following the same steps that she had taken just a few short minutes before, but without the aid of light. When he got to her bedroom, he carefully peered inside and discovered that she was in the bathroom with the door closed. He almost smiled to himself, thinking about his good fortune. As he waited patiently against the wall in the bedroom and on the outside of her bathroom, he noticed her jeans and blouse laying across her bed and removed the belt from the jeans. He continued to wait patiently. He had nothing else to do and all night to do it.

Though she was terrified beyond description at the realization of what was happening, she couldn't scream, because the belt was too tight against her throat. She reached up in a desperate attempt to loosen it, but the man pulled even tighter. She could feel her trachea being crushed and her eyes bulging, and she was powerless to do anything about it. The pain, both in front and behind her neck was excruciating and she began to feel dizzy. The room began to spin as she tried desperately to breathe, but it only made the pain worse and the belt tighter. The dizziness became more intense and soon overcame her to the point of blacking out, causing a sickening calm to wash over her.

He stood there for a few minutes after he felt her body relax and go limp with the belt around her neck, drawn tight to the point that he had lost circulation in his hands, but he continued to hold. When he was certain she was dead, he realized that his grip had been such that she was being held off her feet, her legs unable to support her any longer. He threw her onto the bed as he released her and she bounced like a rag doll across it. He was breathing heavily from the energy he had exerted, but his mind was on a euphoric high. He ripped her gown and panties off her body as she lay across the bed and began to drop his pants immediately. He was ecstatic with anticipation, such to the extent that he thought for a moment he might reach his climax without penetrating her, but he was able to hold it. When he had finished the deed, he brought up his pants, looked around the room and at the dead woman below him on the bed. Seeing that she was wearing no jewelry except a small, diamond cluster ring on her right hand, he pulled it free from her finger, stuck it in his front pocket, and as slowly and quietly as he had come, he left.

@ @ @ @ @ @ @

Linda Strawberry's funeral was set to begin at 10 o'clock at the Interstate Baptist Church. District Attorney Landon Fall, Sheriff L.B. Williams and a host of Bolivar County deputies planned to attend. Not that they knew the family that well or the decedent at all, but for purely political reasons. Their presence there would insure the family and the members of the community that they were concerned or they would not have come. That they were on the job as always and everyone would appreciate them for it. They would remember that at election time, too. It was hard not to be impressed with the squadron of deputies, all in uniform, that lined the front of the small white framed church. Such was southern politics in the Mississippi Delta.

The funeral was gut wrenching for everyone in attendance. Like most funerals, it was an open casket with the body placed at the front of the church, while songs were sung and words about her were spoken. This one was more emotional than most because of the untimely and unexpected death of the girl. Flowers filled the front of the church and down both the sides of the sanctuary. The church was completely filled and the crowd spilled out the door and into the parking lot. It was usually this way when a young person died, but this was extreme. Fortunately, there was no media present and it is doubtful that their presence would have been tolerated. Everyone seemed to be pleased with their absence—except possibly Pastor Kirksey. They were waiting for some news to break on the case, everyone assumed.

When it came time for the eulogy, the pastor held nothing back. He talked of what a lovely girl she was and how she came from the finest family. Pedigrees in the South were extremely important. He talked of her school accomplishments, her character and her sweet personality while leading up to the traditional assurance to family and friends that he had talked with her on many occasions about her faith in Jesus and how he wanted everyone to sleep soundly in the knowledge that she was at this very minute sitting at the table of the Lord God Almighty, feasting with her friends and family that had gone before her to heaven. Then he ended by warning all, that the only way to ever see that child again, the one they loved more than life itself, was to get right with God and join her on the day that they too, were called home. Then, with a strong and heartfelt prayer, it was over. The last chapter in the life of a 17-year-old girl was closed, as was her casket, as the church began to empty.

As the people began heading to their cars and trucks to join the processional into Cleveland for the burial, a man touched Sheriff Williams on the arm.

"Got a second, L.B.?" he whispered.

"Absolutely. How you been friend?" the sheriff answered.

"Fine. Anything developed on this one?" he asked.

"We got some things working," the sheriff responded, hoping he believed it.

"If it's a nigger, we'd like to know, sooner than later. Some of us are sick of the way things are going around here and don't intend to let the sumbitch walk," he said. "You get my drift?"

"You boys do what you gotta do, but you better keep your mouth shut for a change. Otherwise you'll have the FBI swarming down here like ants at a picnic like they did in Neshoba County when them three civil rights workers came up missing back in '64. I can control a lot, but nobody controls them. You get *my* drift?" the sheriff said.

"I gotcha, just keep us in the loop," he said.

"I'll see to it," the sheriff returned, deciding not to go into his thoughts on Tyrone Braid just yet.

Wayne had attended the funeral and sat beside his mother. He rubbed his hands together constantly and fidgeted throughout the service, or so it seemed to the pastor who watched him intently. He didn't go by and view the body like almost everyone else did prior to the start of the service and he got out of the church in somewhat of a rush, foregoing the processional ride to the cemetery with his parents. He left walking in the opposite direction the processional headed.

Paul Lane did not attend the funeral. He had plenty to do to keep him busy, that was for sure. At that very moment that morning, he was trying to run down a photo of Tyrone Braid from the Mississippi Department of Corrections so he could ask around the bus stop and other places if they had seen him. He needed to get one out to Chicago PD and the Cooke County, Illinois Sheriff's Department as well and let them know he was wanted for questioning. He had a stack of notices on his desk that indicated work ahead for him and more would come. The rest of the crime world didn't stop turning because of the Strawberry murder, unfortunately.

@ @ @ @ @ @ @

Steve Pope was about to take a lunch break at the service station in Cleveland where he had worked for the past two years. He worked full-time most of the summer and only part-time during the school year at Delta State where he was currently a senior. Presently, he had taken a summer course which cut into his work hours, but it was now over. While there he had met a girl, and dated her for the past month or so. A good-looking Italian girl named Janice Galtelli, and they had gone to see the new John Wayne movie, *True Grit* at the Ellis Theater in Cleveland the night before. He really liked her, but was a little bit intimidated by her. She was a couple years older than he was, but more importantly, she was divorced. That meant that his sexual prowess was subordinate to hers he thought, and that bothered him a lot. She seemed to be moving too fast for him in the relationship as well. He liked her, no doubt, but she seemed to like him even more, and he wasn't sure how she would be received around the fraternity house in the fall when school was back in session. On top of all that, if they got serious, his family would never accept her, a divorcee from Jackson. He had no intention of getting serious now, anyway. There was simply too much fruit for picking in the sororities and girls' dorms of Delta State. Maybe he needed to back off this one for a while. He would do just that and see what developed. If he didn't call or ask her out for a while, surely that would extinguish the flames of romance for her. He wanted to see her again, but not right now.

CHAPTER 14

Ruleville, Mississippi is located just to the east of Cleveland and the two towns are connected by Highway 8, a state highway that dissects the state from east to west. A local diner, The Mecca, had a separate room for banquets and large gatherings away from its main dining room. A large sign on the north wall of the room in large bold letters read: "This room proudly provided by the Ruleville Citizen's Council." There were similar rooms throughout the Delta and throughout all of the state where members of the Citizen's Council met and transacted their business. It wasn't the Kiwanis Club, the Lion's Club or the Rotary Club, all of whose members, like the Citizen's Council were white by design, but was still totally different. It was soft Klan. They had no robes, hoods or burning crosses, but they were Klan nonetheless.

The purge of the Ku Klux Klan in Mississippi had begun with the federal investigation of the disappearance of three civil rights workers in Neshoba County near Philadelphia, Mississippi in 1964. Paid infiltrators, turned informants, had exposed the Klan's church burnings, bombings, beatings of black residents who tried to vote or even register to do so, as well as the outright murder of blacks in an effort to suppress their rights as United States citizens. Many members fled the Klan to avoid prosecution when it was clear that their brothers couldn't be trusted, while others got out because Klaverns from around the state kept soliciting money from them to aid in the legal defense of those who were eventually prosecuted. "Lawyers don't work for nuthin'," they were told, and it was true. Either way it was analyzed, money brought down the Klan in Mississippi.

While the robed and hooded White Knights of the Ku Klux Klan in Mississippi dwindled away, other groups, nowhere near as conspicuous as the Klan, sprang up across the state in the form of the white Citizen's Council, a philanthropic-seeming social organization that was dedicated to the southern lifestyle and its preservation. Translated, that simply meant it was for the sole purpose of the advancement of white people, which seemed only fair to its members since there was an organization for the advancement of colored people as well. While the Citizen's Council had its faults, it was composed of members of the community who held a place of leadership and trust—like those who had gathered in Brock's Café the night of the Strawberry murder press conference. They were smarter than the cross burning, beer drinking, whoop-it-up members of the Ku Klux Klan at that time who filled their ranks largely from the bars and honkytonks of Mississippi. The members of the Citizen Council were home at night with their wives, helping their children with homework and serving on the Board of Deacons at church. However, often times their goals were the same.

Six men, all in suits, met in the reserved room at The Mecca in Ruleville that night. They were all from Bolivar County, they all were respected businessmen or employed professionally and they all had the same goal, and that was to make the son of a bitch that killed the Strawberry girl pay and pay dearly. That would send the appropriate message to the black community. They already knew the sheriff and his deputies were pursuing a black man, he had pretty much told them that. All they needed now was confirmation and a name. They would have a plan in place so as to act when the time came. They wouldn't do it themselves, that was below them, but they would have it done by someone who would jump at the chance to do it and thank them for the opportunity. It just took a little cash and that was the purpose of the meeting tonight. They would all make a financial commitment to either raise their share or pay it themselves. It didn't matter, as long as it was done. By the time they adjourned at 8:30 that night, the sum was set and their obligations were sealed. It was just a matter of time now and the nigger would pay, they said.

@ @ @ @ @ @ @

Pastor Kirksey went to the church office that next day bright and early at 8:00 a.m. He intended to finish his sermon for the next day, but his mind was occupied. He couldn't get Wayne off his mind and the way he had acted in his car a couple days ago. He didn't think Wayne had any part in the murder, but he must have seen something that bothered him. Getting it out of him, however, would be a feat in itself. He knew from past talks with him that if a subject that he was uncomfortable to talk about was broached, he shut up like an oyster on a pearl. He had once attempted to talk with him about sex after he observed him leering at the girls in the youth Sunday School class and thought he would let him know that it wasn't polite to stare. Surely, he thought, that would be easier than speaking to his mother about it. He was 35 years old at the time, for heaven's sake. The instant he brought up the subject of girls, Wayne crossed his arms, gripped himself and gave him the resulting lip curling sneer that was his habit and tried to change the subject immediately without answering. The pastor's persistence in questioning caused Wayne to leave the office as abruptly as he had left his car the other day. Questioning him would be difficult for sure, but he would try tomorrow after church.

When the following day's service ended, Wayne shook the pastor's hand as everyone did each and every Sunday as the congregation exited the church, the pastor standing at the front door. As he did, Kirksey pulled him close and whispered to him that he needed some help in the office for just a few minutes if he could spare the time. Wayne agreed and the two met in the pastor's study a couple of minutes later.

"Wayne, my friend, you and I need to continue our talk from the other morning, don't we?" the preacher asked.

"What's that?" Wayne asked back.

"You know, Wayne, God knows what's in everybody's heart and he knows everything that we know. We can't see or do anything without God knowing because he is watching over us all the time. You remember those things, don't you?"

Wayne had instantly begun rubbing his hands together, crossing his arms and nervously snarling as he did often, being careful not to make eye contact with the preacher. Kirksey thought himself a pseudo-expert in psychology and human behavior and watched his every move, facial and body expression. He knew Wayne was nervous. Now was the time to go in for the kill.

"Yes, sir I remember about that from the Bible," Wayne responded.

"Don't you think you need to get some things off your chest, son? I know you know something about poor Linda. She can't rest 'til the truth's told, you know," he said with conviction. "Tell me what you know about it."

"I, I, don't know nuthin'. I wasn't on that road that night," he said as tears started to roll down his cheeks.

Nobody said anything about being on a road, Kirksey thought. So, he had to be there and was giving himself away. "What happened, Wayne. Tell me what you know and what happened."

"Wayne, are you riding with us or not?" Mrs. Mullen inquired as she stood at the door to the pastor's study. "You need to come on if you are."

"I'm coming right now," he returned. Before Kirksey could ask him to stay, he was out of his chair and gone with his mom. Kirksey was frustrated, but couldn't make a big deal out of it because he didn't want Mrs. Mullen to know he was quizzing the man. He had been so close, but had been thwarted again. However, this surely wouldn't be his last attempt.

@ @ @ @ @ @ @

Dewitt Strawberry had been acting strange since earlier that afternoon, his wife thought, but really, what was normal these days? The had moved back by necessity into their home after the funeral, but it had been difficult. Everywhere they turned, there were memories of Linda and worse yet, of the awful crime that had been committed there. Carolyn understandably refused to sleep in her and Linda's bedroom and had taken up quarters in the spare bedroom that was luckily next to her parents. It was doubtful at this point if she would ever go back in that bedroom.

Sometime earlier that afternoon, Dewitt had received a phone call from someone, she didn't know who, and he had acted very secretive about it while he was on the phone, talking in a hushed tone. He seemed a little different afterwards, but she really couldn't put her finger on it. She never asked him who had called because neither pried into the other's business. If he wanted her to know, he would tell her, she was sure.

Dewitt had indeed received an important phone call earlier. A man whose voice he recognized, but who told him not to call him by name on the phone, had called and asked him if he could speak for a minute away from everybody.

"Sure," Dewitt said. "Let me step into the bedroom." He hung the phone and made a beeline for the bedroom and picked up the phone back there. "Still there?" Dewitt asked.

"I'm here," the man responded. "Anybody around?"

"Wife and daughter are in the den, but they can't hear. What's going on?"

"Look," the man said, "I know you think like the rest of us and are tired of the niggers doing anything they want and getting away with murder, no pun intended. If the one who killed your daughter happened to be convicted, he probably wouldn't get the death penalty and we'd end up takin' care of him the rest of his life. What kind of message do you think that would send to the brothers? We need to see that he is punished Southern style like we used to do and send the message to the porch monkeys that what happened to him will happen to them if they don't stay in line. Catch is, we don't want to do nuthin' without you as the victim saying you agree. You know it needs to be done, Dewitt, just like we do. What ya thinkin'?"

"What would I have to do?" Dewitt asked.'

"Just tell us you agree with us and we'll take it from there. You'll never know what's happen' 'til it's over and done, unless you want to," the mystery man responded. "Only thing we might want you to do is to give us the name of the suspect as soon as you get it from the sheriff or the DA's office. We need to do this thing before he's taken into custody, if possible. We can probably do it after he's arrested with some other contacts we have, but it will obviously be more difficult."

The image of his dead daughter flashed before him, alive and beautiful, then the image of what he had found when he walked into her bedroom after getting home from the hospital that night flooded his mind. "Do it, dammit," he said. "Send him to hell."

"You got it," the man said in return and the phone clicked leaving only the dial tone.

Dewitt hung up the phone. He had just ordered the execution of a man, or at least acquiesced in it. He had mixed emotions, not being sure how he felt about that. His ego was drunk with the thought of that kind of power. His anger and lust for revenge made him feel righteous while his conscience made him feel sinful. It was the right thing to do, he argued with himself. Somebody had to step up to the plate and call the pitch for the good of the community. The bastard had raped and murdered his little girl, dammit. Besides that, if he changed his mind, he could call it off he assumed, but he was deadly wrong about that.

Immediately after getting off the phone with Dewitt, the mystery caller made one more phone call. This time it was to one of the members of the Citizen's Council that had met at The Mecca in Ruleville previously.

"Dewitt Strawberry is good with it. All we need now is to pool the money and find our nigger's name," the man informed the other one on the line. "We need to meet in a couple of days and draw lots to see who the contact man will be."

"Agreed. Will Dewitt pass the name to us as soon as he knows? You know L.B. will tell him soon as he can, the political fool."

"No problem. Let's meet Tuesday night at The Mecca, again. 8 o'clock. You tell the other four."

"Good deal. See you then."

CHAPTER 15

Tyrone had been in Chicago now for a few days, staying at a cheap hostel on the south side. He had managed to pick up a dollar or two here and there to get by on by doing odd jobs around the neighborhood and the hostel, mostly just cleaning up stores and warehouses. Though he didn't like his situation, it was better than what he had waiting on him in Mississippi, but he rarely thought about it anymore. In the short period of time he had been in Chicago, he had immersed himself in the city and his new life, trying desperately to blend in with the locals. What he failed to understand was that the standard procedure for law enforcement in Mississippi when looking for a black defendant believed to be on the run and no longer in the area, was to look first in the large cities of St. Louis and Chicago, perhaps Memphis as well, because of their abundant black population. When it came to Chicago, the larger of the three which made it the prime target, they focused their search on the south side, again because it was the largest black-populated area of Chicago, blacks composing 75% plus of the population there. Finally, unless it was known that they had relatives in the area, they concentrated their search on the hostels, YMCA and other organizations that offered low income, temporary housing, especially in the initial phases of the search before the suspect could put down roots of any permanency. Tyrone had no way of knowing that he had followed the exact pattern that police would use in their search protocol.

Paul Lane had previously secured photos of Tyrone from the Department of Corrections and forwarded them to the authorities in Chicago. The photo was simply his mugshot from his penitentiary days, but that had been so recent that they should nevertheless be sufficient to help in identify him. He had notified his parole officer that he was wanted for questioning, but did not reveal the nature of the crime for which he was wanted, Paul being extremely careful not to point any more of a suspicious finger at him than was necessary for the time being. His parole officer in turn had advised all his contacts state-wide as well as in Chicago to BOLO, e.g., be on the lookout, for Tyrone Braid. The net was cast.

Paul figured he had done all he could for the time being on the Strawberry murder until he questioned Tyrone. They had simply hit a brick wall in the investigation. He thumbed through notices of other crimes over the last week or so, none of which seemed out of the ordinary for him. There were the usual marijuana possessions as well as a few other drug cases, some juvenile malicious mischief that he was routinely noticed about, but that he thankfully did not have to prosecute since they were not felonies and involved minors. There was also the abundance of property crimes that never seemed to end. Stolen cars, stolen farm equipment and even some embezzlement and bad check cases from some of the businesses in the county. Along with all that, he had just been notified of a break-in near Shaw of a house belonging to a family that had been on vacation for the past week in Panama City, Florida. They had returned to find their house had been broken into and all the electronics of any value as well as some jewelry had been taken. The exact date of the offense was unknown, but had to be within the last seven days since they had been gone. Great, he thought, on top of every other advantage the bad guys had, they had just gotten a possible week's start. Nothing like stacking the odds in their favor, he thought. He was about to look further into it when the phone rang.

"I'm looking for Investigator Lane," the caller said.

"You got him," Paul responded.

"This is Lieutenant Jeffrey Biggs with the Chicago PD. How are you this morning?"

"Been worse, how about yourself?"

"I definitely have been worse. Are you guys looking for a man identified as Tyrone Braid from Mississippi?" he inquired with his thick Yankee accent.

"Damn sure are, my man. Tell me you got him," Paul replied with his best Southern drawl.

"We do not have him in custody, but we think we know where he is located. It appears he is staying at a hostel in the city. I'll be glad to give you the particulars if you want to come up here and question him."

"Keep an eye on him and I'll be there tomorrow," Paul said. They exchanged contact information and addresses after which Paul hung up the phone. He immediately called Landon and told him the news.

"I'm gonna head north this afternoon as soon as I tie up some loose ends, Boss," Paul said. "I don't think we need to let this out until I talk to him and see what he has to say. If we tell L.B., he'll want to go and I don't need that right now. At the same time, I don't want to cause any friction between our office and his. What's your thoughts?" Paul asked.

"You go ahead alone. I may have to throw you under the bus with L.B. if he finds out and stirs up a stink," Landon answered. "You know, my faithful servant acted without tellin' me."

"I hear ya. Blame it all on the renegade investigator. No problem," Paul stated. He hung up the phone and made plans to head to Chicago later in the day. His first matter of business was to inform his secretary that he would be out that afternoon and most of the day tomorrow because he was going to Chicago to talk to someone on the Strawberry case, never divulging who the subject of his interview would be.

"If I have any appointments tomorrow, would you please reschedule them for me," he said.

"The only one you have is with the victim of that home burglary in Shaw last week while he was on vacation. Nothing else. Got something concrete on Strawberry?" she inquired.

"Not really. Just a hunch," he responded, brushing off the question. "See ya tomorrow."

"See ya then and be careful," she cheerfully replied.

He had barely made it to the parking lot when his secretary dialed a familiar number. When a man answered, she said, "Paul's on his way to Chicago on the Strawberry case. Somethings happenin' on it, but I'm not sure what. He was evasive."

"You got to stay on top of it and let us know who they're after. Don't think he is making an arrest, do you?", the man asked.

"No, it doesn't work like that. If the man was arrested out of state, they'd have an extradition hearing or a waiver. Haven't heard anything like that yet, but I'll keep you up on it when I do," she responded.

"Good girl. That's why I love ya," he returned. And with that, the conversation ended.

Paul rushed home, gathered some clothes and left for Chicago. The drive north to Memphis would take about an hour and a half to two hours depending on traffic, where he would cross the river and drive straight through to Chicago. With a little luck, he would get there in nine hours, but would probably take more like ten. He planned to spend the night near there and meet up with Lieutenant Biggs as early as possible the next morning. Hopefully, he could talk to Tyrone then and be back in Cleveland late the next day or early the next evening.

Driving north on Highway 61 to Memphis gave him the seldom offered opportunity to think about and analyze his cases. The Strawberry murder bothered him and it bothered him tremendously. He couldn't recall a murder that he had investigated or defended in his past attorney life that had so few leads. Whoever had committed it was either extremely smart or extremely lucky and left little clues for him. But, as he rationalized in his head, smarts will get you just so far, and luck always runs out. Despite the possible "I told you so" rantings that the sheriff would have the privilege of voicing, he hoped Tyrone was his man. He had never hoped otherwise, but he did want to be sure and not jump to any conclusions. He didn't care about the color of the killer, he could be black, white, brown or yellow, he just wanted his guilt to be determined by the facts and not some preconceived notion.

Almost eleven hours from when Paul had first left Cleveland, he exited off the freeway in Chicago to the welcoming sign of a Motel 6. It was almost midnight and he had no plausible explanation why it had taken that long to arrive. Either way, he was tired and hungry, and ready to get out the car. He checked in to the motel, all the while wishing the DA's office would spring for a Holiday Inn. After dumping his bags in the tiny room, he headed down the street to grab something to eat. Though he wanted to try some of the local hot dogs that he had heard about for years, the possibility of extreme indigestion forced him away from that thought. Instead, he opted for a small Chicago-style pizza and a cold draft beer from a tiny pizzeria that was still opened down the street from the motel. The ensuing heart burn he suffered throughout the night afterwards made him question his sanity for that choice and made him wish he had stuck with the thought of hot dogs. All the *Rolaids* this side of Lake Michigan couldn't suppress it, but it still didn't prevent him from sleeping hard until about 7 o'clock the next morning.

Before he got out of bed, he called the 37th precinct and talked with Lt. Biggs. They agreed to meet in one hour at a *Denny's Restaurant* near the station and would then begin their search to locate Tyrone Braid. The Chicago PD officer would accompany him and open up his office for the man's questioning if he desired.

When they met in the restaurant, they exchanged pleasantries over coffee and after a short time, headed out to the hostel where Tyrone had been staying. The older man at the front desk was most helpful.

"I'm Lt. Biggs with the Chicago PD, this is Investigator Paul Lane," he said, both men showing him their badges and identification. "Do you have this man, Tyrone Braid, staying here?"

"He looks familiar, but the man I know doesn't go by that name. That looks like Henry Baines who stayed here for a while, but he left about two days ago, the man said.

Feeling his hopes deflate, Paul interjected, "Do you know where he might have gone?"

"No, I don't, but he had a part time job for Kruger Company at their warehouse doing something. Don't know if you can find him there, but I can give you the address of the place if you would like," the elderly gentleman answered.

"We would be most appreciative," Paul said.

The man gave them the information, they thanked him and the two men left. They proceeded directly to the warehouse in the Chicago PD's black and white cruiser and arrived about ten minutes later. As they entered the warehouse, they observed several men working with a forklift operator clearing an area and Paul immediately recognized one as the long-sought Tyrone Braid. He wore a hard hat and denim coveralls, but Paul had committed his face to memory after several days of looking at his mugshot. He told Lt. Biggs which one he was by pointing him out to him.

"Tyrone Braid! Chicago Police Department. We need to speak with you," Biggs called out to him, a move he would soon regret.

Paul Lane and the Chicago PD Lieutenant had apprehended many suspects in their combined careers, but Tyrone Braid would not be one of them on that day. As soon as Biggs had called out to him, Tyrone knew there was trouble brewing and ran. He dropped his hard hat and fled from the warehouse through a back hall and out into the street. He headed east down the street and cut through an open-air market of knock off t-shirts, fake watches and other flea market specials. When he cleared the market, he ran north into an oriental laundry and through the back heading, east again. He didn't slow down until he knew he had left the men far behind and unsure of the direction he had fled. It didn't take Biggs and Paul long to figure out they were no match for the fleet footed Tyrone who, unlike them, was literally running for his life. Two blocks from the warehouse, they slowed their chase, unsure of the direction he had taken. They couldn't have caught up with Tyrone if they had wheels on their shoes. Two middle-aged, overweight chaps versus a former high school running back that *needed* to get the hell away was a mismatch from the start.

"Damn," Paul exclaimed. "There goes our one shot at him."

"He caught me off guard when he ran that quickly," Biggs said. "I'm losing it," he confessed. Paul wondered if Biggs ever had it, considering the shape he was in now.

"We don't know where to look for him now, either. If the old man at the hostel was telling the truth, and I have no reason to doubt him, he won't be going back there since he's not staying there anymore. Looks like I wasted a trip and you wasted a morning's work," Paul apologetically said.

"Pay is the same, my man," Biggs laughed. "We will watch for him. He might turn up again. If he does, I'll be sure to let you know." Neither man had been able to catch their breath just yet and were huffing and puffing while down on one knee..

Paul returned to Cleveland that night, arriving just before 11 o'clock. He didn't bother to go by the office as he usually did, regardless of the time, after being away. He was tired and disgusted from his failed mission to question Tyrone and was in no mood to read phone messages from police officers and crime victims questioning him of the status of their cases. He would check in early enough tomorrow, but for now, he needed some sleep in his own bed after a whirlwind trip to the Windy City.

CHAPTER 15

Though Janice Galtelli was dead, she managed to play mind games with Steve Pope and send him into a tailspin of confusion, anyway. He had intentionally refused to call her or contact her after their last date in an effort to discourage her from pursuing him, at least for any long-term relationship, but instead he never received any calls or contacts from her since, and that was not part of his plan. He was so certain that she would chase after him when he quit calling her that he was stunned when she didn't and his male ego was crushed. She had gone from making daily contact with him, sometimes as much as twice a day, to going totally silent over the last five. What the hell was wrong with this woman, he asked himself? He was a damn fine catch and she was turning her nose up at him, or so it seemed. Curiosity and Budweiser convinced him, on the fifth day of their reciprocal silence to ride out to her house and see if she happened to be entertaining anyone that he needed to know about. That had to be it. That was the only explanation he could conceive. Someone else had moved onto his territory and was at that moment attempting to root him out of her favor, the bastard. Though he didn't want her, his ego didn't want anyone else having her either.

He took the fifteen-minute drive out to Interstate and slowed as he passed her house. Her car was under the carport, but the house was dark. It was about 9 o'clock, too early for her to be in bed, but if she wasn't and was there, she would certainly not be sitting in the dark. His hunch must have been right and she was out on a date with someone else, the bitch! He accelerated past her house and returned to his apartment to finish off what was left of his six-pack. A couple hours later, he tried to call. After the phone rang eight times he hung it up and tried not to think about what or who she may be doing, and fell asleep.

During his lunch break the next day, Steve went to a pay phone and tried Janice again. Still no answer. For someone uninterested in her, he was persistent and seemed to know all about her daily schedule because he couldn't think of a single reason why she would not be home at that time of day. She wasn't working anywhere and he had often called during his lunch hour. When he got home, he tried her again with the same result, no answer. Now he was wondering if she had gone out of town with her new suitor, the little slut! He tried on seven different occasions between his returning home from work that day and getting off his job the following day, including a repeat of the lunchtime attempt with no success. Only after those failed attempts did it enter his mind that something may be wrong, and he decided to repeat his drive-by from a couple days ago.

He went straight from work out to the country, passing the usual array of cotton fields, soybeans and the occasional pasture as he drove. As he approached her house, this time in broad daylight, he noticed that the grass in her yard was unusually overgrown and appeared not to have been mowed for quite a while, uncustomary for someone who had always kept it neat and trimmed because she had so much time on her hands with no full-time job. Even stranger, her mailbox was overflowing with magazines, letters, bills and the usual junk mail everyone received over time. Even if she had gone out of town with Romeo she would have made arrangements for someone to pick up the mail or have it temporarily halted. He passed the house, went to the next drive a half mile away and turned around, then proceeded back toward her house. This time, he pulled into her drive and decided to leave her a note on the door that he had "been in the neighborhood" and just stopped by to visit, only to find she was away. As soon as he approached the door under the carport, the overpowering smell of decomposing flesh filled his nostrils, causing him to almost vomit. The smell, enhanced by the near one-hundred-degree heat and ninety percent humidity, made him step backward toward his car and look for a dead animal around the carport or in the yard, all the while holding his hand over his mouth and nose. Unable to find anything dead there, he realized the smell was coming from within the house and he panicked. Jumping into his car, he wheeled out of the drive and headed back toward Cleveland to the nearest law enforcement officer he could find.

@ @ @ @ @ @ @

Wayne had run from the pastor's study that day and purposely avoided him after that. He was visibly shaken after he left and had no intentions of going back through that inquisition again. He remained at home for the most part in order to do so, but soon, he was back on the road between his home and Cleveland, walking, watching and listening. The heat and humidity were staggering, and the occasional clouds brought a little relief every now and then, but they didn't linger very long. The blacktop road had become so hot, it was sticking to his shoes along with tiny rocks of gravel. As he neared the north end of Interstate Road, he passed the residence of Janice Galtelli, and stopped at the end of her driveway, looking and listening as he always did, unaware that Steve Pope had left only a short time ago. As he did so, a swirl of wind brought the pungent smell of rotting flesh to him, and like Steve had done, be backed away and cast his eyes across the lawn for a dead animal. He walked under the carport to where the car was parked and looked around it among the empty paint cans, tools and a gas can that was stored there. The odor was stronger there, but he didn't see the source. Not really thinking, he walked around into the back yard to investigate further, wading the somewhat overgrown grass, and was returning to the front when a sheriff's deputy pulled into the drive, followed by Pope. Alarmed at their presence, Wayne broke into a run and headed back south down the road, quickly pursued by the deputy who had no idea who he was or why he was there, much less why he had run.

"Stop! Get your hands up!" the deputy shouted, which only caused Wayne to run faster. "I'm warning you! Stop!" Seeing that his verbal commands were having no effect, the deputy, who was slightly more than half Wayne's age and in much better shape, overtook his target and tackled him in the ditch on the side of the road.

"I give up! I give up!" Wayne yelled as the officer rolled him over onto his stomach and pressed his knee into Wayne's back near his neck in order to restrain him temporarily. He then brought the suspect's arms to his back and cuffed both of his hands.

"Get up," the officer commanded and as he pulled on the cuffed man's arms to assist him. "Why were you running?" he asked.

"Just scared," Wayne responded.

The deputy escorted Wayne back to his patrol car and placed him in the backseat.

"You stay here until we sort this thing out. Right now, you are looking at a resisting arrest charge. You better hope that's all you are charged with," he warned, as he headed toward the house.

He approached the carport door and knocked, barely able to withstand the assault on his senses by the smell that permeated the humid air. He walked around the house and tried to look into the windows, but the curtains had been drawn tight. Finally, he returned to the door under the carport and found it was unlocked. He slowly opened it and announced, "Sheriff's Office, anyone here?" He walked a few steps more into the kitchen area and made the same announcement with similar results. He began a room to room search of the premises, service weapon drawn, announcing his presence as he entered each room. When he entered the master bedroom in the rear of the house, he was confronted with a sight that would turn the stomach of even the most seasoned law enforcement official.

The body of Janice Galtelli was sprawled across the bed, legs spread open and head turned to its side, eyes opened. Her nightgown and underwear were piled up toward the bathroom door and her jeans and blouse were scattered on the opposite side of the room. Importantly, her belt lay at the foot of the bed, curled into a circle. To the layman, it couldn't be readily determined whether the girl had died of natural causes or by some criminal act, but to a trained eye, the position of the body and legs, the presence of the belt out of the jeans and the ripped underwear were tell-tale signs of a brutal assault and rape culminating in murder. The condition of the body because of the advanced decomposition would make physical evidence collection more difficult, but certainly not impossible. The officer gagged but held his lunch as he left the room, went back through the house and out to his car.

From the look on the face of the officer, Steve Pope knew she was dead. The officer confirmed that to him in a cold professional manner as he had been trained, warned him not to go inside and sat down under the wheel of his car. He grabbed the microphone of his radio and called the dispatcher, requested backup officers, and an ambulance to the location and reported his findings.

"SO 27, SO. I need backup and an ambulance out on Interstate Road. Address is Route 3, box 267, Shaw. Probable 187 as well as a possible 261. I'm at the scene now and have a suspect in custody. Need to notify SO-1 and DA as well," he told the dispatcher, trying desperately to sound professional, but being physically shaken.

"10-4, SO 27. I receive and will dispatch backup and ambulance," the dispatcher returned. "Please keep the scene secure."

"10-4, SO, I copy."

Hanging up the radio mike, the officer turned to Wayne who was cuffed in the backseat, sweating profusely, and said, "I believe you are going to have some explaining to do my man."

"What's that," Wayne asked, unaware of the situation, though he had heard the officer's conversation with the dispatcher. Being unfamiliar with police lingo, the conversation may have well been in Spanish.

"Don't play ignorant, Dumbo, there's a dead girl in that house and I arrive to find you running from the backyard. You refused to stop, forcing me to take you down. You don't think that looks just a little bit suspicious?"

"I never seen her before," Wayne said.

"Right. You just make yourself comfortable for the time being. I'll be taking you in for some questions, shortly. You just relax."

For the next 30 minutes, they waited for the requested backup and ambulance, everyone in a vehicle with the air conditioner running at full blast to escape the heat and the odor. When the ambulance arrived, it was escorted by L.B. Williams, and two other sheriff's units. Paul Lane arrived within fifteen minutes of their arrival. Four patrol cars, an ambulance, and an unmarked vehicle, all with lights flashing, sat in the drive and in the yard of the Galtelli residence at the time. The news of the activity there spread through the community and the county like the flu. The reality that there was another murder coming on the heels of the Strawberry murder, sent shock waves through the area. Yellow police tape around a local residence was becoming a sickening scene too often repeated. The coroner was dispatched almost immediately and performed his duties at the Galtelli residence before the body was transported to the morgue.

CHAPTER 16

The investigation team, led by Paul, carefully went through the Galtelli home and particularly the master bedroom and bathroom, photographing everything as they went. There was no way by mere observation that they could determine whether the victim had been raped because of the length of time that had passed since the crime occurred. If there were traces of semen, it would have to be detected by the lab. Unlike the Strawberry murder which had been discovered virtually within minutes of its occurrence, they could only speculate at this point about the time of death, and the advanced decomposition made even the cause of death questionable, though everything pointed to strangulation. The scene resembled the Strawberry murder scene in many eerie ways, however. Both victims were young, attractive females who were caught in their bedrooms alone when they were murdered. Both were at night, near bedtime for the victims, apparently. Strangulation was the manner of death of choice of the perpetrator, or all evidence pointed to it at the time. Both had their panties ripped off of them and tossed aside with the remainder of the clothing they were apparently wearing. There were very little, if any, signs of a struggle at either scene and there was no evidence of forced entry in either case. Though they could not know it at the time, no fingerprints would be found at either scene other than those that would be expected, such as family members, leading to a conclusion that gloves were used by the assailant.

"We have a second victim murdered by the same suspect in all likelihood," Paul surmised outside the home to the sheriff. We'll find out soon enough when the crime occurred from the lab. She'll go to Jackson first thing tomorrow for an autopsy. What about the suspect they arrested?"

"Wayne Milton, aged 38. Lives down the road here. I've seen him in Cleveland roaming around for years. He's retarded. We'll get him a public defender before we really ask him anything because of that. You know how they are, soon as he says something to incriminate himself some lawyer will be hollering about how we knew he was touched in the head and forced him to talk. That's all we got on him," the sheriff said.

"Good thing he's white, huh L.B.? If he'd have been black running from the scene of a murder, you'd be ready to pin the Lindbergh kidnapping on him, too," Paul surmised.

"Got a helluva lot more on that Braid kid than running from the scene," L.B. said. I'll be anxious to hear where he was when the time of death on this one is determined. What do you bet he can't account for his whereabouts?"

The memory of the Braid kid running out of the warehouse to his and Biggs shock and disbelief was still fresh in Paul's mind, making Paul even more eager than the sheriff to talk to him. A twin murderer in Bolivar County? That was hard to fathom, but it certainly appeared that way.

@ @ @ @ @ @ @

As promised, the body of Janice Galtelli was transported the following morning to the State Crime Lab in Jackson, an understaffed and underfunded bunch that was expected to produce miracles for law enforcement across the state. Unless the case had serious questions that need to be answered about the death, officials were cautioned not to request an autopsy to prevent any more of a backlog of cases than they already had. The Strawberry murder had very few questions, except the identity of the killer, but this one certainly qualified. A preliminary report could be expected in ten days. It came by telephone in eight days.

"Dr. Luther Cromwell with the State Crime Lab calling, may I speak to Paul Lane?" the caller asked.

"Yes, sir. One minute," the secretary stated.

"Paul Lane," he said.

"Mr. Lane, Dr. Cromwell in Jackson. I can give you some preliminary facts on the Galtelli murder over the phone and follow-up later with a written preliminary if you'd like."

"Absolutely, thank you, sir."

"Ok, it looks like we are going to have a death by strangulation as you suspected. Contusions to the neck consistent with a ligature of approximately three-quarter inch indicates it was flat, uh, maybe a belt of some type that was used. Ruptured blood vessels in the eyes corroborate the strangulation finding. There was trauma to the genital area indicating forcible penetration that was most likely postmortem due to the lack of bleeding. Sperm traces were found in the vaginal canal as well as on the bed sheet that you submitted. There was no hair or skin samples that could be connected to the suspect found on the body or under the nails of the victim. She apparently struggled very little with the suspect, if at all, indicated by the lack of wounds on her body that he likely would have inflicted. Time of death seems to be within seven to nine days from discovery of the body. Oh, one other thing. Best we can tell, there is an abrasion on her right hand, the ring finger, that is consistent with someone forcibly removing a ring following death."

"Seven to ten days," Paul said thinking out loud. That put it just before or just after the Strawberry murder.

"Yep, you got yourself a multiple murderer or a good copycat. If it is a multiple murderer, he's on a binge, because you usually don't see murders by psychologically driven killers that close together unless they have lost complete control after a string of murders over a long period of time," Dr. Cromwell said. "Haven't had any similar ones in your area previously have, you?"

"None that I'm aware of," Paul replied. "I'll do some checking around the state, though."

"Multiple murderer or copycat, you've got one bad hombre' on your hands," the doctor speculated. "Better catch him quick."

"I intend to. Thanks for the prelim," Paul replied, and hung up the phone.

@ @ @ @ @ @ @

When Wayne was transported to the Bolivar County jail that night to be held for questioning, the sheriff saw that one of the local attorneys who routinely served as a public defender was summoned and talked to him before he was questioned. Then, after being advised of his rights pursuant to the directives of the recent U.S. Supreme Court case of *Miranda vs. Arizona* and with his attorney present, he underwent questioning by the sheriff.

"Wayne, you need to be honest with me and we'll get this thing over with quick as possible, okay? You were out at the Galtelli residence when my deputy showed up and he saw you running from behind the house. He ordered you to stop and you didn't, but he caught up with you and brought you in. All that right, so far?" the sheriff asked.

Wayne, who was bent at the waist as he sat rubbing his hand furiously replied, "Yes sir, that's right."

"What was you doing back there anyway?"

"I was just looking for that smell. I knew something was dead, but I couldn't find it."

"You know the girl, Wayne?" the sheriff asked. "Ever met her?"

"No, sir."

"Sure, about that?" the sheriff inquired further.

"No, sir, never have." He was switching from crossing his arms and sneering to rubbing his hands like a man possessed now.

"How long had you been there," L.B. asked.

"Just got there just before the law came," he said.

"Why didn't you stop when he told you to?"

"I don't know, scared," Wayne replied. "I'm sorry 'bout that."

"Let me talk to your lawyer here for a minute outside, Wayne. We'll be right back."

The sheriff and the young lawyer stepped outside and talked. From the albeit weak questioning by the sheriff, it appeared Wayne was simply at the wrong place at the wrong time and had nothing to do with the

Galtelli murder. It was agreed that he would be released and allowed to return home, having spent most of the first night away from home in his life that he could remember.

Word of his being taken for questioning brought differing opinions from the people in the county and especially the community of Interstate. Those that knew him thought it preposterous that he had even been considered as a suspect. Others who didn't know him so well were not so sure. Pastor Kirksey was among those who were concerned that he might need to be checked out more thoroughly, but kept his opinion to himself for the time being. The sheriff had no concerns, not yet anyway.

@ @ @ @ @

Tyrone Braid was dumbfounded that he had been located so far away from home and so soon. He was scared to return to the tiny apartment he now shared with one of his co-workers from the warehouse for fear they would be waiting there. He decided to move from that area of the city to another as for now and would move from the city completely if he felt it necessary. Whether he was aware or not, the MS Department of Corrections had placed a hold on him for a parole violation for leaving the state if he happened to be picked up by any agency for any offense. Paul Lane had seen to that upon return from his failed trip to Chicago. Someone would catch up with him one way or the other.

Tyrone needed to get in touch with someone back home and find out what was going on there and maybe solve the mystery of how he had been located. His only confidante there was
Darcel.

"Long distance call from Tyrone, will you accept the charges?" the operator asked.
"Yes ma'am, I will," Darcel responded. This time she didn't bother to complain about the cost of the call to him.
"Darcel, how's things at home?" he asked.

"Good, how about you?" she responded.

"Darcel, a cop came looking for me today with someone else. Do you know who it was or how they found me?"

"Tyrone, I don't even know where you are. Somebody came by here after you left asking questions about where you been, some investigator from Cleveland. I told him you had gone to Leland to look for a job and put him off. He ain't been back," she informed him.

"Didn't say why he was lookin' for me?"

"Did not."

"Ok, that was probably him up here. That or somebody with the parole office. I'll get a number for you to call me if something happens, soon as I get it. I'm moving around right now. Gotta go now."

"Be careful, Tyrone."

They both hung up the phones.

CHAPTER 17

Paul was reeling from the preliminary information that he had received from the Crime Lab, especially the time of death. Though highly unlikely, it was possible from Dr. Cromwell's estimate that both girls were murdered on the same day, a homicidal appetite he did not want to even think about if that was the case. This was one brutal, vicious SOB and he was still out there. It was time he and L.B. got on the same page, so he arranged a meeting with the sheriff later that afternoon in Paul's office. They both agreed to bring their respective investigation files and without holding anything back from the other, share their findings, theories of guilt and collected evidence. The sheriff was more than agreeable and was anxious to hear the preliminary findings of the Crime Lab that Paul had indicated he had received. Paul began to prep for his meeting when his Secretary buzzed him.

"Mr. Lane, you have Ralph West here for your 2 o'clock appointment. Shall I send him in?" she said.

"Please do," he responded, though it irritated him that he had forgotten about the appointment and was trying to concentrate on the murders.

Ralph West was the man who lived just outside of Shaw and had returned from vacation to find his home burglarized, the same person whom Paul had cancelled his appointment with on the day he drove to Chicago, and he didn't want to keep him waiting.

"Good afternoon, Mr. West, I'm Paul Lane. How can I help you?"

"You can catch the thugs that ransacked my house while I was on vacation for starters," he responded, half joking, but obviously serious.

"Let me tell you where we are. We have sent notices to all the pawn shops in the county as well as in Washington and Sunflower County with descriptions of the things taken from your house. So far, they haven't attempted to be pawned, yet. We dusted for some prints, compared them to your family's prints that ya'll graciously gave us for comparison purposes and have come up with nothing there as far as any other prints are concerned. It makes it difficult not to know the date of the crime as well. We're really hoping we can catch the thieves," Paul said.

"Basically, if I'm hearing you right, you've taken prints and checked the pawn shops and that's about it, huh. You don't have anybody in particular in mind as a suspect and don't have anything else you can do. Am I getting' this right?" West asked with his frustrations exposed.

"I wish I could say you are wrong, but unfortunately, without some witnesses, some fingerprints, some pictures, there really isn't a whole lot that we can do. Hope we can get lucky and he tries to sell or pawn the property," Paul responded. "I know it's frustrating."

"Damn right it is. I don't mean to be critical of you. I see what you mean, it's just a shame when some thief comes in and takes what you worked hard to get for yourself. Thanks for your time and please let me know if something develops."

He shook Paul's hand and went out the door. Paul hated that part of the job. The part where you had to tell someone who has been a victim of a crime that the bad guys were likely going to win and get away with it, whether they liked it or not. The truth is somehow hard to take, but it must be told. He shut the door to the office and returned to his files on the two murders, Strawberry and Galtelli in preparation for his meeting with the sheriff.

The sheriff came to his office right on time, an expandable file filled with documents under his left arm. His secretary showed him into the conference room and Paul appeared a minute later. Together they spread the materials they had across the 8-foot walnut table.

"Let's talk about Galtelli first, since we haven't had a chance to talk about it together before now," Paul suggested.

"Fine with me," the sheriff said, and Paul began to repeat in as much detail as he could the information revealed to him by Dr. Cromwell with the State Crime Lab. When he was finished, they both were silent for a second.

"So, here's what we know for sure: The two murders are by far too much alike to conceive that they were done by two people, even someone trying to copy the first, whichever one was first. The removal of the rings from both girls has not been made known to the public, so there is no way anyone knew that in order to duplicate it. Also, both girls were strangled from behind, which may have been assumed, but has not been revealed to the public. The way the bodies were both stripped of their underwear is identical. I'm convinced we are looking for a single killer who, unfortunately for everyone, committed the murders pretty much near the same time, no more than seven days apart," Paul surmised.

"Five," corrected the sheriff, the boyfriend says they had a date on Thursday night, 3 days after the Strawberry murder. Hadn't heard from her or talked to her since that day." It was ironic that Steve Pope, the man that didn't want to be connected to Janice Galtelli on a permanent basis, would now always be thought of as her boyfriend.

"So, you talked to the boyfriend. His story check out? You don't believe he had any involvement?" Paul asked the sheriff.

"Naw. He's just a jealous kid that came out to the house to see if she was screwing around on him," the sheriff returned.

"What about Milton, the one they caught at the scene?"

"Talked to him, too. He hasn't got enough sense to do the deed. He's just a local dumdum that walks the roads and is nosey as hell. Happened by and smelled the body, that's what he says. Got no reason not to believe him," the sheriff said. Paul had to talk himself out of asking L.B. if either of the two they had just talked about had been black would he have a reason to disbelieve their stories. He knew the answer anyway.

"So, the bottom line on both cases is that we really don't have a suspect at all, except maybe the Braid boy, right?" Paul asked.

"That's the way I see it," L.B. agreed with a smirk.

"I think we may possibly rule out Braid as well."

"How's that?"

"I happen to know that he's been in Chicago for a little while, possibly during the time of the Galtelli murder, and if he's not guilty of Galtelli, he can't be guilty of Strawberry, either," Paul announced. "Looks like he might have gone to Chicago about the same time as the Galtelli murder. I've got to confirm when he actually left here for Chicago, but it looks like it's gonna be close to that time," Paul explained. "Right now, I just don't know, but I will eventually."

"And just how long have you known this little tidbit of information? I've been running up and down the road between here and the other end of the county trying to catch him at his house. When were you going to tell me?" the sheriff asked, his face flushed from obvious anger.

"Just been busy L.B., with this new murder and all. I promise I wasn't trying to keep it from you," Paul lied with a straight face. He wouldn't be telling him now if he thought he didn't have to eventually. The sheriff pounded his fist on the table in aggravation.

"I'm going to talk to Landon about this. I'm sorry, Paul, I thought we were on the same team, but I guess that ain't the case. I'm trying to catch a killer and you're more interested in defending a nigger. We're through here today. We're either going to work together or I'll do my thing and you do yours." The more he thought about it, the angrier he became.

"Look L.B., I'm sorry. I just want to be sure when we make an arrest that we are sure, that's all," Paul somewhat pleaded. He had not expected this.

The sheriff had gathered up his papers and returned them to their original place in his file. He stormed to the door and while standing in the reception area of the office, yelled back to Paul, "You take good care of your nigger, you hear. I wouldn't get too attached to him, though.

When I get through, I'll have Tyrone Braid where he needs to be, you hear me? Right where he needs to be, waiting to sniff gas at Parchman," he said just before he stormed out, slamming the outer door to the office so violently that the pictures in the office shook.

Paul gathered his documents from the conference table, returned them to the file and went into his secretary's office which adjoined the reception area. She was casually playing with an ink pen on her desk pretending that she didn't hear the obvious tirade.

"Sorry you had to hear that. Our meeting obviously didn't go as planned," he apologetically said.
"No problem," she said. "I've heard worse."

Paul took the files back to his office, grabbed his car keys and said, "I probably won't t be back until in the morning. I hear a cold beer calling."
"See you then," she said.

As soon as she was sure he had left the building, she dialed a familiar number, listening as the rotary dial phone clicked in her ear after every number she dialed. When a man answered, she said, "I got you a name. Tyrone Braid. Don't know nothing else about him, but that's the man. Thought you might want to know as soon as you could. Sheriff's convinced he's the one."

"That's what we been waitin' for, darling. Wish I had two more just like you," the man flirted.
"Honey, you couldn't handle any more than me," she giggled, "but you're welcome to try me anytime," and hung up the phone.

@ @ @ @ @ @ @

Paul drove to a nearby country bar known as "The Thicket" out on Highway 446. The bar was nothing more than a pre-fab metal building along the side of the highway, decorated with a host of beer signs, neon and painted, depicting hunting and fishing scenes and had the usual gravel parking area. Apparently, one couldn't fish without drinking and despite the inherent danger, hunting was the same. Though there was nothing that indicated so, the bar was for whites only, although no black person alive would even try to come in and subject himself to the recorded sounds of Elvis, Three Dog Night or Neil Diamond. Frankly, white people wouldn't have been welcomed at P. Willie's Place and certainly would not have cared for the jive music played there either. The most segregated places in the South were the bars, funeral homes and the churches.

Paul needed to decompress from the volatile ending of his meeting with the sheriff, and a beer with a fried ham sandwich with lettuce and tomato, even at this early hour, was just the ticket. He walked in, bellied up to the bar, and placed his order. The lady behind the counter handed him a beer from a vat of crushed ice and took his money.

I'll bring the sandwich to your table, hon," she said with a smile. She was probably his age but with many, many more miles than him.
"Thank, you ma'am. Can you add cheese to it, too?" Paul asked.
"Sure thing" she responded.

Paul took his beer and sat at a table toward the back. The longneck was dripping in moisture and so was Paul, just from the walk from his car to the bar. He drank a swallow of beer, finally relaxed completely in the chair, then chugged another swallow. He would need a second one by the time his food got there he thought to himself, so he called for another to be brought at that time.

"I'll bring it, hon" the lady called back. "Sandwich is almost ready." With that assurance, he killed the remainder of the beer he had and pushed the bottle to the opposite side of the table.

The sandwich was nothing more than a BLT with cheese, ham instead of bacon, but looked and tasted delicious. He was just into his second bite when a man tapped him on the shoulder.

"How goes it, Paul? Must be nice having banker's hours!" he exclaimed.

"I started work at 5 this morning," Paul shot back, again lying, but knowing the man didn't believe it.

"Haven't seen you but a couple times since you moved back here. Still puttin' bad guys away?"

"Only when we catch em'," Paul laughed.

Larry Doyle was an old high school classmate of Paul's from Cleveland High who, like most of the ones in his class, had never left the Delta since their birth and had never really even thought of such. He was employed at the local medical supply factory rotating shift work every fourteen days, a job he had taken right out of high school and been with ever since. He seemed happy with a small house in a subdivision, two children and a wife that worked as a teller at one of the local banks. It didn't take much to make him happy, though. He was one of those guys that took life as it came and was satisfied with whatever he got. Best of all, you could count on him to bail you out of jail if need be. Just a good ole boy.

"Ya'll gonna catch that son of a bitch that killed the girl out towards Shaw?"

'Which girl?" Paul joked.

"Both of 'em, I guess."

"Damn sure hope so, eventually. Just ain't got much to go on now."

"That's not what I'm hearing, Paul," Larry said as he pulled out a chair at the table and sat down.

"What's the word on the street, then?" Paul asked, as he bit off another bite of sandwich.

"Word is you got a nigger boy you trying to run down, but ain't caught up with yet," Larry said, taking a swig from the Miller beer he was holding and wiping his mouth with his sleeve.

"I promise you we don't have enough on anybody to make an arrest," Paul reiterated, wondering just how much information was out there. "I don't suppose you know who this guy is supposed to be do you?"

"Nope, that's your business. But I'll tell you something friend to friend and it don't go no further than here. If you say I told you, I'll call you a liar to your face," Larry warned. "My wife tells me that her boss at the bank and some of the others are settin' back waitin' to find out who it is, and if he's black as they suspect, he's a dead man." Larry had lowered his voice to such an extent that Paul was barely able to hear, but he got the message.

"Klan, Citizen's Council, or just a group of good ole boys with too much time and beer on their hands?" Paul asked further.

"Does it really matter, Paul? Either way, the nigger's dead and you get stuck with trying to find out who killed him and indicting friends and neighbors, all of which would probably be hard to convict in this county. Don't know what they payin' you, but you fixin' to need a raise," Larry observed. "Makes my job look easy compared to yours."

"How good do you think your information is, Larry?" Paul asked.

"If it was a tip at the dog track, I'd bet my house on the trifecta."

"Damn," Paul said. "Thanks for the warning."

"Not a warning, a promise. And remember what I said about calling you a liar."

"No problem," Paul assured him. He purposely turned the conversation to Larry's success in the deer woods last fall and his prospects for the season coming up. The two never broached the subject of the case again, though they sat and talked for an hour afterwards before promising to get together in the future and go fishing, a promise both knew they would never keep. Just before they parted ways, Paul asked, "By the way, you still frog giggin' like you used to?"

"Damn right," Larry responded. "A man just can't eat squirrel every day," he added with a big grin. Damn, it was good to grow up in the South, Paul thought.

The drive home gave Paul the opportunity to consider the ramifications of what he had been told. If Tyrone was the killer, who cared what happened to him? If the vigilantes took him out it might save his office and the state a lot of work and achieve the same result. But then his ethical conscience played hardball. Tyrone could never be the killer until a jury of his peers said so, and that could never be accomplished if he couldn't be brought to trial. Paul's duty was to protect Tyrone, as disgusting as that may be if he, in fact, was the killer, and see that he has his day in court. The Klan, the Citizen's Council or whatever name the boys were going by these days would have to wait and see what the jury said, whether they wanted to or not. If they acted as soon as they discovered his name, Larry was right and Paul would have to investigate and bring them to justice, whoever they were, even friends, relatives or community leaders. He tried not to think of the consequences to his career and even his life if that happened.

CHAPTER 18

Wayne had been released from custody and allowed to go home early in the morning hours. When he got home, around 4:30 that morning, he went straight to bed, having been up all night. His mother didn't ask him about where he had been. She was afraid to ask her son about it since he had not volunteered to tell her in the first place. She figured he would approach her about it later if he needed to talk.

James Weeks had heard about the Galtelli murder not far from his home, and more importantly, had heard about Wayne's questioning. James wasn't that familiar with him, nor was he aware of Wayne's propensity to walk, watch and listen. But when he heard he had been at the Galtelli home when her body was found, he began to do some investigation of his own, so he thought he might start with the sheriff's office. As luck would have it, he and Pastor Kirksey had arrived at the sheriff's office at virtually the same time to voice their concerns about the abnormal activities of Wayne Milton and his connection to the Galtelli and Strawberry murders. While seated in the reception area of the sheriff's office and jail, they had a chance to meet and converse.

"I'm W.D. Kirksey, pastor at the Interstate Baptist Church," the preacher said.

"Good to meet you, sir, James Weeks, here," he replied. I live on Interstate Road, myself."

"Hope you can come visit us sometime," Kirksey said, always eager to add to the flock.

"I appreciate it, but me and my family go to the Methodist Church in Shaw," Weeks returned, shifting uncomfortably. He had put down the *Field and Stream* magazine he had picked up to read. "Are you visiting someone here at the jail?" He was looking for common ground that he and the preacher might have.

"No, not today, fortunately. Since you live out my way you're aware of the tragedy we've had over the last couple of weeks. I'm here to address the sheriff with some concerns I have about a man he questioned earlier."

"Me, too," replied Weeks. I had an incident at my house last week that involved a prowler and I want the sheriff to be aware. Happened about the time they say the Galtelli girl was killed."

Weeks proceeded to tell the story of the incident with the prowler that he had run off with a blast of his shotgun, leaving so fast that he had left behind his straw hat. The deputy had picked it up and taken it with him. The more he talked, the more the preacher was infatuated.

"Where did he go when you ran him off?" the preacher asked.

"Back south up Interstate Road, but he had to cut through the cotton field because I looked for him for almost an hour and didn't find him. Then I hear that this Milton fella was found at the scene of a murder. Lots of coincidence to me."

Kirksey, flabbergasted at his tale, began to relay his story of Wayne's nervous behavior when he was questioned about the Strawberry murder, and yes, Wayne *always* wore a straw hat. Both men suddenly were becoming more and more convinced by their suspicions that the sheriff had let Wayne go too soon. When they were called back to talk to the sheriff, they went together and again relayed their suspicions based on speculation and pure circumstantial evidence. Their question to the sheriff was simply, should he not look further into the possibility that Wayne Milton was connected to the murders? The sheriff promised them he would look further and they left satisfied for the time being upon that promise.

@ @ @ @ @ @

The round table at Brock's Café in Cleveland was crowded and abuzz with conversation, even more than usual. Nine men, including the six who had recently met in Ruleville at The Mecca in the Citizen's Council room, were gathered for their daily ritual of breakfast consisting of eggs, biscuits, grits, bacon and coffee, but today the conversation was not nearly as raucous and noisy, but was to the veteran observer, subdued and moderated. There was a definite attempt by all to whisper among the group, as well as an attempt to restrict certain topics from discussion by the apparent leader, Stanton Merriweather.

Merriweather, dressed in a black pinstripe suit, the requisite white shirt, striped red and black tie and black wingtip shoes, could have been picked out in a lineup as the emblematic attorney. His hair would have been solid gray, but had been dyed Labrador retriever black for years, enhancing his look of untrustworthiness, especially since his heavy eyebrows remained their natural color. He sat with his back closest to the wall at the table and served as the mythical chairman of the group, reminding them all at times to lower their voices or admonishing each of them not to discuss certain subjects, lest they be overheard or worse yet, recorded. Today, he was most cognizant of his role.

"Gentlemen, we need to keep it low so we don't disturb our neighbors in here and they don't get the wrong idea of the subject of our discussion," he said, as if federal agents were hearing their every word.

"I'm sick and tired of keeping silent about the way some niggers believe themselves above the law," one opined with no illustration given. Merriweather winced at the statement and did his best to ignore it.

"I believe we have now discovered the identity of the individual who has breached the contract in which each of us are privy," Merriweather responded, trying to direct the conversation from the obvious to the symbolic. "Perhaps we should work toward a resolution of that breach." He simply couldn't resist using an expanded vocabulary in order to appear wise. He was truly a legend in his own mind.

"I agree," one of the group added with a mouth full of food. "This is serious business," he added, as if making an astute observation.

"Might I suggest a meeting in the immediate future in say, Ruleville, perhaps?" Merriweather said with a wink. "I'll be happy to answer any questions anyone may have at that time concerning the issues of liability and causation." He certainly believed himself to be one smooth, smug operator.

"Tomorrow night at 7 o'clock at The Mecca," another suggested.

"Good as any," Merriweather agreed. "And I don't anticipate we will need another meeting on this case thereafter, provided everyone has fulfilled their financial obligations. The retainer must be paid." Secretly, Merriweather hoped these simpletons understood what he was trying to say. Where would they be without him?

Everyone agreed and the group slowly disbanded their meeting and returned to their various jobs to start the day.

@ @ @ @ @ @

Paul had gotten to his office at the usual time of 6:30 and reviewed the phone messages from the previous day, particularly the time after he left to go to The Thicket. He returned the ones he could return at that early hour and made plans to call the rest after normal working hours began. Though everyone in Cleveland believed him to be a workaholic and dedicated to his job, the truth was, he had started those early hours when he began his solo practice of law, and had not been able to break the habit since that time. What he intended to do that day, if he did nothing else, was to talk with Landon about the "word on the street" that Larry had shared with him the night before. Landon may not be able to resolve the possible crisis, but he had a way of helping Paul deal with such problems by simply bouncing the possibilities and ramifications off him. A call to Landon's office set their appointment at 10 o'clock, just enough time to return the remainder of his calls and plan the remainder of his day. He arrived, and after pouring himself a cup of coffee from the reception area of the DA's office, sat across the desk from him.

"So, what brings the finest investigator in the district to the boss's office without a summons?" Landon asked. "Looking for a raise?"

"No, but if you're offering. ...," his voice trailing off.

"Not a chance. What's on your mind?" Landon inquired.

"We may have a problem. I got it on best authority that some of our outstanding citizens don't want to wait until a trial to convict and sentence our suspect in the Strawberry and Galtelli murders," Paul advised. "He's not their favorite color."

"Wasn't sure we had a suspect to speak of. Who are we talking about so we're both on the same page? L.B.'s man?" Landon asked.

"Tyrone Braid. Yep, the one L.B. has been crowing about the whole time. I think he's a longshot, but I guess it is possible. He's been laying low in Chicago for a little while and ran from me and a CPD officer when we tried to question him up there. Everything we have is circumstantial and I think he may have already gone to Chicago by the time the Galtelli girl was murdered. Appears to be the same man who killed Strawberry and Galtelli, so if he was gone when Galtelli was killed, he's not going to be guilty of the Strawberry murder either. Anyway, that's for another day. The problem now is, if his name gets out, he may be a walking dead man and not know it if some of these people act on their threats. Wouldn't be the first time, you know. Same thing we talked about after the press conference on Strawberry when L.B. seemed to do his best to let everyone know he had a black suspect. Problem is, this time we may have a credible threat and not just my speculation. And concern."

"How good is your information?" Landon asked.

"On a scale of one to ten, with ten being the most reliable, I'd say a seven or even an eight. Old friend from school who doesn't really have a dog in the fight, just told me because we happened to bump into each other. I'm damned concerned."

"Did he give you any names?" Landon asked.

"No, but his wife told him her boss at the bank mentioned it. Don't know if he is involved or just privy to the information."

"Are you concerned for this man's safety? Is that all?" Landon knew Paul's predicament, but wanted him to admit it.

Paul sipped his coffee while holding his cup with both hands. "Look, if this guy's guilty, my gut reaction is 'good riddance', but we both know we can't sit back and let some vigilante force do the law's job. If he's innocent, we condone murder by this bunch if we do nothing to protect him. Worse yet, if they're successful in taking Braid out, how do you feel about going after that group and prosecuting them? It could be political suicide for you and the end of a career for me as well. The reality of it is, I don't want to prosecute friends and business acquaintances, but it may come to it. You see my concern?" Paul asked.

"Oh yeah, I see it, and it's my concern too," Landon observed. "But let me tell you a story about a friend of mine that used to live up your way before you moved back here. Gerald Chatham was district attorney in the 17th District that included Tallahatchie County. Fifteen years ago, he got stuck prosecuting a case where a young black kid named Till, was killed by two white men because he whistled at one of their wives. Media from everywhere turned it into a circus. Nobody local even wanted the two to be tried. Ended up acquitting the two who later admitted to doing it. Bottom line was, nobody wanted to touch the case because everyone in that time and place, believed the kid got what he deserved. But, Chatham knew it was his job to do and handled it fairly throughout by everyone's reasoning. Most figured that was the end of the line for Chatham as an elected official, but when it was all over, most everybody actually thought more of him. What I'm trying to tell you is this: We are gonna do what we think is right and let the chips fall where they may. If they run us out of town afterwards, they'll have to do it knowing we did the right thing. I'm willing to bet right now that the vast majority of the people will respect us."

"Ok, I'm with you. But in the meantime, what do we do about Tyrone?" Paul asked.

"Well, for right now, he's tucked away in Chicago, correct? Best thing he can do is stay there until we or L.B. arrest him, if we ever do. Then he's in custody either here or in Chicago, pending extradition, and I doubt there will be anyone that will try to bust him out of jail just so they can kill him. He obviously knows you're after him, so he's not likely to come back. If he's there or in custody, I think he'll be fine. Besides, I don't think it's common knowledge that he's even a suspect, is it? Landon asked.

"Not unless L.B. lets it out. We had a meeting yesterday and I had to tell him I went to Chicago to try and question the man. He left my office quite pissed. I assumed you'd gotten a call late yesterday. If you didn't, I'm sure you will today."

"Great. Now I've got that to look forward to all day. What else you got?"

"That's it. Thanks, Landon. I hope the boy has the good sense to stay in the Windy City."

"Me, too. Now get out of here so I can do some work."

CHAPTER 19

Wayne had remained at home for the most part for the past few days after his debacle at the Galtelli residence that resulted in his being taken in for questioning. It took that long for him to feel comfortable about roaming the roads in the community without feeling as if everyone was whispering about him or trying to ignore him after that incident. When he finally felt as if he could get back to his normal routine of rambling, eavesdropping and watching, it didn't take him long to put the memories of that day and night behind him. He was on a roll again. On a roll, that is, until he walked past the church and Pastor Kirksey saw him and called him over from the side door of his study.

"Wayne, my friend, we need to talk, don't we?" the preacher asked while walking out to the road to meet Wayne. His tie was loosened and the sleeves of his white shirt were rolled up to the elbow of each arm to ease the sting of the heat at that time of the day.

"I don't know," Wayne replied, obviously confused.

"We didn't finish our conversation the other Sunday and I think you have undergone some trials and trouble this week. Am I right, my friend? You know I am always available to help you or any other member with their problems, don't you, Wayne? I just want to help."

"Yes, sir, I know."

"Come on in and let's get out of the heat," the pastor suggested. Even though the last thing Wayne wanted to discuss was his problems with the law, like a child that is easily herded in a certain direction, he felt compelled to do as the pastor suggested. When they got into the office, Kirksey offered him a coke and some cookies which Wayne gladly accepted.

"Tell me what's bothering you, Wayne?"

"Nothing. Nothing," he responded.

"You can tell me. I want to help. Is there something about the Galtelli girl *and* Linda Strawberry that is bothering you? You know before your sins can be forgiven, they must be confessed, don't you? You need to lay it all on God and he will carry you through it, no matter how big a problem or burden you are carrying," the pastor pleaded. He continued to lay the guilt trip on Wayne for the next few minutes, and when he saw Wayne begin to cry, he knew he was making progress.

"You know all about them, don't you, Wayne? You can bring so much peace to their families by telling what you know or have done. Only you can do that, no one else," he told the crying man, apparently failing to remember that God was the one who forgives and eases burdens for people, and not Wayne himself. "Tell me what happened, I won't judge you."

Wayne was sobbing, now, his conscience or his mental stability broken down by the prying preacher.

"You hurt them, didn't you, son? I know you didn't mean to, but you hurt them, didn't you? God will take away your pain if you only trust him and put your faith in him by confessing your guilt."

Few veteran police interrogators could have accomplished what Pastor Kirksey did at that meeting with Wayne, largely due to the fact that it wouldn't have been legal. But Kirksey wasn't bound by the constitutional safeguards that often inhibit law enforcement and their tactics. Kirksey had a free rein to talk as he felt the need in order to get to the truth about the heinous crimes committed against the two women. Consequently, in the pastor's study of a small Baptist church within sight of the scene of the first murder and not that much further from the second, Wayne Milton looked to his God as instructed by the preacher and did something that would most likely stun most of his friends and neighbors. Wayne Milton confessed to the murders of both Linda Strawberry and Janice Galtelli.

@ @ @ @ @ @ @

Kirksey told Wayne to go back to his house after their meeting, wait on him to come by, and in the meantime, pray for forgiveness for the terrible wrongs he had committed. He had reservations about letting an admitted killer go his own way, but where was he going to go, anyway? Wayne realized he was in the crosshairs of the sheriff because of the recent questioning and now, after the confession to the preacher, he surely wouldn't try to hurt anyone else, not before the sheriff could get out there to arrest him and hold him for trial. Regardless, Kirksey made a beeline for his Volkswagen Beetle and headed straight to the sheriff's office in Cleveland to break the news. His head swirled with tasks he had to do in light of the revelation, like contacting the media, notifying the Strawberry family and generally putting out the word that he, alone, had cracked the first case of a mass murderer in Bolivar County.

When he arrived at the sheriff's office, no less than thirty minutes from the time he had sent Wayne home, the receptionist advised him that the sheriff was out and was not likely to be back until shortly after lunch. Kirksey took a seat in the lobby and waited. His astounding news could wait an hour, if need be, as long as it was able to get out to the media before the five o'clock news, he thought. It was shortly after 1:30 p.m. when L.B. Williams strode into the office and greeted the pastor with a firm handshake and invited him back to his private office.

"What brings you here today, pastor," the sheriff asked.

"I have some startling information that I'm sure you will find beneficial in your investigation of the Strawberry and Galtelli murders," the preacher responded. "Startling and tragic for our community in particular." He then began to spin his tale of discovery he had gleaned from his meeting with Wayne earlier that morning. The more he talked, the more mesmerized the sheriff became in the facts as they unfolded from the pastor.

The sheriff's mind was whirling. He had questioned Wayne just days ago and had seen nothing in his answers that indicated he had any knowledge whatsoever of the murders, let alone participated alone in them. Damage control came first to his mind. What would the public surmise of him for returning a killer to the streets after his questioning? Why had he not been more thorough? He had taken the necessary steps to insure Wayne's rights were protected by seeing that he had legal counsel present, but that may compound his public perception problem. He could hear his opponent now, speaking at the many fish fries and BBQ functions he would have to attend as a candidate, "Your sheriff was more interested in a criminal's rights than he was protecting you as citizens from a dangerous killer." A lot of horseshit could be made from a small amount of hay when it came to politics. What about the Strawberry family? How could he explain that he had their daughter's killer in custody and just let him go, possibly to continue his killing? And that damn James Weeks. He had been crowing all over the south part of the county that Wayne was the culprit from the beginning after that incident at his house. He would be on every newscast and in every newspaper, that would give him a chance to speak saying he warned this office of the danger. Last, but certainly not the least concern, L.B. had made it well-known to all who would listen that the culprit was a black man and he was on the run. His statement made at the press conference haunted him like a cemetery at midnight.

Politics, they say, makes strange bedfellows, so it was not surprising to anyone that L.B. excused himself from the meeting with Kirksey and called, up to that point, his nemesis, Paul Lane.

"Paul, I need your help down here at my office right away if you can come," the sheriff said into the phone, almost pleading. "We've got a break in the Strawberry/Galtelli case you need to hear and advise me how to proceed. Like you said before, we need to be thorough on this one 'cause everybody's watching."

"I was just heading out to grab a bite of a late lunch," Paul responded. "Can it wait thirty or forty minutes?"

"It can't. I'll have Barbara bring something in for you if you can get over here," the sheriff said, again sounding a little desperate.

"Tell her I want a burger from the Pool Hall Grill with everything on it and some fries. I'm on my way."

Paul knew it was a big deal for the sheriff to ask for his advice on this case, much less to up the ante with a free burger and fries, catered no less. He drove over to the courthouse, parked in front because of the unavailability of open parking spaces in the back where the sheriff's office was located, and walked through the interior of the courthouse back into the office. He walked past the receptionist and into L.B.'s office where he was introduced to W.D. Kirksey. The sheriff then asked Paul to step outside to an adjoining office and the two excused themselves from the preacher once again.

It took at least fifteen minutes for the sheriff to fill Paul in on the details of the preacher's story to him, but it took another fifteen for L.B. to point out his political concerns from the news that was about to be dropped on the public. Paul listened and at least appeared to care for the election ramifications from his counterpart while he downed the burger and fries that was brought to him in the interim. Then, after hearing the entirety of the story from the sheriff as well as the pastor, Paul began a lecture on criminal procedure and evidence as simple as he could make it for the two laymen.

"Gentlemen, we have a very, very basic problem with the confession here. There is a longstanding rule of evidence that prevents our use of Mr. Milton's confession to the pastor here. Very simply, when a person tells his pastor something while that pastor is acting in the capacity as the person's spiritual advisor, anything learned from comments made by that person to the pastor is privileged communication and accordingly, is inadmissible as evidence in any criminal prosecution. Very simply, although he has admitted to the murders, we cannot use that confession as evidence against him. Any first-year lawyer will object if we do or face a lawsuit for malpractice. Without that confession, we have very little evidence to implicate him. All we really have is his straw hat on the side of the road and his snooping around the Galtelli house. Nothing else," Paul advised.

"Are you telling me we are going to have to let a murderer walk free because of a little technicality?" Kirksey asked, seemingly stunned.

"The United States Supreme Court does not look upon it as a little technicality. And yes, we have to let him go free, at least until we find something else to hang our hat on in the case," Paul responded. "Sheriff, there is nothing to prevent you from questioning him further, provided, of course, that his attorney you got for him doesn't object."

L.B. felt the barb thrown by Paul sink deep into him and replied, "I'll get in touch with him and see."

"I'm not believing this," Kirksey continued. "What do we do in the meantime? What if he does it again? We've got to let people know, don't we?"

"Not a lot we can do right now. I wouldn't let anyone know if I were you Pastor Kirksey. Most people won't believe you because he hasn't been arrested. Other people will be wary about being counseled by you for fear of you disclosing what they tell you. You're kind of in a catch-22. Let's hold up on any news of this getting out for everyone's sake," Paul said.

All three agreed that, though it wasn't preferable, the best plan was to sit on the information for the near future. L.B. agreed to have a deputy shadow Wayne as much as possible to see where he went and what he did in the interim. A quick call to Wayne's public defender resulted in an immediate denial of any further questioning of his client by the sheriff or anyone else unless they could give him a good reason why he should. No one dared inform him of the illicit confession that had been obtained by the preacher, so that was the end of that.

L.B. seemed happy with the outcome, actually. He wouldn't have to face any political ramifications about letting Wayne go and without the confession, there was no reason to look at him as a possible suspect without something more, leaving him free to pursue putting a case together against Tyrone Braid who he believed all along was the culprit. Besides, after the preacher had left, disappointed in his media frenzy fizzling, he and Paul had discussed the likelihood of Wayne Milton as the murderer of not one, but two women, and both were of the opinion that these attacks were, in all likelihood, much too sophisticated and flawless to be accomplished by a middle aged, mentally challenged man such as him. As for the confession, it was most likely the result of an overbearing minister who had already expressed suspicions of Wayne earlier. Still, it could not be completely overlooked.

CHAPTER 20

At precisely 7 o'clock p.m., two vehicles pulled into the rear parking lot of The Mecca in Ruleville, a black Cadillac and a gray Oldsmobile with a total of three passengers between them. They were met by the driver of a pickup and a Chevrolet Impala with a passenger that had arrived just minutes before them, bringing the total people meeting that night to six. Stanton Merriweather got out of the Cadillac, greeted each person with a handshake and then led them all to the Citizen's Council room in the back of the restaurant, where they were seated at a round table not unlike their usual accommodations at Brock's in Cleveland. Soon thereafter, they were all brought soft drinks and sweet rolls to enjoy as they were met by the restaurant owner.

After a few minutes of pleasantries between the group, Merriweather began to speak.

"Gentlemen, I believe the first order of business should be the balancing of the books between us," he said, as he reached into his inside pocket of the suit coat that he was wearing and withdrew a stack of currency bound by a wide rubber band. He removed the band and began to count the cash out on the table before him so that everyone could clearly see and acknowledge the total amount. The cash was all in $100 bills and totaled exactly one thousand dollars. When he was finished, he pushed it to the center of the table and looked to the man on his right who, without being told, did exactly as Merriweather had done, counting out a neat stack of bills totaling one thousand dollars. When he pushed his stack to the center of the table as Merriweather had done before, the man to his right repeated the same performance with the same result. This continued for the next member and the next in like manner, except that the last member had numerous denominations of bills which had to be recounted twice to insure a total of one thousand dollars was there. Before the group, upon completion of the donations by five of the six members present, sat a total of five thousand dollars in cash, neatly stacked in denominations one hundred-dollar bills, except for the last member's contribution.

"I believe that was our goal, was it not?" Merriweather asked, and all present agreed.

"Now, let's go over what we know and what we would like to accomplish, so that all of us are on the same page," Merriweather stated, so proud that he was the leader of the group. "We have been advised that the man who committed these murders is a nigger by the name of Tyrone Braid who was convicted in the past of a sex crime and served time in Parchman. This information comes directly from the DA's office or at least from his investigator's office through our contact there. We all need to thank Sam for going the extra mile and banging the old girl who has helped us," Merriweather laughed, bringing out guffaws from the entire group.

"He's currently on the run, probably somewhere up north, and we need to get him back down here so we can do what we have to do," Merriweather observed.

"Sounds like we need to lean on his family. You lean hard enough, they'll give him away and we can go from there," one member said pointedly.

"Won't do us no good to find out where he is up north. We need him back here in Mississippi before we can do it," another member said, a statement that brought nodding agreements from most of the group.

"Ok then, lean on his family in a way that makes him come back to check on them. Say, if one of his family members was involved in a car wreck, that might flush him out and back down here," the first member who had spoken said.

"You could be on to something there," Merriweather chimed in. "How about the two of you coming up with a plan along those lines and let's see how it goes?"

"No problem," they both said at the same time.

"Our next order of business should be to draw lots for the delivery of the money to our friend. I'll take the entire amount, and place it in my mailbox in front of my house. Whoever draws the black ball can come by tonight after midnight and retrieve it, deliver it to our man and make the arrangements. I can assure you I will be in bed and will not see who picks it up. If I draw it, I will do my job and we won't have to worry about someone stealing it out of the mailbox. None of us will ever know which one of us made the drop to our man. Everyone agreed?" Merriweather asked. He was enjoying these clandestine exploits way too much.

One of the men went to a broom closet in the room and removed a wooden box with a hinged lid on it. Inside the box, he placed four white marbles and one black one. He held the lid open for everyone to see and verify what had been placed in the box and then closed the lid, shaking the box with both hands. One by one, beginning with Merriweather, each man ran his hand under the lid of the box and retrieved a marble, immediately tucking it into their pocket so that no one saw it. When all five had drawn their lot, the box was returned to the broom closet, everyone shook hands and they all eventually departed. The last two to leave were Stanton Merriweather, laden with cash, and the sixth person who had attended but took no part in the meeting except to observe as an invited guest.

"I want to tell you again how sorry we all are about your tragedy," Merriweather told him. "I'm glad you could come just to see that there are people who care about this county and this state and are willing to go the extra mile for all of us."

"I thank you for the invitation, Stanton. I'm proud of all of you. God bless ya'll." And with that, Dewitt Strawberry shook hands with Stanton Merriweather, walked over to his pickup, climbed inside and drove away.

@ @ @ @ @ @ @

Wayne Milton had acted strange to his mother from the moment he had come in about lunchtime the previous day. He ate, but refused to make eye contact or speak during that meal and then made a hasty retreat to his room for the remainder of the day. He had left late that afternoon, but had come in earlier than usual and again holed up in his room for the rest of the night. His actions were as strange and as similar as they had been shortly after Linda Strawberry had died, but she was puzzled as to what the problem was this time. Her worry was about to be compounded minutes after the unmarked county vehicle pulled into the driveway of her home. A man, dressed in khakis and blazer with no tie got out of the vehicle and proceeded to her door, but before he was able to knock, she met him there.

"May I help you?" she asked.

"Yes ma'am. I'm Paul Lane, investigator for the DA's office in Cleveland and I need to speak with you for a few minutes, if I may," he responded, presenting his badge and identification to her simultaneously.

"What on earth about?'

"I believe your son, Wayne Milton, lives here with you, doesn't he?"

"Yes, he does. My God, is there something wrong? Has something happened to him?" she asked in a panic.

"No ma'am, but may I come in and sit down with you? I think it would be better if we talked there," he said.

"Please," she replied, "Come in." They proceeded to the den just inside the front door and both took seats on opposite ends of the sofa. The front room was furnished with cheap furniture of vinyl and cloth and smelled of a mixture of cigarette smoke, dust and mold.

"I take it Wayne is not here now?" Paul inquired, as his eyes roamed the room of the old house.

"No, he's been gone since early this morning, probably 7 or 8 o'clock. What is the problem?" she inquired, the tension starting to obviously build in her voice.

"Ma'am, I'm investigating the murder of Linda Strawberry and Janice Galtelli, both recently killed at their homes near here. I'm sure you are familiar with them," he began.

"Yes, I'm familiar with them, but surely you don't think Wayne had anything to do with them," she retorted, her voice going from concern to resentment quickly.

"Ma'am, I'm just checking all possibilities right now. Do you know where he was on Monday, August 4th somewhere between 8 and 10 o'clock p.m.?" he asked, sounding too much like Jack Webb than was necessary.

"I couldn't tell you where he was that day or most any other day. He's a grown man and comes and goes as he pleases. He doesn't have to report to me or anyone else," she shot back.

"Is he out most nights?" Paul asked.

"At times he is, but that doesn't prove anything," she responded rather indignantly. "He loved that Strawberry girl and was most upset when she died. He asked me if she went to heaven and also would the man that killed her go to heaven or hell. He's slow, you know, but he was concerned for the souls of both, and I thought that admirable," she said defiantly.

"What about the Galtelli girl, did he know her?" Paul asked.

"No, he did not and probably didn't know where she lived," she returned.

"Did you ever talk to him about her, or are you just speculating?" Paul inquired.

"Never talked to him about her. He hasn't mentioned anything about her," she replied. "I'm not even sure he knows anything about her death at all," she added.

"So, he hasn't mentioned to you that he may have been seen at her residence when her body was discovered?" he asked with amazement.

"Absolutely not. That is a lie. He would have told me about the news of her death. Again, he doesn't even know about her death," she angrily responded.

"Would he try to keep that from you if he had?"

"No way, he tells me everything. You are barking up the wrong tree, mister," she said, again indignantly.

"If he doesn't tell you something, does that indicate to you that he doesn't want you to know?" Paul asked.

"He tells me everything, I said. I think you should go, sir."

"Yes ma'am. Sorry to have upset you," he said, and proceeded toward the door.

As he backed his car into the road, he couldn't help but wonder what else Wayne had neglected to tell his mother. Maybe this guy was smarter than everyone gave him credit for being. It came down to this, so far: 1) He knew the Strawberry victim well; 2) His whereabouts were unknown at the time of the Strawberry and Galtelli murders; 3) He had the physical characteristics that would allow him to perform such an attack on either petite girl; 4) He was visibly upset shortly after the murders; 5) He's normally open and truthful with his mother, but has obviously hidden the Galtelli residence incident from her; 6) His characteristics of walking the roads and watching the houses in the community were well documented; 7) He was originally extremely nervous and evasive about the subject with his pastor; 8) He was involved in a stalking incident of sorts at the Weeks residence about the time of the Galtelli murder and finally, 9) He has confessed to both murders. The confession was inadmissible, but couldn't be discounted completely. Hell, either he was basing his whole case on circumstantial evidence as L.B. was with Tyrone Braid or he was correctly on the trail of a multiple murder who was walking the roads of the county at this minute. He could comprehend a possible circumstantial conviction from what he had or he could keep looking. When he got back to the office, he had a phone memo from Landon who wanted an update on Strawberry and Galtelli murders. Since the discussion of the Strawberry murder now seemed to always include the Galtelli murder, it was becoming annoying to refer to each by the full name. As Landon wanted to make their reference easier for everyone, particularly himself, he combined the two murders into one name, "GalBerry", using a part of each name. With Landon's update in mind, Paul decided it best to keep looking.

CHAPTER 21

Darcel Braid had never been lucky in her life, but somehow, she had secured a job at the Delta Drugstore in Shaw as a stocker and janitor. It paid a whopping $1.65 per hour, five cents more than the federally mandated minimum wage, and was for a total of twelve hours per day. There was no overtime pay, but she was glad to get the hours, regardless. She had applied, expecting the usual response of "not hiring now" and had been ecstatic when the call came telling her that the job was hers and asking her when could she start. Two weeks into the job, she couldn't have been happier with the hours, the work and her employer as well.

When Darcel had gotten off work that Thursday night, she used the time and the convenience of already being in town to pick up what groceries she had needed at the Piggly Wiggly Grocery located a couple doors down from her job. The task took more time than she had planned or imagined, and by the time she headed back home down Highway 442, darkness had fallen over the Delta. She gave little thought to the pickup parked on the side of the road about two miles out of town as she passed it, nor did she notice that it pulled into the highway behind her as she sped toward home. As she got within a mile of her home, the pickup pulled alongside her in an attempt to pass her, or so she thought, and then quickly clipped the front of the car she was driving, causing her to lose control and sending her careening off a steep embankment on the right side of the road. Unable to control it at all, Darcel was helpless as the car flipped at least twice and landed in a deep ditch, coming to rest on the driver's side of the vehicle. The pickup that made contact with the car Darcel was driving sported a heavy steel bumper and sped quickly away into the night, never bothering to see what damage it may have caused.

"Maybe that will bring Mr. Tyrone Braid out of hiding. Surely, he'll come to check on his sister in the hospital or at her funeral," the driver of the pickup laughingly said.

"If it don't," the passenger said, "We'll keep looking 'til we find somebody he gives a damn about," his passenger laughed back. In seconds the pickup was out of sight on the deserted stretch of highway, leaving nothing to indicate it had ever been there. The sound of skidding tires, crushing metal, breaking glass and revved engine noise was once again replaced by the tranquil sounds of croaking frogs, cicadas and the wind.

John Braid knew Darcel's schedule and was keenly aware that she was late coming home that night. He had waited on her with anticipation, not so much because he was concerned about her, but because he relied on her to fix supper and that as well was late. When she had not arrived home by 9 o'clock, he called a friend to go look for her. When the friend arrived, he told John of an auto accident just up the road he had passed that had a couple of Mississippi Highway Patrol vehicles, an ambulance and a wrecker on the scene. John's instincts told him it was Darcel and they headed in that direction to see. When they arrived, the ambulance had departed a short while before. One of the patrolmen advised them that a young black female was currently being transported to the hospital in Cleveland in critical condition, but he was unaware of her identity. When John looked at the vehicle being dragged from the ditch by the wrecker, his heart sank.

"Do you know how it happened?" John asked the patrolman.

"Nope. We suspect that alcohol played a role. Just the one vehicle involved," he informed him. And with that, John and his friend headed to Cleveland to the hospital to see about Darcel.

@ @ @ @ @ @

Tyrone had settled in a new apartment with a new roommate as well as a new job, still on Chicago's south side, but far from his original place of residence he had taken up when he first arrived in the Windy City. He had luckily found a job loading trucks at a service that specialized mainly in shipping produce and meats across the state of Illinois and beyond. It seems there was no shortage of available jobs if one could stand the physical labor. He had tried earlier to call Darcel and John and give them his number to call if they needed to reach him, but so far, he had been unsuccessful. He felt initially uneasy about neither of them being home during the week at night, but brushed it off as their maybe being in the yard and out of earshot of the ringing phone. Five attempts later that night to contact them without success rekindled his uneasiness and it frustrated him to no end that he could call no one else to check on them. Consequently, he went to bed and lay there, eyes wide open, wondering what the problem might be. Two hours later and still no sleep, he called his Uncle Lonnie as a last resort.

Lonnie Braid had been asleep for hours, knowing he had to get up at 4:30 in order to start his day at the store, and when the phone rang, he was both shocked and annoyed.

"Hello, and this better be important," he groggily said into the receiver.

"Uncle Lonnie, this Tyrone. I hated to wake you up, but I need to talk to Darcel or John and I can't get either one to answer the phone," Tyrone said.

"What time is it and where are you?" Lonnie asked, still annoyed and not understanding the emergency.

"I'm in Chicago. It's 2 o'clock in the morning. Do you have any idea where they may be?" Tyrone asked.

"I haven't seen either since early this week. How long have you been trying to get in touch with them?" Lonnie wanted to know.

"Just since earlier this evening," Tyrone responded. "John may be out partying, but you know Darcel would be home if there wasn't a problem," Tyrone observed.

"Ok, ok. I'll get dressed and run down to their house and see what's going on," Lonnie said. "Where can I call you?" Tyrone rolled off the new phone number he had secured and asked his uncle not to share it with anyone. "I'll keep it to myself. I don't even want to know why you are in Chicago and why you don't want this number given out."

"Thanks, Uncle Lonnie. Let me know something."

Lonnie got out of bed and pulled on his blue jeans and t-shirt, slipped on some shoes and after finding his keys in the dark so as not to awaken his wife, he went outside and got into his truck. A minute later, he pulled into the drive of Tyrone's home to find another vehicle there, lights on and engine idling. He pulled in behind the vehicle and was apprehensive about its presence because he certainly didn't recognize it. It was a green 1960 Oldsmobile Cutlass with Bolivar County, Mississippi license plates. He sat there in his truck for a second and then saw a figure emerge from the passenger side of the car and walk toward his truck. Breathing a sigh of relief, he recognized the man as John Braid, his nephew.

"Is that you Uncle Lonnie?" John shouted at the truck.

"It's me, John," Lonnie said as he got out of his truck and strode toward the Oldsmobile. "I'm checking on you and Darcel. Tyrone's been trying to get in touch with ya'll and couldn't. Is she with you?"

"No, sir, Uncle Lonnie," he said. "She's been in a bad car wreck tonight. Me and Jerome just got back from the hospital. That's him in the car."

John went on to inform his uncle of the events as he knew them from earlier in the night. According to the staff at the emergency room at the hospital, Darcel had been admitted with multiple lacerations on her face and arms from broken glass, had an apparent broken leg and a head injury that had rendered her unconscious since the accident. The doctors were optimistic she would awaken tonight or tomorrow, but they just didn't know. They were told to check back tomorrow and pray in the meantime. Meanwhile, Darcel would be in intensive care and she would be afforded no visitors until sometime tomorrow and then on a very limited basis.

As for what caused the accident, it was unknown except for some speculation that she had been intoxicated. Because they knew that Darcel never drank, John and Jerome knew for certain that wasn't the case and advised the hospital staff. Other than that, until Darcel was able to tell them something, they could only speculate that the accident was the result of inattention on her part or possibly that she had swerved to miss an animal such as a deer, and lost control. It was anybody's guess at this point, but the thought that she may have been intentionally run off the road was never considered.

Lonnie left the two and returned home a few minutes later. Digging the number Tyrone had given him earlier from the backside of his wallet, he dialed it. It only had to ring once before Tyrone answered.

"I've got some bad news, Tyrone," Lonnie began. "Darcel's been in a horrible car wreck tonight and she is in the hospital in Cleveland. I just talked to John at their house who filled me in on it."

He went on to recount the facts concerning the accident as he knew them, repeating them to Tyrone as John had given them to him, as best he could. Tyrone listened in silence until Lonnie finished, and then struck his fist against the headboard of the bed he was sitting on while talking, the frustration and shock boiling over in him.

"I can't believe it, Uncle Lonnie. She gonna make it ain't she? Tell me she gone make it," Tyrone said hopefully.

"I just don't know, Tyrone. You know as much as I do right now. Hopefully we will know more tomorrow and it will look better for her in the daylight," Lonnie said. "I'm glad you called me earlier now."

"I'm coming home, Uncle Lonnie, I can't just stay up here and do nothing. I got to see about her. I'm coming home soon as I can get a bus ticket in the morning," Tyrone announced.

"I'll see you when you get here, Tyrone. You be careful 'til then. We don't need another tragedy," Lonnie responded.

"I'll see you soon as I can get there, Uncle Lonnie. Bye." Tyrone hung up the phone and immediately started to gather some clothes and belongings to take with him back to Mississippi. He would have to be careful going home, but he had to go. He had dodged the law many times in his life and could do it again. Besides, everybody seemed to know he wasn't around Bolivar County anymore and wouldn't be looking for him there.

CHAPTER 22

"Ｅast Bolivar County Hospital, how may I direct your call," the operator said.

"I need to check on Darcel Braid," the caller said. "Can you tell me what her room number is."

"I certainly can," the hospital operator responded. "Give me just a second and I'll look that up for you. The phone went silent, but the caller could hear pages being flipped as the operator looked up the room. Soon she returned to the line. "I'm sorry, but she hasn't been placed in a private room, yet. She is in ICU and unable to receive calls. Can I connect you to that waiting room so you might talk to a family member?"

The other end of the line was silent until the recognized dial tone sounded, indicating the caller had hung up.

"Well just be that way," the operator said and hung up as well.

"She's in the hospital and better yet, she's in intensive care," the man said to his partner. "He'll come running. Now all we have to do is sit back and watch for him riding in like Sir Lancelot to see about the sister he used to live with."

"Great," said his partner, an older man who was chain smoking cigarettes the entire time they were talking. "I'll let Merriweather know so he can get word to our man on the street."

Edker Bentley had been retired from the telephone company for 10 years, but was only 65 years old. His weathered face with its many wrinkles and gray hair reflected he had more miles on him than most his age. He had been a long-time member of the Leflore County, Mississippi Klavern of the Ku Klux Klan, but like most in the mid-sixties, had gotten out after the Klan had been infiltrated by federal agents under the direction of J. Edgar Hoover and United States Attorney General Robert Kennedy. Edker was different though. Unlike most who were glad to get out because of the distrust of other members and distinct possibility of going to federal prison, Edker wanted to stay. He had risen to the rank of Exalted Cyklops in the klavern and would still be there and active today if he had his choice. However, when every member but him abandoned the klavern, there was no reason to remain, but he just could not let go of his feelings of resentment toward the black community in general. Old habits were incredibly hard to break. His enduring legacy however, would be written by his conduct afterwards, conduct that was known by few, but suspected by all. He was the man that others turned to for the performance of distasteful duties such as the burning of old homes and buildings that needed to be rid of unsavory tenants, threatening notes and letters to activists, black or white, who dared to challenge the hierarchy of the status quo in the community, and even elimination for the right price and reason. If the job was too extreme, offensive or repugnant, he was the man you wanted. The persecution of a black man who had allegedly raped and murdered a white woman and perhaps even two, was reason enough and the price was well worth it to him. The initial payment of one half his fee had been tendered a night or so ago, and he was ready to do what had to be done. He just needed to know where to find his suspect. He was watching television when the phone rang, casually sipping a small glass of Jack Daniels whiskey.

"Hello," he answered.

"We have made arrangements for our man to return from his business trip up north. A close member of his family was involved in an automobile accident and we believe he is, at this moment, rushing home to check on her. She is in the East Bolivar County Hospital, so you may want to try to meet up with him there or close by to finalize our business with him. Not sure when he will arrive, but we anticipate very soon," a voice said. The caller never identified himself, but Edker was familiar with the voice—and the procedure he needed to follow.

"That will be great. I have looked forward to closing this transaction now for a while," he responded. "Do you know what type of car he will be traveling in?"

"I don't. We believe he took a bus to begin with so he may well return that way," the voice said. "We will update you as soon as we know more, just wanted you to be aware. I believe you have a photograph and list of his known family members and acquaintances."

"And I appreciate that more than you can know, old buddy. More than you know," he repeated and hung up the phone. He swallowed the last bit of whiskey he had in his glass and grimaced at the burn. There was really nothing like being a true patriot, he thought to himself. It was so rewarding to him.

Dewitt Strawberry on the other side of the county, like Edker, sat in his imitation leather recliner and stared at the television in his living room. He had no idea what was playing on it at that particular time, because he was paying no attention to it at all, simply staring at the screen. His mind was occupied by the events he had witnessed a few nights ago in Ruleville. The phone call, a week or so back asking him if he consented to the elimination of the man who killed his daughter, had been a shrill wake-up call for him and he had felt uneasy about agreeing. Now he had actually witnessed the act being placed into motion by his attendance at the Citizen's Council meeting and it shook him to the core. He thought that was what he had always wanted since the bastard killed his daughter, and why not? The Bible said an eye for an eye, didn't it? Why should he live, even in the penitentiary, while his daughter lay dead in the cemetery? Who could blame him? Still, his conscience bothered him like it never had before now. My God, what if they had the wrong man? Wouldn't he be an accomplice to premeditated murder? He tried to put the thought from his mind, but it kept nagging at him like a buzzing mosquito. Anyway, he really didn't have anything to do with the vote, the finances or the actual act of murder, he consoled himself. Why should he care if the son of a bitch was killed? If he wasn't guilty of that crime, he was probably guilty of something else he had not been prosecuted for just yet.

Back in Cleveland, Paul Lane sat at his desk in the darkness, contemplating his next move on GalBerry. He was frustrated at the lack of progress in the cases and his frustrations had caused him to neglect other cases that he had. Everyone was gone for the day and had been gone for several hours, so it was just him and his thoughts, alone in his office with the lights off. He wheeled around in his high-back chair and looked at the framed documents he had on his wall behind him. His undergraduate diploma, his law school diploma, his admission certificates to various courts and his license to practice law in Mississippi. Boy, that was a piece of paper that at present was more suited to lining a bird cage than anything else! He had abandoned the practice of law and normally had few regrets, but at times like these, he found himself playing the devil's advocate and arguing against his findings in a case such as this. He could rip a prosecutor's case to shreds simply by cross examining witnesses on the GalBerry prosecution that would testify only to circumstantial evidence. And that alone made him work that much harder in order to solve the case. He walked to the window and stared across the courthouse square at the humongous oak trees that filled the courthouse yard. He looked at the old Confederate statue standing guard for the people of the county as he had done for dozens of years. Those same people were counting on him, paying him nicely, to see that they were protected from the likes of the GalBerry killer. It was time to quit feeling sorry for himself for being unable to solve a difficult case and get back to doing just that. He walked to the door of his office, locked it behind him and headed home. Tomorrow was a new day and he would meet it with renewed vigor.

@ @ @ @ @ @ @

Wayne Milton quietly eased into his house about midnight, intent on getting in the bed without disturbing anyone. He had been able to avoid contact with his parents for the last day or so, except for breakfast when no one said much any way. He wouldn't avoid his mother tonight.

As soon as he stepped into the hallway on the old pine plank floor, his mother heard the squeak of his heavy feet against the boards. She gave him a minute or two to get settled in bed in his room, then put on her housecoat and slippers and eased into his room. She flipped the switch that turned the overhead light on in his room, flooding it with light. Wayne was startled when she came in, especially after the light was turned, but lay there as if asleep.

"We've got to talk, son. I know you just came in and you're not asleep, so stop faking," she said rather sternly. "You've been avoiding me for the last few days and I generally don't pry into your business. You know that, but I had a visitor yesterday that asked some questions and told me some things that you need to explain."

Not absolutely sure what she was talking about, but fearing the worst, he said, "I don't know. . ."

"You let me finish," she interrupted.

"Yes, ma'am."

"This man was from the prosecutor's office and was asking me all about you and what you knew about Linda Strawberry and the other girl that was killed. I've never been so shocked in my life. What do you know about them?" she asked him.

"Nothing, Momma," he replied, refusing to make eye contact with her.

"Why don't I believe you, son? Something tells me you know more than you want me to know. What do you know about those girls?" she asked again. "Did you see who done it?"

He had sat up when she had begun her inquisition and was now scared about where this conversation would lead. He nervously ran his fingers through his red hair and said,"I don't think I know anything. I know I don't."

"Have you ever been to the house where that second girl was killed? Do you know where she lived?" she asked. The expression on his face immediately fell and she could actually see the blood rushing from it. He knew!

"I'm sorry, Momma, I'm so sorry," he said, breaking into tears. "I should have told you, but I was afraid I was going to hell!" he exclaimed.

"Told me what?" she asked, afraid herself now as to what secrets he had been keeping.

"I killed 'em, Momma, I killed 'em," he wailed. "I don't know why, but I did. I felt so bad 'til you told me I could still go to heaven and then I felt better. Now I'm scared all over again and I feel worse," he continued to cry out. "What they gone do with me?"

Mrs. Mullen had never felt the combined shock, disbelief and fear her entire life that she felt that very minute. She didn't know whether to hug him, call the police or run from him in fear. She had never in her life suspected that he was capable of anything anywhere near as violent or heinous as this, but she had heard him with her own ears. She backed away from him until she backed into the closed door to his room behind her, her hand clasped over her mouth in disbelief.

"Oh, God!" she cried, partly in shock and astonishment at the revelation and partly calling on her deity to do something. She wasn't sure what to do, so she wheeled around, opened his bedroom door and fled back to her room and her husband who was oblivious to the catastrophic news that had just been revealed. She dove into the bed sobbing.

"Oh, God, oh my God."

CHAPTER 23

Tyrone Braid sat toward the middle of the bus trying to nap. He had gotten little sleep the night before because he had stayed up so long trying to get in touch with Darcel and John. When he learned the news about Darcel from his Uncle Lonnie, the thought of sleep was not even a consideration for him. As soon as he could in the morning, he had contacted his boss at the shipping company and told him he would be out of town for the next three or four days, purchased a one-way ticket on Greyhound at the station, and headed out. He caught the 9:15 a.m. southbound toward Memphis. He only had the one carryon bag, so he didn't have a baggage charge. He had his jeans on from the day before and a blue t-shirt that helped him stand the heat in the bus that was enhanced by the lack of air conditioning. He pulled his cap down over his face as the bus left Chicago behind and tried to sleep, but it avoided him until somewhere near the Kentucky state line, shortly after the bus made one of its many stops on the way south.

In Cleveland, Darcel had yet to regain consciousness and consequently had been moved from intensive care to a private room for further observation. John, his Uncle Lonnie and Lonnie's wife Victoria, had been at the hospital in the intensive care waiting room for most of the past few days and were relieved when she was moved to a private room so they could be there with her at bedside. Neither said much to the other, but they obviously were greatly concerned with their relative who they hoped would have come around by now. Every now and then, one of them would speculate as to when Tyrone might get there, but nobody had any clue at that point. They sat around waiting for something, anything by Darcel to show some signs of recovery and snacked on peanut butter and crackers Lonnie had brought from the store in the meantime.

The Greyhound bus station in Cleveland was located a block or two west off Highway 61 near the south end of town. There were usually no more than two buses, three at the most that came through each day, but generally one northbound and one southbound. The southbound bus would arrive somewhere around 10:15 a.m. each and every morning, roughly twenty-four hours from when Tyrone left Chicago. Tyrone intended to get over to the hospital, about a mile from the bus station, as soon as he arrived. He would have to walk since no one knew when to meet him, but that was no great distance for him, his job being further than that from his shared apartment in Chicago. He got off the bus occasionally at its stops to use the bathroom and get a snack to curb his appetite.

About 9:30 a.m. the day after Tyrone left Chicago, an old white pickup pulled into a parking spot across the street from the bus station in Cleveland. It was no less than a dozen years old and showed the scars and dents of years of use on a farm, smoking from oil loss through the exhaust. The back end was cluttered with empty beer cans, a tool box, spare tire and assorted pieces of trash that were obviously intended to be dumped at a trash bin but had never made it. The driver was Edker Bentley. Between him and the driver's side door, he had placed a .38 caliber revolver, loaded with five rounds of ammo, which he always carried, but usually could be found hidden under the seat. Today, he intended to use it, so he made it accessible. Shortly after ten o'clock, he saw the long bus make its turn off of Highway 61 and head for the bus station, eventually pulling in to it. He watched closely as passengers, mostly black, unloaded one by one and either retrieve their luggage from the driver on the bus's passenger side, and enter the terminal building or head out down the street. He watched with increased interest as they unloaded and went their separate ways, scanning each face for a recognizable one that would match the photo he had been given. He had preferred to complete this mission at night for the sake of secrecy, but had little option because of the bus schedules. On the positive side, identifying his target in the daylight was much easier than it would have been if performed at night.

When Tyrone stepped off of the bus carrying his bag, Edker instantly recognized him.

"Hello, you unlucky bastard," Edker said to himself under his breath. He watched as Tyrone headed east up the street back toward Highway 61. He watched him cross the highway and head back north toward Highway 8 and the hospital. Edker could read him like a book and waited for him to get a block and a half up the highway before pulling out and duplicating his route. As he passed Tyrone on the side of the highway, he pulled over quickly and waited for him to walk alongside his truck.

"You look like you may be in the army, and I always give army boys a ride. Where you headin'?" Edker asked with a smile that revealed a missing tooth on his lower jaw.

"No, sir, not in the army," Tyrone said, grinning back, pleased that someone might think he was military material.

"Well, I'm stopped now, anyway. Where you headin'?" Edker asked again.

"Just over to the hospital on Highway 8," Tyrone said.

"Come on, I'll take you. I'm going that direction anyway," returned Edker.

Tyrone ran behind the pickup, opened the passenger door and slid in the cab. He closed the door and Edker shifted into first and pulled back onto the highway.

@ @ @ @ @ @ @

Paul Lane called Landon Fall's office as soon as he felt Landon had checked in and was there, but before he became engrossed in trial preparation. He had wanted to put this meeting off because he really had nothing to report, but Landon's secretary had called again late the afternoon before and advised that Landon still needed that update on GalBerry. He set up a status meeting with Landon at 9:30 that morning and then spent the next two hours before then prepping for the meeting, perusing all his notes and making mental ones about what to say and what was probably best unsaid at the time. At precisely 9:30, Paul walked into Landon's office and spoke to his secretary.

"Good morning, Tracey," he said, finding a seat in one of the plush office chairs in the reception area.

"Good morning, Paul," she returned. "He's on the phone and will be with you as soon as he gets off it," she said.

"Where's the coffee?" Paul asked. "Landon hasn't gone cheap on me, has he?" Paul snipped. He really didn't want any, having had three cups already that morning, but he was just trying to fill in the dead air in the room. Before she could answer back, Landon's voice came over the intercom.

"Ask Paul to step back here, please," he said.

When Paul entered the office, he could sense that something was awry. The normal jovial mood of his boss was missing and he seemed all business on this occasion. Paul quickly took a seat in front of Landon's desk in an office chair and waited for Landon to begin.

"Paul, I'm hearing a lot of grumbling from constituents, the press and L.B. about our lack of progress on these two murders. Most people say we couldn't catch this man with a net if he was sitting in my office. Now, I'm used to the press and L.B. bitchin' about us, but when it comes to my constituents, excuse me, *our* constituents, my political radar goes haywire and I start thinking about forced early retirement, or God help me, practicing law again. I also think about you sharing expenses with me in a law office at that point. You follow what I'm saying?" Landon asked.

"I hear you, boss, I just don't know what to tell you. Realistically we have two possible suspects, Tyrone Braid and Wayne Milton and not a shred of direct proof against either one. Just a whole lot of suspicions and circumstances—no motive, no propensity for violence, no fingerprints, no nothing. I've got a confession I can't use from a retard that probably was coerced by his minister and whose lawyer won't let me near him to question him further. I've got a suspect I can't even catch up with to interrogate. Neither can his parole officer. Hell, I was thinking the other night if I was still in the game as a defense attorney, I'd love to defend either one of these clowns in court against me with the evidence I have," Paul surmised.

"We're going to have to get everyone involved in finding this Braid kid," Landon announced. "I know your concerns about vigilante justice against a niggah, but though I might agree with your fears, I don't know that we really have a choice at this stage of the game. We've been kind enough to keep his name out of the limelight to our detriment and he repays us by running from us. We're starting to look like a couple of jackasses to the public because of this little thug and I'm tired of it. We can call him a person of interest, not a suspect if you think that will help, but we've got to get his ass caught and in here so we can interrogate him."

"You call the shots, boss. That's why they give you the big bucks," Paul responded. "What's your pleasure?"

"From this moment until further notice, I want you working 100% of the time on GalBerry," Landon stated. "No other cases until this one's in the bag. I want you to get to Chicago and find this little thug and interrogate the hell out of him. I want you to tell me he is purer than the Virgin Mary or have his ass in jail when you're through with him, no doubt either way. I'll see that his parole officer puts out a warrant for him as well and I'll do a press release announcing that we would like to talk to him as a person of interest. That should appease the public for the time being. You understand what to do, now? I want the heat turned up on him until it's boiling."

"I got you, boss," Paul said and got up from his chair. He looked back into the seat to see if part of his ass remained there after Landon had chewed it off and was pleased to find that he still had it intact. He headed out the door, speaking to Tracey as he exited.

CHAPTER 24

Chollie Mullen awoke to the constant sobbing of his wife as she lay next to him in the bed. He was a heavy sleeper, partly due to his drinking, but nobody could sleep through the kind of commotion she was stirring. Shaking his wife and pleading with her to tell him what the trouble was finally produced a response.

"My boy killed 'em," she wailed. "He killed both of 'em. He told me he did."

"Killed who?" Chollie asked.

"Those two girls, Chollie. Wayne killed 'em. He told me he did. My boy killed 'em. Oh, God what are we gonna do?" she asked in return.

Chollie got up out of the bed and strode to Wayne's room in his boxers and wife beater T-shirt. He was as stunned as his wife and had to verify what she told him. She lay still and heard their muffled voices through the closed door and walls, unable to hear what was being said between the two, but able to imagine. The tone of her husband's voice went from soft, but stern to loud and angry and then retreated back to soft. She couldn't hear Wayne very clearly, but she had heard enough to know what her husband was hearing at the time. Then their voices fell silent or else so low they could not be picked up by her. She waited with eager anticipation for her husband to return to the bed and tell her what had transpired, but he did not. Finally, after what seemed like forever, she heard the sound of his steps as he left Wayne's room, entered their bedroom again and laid back down.

"What did he say, Chollie," she asked since he didn't quickly volunteer.

"Same as he told you. I'm just not sure I believe him," Chollie said.

"Why in God's name would he say something like that if he didn't do it?" she shot back.

"Dammit," Chollie said. "He's got the mind of a ten-year old, who the hell knows why he does anything. Maybe he saw something about it on the television and thought it might be fun to say it."

"That's not it, Chollie," she said. "He was upset when he told me. He's never lied to me that I know of and I don't think he's lying now."

"What do you want me to tell you, that your son is a murderer that has killed twice in the last month and will likely kill again? I don't know what to think right now either. We either have to cover for him or turn him in if what we are hearing is the truth. You tell me—what do you want to do?" Chollie asked while sitting on the side of the bed fumbling for a cigarette.

"Oh, God," she said. "I can't send my boy to jail for the rest of his life or worse yet to the gas chamber. Nobody can expect me to can they? Oh my God!"

"Look, we ain"t doing a damn thing until we are sure he has done something," Chollie decided. "He needs to stay home and quit runnin' the roads until we can see what really happened and then decide from there."

"I agree," she said. "I'll tell him and if he leaves here, we may not have a choice then," she said forebodingly. They talked together about their options and the ramifications of each for at least another hour.

"Well, I guess sleep is out of the question. Might as well get up," Chollie said as he pulled his pants on.

@ @ @ @ @ @

Though a brief ride to the hospital, Edker and his passenger carried on a conversation like two good friends until Tyrone saw that they were passing the hospital without stopping.

"Anywhere right along here will be fine," Tyrone said as he peered through the windshield and the driver's side glass at the hospital they were about to pass. Edker ignored him and continued to look straight ahead.

"This good right here," Tyrone repeated as the truck continued straight ahead. "Hey, man where you goin'," Tyrone asked. Edker drew the pistol from beside him and pointed it at Tyrone's midsection.

"I'm probably going straight to hell with you, eventually," Edker responded, "but in the meantime, me and you are going for a little ride in the country. I need your wallet."

"Man, I ain't got no money!" Tyrone exclaimed, all the time reaching for his wallet in his back pocket.

"You won't need any," Edker responded, holding the steering wheel of the truck with one hand and pointing the pistol at Tyrone with the other. He began accelerating the truck and was out of the city limits and into the countryside in seconds.

Tyrone withdrew his wallet and attempted to hand it over at the same time that Edker was attempting a left turn onto a gravel road off the highway. Whether it was fear or anger that made him react, Tyrone couldn't say, but in that instant he pushed the pistol in Edker's hand down onto the seat with the hand that held his wallet while at the same time fighting with him for control of the vehicle. The timing was perfect as Edker lost his grip on the pistol and it fell to the floorboard of the old pickup. Likewise, Tyrone lost his wallet at the same time Edker dropped the pistol in the scuffle, a trade he would make any day of the week and twice on Sunday if he had the opportunity. As the men fought for control of the steering wheel, the truck careened off the highway, onto to the gravel road, and came to rest in a ditch. Tyrone jumped from the vehicle through the passenger door, sprawled into the cotton field across the ditch and made a mad dash for safety. Edker fumbled with the pistol in an attempt to recover it from the floor of the pickup. By the time he retrieved it and got out, he could hear the swishing sound of cotton plants being pushed aside as someone ran through them, but he was unable to see Tyrone. In desperation, he leveled the pistol and fired three shots in the direction of the sound. None found their mark, but they succeeded in pushing Tyrone to top speed in his getaway.

In the midmorning heat and humidity, Tyrone's clothes were drenched in sweat in a matter of seconds and his breathing was labored just as quickly. He pushed himself until he was certain that the old man had not, even if he could have, pursued him as far as he had run. He stopped and listened for sounds of movement but heard nothing. He tried to see if the truck was still there or if it had been moved, but he had gone too far into the cotton and high weeds along the field to see back that far. He looked around to get his bearings and could hear nothing but the passing vehicles along Highway 8. He decided the best direction to go was east, away from Cleveland as he believed the old man would return in the direction he originally came. He was correct.

Edker had returned to his truck immediately after firing into the field in his desperate attempt to hit the fleeing Tyrone. He climbed inside, stuck the pistol in his belt, and floored it. He was able to free the truck from the ditch because of its lack of water, by rocking it back and forth from forward gear to reverse, then flooring it as he gained traction. He cursed the situation under his breath as the truck leaped onto the gravel road, spun around and turned onto the highway. Edker again mashed the accelerator and sped back into the city limits of Cleveland, cursing himself the entire time for his failure in not carrying out his planned execution of Tyrone.

Tyrone had continued walking east along the highway, inside the field and out of the view of anyone passing by him. The last thing he needed now was for someone to see him and report him to the authorities for trespassing. He had managed to lose his wallet with what little money he had along with his clothes and for the time being, his ability to check on Darcel. He needed to call the hospital, not only to see about Darcel, but for some help for himself from any family member who might be there. He knew The Half-Way Store was a few miles up the road and they would have a pay phone, so he headed to it.

It would take him the better part of an hour and a half to get there in 96-degree heat and high humidity, but he finally arrived, tired, exhausted, thirsty and soaked to the bone from sweat. He wanted to tell the lady behind the counter, a squatty white woman in her sixties, the truth: That he had been robbed up the road, lost his money and see if he could borrow a phone. However, a man wanted by the cops as well as his parole officer couldn't afford to report anything to the police, so he decided against it. Instead, he walked up to a phone that hung at the back of the store and checked the coin return slot. Up until this time he had experienced nothing but hard luck, but that changed instantly. As luck would have it, a dime was in the slot, apparently left by someone who had been unable to complete a call and failed to collect the returned coin. He glanced upward in a mock attempt to thank God for his luck, and looked up the number of the hospital in Cleveland from the phone book that hung by a small chain alongside the pay phone. He had one shot, so a wrong number couldn't be risked.

"East Bolivar County Hospital," the receptionist answered.

"Yes ma'am, can you connect me to the room of Darcel Braid?" Tyrone asked.

"One moment, please," she responded. The phone fell silent and then began to ring inside the receiver. After the third ring, he was about to lose hope when it was answered.

"Hello," the voice said.

"Uncle Lonnie!" Tyrone exclaimed. "It's Tyrone. How's Darcel?"

"She's still in a coma, Tyrone. Where are you?" Lonnie asked. Tyrone began the story of arriving in Cleveland on the Greyhound bus, being robbed at gunpoint, and the long walk to The Half-Way Store.

"Just stay there for a few more minutes, Tyrone. I'll send John to get you in my car," his uncle told him.

"Thanks, Uncle Lonnie."

Tyrone hung up the phone, walked out of the store and drank heavily from a faucet by the gas pumps. He found a seat on a bench along the front of the store beneath an awning and waited for his ride. Twenty minutes later a dark brown Cadillac pulled into the gravel parking lot of the store and alongside where he sat, driven by John. Tyrone opened the passenger side door and climbed in.

"Never thought I'd be this glad to see you. Hope you takin' better care of Uncle Lonnie's car than you did mine," Tyrone said, half-jokingly.

The two talked as they headed back to Cleveland and the hospital. John asked about Chicago while Tyrone asked about Darcel and the details of her accident. Both had plenty of catching up to do just from the events of that day if nothing else.

"That man just robbed you, just like that?" John asked.
"Never knew what was happening until he pulled the gun on me," replied Tyrone.
"How much did he get?"
"Thirty-two dollars, man. All I had in the world."
"You think he would have killed you for it?'"

"Damn right he would have. He tried to shoot me when I ran."
"Would you recognize him or the truck?"
"I'd recognize him, but maybe not the truck. Didn't get no tag number or anything."
"How long you stayin'?" asked John.
"Don't know. Ain't got no money to get back on now," Tyrone answered.

He had no idea that the incident earlier was a hit on his life as opposed to a simple robbery, and at that very instant, Edker was eating a hamburger at a drive-in diner, Bob's Drive-In, contemplating his second attempt. He would have to call Merriweather and give him the news of his failure and he dreaded that; not because he was afraid of Merriweather, or anyone else for that matter, but because he hated to admit failure. Soon enough, he would plan and execute his next attempt to get Tyrone, the biggest problem now being where to find him. Perhaps it was best to start where he left off earlier—at the hospital.

CHAPTER 25

Having had little, if any, sleep since the events of the night before, Wayne's parents were up and waiting on him when he got out of bed the next morning. His mother had prepared the usual array of foods for breakfast that included eggs, biscuits with homemade blackberry jam and bacon, all of which was spread upon the kitchen table like a buffet. Wayne walked in without saying anything or making eye contact, perhaps hoping that what had transpired last night was all a bad dream. There was no chance of that. As soon as he sat down, fixed his plate and began eating, both his parents began their verbal assault of questions and demands.

"Wayne, son, me and your father have talked about it, and we believe you need to stay home, at least in the yard, for the next few days," his mother said.

"Why, Momma?" he asked, appearing oblivious to the problem, at least outwardly.

"We've got to protect you from those that might want you to go to jail, son," Chollie answered, being blunt in his response. "The law could come pick you up any minute if they saw you walking down the road like you do usually." He was trying desperately to be truthful with his son but not say the truth: That he and his Momma were afraid he might do something violent again.

"I don't want to go to jail," Wayne stammered, "and I don't want to go to Hell either."

"Then you best stay right here for the time being, we'll let you know when it's safe to travel around again," his Momma said. Neither one could believe they were actually hiding the fact that their son might be a killer, but consoled themselves with the thought that they certainly were not sure at this point. Both of them wanted to dive right in to an intense interrogation of the man to convince themselves that he was or was not guilty by asking him specifics about the crimes, but neither wanted to taint his memory with answers that he made up in order to tell them what they wanted to hear. That type of questioning would best be performed by a counselor or psychologist of some sort who knew what to say or do to ascertain the truth and they both had decided to hire one for that purpose. Since medical records are privileged, they couldn't be used against him in a trial, could they? They both were certain that they had heard that on one of their television shows.

"I'm gonna hate it, but if it will keep me from going to jail, I'll do it, especially if it will keep me from going to Hell as well," Wayne decided. His rationale and reasoning were beginning to reveal the level that his mind actually functioned, and it was incredibly low.

"We're going to have to take you to a doctor before too long, son, to help you with all this," Chollie said. He didn't specify what "all this" was, but it appeared that Wayne understood. When Wayne began to weep shortly afterwards, they both left him alone to finish his breakfast without any more discussion.

Chollie Mullen called the church looking for the pastor. He would surely know who they could talk to about Wayne's problem and might be able to shed some light on the subject himself, as long as he didn't have to know what Wayne's "problem" was. They couldn't afford to let word of this event getting out into the community, having no idea that the possibility of his involvement in the two murders had already been discussed with a large portion of the residents, courtesy of wagging tongues that could be traced back to James Weeks and the very pastor they now sought help from at the moment. There was no answer by the pastor at his phone in his study, so they decided to try later.

@ @ @ @ @ @ @

Dewitt Strawberry had come in from plowing that afternoon with nothing on his mind but his recliner and a glass of sweet tea. Estelle met him at the door with an ice-filled glass of it in her hand and gave it to him as he deposited his John Deere cap on the hat rack by the door, stepped out of his boots and collapsed into his chair. The window unit air conditioner mounted in a side window of the den was set on high with the thermostat on it turned down as low as it could get. The roar of the fan made listening to the television hard unless the volume was cranked up to almost the maximum, so he adjusted it to just that and sat back in his chair.

"I've gotten two strange calls the last thirty minutes. The caller don't say nothing, just hangs up when I answer," his wife informed him. "If you were younger or had more money, I'd think you were having an affair," she laughed.

"Probably kids playing pranks," he observed. "When's supper?"

"'Bout fifteen minutes," she answered.

Several minutes later, the phone rang again. "I'll get it," Dewitt called out, "probably my girlfriend, again." He answered the phone on the wall near his chair in the den. A familiar voice began to talk, never announcing who he was.

"Just wanted to let you know that our client is in town and we have made initial contact with him." Dewitt's face turned pale as the blood from it rushed to his feet. As before, he recognized the voice, though the caller did not identify himself. Before he could say anything, the voice continued, "We were unable to close the transaction at that time, but we are planning on continuing further negotiations. As long as he is in town, we feel like there is a high likelihood of success."

Dewitt broke in, "What happened?" he asked.

"No need to go into the specifics of the failed attempt to close the deal at this time. I just wanted you to know that we are working to get it closed. I knew you would be concerned and wanted the negotiations over. Just wanted to update you," the voice said.

"Uh, uh, ...," Dewitt stuttered.

"I'll keep you updated and contact you again as soon as something new develops," the voice promised. "Good, day." Dewitt heard the familiar dial tone afterwards and hung up the phone himself. He sat back in his recliner with his iced tea and reared back in it.

"Who was that, Dewitt?" Estelle asked.

"Uh, somebody wanting to know if I was hiring on the farm," he lied.

That seemed to pacify Estelle and she inquired no further. Had she come into the room and talked directly to her husband, she would more than likely have noticed how upset he was from the paleness of his face, his stuttering and stammering speech and the renewed sweat across his brow. The reality of the seriousness of his involvement in the planned hit, though at the outset seemed appropriate and acceptable to him, now seemed too real for him. Anyone could brag about wanting to kill someone for hurting or killing a loved one, but to actually consent and participate in its accomplishment was something else. He had lost many hours of sleep over it since his meeting with the boys in Ruleville, but it looked like his insomnia might reach a new level now, with the fact that apparently, they had tried, though unsuccessfully, to eliminate a human being. Worse yet, they appeared to be doing it, among other reasons, for his sake and at his command. His conscience would not let the situation die, either. As much as he tried to justify it by reminding himself that he wasn't doing the killing or wasn't even paying to have it done as others were, he still felt responsible. He just wasn't wired for that kind of action.

He tried to get his mind off the call by watching television, to no avail. When he finally went to bed, he lay awake for hours, turning over and over beside his wife. Somewhere in the early hours of the morning, he decided that he had to call Stanton Merriweather and do what he could to call off the whole thing. Surely, they would understand. He couldn't be the first person to change his mind about something like this, could he? He would do it first thing in the morning as soon as he left for the fields. He would drive to a pay phone and make the call before anything further could happen. He couldn't risk using his home phone for fear of Estelle hearing his conversation. Then his mind would be clear and conscience would leave him alone. With that plan, he turned over for the final time that night and drifted off to sleep.

@ @ @ @ @ @ @

Paul Lane was accomplishing two tasks at the same time that morning with equal vigor. He was looking over the written preliminary report of the autopsy on Janice Galtelli while devouring an apple fritter he had picked up at the Delta Cream Donut Shoppe that morning. The timeline between the Strawberry murder and the Galtelli murder had bothered him from the beginning, the time of death on Strawberry being fixed, the time of death on Galtelli being the variable. Based on his own expert, he had unwillingly convinced himself that neither Braid *nor* Milton could be excluded as suspects in both murders based on their presence in the area during that timeline. He was sick of second-guessing himself and had to move forward on the sheriff's theory that the more likely suspect was Tyrone Braid at the present time, even though Wayne Milton could not be excluded.

His thoughts were interrupted, as they often were, by the intercom call from his receptionist.

"Mr. Ralph West would like to know if you a minute to talk to him," she said.

"West, West, West," he wondered aloud, but to himself, "who the hell is that, anyway." Then his mind clicked and he remembered the vacationing man from Shaw who had lost his home electronics in a burglary while he was away.

"Uh, ask him if he can give me about ten minutes and I'll see him," he answered back to the receptionist on the intercom. He hated people who dropped by to see him without an appointment, but at the same time, he hated appointments because they restricted his freedom to come and go. In this case he felt sorry for the poor guy and decided he would see him, if for no other reason than public relations. He sure didn't have any progress on his case to report. Shortly thereafter, he greeted Mr. West in the reception area and escorted him back to his own office. They made small talk and then West announced the reason for his visit.

'I understand they found a good stack of stuff probably taken from a burglary in an empty soybean storage bin out on the southeast end of the county." Mr. West said. "Have you looked at what they found?"

"I have not, Mr. West. Do you know by chance what officer did the initial report on the find?" Paul asked.

"I hoped you could tell me. Had to be someone from the sheriff's department. There ain't no city police in that area. Friend of mine from over 'round Indianola told me about it. Said it was found by the owner who was cleaning it out for when he combined his beans and found all kinds of stereos, tape decks and televisions," West elaborated.

"It is certainly possible for our sheriff's department to drop the ball or screw up, but they are pretty good about letting me know anything that might help them prosecute their cases and I've not heard a single word about that. I hate to be ignorant, but this is the first I've heard about it," Paul told him, thinking in his mind that the dumbasses over at L.B.'s office couldn't solve a crime if they witnessed it.

"Do you mind checking on it for me? I was just hoping I might get some of my stuff back," he said, being extremely humble and not critical.

"Absolutely. If you'll give me a week, I'll get to the bottom of it and give you a call to come look if I find it. I certainly will," Paul reiterated.

"That works for me," Mr. West said. "Sorry to drop in on you without calling first."

"No problem at all," Paul said. "Happy to help if I can."

He walked the man out to the reception area carrying on small talk, opened the door to the outside for him and promised again that he would get in touch with him within a week.

CHAPTER 26

John and Tyrone arrived at the hospital and promptly parked in the back where the hospital employees parked. They avoided the reserved parking spaces as they would never be mistaken for doctors, but the maintenance staff likewise parked back there and there would be nothing unusual about a couple of black boys in their twenties parking back there. They entered the hospital through the back door, took the elevator to the third floor and headed down the hall to room 316. When they entered the room, a rush of emotions went over Tyrone at the sight of the family that he had sorely missed, his aunt and uncle, with the shock of seeing Darcel, her leg in an elevated cast, IVs in her arm, bandaged, on oxygen and comatose.

He hugged his aunt, shook hands with his uncle and then knelt by Darcel's bed, not sure what to do at that point. Had he known she had been intentionally injured to this extent as a means of getting him back to the Delta, he would not have been able to contain the guilt.

"What the doctor say?" he asked to no one and everyone.

"They still can't say. Except for the fact that she is unconscious, she is doing well, apparently. One of her doctors described her brain as an egg that had been thrown against the wall and spattered. It takes time for it to heal by drawing itself together. Until then, she may be out," Lonnie told him. "I know that's a little plain, but that's what he said." No one said anything for a few minutes and then Lonnie broke the silence.

"Tyrone, are you ok, son?" Lonnie asked. "We need to get the police to work on the robbery. You shouldn't have to go through that, and he shouldn't get away with it," Lonnie observed

"I can't report it Uncle Lonnie," Tyrone said, rising from the side of Darcel's bed and walking to the window, looking out at the parking lot. "I'm in violation of my parole for leaving the state and not reporting to my parole officer. He probably got a warrant out for me and they'd pick me up as soon as I walked into the sheriff's office. I can't do that."

"What else are you running from, Tyrone. Why did you go to Chicago?" asked Lonnie.

"It don't matter, Uncle Lonnie. All that matters right now is that Darcel gets better," Tyrone said. Lonnie knew he would tell him one day if he felt the need, but obviously not today, so he didn't push the issue.

"How long can you stay and how are you getting back? Are you even going back?" Lonnie inquired.

"I can't stay but a couple days or I'll lose my job," he answered. "I really don't know how I'm going to get back after that damn robbery. I'll think of something, though."

"Here, boy. Put this in your pocket. We've all got enough problems with Darcel and we don't need to make them worse," Lonnie said. He took a number of bills from his wallet, folded them in half and handed them to Tyrone, who stuck them in his pants' pocket without looking at them to see how much it was.

"Thanks, Uncle Lonnie. You're too good to me. I'll pay you back."

"Sure, you will," Lonnie laughed, "Sure you will."

"I promise," Tyrone said. That brought a laugh from everyone in the room, including Tyrone and it seemed to lift the mood, at least for a short while.

They all stayed the remainder of the day and when visiting hours were over, Tyrone volunteered to stay there with Darcel so all the others could go home for some much-needed sleep. It made perfect sense since Tyrone couldn't chance going home with John to their house and he had nowhere else to sleep. They all said their goodbyes and left Tyrone there alone with Darcel. He stretched out on the vinyl chair by her bed and started to doze. He was used to sleeping upright and with the events of the day, it didn't take him long to fall asleep.

Somewhere during the night, Tyrone woke to a gnawing hunger and decided he would go down to the snack machines. He knew there were chips, candy, sodas and even cold sandwiches available in the vending machines on the first floor near the emergency room, so he left the room and headed in that direction. He walked past the nurse's station, got in the elevator, and punched the first-floor button. The elevator stopped momentarily on the second floor and two candy stripers got on, chatting constantly as they rode down to the first floor with him. On the first floor, they went in the opposite direction as he headed for the snack room.

He had to get change from a dollar changer and then bought a coke and a package of peanut butter crackers. He opened the coke, but put the crackers in his pocket and headed back upstairs. When he exited the snack room, he passed a couple coming in to it, apparently from the emergency room, made a beeline for the elevator and was back in Darcel's room in a matter of minutes. There he ate his late supper while looking back out onto the parking lot where nurses and staff were coming and going as shifts changed.

On the first floor, a man was making a telephone call on a pay phone.

"I hate to wake you, but this is important. I just passed our client coming out of the snack room on the first floor of the hospital," he said.

"Are you stalking him or something?" the voice on the other end said.

"No, I'm at the hospital with my son. Me and my wife brought him to the emergency room with some severe pain in his abdomen. They think it may be appendicitis. Anyway, we just happened to go to the snack room for a coke, and we ran into him coming out. Visiting hours are over, so he must be spending the night here," the caller said.

"Not much we can do there, but our man needs to know when our client leaves. There may be some room to close the deal then. I know you can't keep an eye on him with your son being sick, but just keep your eyes open. If he leaves the hospital and you happen to see him go, give me a call. I'm calling our man now."

"Good deal," the caller said and hung up.

A call was then placed to Edker Bentley who had yet to go to bed and was sitting up drinking whiskey in an effort to drown the memory of his failure earlier that day.

"Might be too risky to take him at the hospital, even on the outside of it. I'd rather catch him on the road where there aren't as many possible witnesses. I'll go there first thing in the morning and at least do a little recognizance, you know, see who he's with, what's he riding in or driving, that kind of thing. I spent a little time there a little earlier today and didn't see him. Good to know he's still following the routine we thought he would follow. He's a walking dead man, sooner or later," Edker observed.

"You're the pro. I delivered the info, you use it to your advantage, the caller said.

"I'll do it, old friend, thanks," Edker said, and the call was terminated.

@ @ @ @ @ @

Maybe it was the thought of being home, or maybe it was just his nature to roam, Tyrone desperately needed some fresh air and to walk around. Nobody that would cause him to be arrested could possibly know he was home, so he felt the need to go for a little walk around. Darcel would not know he was gone and there seemed little that he his presence in the room could do for her anyway. He wouldn't be gone too long anyway and he would be careful.

@ @ @ @ @ @

The man watched with eager anticipation. He had walked these roads and watched these houses so much, that they were familiar to him to the point of being monotonous. He stood at the end of the drive, just inside the field, and watched as one by one the lights in the house were turned off. He knew the girl that lived there, though they had never spoken. She was a petite brunette soon to begin her senior year in school and as beautiful as a magnolia blossom. More importantly, he knew she was alone, her parents and two siblings having left earlier for parts unknown as he watched from his cotton field vantage point. He emerged from the cotton and strode confidently up the drive with a credit card in his hand, ready to use it to unlatch the front door if it happened to be locked. His anticipation was almost more than he could stand and he was totally aroused.

He was almost to the front door when he heard the distant crunch of gravel from an approaching automobile. "Damn it to hell!", he seethed, as he began to back away and look for a spot to hide until the car passed. He planted himself three rows deep in the cotton field on the side of the house and waited.

The car stopped at the end of the drive where he had just come and two young boys got out. They had turned the lights of the car off just before they arrived and he wondered why. Methodically, the boys began flinging roll after roll of toilet paper into the trees in the yard and across the freshly mowed lawn, laughing as they went while trying to keep quiet nonetheless. They continued "rolling" the young girl's yard for several minutes, whispering back and forth about how the cutie would be so surprised when she got up in the morning and would surely think of them first. They were so enthralled in their task that they never heard or saw the shadowy figure as he faded further into the cotton field and headed back home, frustrated that his attempt at satisfaction had been thwarted on this night. There would be another day, he thought, and that seemed to pacify him for the moment.

@ @ @ @ @ @

Shortly after sunup, a beige Plymouth pulled into the front parking lot of the hospital and parked. The driver put the car in park, pulled out a pair of binoculars, and began scanning the parking lot and paying close attention to anyone who arrived or left it. He had some biscuits and sausage next to him that he slowly ate as he continued to watch, being careful to put the binoculars down when someone rode or parked close by so as to not be noticed. He opened a thermos of coffee, poured a cup into the cap and sipped it. He had learned many things in his life, but the best lesson taught to him by experience was patience and he had perfected it. Three hours later he had not seen the subject he was looking for, nor anyone that may have come with him, but he continued to watch. Though he did not know it, Lonnie Braid, his wife and nephew John had returned to the hospital and parked no less than six spaces away from him, gotten out and went inside. They were now back in Darcel's room with Tyrone. Edker had seen the brown Caddy pull up, watched the entourage arrive and go inside, but had no idea who they were. In another hour or so, he would give up for the time being and leave the parking lot.

Lonnie and Tyrone talked outside of Darcel's room in the hall.

"You got to go get some rest, Tyrone. You need a change of clothes, a shower and you need to decide what you are going to do in the immediate future. There's nothing you can do for Darcel here right now. I want you to stay, but I'd rather see you come back when she wakes up. She would, too," Lonnie advised him.

"I just hate to leave her, Uncle Lonnie. She and you are the only two people in the world I could count on to help me every time I screwed up," he said.

"Take my car, go to John's and get you some more clothes and take a shower. Get some sleep if you want to and then come back here and we'll see what's changed, if anything," Lonnie instructed.

"I know you're right. Are you sure you don't mind?" Tyrone asked.

"Go, boy," Lonnie commanded. "Take John with you so you can get in the house. I know you don't have any keys."

Yes, sir," Tyrone said. He went back into the room, got John and the two headed out.

When they got down on the first floor, John motioned for Tyrone to follow him out the front.

"We parked in front. It'll be all right," he told Tyrone.

They exited the front of the hospital and headed to Lonnie's car. As they did, Edker's binoculars were focused on them. He recognized Tyrone instantly, but was more interested in John. He needed to know who the guy was and he needed to remember his face. When they pulled out of the parking space, Edker was behind them and committed the license plate to memory. He followed them out onto the highway, got behind them until they reached the intersection of Highways 61 and 8. When they turned left to go south, Edker continued west. He had the info he needed, he just needed time to run the plates and figure out who Tyrone was hanging with while he was here. Then, and only then would he know how and where to take him out. When he got back home, he called his connection in law enforcement and asked if it would be too much trouble to run a license plate number for him. No problem, they would have it for him in a few minutes and call him back. Edker was ecstatic and couldn't wait.

"Now, you niggah bastard, I'll have your black ass this time," he said to himself.

CHAPTER 27

A call to the pastor the next day bore fruit for Mr. and Mrs. Mullen. Not only was he in the study, but he was never too busy to talk to his church members, or so he said. He invited them to come on down and he would be happy to talk to them about any problem they had, he insisted. They instructed Wayne to remain at the house and not go anywhere, assuring him they would be back in probably an hour or so. If anything, Wayne was obedient to his parents, particularly his mother, and they had no doubt he would remain in the yard and be there when they returned later that morning.

They were greeted at the church door by Kirksey, who hugged the Mrs. and shook hands with the Mr. who he did not know well because of his lack of attendance on Sundays. He invited them back into his study where the air conditioner was blasting on high already this morning, in sharp contrast to the church sanctuary which was hot because the air had not been on since the Wednesday night prayer meeting two days ago. He ushered them in and seated them in the large club chairs in front of his desk, took his place behind the desk in the high-back judge's chair that he loved and asked them how he could help. Neither knew how to broach the subject and was somewhat embarrassed to bring it up. Finally, Mrs. Mullen spoke.

"Brother Kirksey, my husband and I are concerned about our son, Wayne, for a number of reasons. Lately, he has acted very reserved and quiet and seems to be greatly troubled by the death of Linda Strawberry. We don't know what to do for him, and we thought you might could refer us to a professional counselor of some sorts that could talk to him and get a feel for what is troubling him," she said cautiously.

"It's funny you should say that, Mrs. Mullen because I have been concerned about him for a while myself," the preacher said. "What type of behavior has he shown that troubles you or what has he said that causes concern?" he pried.

"He just asks is she in heaven and is the man that killed her going to Hell, things like that," she responded as she shifted uncomfortably in her chair. She did not want to tell him that Wayne had confessed to the murders under any circumstances. "He's been crying a lot, too, something he never used to do."

"I understand, completely. Does he appear to be hiding anything from you?" the preacher inquired.

"Oh, no, not at all as far as we know," she truthfully stated. "He's very open with us."

If that was the case, surely Wayne told them what he had told him in his study previously. He wanted to ask them, but he didn't want them to know that he had solicited a confession from their son and not told them about it. It seemed to him that half the county already knew it because of James Weeks and his ability to tell anyone that would listen, but somehow, because of their reclusive nature, his own parents may not know.

"What would you like me to do?" the preacher asked.

"Maybe you have a friend who is a psychiatrist or something and can get us an appointment with him to see Wayne," she stated.

"I can certainly do that for you. I know just the person in Cleveland. She's not a doctor but a licensed social worker who counsels children through her job," he said, not really thinking of what he had just said. "I'm sorry, Mr. and Mrs. Mullen, I didn't mean to imply that your son is a child. I'm very sorry for the way that came out."

"No apology is necessary Brother Kirksey, we are well aware of Wayne's disability," Mrs. Mullen said. "If you can get me her name and phone number, I'll give her office a call."

"I'll do better than that. I'll call her for you," he said. He picked up the phone on his desk after looking her number up on his rolodex and dialed. Before it could ring, he slowly pushed the button on the base of the phone, causing it to hang up, and then began a conversation with no one.

"Yes, I'd like to speak with Ms. Leonard," he said to the dial tone. "Ok, do you know when she will return? Well, would you tell her Reverend W.D. Kirksey called and ask her to call me at 601-754-6534? That will be fine, and thank you very much." He replaced the receiver on the base and announced, "It appears she is out now, but will return this afternoon. She will return my call and I will call you afterwards with the appointment. Hopefully the appointment will be tomorrow, is that ok?"

"That would be great," Mrs. Mullen said. "We thank you so much."

"I'll call you as soon as she calls me," he promised. "Can I do anything else for you?"

"No, that will be all, you've done plenty. I feel better about him already," she returned.

They both got up, followed by the pastor, and made their way to the door of his study. After saying their goodbyes, they left and returned home, anxiously awaiting the pastor's call later that day.

Kirksey returned to his chair in the study and called the number of Ms. Leonard's office again. This time he let it ring and asked to speak to her when the phone was answered by her secretary. When she was on the line and the pleasantries were exchanged, he got right to the point.

"Norma, I have some church members that have a retarded son, nearly 40 years old, I believe. A week ago, during a counseling session, he confessed to me that he killed the two girls that were murdered around here this past month. I went to the sheriff and the DA, but his confession to me is inadmissible, but I don't think they believe him anyway. Now his parents have come to me for a referral to you for counseling because he has been acting strange to them and they are concerned. They didn't say he confessed to them, just that he is acting strange, crying and asking lots of questions about the first girl murdered. I know this is a lot for you to digest, but you need to talk to them and corroborate what I am telling the sheriff. This man could be very dangerous. Can you see him for a session and what day and time can you?" The pastor was practically out of breath after that long statement.

"Sounds interesting," Norma replied. "Beats the typical custody evaluations and kid interviews I usually do. How about in the morning at 9 o'clock? My office, of course."

"I'll have them there," Kirksey replied. "And let's keep this conversation between us, ok?" he asked.

"Sure thing. Thanks for the business and I'll see them tomorrow," she replied.

@ @ @ @ @

Dewitt Strawberry had driven into the town of Shaw that morning in an effort to make a private phone call under the guise of picking up a part at the tractor repair shop. He pulled his truck into the parking lot of Midway Grocery along Highway 61 that had a phone booth with a pay phone out front. He got out of his truck, entered the phone booth and made sure the folding door was completely closed. He deposited a coin and then dialed the number of Stanton Merriweather, attorney at law in Cleveland.

"That will be seventy-five cents for the first ten minutes," the operator said.

He deposited the coins and the phone began to ring. He asked the secretary if he could speak to Mr. Merriweather, and without asking who was calling, put Dewitt through to him. When Stanton answered the phone, Dewitt blurted out his purpose in calling.

"Stanton, I need to meet with you, it's extremely urgent," he said.

"What's it about?" Merriweather asked.

"Our contract negotiations," DeWitt replied. There's a problem."

"How about you meet me for lunch at 11:30 this morning, then. At Brock's," Merriweather offered.

"I'll be there," Dewitt responded and hung up the phone.

Dewitt climbed back into his four-wheeled drive pickup and turned around heading back toward his farm. It was only 8:30 now, so he had three hours before his meeting. He said a silent prayer that nothing would happen before they met and he was able to call the thing off. He went to work, but his mind was occupied so his work was minimal at best. Time slowly dragged by as it always seems to do when you watch the clock in anticipation of something, but finally at 11 o'clock, he washed his hands at the barn and took off for Cleveland and Brock's café.

When he arrived at Brock's the noon time lunch crowd was beginning to show, but Merriweather was already there and seated at a booth in the back, not at his usual table. He walked over and slid into the booth opposite Merriweather and asked the waitress for an iced sweet tea for the time being.

"What on earth is the problem?" Merriweather asked.

"We've got to call it off, Stanton. I can't go through with it," Dewitt said.

"What!" Merriweather exclaimed.

"I can't do it, Stanton. I've thought about, prayed about it, I just can't let ya'll do this," he said.

"Do you have any idea what you are asking?" Merriweather said. "The impossible," he answered for Dewitt.

"You've got to stop it Stanton, I can't go through with it," Dewitt repeated. Merriweather's face grew tense and he furrowed his forehead. He leaned toward Dewitt, speaking low but very sternly.

"Now you listen to me and you listen really good, you son of a bitch. I asked you from the beginning if this is what you wanted and what did you tell me? You said yes, this is what I want. I invited you to our meeting and advised you what the procedure for the finances would be and who would be the financiers. You told me afterward you were all about it and thanked us for doing our duty. You shot your mouth off about what you would do to the bastard if you caught him, beginning the day after they found your daughter's body spread-eagle on the bed in your house. And now, you have the audacity to tell me I need to stop it? Why, you egotistical son of a bitch, who do you think you are, some kind of Imperial Wizard? The time for thinking about it and praying about it has long passed. You consented to setting the wheels in motion to rid the world of this good for nothing thug, not me or anyone else. It would have never started if you had not been in agreement—you were given that privilege. That was then and this is now. You can't stop it and neither can I or anyone else. The lots have been drawn, you saw that. The order has been put forth by vote with your full agreement, so you sit back and let nature take its course like you agreed. I promise you Dewitt, if you rock this boat at this point, your life won't be worth a damn nickel more than Tyrone Braid's, do you understand me?" Merriweather spewed forth in a tirade.

"I've never seen this side of you, Stanton," Dewitt said in astonishment. "We've always been friends."

"And we always will be unless you continue on this course of derailing our project," Merriweather said, converting his conversation to code. "Don't interfere, Dewitt. It's a done deal, so get used to it."

"I don't know that I can," Dewitt said in wonder. "I'll try."

"You better try damn hard, too. You do not want to wade off into this one, Dewitt. Let it go and let it happen. Don't sacrifice yourself for some damn nigger that killed your own offspring. He is not worth it," Merriweather said, no longer talking in code.

"I know you are right, it's just hard to deal with, that's all," he said.

"I'm going to do you a favor and forget this little meeting ever happened and nothing we discussed today ever came up. I would most strongly suggest you do likewise. I need to get back to the office, now. Good day, Dewitt," Merriweather stated. Stanton got up and left, leaving Dewitt alone with his tea.

CHAPTER 28

Tyrone and John arrived back at their house and Tyrone wasted no time in hitting the shower. He sat flat on the floor of the tub and allowed the shower to cover him with the hot water and nearly fell asleep in that position. John rumbled through the cabinets and refrigerator for something to eat and came up with rag bologna and hoop cheese for sandwiches. He made each of them two apiece and got them a beer from out of the fridge. He began eating while Tyrone was still in the shower. When he heard the water shut off and the shower curtain being pulled back on the rod, he called out to Tyrone to come ahead and eat. After drying off and pulling on fresh underwear, Tyrone was at the table eating the first real meal he had eaten since before leaving Chicago.

When he finished eating, he scrambled around the house for what few clothes he had remaining there and packed them into an "Arkansas suitcase" known locally as a paper bag. He downed the remainder of the beer John had set before him earlier and flopped onto the bed in his room. It felt good to be home in the comfort of his own bed and didn't take him long to drift off into a deep sleep, unlike anything he had experienced since before Darcel had her wreck.

John busied himself by picking up the dishes in the kitchen and putting them in the sink before sitting in front of the television in the front room. He knew Tyrone would be asleep for a while and he knew he needed the rest. He would let him be until he awoke on his own and then they would do whatever Tyrone thought they needed to do to get him ready to head back to Chicago. He had no way of knowing, but the same beige Plymouth that had followed them out of the parking lot of the hospital earlier, was now about a mile away, parked at Braid's Grocery after finding the Caddy at their house.

Edker Bentley had gone inside the store and purchased a beer, struck up a conversation with the middle-aged black woman behind the counter and lingered there. The woman was friendly, like Lonnie Braid expected all his employees to be, and had no hesitation in talking to the stranger who seemed more than eager to talk that day.

"Mr. Braid's not in, is he?" Edker asked.

"Naw sir, he at the hospital with his niece. She in a car wreck," the lady said as she put the money for his beer in the register.

"Doesn't he drive a brown Cadillac sometimes?" he asked further, knowing full well

that he did from the license plate check.

"Yes sir, he do. That and a dark blue Chevy pickup," she answered, as she walked toward the end of the counter and began stacking cigarettes onto a shelf.

"I thought I saw him in his car about an hour or so ago this morning down the road," Edker advised.

"I don't think so, 'cause he been at the hospital since real early this morning, right after he helped me open the store at 6 o'clock," she said. "You might have seen the car, but that was probably his nephew John driving it. He lives down the road a ways and Lonnie gets him to run errands for him, especially since his niece been in the hospital."

"It probably was," Edker agreed and smiled to himself.

"You need to leave a message for Lonnie?" she asked.

"No, ma'am. I'll catch up with him later. No big deal," he said. He walked out the door, pulled the tab on his beer and threw it to the ground, then took a long slug of it. He got in his car, pulled out onto the highway and headed back to Cleveland. He knew to watch for John Braid now and he would likely run into Tyrone in the process, then Tyrone's ass would belong to him.

Tyrone awoke after a good two-hour nap and was ready to roll when he did. He needed to go to the bus station and get his ticket back to Chicago so he could be at work the day after tomorrow. He didn't want to take a chance on losing his job and he needed the money it would generate to live on. He garnered his clothes that he had bagged, got John moving, and they both headed out in Lonnie's car back to Cleveland. Thirty minutes later he had his one-way ticket back to Chicago, leaving northbound from Cleveland at 10:30 in the morning. He hated to leave with Darcel showing no signs of improvement, but as Uncle Lonnie had said, there was nothing he could do for her right now, and he would certainly want to come back when she woke up. He and John returned to the hospital in the late afternoon, and he stayed through the night and in to the next morning.

About 10 o'clock, John took Tyrone to the bus station in Lonnie's car, dropped him off and went back to the hospital. With pangs of homesickness, Tyrone sat on the bench inside the station waiting on the bus from the south that would take him back to the Windy City and hopefully, anonymity. Just before 10:30, the bus arrived, loaded its ticketed passengers and their luggage, and pulled out at precisely 10:30.

Tyrone had no need to check any luggage, keeping his bag of clothes with him on board the bus and used them as a pillow to catch some more needed sleep as the bus rumbled north, stopping all too often at small hole-in-the road towns as it made its way north to Chicago. The bus was never more than three fourths full the entire way, making it easy to stretch out on unsold seats for comfort. Greyhound's loss was Tyrone's gain.

@ @ @ @ @ @ @

Dewitt Strawberry had been in shock since his talk with Stanton Merriweather the previous day. He had failed to catch any sleep that night as visions of hooded Klansmen and the various law enforcement departments descended on him for his transgressions of either planning and conspiring with others for a hit or refusing to go through with it. Either way, he was toast. He had gotten up at one point in the night and thrown up in the bathroom adjoining his bedroom. Estelle had heard him and asked if he was all right causing him to lie to her by saying he was fine. He prayed that God would lead him and direct him in this situation and forgive him for his part in it. Though it was distasteful, he prayed that God would protect Tyrone, something he could not have imagined a few weeks ago. He cried, he thought, he prayed again and then he cried some more.

There was one poisonous pill that he could not escape and knew that he would have to swallow eventually: If he was truly repenting of his sin to God, he had to make things right by doing what he could to stop the hit. And that meant going to the police. He couldn't escape the images of Parchman Farm in his mind, having visited there on a couple of occasions when he went with other church members to witness to the inmates. My God, how could he have fallen this far! He knew he had to do it, though the jaws of Parchman yawned at him in anticipation of his arrival and he made a solemn vow that night to contact some law enforcement agency in the morning. By doing so, he would surely be indicted as a conspirator, but if it meant his salvation and saving the life of a human being, even a black one, he would do so. After making that promise to God and to himself, he thought he might be able to sleep. God would surely do that for him, wouldn't he? When he failed to find sleep after a couple more hours, he knew his or anyone else's bargaining power with God was worthless. He accepted his fate and got up at the usual time, never having gotten the first minute of rest.

So as not to alarm or tip off his wife as to his motives or actions that morning, he left as usual, dressed in work clothes, jeans and a short-sleeved khaki shirt, and when out of sight of the house, made a run again to Midway Grocery in Shaw and the phone booth near the highway there. He had thought it through and as opposed to calling the sheriff directly, decided it best to talk to the officer or detective in charge of his daughter's murder. He wouldn't do it over the phone, but merely wanted to come in and tell his story. As far as he knew, he may never be allowed to leave that office, never being a free man again after doing so.

"I need to speak to the officer in charge of the Strawberry murder, please. I have some important information he may need to know," he told the person answering the phone at the sheriff's office.

"That would actually be investigator Paul Lane with the District Attorney's office. Would you like his office number?" she asked.

"That would be fine," Dewitt responded.

He obtained the number, called it and spoke to his receptionist. She advised that Paul was out at the moment, but would be in shortly, made him an appointment for 1 o'clock that afternoon and thanked him for calling. Dewitt was a lost man for the remainder of the morning, not even having the will or the energy to return to his farm and try to get some work done. Instead, he went to downtown Shaw and spent the morning in the old swing of the Shady Nook Liars Park, a small gazebo on Main Street in Shaw. If it was Saturday night he thought, this street would be void of any whites, but completely filled with blacks who traditionally came to town after being paid earlier in the afternoon. Any Delta town would have the same crowd that time of the week, all of them spending whatever they could spare until the following Saturday when they would do it all over again.

He watched the people going back and forth to stores and businesses, fed some sparrows a piece of a biscuit he had brought with him from home that he couldn't eat, and killed the morning. By noon he wanted something to eat, not because he was hungry, but because he was bored, so he went into the Blue Front Café down the street, entered on the "whites only" side and ate most of a hamburger with a side of crinkle-cut fries at the counter. Afterwards, there was nothing else to do but head for Cleveland and his meeting with Paul Lane.

"How do you do, Mr. Strawberry, I'm Paul Lane with the District Attorney's office. Please come in and sit down," Paul said to Dewitt as the two shook hands in the reception area. They walked in to Paul's office, were seated and Paul began to speak in order to break the uncomfortable silence that seemed to permeate the room.

"I want to tell you how sorry I am about your loss, Mr. Strawberry, I don't believe I have spoken to you since that night at your house." Paul said. "I had hoped to update you on our ongoing investigation before now." He had already made up his mind that Dewitt, like half the people in the county, wanted an update on the investigation into his daughter's murder and wanted to know further, just exactly what was taking so long to make an arrest.

"I appreciate that," Dewitt said, "But that's not why I'm here.
"Ok, I just assumed …," Paul started.
"I'm afraid I have some terrible information to share with you," Dewitt interrupted. He started at the beginning about being contacted about taking Tyrone out and his acquiescence, about the updates to the information the group had become privy to, about the meeting in Ruleville, who the cast of characters included, the amount of the payment and the failed hit on Tyrone. He then recited almost verbatim the conversation he had with Merriweather in Brock's over lunch and the enormous guilt he had felt afterwards. He was all-inclusive in his story and pulled no punches with anything, not even when it may have been favorable to him personally.

Paul listened with great interest and with his bottom jaw resting on the floor at the story the man told. He had no qualms about its believability because it greatly incriminated him as a conspirator. He let the man talk without interruption while the thoughts and legal questions rushed through his head as he continued spinning his tale. He looked at the man and tried to imagine the immense pressure he was under without feeling sorry for him. After all, he was a grown man that knew or should have known what he was getting himself into or doing. Forget the fact that his daughter had been brutally killed, you just couldn't take the law into your own hands.

When Dewitt finished he said to Paul, "I know I am probably going to prison, but this is something I have to try and stop if I can. Do you understand?"

"I can't say that I understand what you have done, but I certainly understand what you are trying to do now and why," Paul replied.

"Thank you for that, at least," Dewitt said as he shifted uncomfortably in his chair and brushed a fly from his arm.

The two men talked a while with Paul asking a few questions and Dewitt willingly answering them as best he could. Eventually, Paul retrieved a reel to reel tape recorder from the bottom drawer of his desk, took out a new reel of tape and threaded it through the machine. When he had finished, he asked Dewitt to repeat his story so that it could be saved for future use. Although Paul did not advise him of his rights under *Arizona vs. Miranda*, he did ask him if he understood he was not in custody or under arrest at this time, that he was free to leave without saying anything further and finished by offering him a coke from his office refrigerator, an offer Dewitt gladly accepted. The tape session took a little longer than the original story took to be told because of the questions Paul interjected into the story, causing Dewitt to stop and answer before returning to his soliloquy. By the time they had finished, an appointment that had begun promptly at one o'clock, finally came to a conclusion three and one-half hours later.

"I need you to go home and as best you can, I need you to live your life for the time being as normally as you can. If you feel the need to tell your wife these things, I can do nothing about it. That is your decision. However, I want you to understand that if these people believe you have breached their trust, your life will be as worthless as Tyrone Braid's life is, just like Stanton Merriweather told you. I need you to talk about this to no one and advise me if anything out of the ordinary should occur, regardless of how insignificant you may think it is," Paul warned.

"Am I going to prison?" Dewitt asked.

"Very possibly, Mr. Strawberry, but there are a lot of things that I'm concerned with right now without thinking about that. Mainly your life and Tyrone Braid's life," Paul said.

"I understand," Dewitt returned.

The two arose from their chairs, shook hands again, and said their pleasantries. Paul walked Dewitt to the door and closed it as the man left.

Turning to his receptionist, he grimly told her, "See if you can get L.B. on the phone. There is a hit out on our GalBerry suspect. See if he can meet me for dinner at Brock's at 6:00 tonight. I'm going over to Landon's to talk to him and won't be back until in the morning."

"I'll call right now," she said. As soon as Paul had walked out and she was sure he wasn't coming back, she called a familiar number.

"Ya'll have a problem," she said to the man who answered the phone. Dewitt Strawberry just left this office and was here all afternoon. He told Paul about the job."

"How much did he tell him?" the man asked.

"I have no idea, but he was in there long enough to read him *War and Peace*, she said.

"What the hell does that mean?" the man asked.

"Dammit, he was in there ALL AFTERNOON," she said in frustration.

"Damn him, the son of a bitch," he said. "Thanks for calling and let me know if you find out anything else. Got some calls to make myself, now."

"I will, Sweetie," she said.

"You're such a doll," he added and hung up the phone.

CHAPTER 29

As had been arranged, the Mullens, with Wayne in tow, arrived at the office of Norma Leonard, a licensed social worker employed with the Family and Children Services Division of the Mississippi Department of Human Services. She was employed by the State of Mississippi and on their clock, but occasionally she would see private patients to supplement her income. Since the state paid so little, she rationalized, it was only fair that she does so, even if it meant doing it on the State's time. Besides, what the state didn't know wouldn't hurt the state and everybody did it anyway. She greeted them and welcomed them to sit down, got the appropriate paperwork signed, and had the parents tell her again the purpose of her counseling their son. Then she asked that the Mullens leave without Wayne and allow her to speak to him alone for about an hour, or so.

"You are welcome to shop around town or run errands if you would like. We should not be very long," she advised them. The Mullens thanked her, left her office without Wayne and did just as she had suggested, beginning with a trip to the supermarket for groceries.

"Tell me why you think you are here, Wayne?" she asked him.

"I don't know. 'Cause I killed them girls, I guess," he returned.

"Did you do that, Wayne? Did you kill those girls?" she asked.

"I think so," he responded, beginning to rub his hands profusely.

"You think so?" she asked.

"Yes'm," he answered.

"Let's talk about Linda Strawberry, first," she stated. "How did you know her?"

"I went to church with her. Seen her there," he said. He began to cry, wiping his eyes with the back of his hands until she passed him a box of tissues. She was so far out her league in questioning him, so far from acceptable practices in questioning a mental patient, but she felt like Perry Mason, about to break down a killer in the courtroom. She was on an egotistical high and kept at him.

"When you killed her, Wayne, how did you do it?" she asked, ever ready for the gory details.

"I stabbed her, he said." "I didn't mean to."

She was taken aback by his response, but pushed forward.

"What did you stab her with?"
"A knife."
"And where did you get the knife?"
"I don't remember."
"Did you get it from her house?"
"I don't remember."
"Very well, what happened after you stabbed her, Wayne?" she asked.
"She died." Wayne had begun to openly weep at this point. Norma Leonard never changed expressions or the tone of her voice because that is how she saw people on television do it.
"How soon after you stabbed her did she die?"
"Soon as I did."
"How many times did you stab her with the knife?" she asked, pushing him for more details.
"I don't know, maybe a couple of times. Maybe three"
"Did she say anything when you stabbed her?"
"She said it hurt."
"What happened after she died?"
"She just laid there in the living room floor."
"And what did you do after she died?" Norma asked. This was certainly not going as she had planned, or had hoped.

"I told her I was sorry and left. Went back home."

"What did you do about all the blood, Wayne?" she asked.

"I washed it off when I got home. Took a shower at home. His crying had subsided for the moment.

"What about Janice Galtelli? How did you know her?" she asked him.

"Who?" he asked back.

"Janice Galtelli. Do you remember her?"

"No ma'am, I don't know her," he answered.

"What about the other girl that you killed, do you remember her?"

"Yes ma'am, I killed her," he said

"How did you know her?"

"I didn't, I just went into her house and stabbed her," he said. "She smelled bad."

"What do you mean she smelled bad?"

"She had something dead in her house or in her yard. I liked to have got sick."

"Do you remember where she was when you stabbed her, Wayne?" she asked as before.

"Yes'm. In the living room watching tv."

"How did you get into the house, Wayne, tell me that," she said.

"I broke a window out in the back of the house," he answered. He was not crying at all at this point, but had begun the habit of crossing his arms and curling his lips into a sneer.

"How about at the Strawberry house, how did you get in there?" she asked.

"Same way, broke out a window."

She had been questioning him now for over an hour and had to change the tape on the recorder twice. She was frustrated and bewildered at the same time, not hearing the answers she thought that she would after having the earlier conversation with the preacher. Maybe she needed to be more brazen with him and lead him to the answers. As it was, she couldn't say with any degree of certainty that he was aware of any detail involving the murder of the two girls. The only thing he was correct or certain about, was that they were dead.

Norma walked out into the waiting area of her office and talked to the Mullens who had returned as she requested after an hour or so.

"I think we are doing good with Wayne, but I probably need to see him in a few days again. I think it best if you not question him about our session as that may cause him to lose ground that I believe we gained today," she instructed them. They carried on some small talk, the Mullens paid their bill to her and they made an appointment for two days later at the same time.

"Did Wayne give any indication as to what may be bothering him at this time. Any revelations?" Mrs. Mullen asked, hoping to see an indication that he had likewise confessed to her during the session.

"No," Norma said. "We are taking it slow right now and will see what the next session brings."

Truthfully, Wayne seemed a little happier and less withdrawn which pleased his parents to no end. They looked forward to their return. They left with Wayne and headed home.

The Mullens could not have possibly gotten out of the small city before Norma had called Pastor Kirksey.

"W.D., this is Norma. Look, the Mullens just left my office with their son. I talked to him for over an hour alone and I have to tell you, though he was quick to tell me that he had killed the two girls, when I questioned him further, he didn't know the slightest bit of information that he would be privy to had he killed them. He even told me he stabbed them as opposed to strangling them. What did he tell you?"

"I did not get into specifics with him after he told me he was responsible. Are you sure you approached him correctly about it?" W.D. wondered aloud.

"I am a professional, sir. I know what I'm doing and I certainly know how to question someone as retarded as he is," she snapped. How dare he question her method or ability!

"I didn't mean it that way. I'm just confused. Maybe he is trying to make you think he is crazy or something," he speculated.

"W.D., he IS crazy, therefore he doesn't have the mental ability to play mind games. It appears he will tell you whatever he thinks you want to hear, like any 4 or 5-year-old child will when you corner them," she espoused in a desperate attempt to prove to him she was capable.

"When do you meet with him again, or do you?" he asked.

"Oh, yes, day after tomorrow. I need to milk this little cash cow for a little while," she laughed.

"Ok, then. Let me know what happens," he said.

"Hopefully more than happened today," she said. "I'll call you."

Despite the warning of the good counselor, Mr. and Mrs. Mullen began picking Wayne for information as soon as they got back to their car. As they rode out of town back home, Mrs. Mullen started in on him.

"Did you like Ms. Leonard, son?" she asked him.

"Yes'm," he said.

"Did you tell her what was bothering you, like you told me?" She prodded further.

"Yes'm," he said.

"What did she think?"

"I don't know, Momma."

"Did she seem surprised?"

"I don't know."

Try as she might, she couldn't get anything out of him. He had withdrawn and was not about to open up to her or anyone else. She wondered if that is how he responded to any of the counselor's questions or if he had at least been open enough to admit his guilt so that she could verify it.

"Can I leave the yard now, Momma?" he asked as they continued toward home.

"No, son. You have to stay home for a little while. It may not be too long. We'll see," she answered.

Yes'm," he said. He was miserable without being able to ramble at will and she knew it, but for everyone's concern, it was best that he remained within sight of her.

CHAPTER 30

When Paul had met with Landon Fall and had given him the rundown on the hit planned on Tyrone Braid, they both agreed that the number one goal was to protect Dewitt Strawberry as much as possible from retaliation by Merriweather and the boys. It wasn't that they weren't concerned for Tyrone, because they were, but Tyrone was in Chicago away from the reach of the hit for the time being. Furthermore, and just as importantly, the sheriff would not be as easy to convince that he should go out of his way to protect or help, as he put it, "a thug nigger that needed killin'." He would surely want to protect a local white voter, but could care less about an out of county black guy that would end up in Parchman's gas chamber if he had anything to do with it. Paul's secretary had advised him that the sheriff was not in town at the present and could not meet him for supper as planned so he could fill him in on the latest happenings. That was no big problem, Paul had decided, he needed time to consider a strategy before informing the sheriff. The meeting with Landon had been short, but some hard decisions had been made regarding their immediate actions.

"How the hell did Merriweather and the boys get Tyrone's name in the first place? I haven't released anything naming him as a person of interest or a suspect. Do you think we have a mole?" Landon had wondered.

"I don't see how, unless its L.B. shooting off his mouth or someone in his department. Those deputies love to talk about things no one else knows about. Makes 'em look like they are privileged to have that information. Either way, we knew we couldn't keep it a secret forever. We're just lucky the first attempt on Tyrone failed."

"Call Sheriff Holder when you get back and ask him who Tyrone's people are over there in Sunflower County. We've got to get in touch with this kid and take him into protective custody for the time being or he won't make it a week. Never know when he might come home," Landon told Paul.

"Will do, Boss."

Because it was after office hours, Paul decided to drive from Cleveland over to Indianola and see if he could meet up with Sheriff Holder there, or at least some of his deputies that might give him some information on Tyrone's family so he could get word to him that he was a hunted man, not by law enforcement with laws and regulations regarding his rights, but by a virtual lynch mob that had already passed judgment and sentence on him, whether he was guilty or not. Surrendering to law enforcement had to be preferable to being taken out in a hit, Paul thought.

His unmarked Ford Galaxy was detectable by a layman as a law enforcement vehicle only by the extended antenna on the back that served his police radio, and nothing else. He headed toward Shaw and then to Indianola, the county seat of Sunflower County. He had called the sheriff's office there by radio and asked for Sunflower-1, the sheriff's designated call sign and gotten no answer, but the dispatcher there had responded and said that she would try to get in touch with him and have him come to the office to meet him if he could. Other than the one call, he didn't talk with anyone and didn't elaborate over the air the nature of his business with the sheriff for fear as to who might be listening and advise Merriweather's boys.

When he arrived at the sheriff's office, which like Bolivar County was part of the county courthouse, he met with Chief Deputy Macon Maroney who had been employed in that office for ten years, a carryover from the previous sheriff's administration, something that spoke highly of his ability to steer political waters. They stepped back into his office and Paul pulled the tab on a coke he had been given by Macon as the two began to talk. Paul laid it all out about the hit and he and Landon's concern for both the suspect, Tyrone and the conspirator, Dewitt.

"I believe you have hit the nail on the head, Paul. Your victim's father is probably in more or at least as much danger as your suspect is," Macon proclaimed. "You got the goods on your suspect for the murder?"

"Not by any stretch of the imagination," Paul responded. "On a scale of 1 to ten, with ten being guilty, I'd put the case at a five at best now. Of course, as you well know, if I get a chance to interrogate him, he might rise quickly to a nine or ten."

"I feel your pain," Macon laughed. "Without a confession, more than half our indictments around here would walk. They just can't keep their mouth shut. If they are smart enough to talk to a lawyer before we get the chance to talk to 'em first, we're sunk. Anyway, how can I help with your situation?"

"I need to know who my suspect's people are so I can talk to them and try to get him to come in for his own sake. Thought maybe the sheriff would know. How about you, you got any idea who one, Tyrone Braid, might be kin to around here? I understand he's been in Sunflower County all his life," Paul inquired.

"Braid, Braid," Macon said to himself. "He's got to be kin to Lonnie Braid down near your county line. One of the nicest guys you'll ever meet, black or white. First class all the way. Straight as an arrow and just one hell of a good guy. Let me see if I can get his address and maybe some info on his car so you can try and catch up with him. Runs a small country store out highway 442."

As this possibility was being announced, the dispatcher stuck her head in the office.

"Sharpe needs to see Mr. Lane before he leaves, Macon.," she said.

"All right, let me finish with him and Sharpe can have what's left," Macon laughed along with Paul.

"Whose Sharpe?" asked Paul, downing the last of the coke.

"Young deputy we have here. Green as an onion, but pretty good at the same time. He handles most of our burglaries and property crimes. We can't let him get into the violent crimes yet, he ain't THAT good," Macon again laughed. "I have no idea whatsoever what he wants with you."

Macon left the office to get Lonnie Braid's address and car tag number, leaving Paul alone to thumb through an old issue of *Outdoor Life* that was on the corner of Macon's desk. He looked around the office and thought to himself how lucky he was to work in an office like the one he had in Cleveland that was much more modern and plush, a sign that Bolivar County had more tax money available than Sunflower County. Then he laughed to himself when he thought comparing the two counties' tax base was synonymous to saying that Mississippi was more preferable than Arkansas—both were routinely at the bottom of the barrel nationally when it came to socio-economic conditions. Thank God for Arkansas, he thought.

His thoughts were interrupted by Macon's return, so he put the magazine down and paid attention to the information Macon shared.

"Just like I thought. One of the other deputies says Tyrone is the nephew of Lonnie Braid. He has a store out on Highway 442 near Shaw and his house is right next to it. Tyrone is on parole and lists his address as not far from Lonnie," Macon said.

"Yeah, I know where Tyrone lived before, I've been there to try to find and talk to him earlier. Young lady was there, so I talked to her, but got nothing," Paul said.

"That was probably Darcel, his sister or niece or something they tell me. She was in a bad car wreck a short while ago, but lived. Don't know if she is home now or what," Macon replied. "Other than Lonnie's tag number, that's about all I got right now."

"That's plenty to go on," Paul responded. Thanks a million. Now where can I find this ace of yours, what's his name, Sharpe?" Paul asked.

"I'll get his highness and send him in. You call me if you need anything, Paul," Macon said as the two shook hands.

"Same here," Paul returned.

Within a couple of minutes, the infamous Deputy Sharpe came into the office. His uniform was starched and ironed with a necktie on to boot. He looked as if he was ready to pose for the cover of **Police World** and would be just as happy if he was in the Marine Corps. Barney Fife definitely had competition.

"I'm Deputy Sharpe," he said to Paul as he stuck out his hand.

"And I'm impressed," Paul said with a smirk and a short laugh. "No really, I'm Paul Lane with the DA's office over in Cleveland. How are you?'

"I'm good," he said. "I've been investigating the recovery of what I believe to be stolen merchandise from a grain bin over near the county line with us and Bolivar. I believe it was the product of a burglary or burglaries in one or both of our counties, but haven't been able to determine where. I don't want to get into a jurisdiction question so I thought I would talk with you after someone said you were here from Cleveland. Are you aware of any thefts or burglaries occurring in your jurisdiction in the last few weeks?"

God, Jack Webb would be proud, thought Paul. Then the light bulb came on in his head—Ralph West, the vacation burglary in Shaw, the one that he had completely neglected.

"As a matter of fact, I do know of one in Shaw. A burglary while the owner of a home was away on vacation. Happened the week of August 3-9, this year. Don't know the exact date because the homeowner was out of town during that time and it occurred while he was gone. Seems like a bunch of electronics were stolen from him. We dusted for prints, but didn't find any. Sound like anything you might have?" Paul asked.

"Very possibly. There were a couple of televisions, a tape deck, some speakers, the general take for items that can be pawned, but we found them before he tried to pawn them. I guess he was waiting on them to cool off a little before he moved them. We got some prints from the equipment, but haven't had a chance to study them and compare them. You think your victim might want to look and see if they are his? We know they were taken the night of Monday, August 4 because they were placed in the grain bin on that night. Just by chance, the farmer had been cleaning it up during the day and didn't finish. When he went back there on the morning of the fifth, he found them and called us. We haven't had anyone claim them, yet," Sharpe said.

Something about August 4 seemed familiar, but he couldn't place it. Nevertheless, it appeared that the timeline was correct for the West burglary.

"I want a man named Ralph West to have a look. It may or may not be his, but it's worth a shot," Paul Lane said. "I'll get in touch with him in the morning and have him contact you if you don't mind."

"Perfect," said Sharpe. He handed him his business card with his telephone number, shook his hand and walked with Paul to the door. Paul left the building and got into his car. Great, he thought. Just one more thing to do now with everything else. He sped through the countryside among the cotton and beans, occasionally smelling the pungent odor of insecticides and herbicides the farmers utilized. Alone in the car in the darkness, his mind drifted from the day's events and he thought back to his childhood, wishing he could return to that carefree time where his biggest concern was what time supper was going to be ready and how much longer was it until Christmas. Before he knew it, the backroads had led to his house and he went in for the night. Tomorrow, he would have to bust his ass because lives depended on it, and that was unfair, he thought. Not only to him, but to the people whose lives were at stake, but that was the hand they were all dealt and they had no choice but to play the round.

CHAPTER 31

Tyrone had finally made it back to the south side of Chicago after a long bus ride that was permeated with so many stops he had lost count. He had the long walk from the station back to his apartment that he shared and he needed to get some kind of rest before going back to work in the morning. The walk gave him the opportunity to think about the problems he had on his mind, Darcel, his job and his ever-present legal problems. The paranoia of being apprehended was always with him, and in Cleveland, it had reached its zenith. Now, back in Chicago, he wasn't as concerned with the law, perhaps because of the feeling of anonymity that comes to one in a large city, but the feeling was still with him nonetheless. He was reminded of the time he had sneaked into a farmer's catfish pond and relieved him of a string of channel cats. The fishing had been fun, but he was always looking over his shoulder for the farmer to catch him and have him hauled away for trespassing. Fun, but tainted with the thought of being caught. That was his life now. He got to his address, climbed to the fourth floor of the tenement building, went inside and lay down on his bed, a mattress with no sheets, a knitted comforter and a pillow he had picked up at Goodwill. He closed his eyes and fell asleep, never awakening until just before six o'clock in the morning, just in time to get dressed and head back to work. He was back in the grind.

Back in Cleveland, the hospital scenario had not changed. Lonnie, his wife and John arrived early every morning to a sleeping Darcel, IV in her arm, bandaged and with her leg in a cast and raised slightly in the bed. They sat throughout the day watching her for any sign of movement, hoping and praying that she would come around and speak to them. At night, they would go home at the end of visitor's hours and would return the next day, repeating the process all over. It was wearing on the family, but it was something they felt like they needed to do.

About 9 o'clock in the morning, the phone in the hospital room rang. Lonnie answered and listened while one of his employees told him that a policeman with the Sheriff's office or something in Bolivar County had come by earlier looking for him. He had not told the man where Lonnie was, but told him he would get a message to him and see if Lonnie could call him. The man had told him it was very important and real urgent that he speak with Lonnie. Didn't say what it was, just real important. He had left a business card.

"What's the name and the number to reach him?" Lonnie asked curiously.

"Paul Lane. 843-4208 is his number," the caller replied. "Card says he is with the District Attorney's office." Hope there ain't no trouble comin'," he said wishfully.

"I'm sure they are trying to run down my nephew," Lonnie said. "He can't run forever. Anyway, thanks for calling."

Lonnie had no way to know how right he was in his thoughts on the call. Paul was trying to run Tyrone down, but not to put him in jail, just to save his life.

@ @ @ @ @ @ @

Breakfast at Brock's café that morning was more solemn than usual. The boys, with Merriweather at the center of the discussion at the round table had their heads down and their voices low. The basket of homemade biscuits in the middle of the table had barely been touched, a sign that they were more occupied with conversation than eating.

"We can only conclude that the very terms of our project have been laid out to the Court," Merriweather, observed. "There would be no need for a discussion with the court all afternoon unless the terms were discussed in great detail." He stuck a fork in a biscuit and drew it from the basket over to his plate.

"I would have to agree. Can we then assume that some type of side deal has been cut?" one of the boys asked. Merriweather had obviously taught them well in ways of speaking in code.

"I don't know. When I last talked to the breaching party he was genuinely upset and thought his position was strong enough to call the whole project off. He may have just thrown in the towel regardless of the consequences. I'm not aware of any legal counsel he may have had," admitted Merriweather, all the while spreading butter and jam on the biscuit.

"We have to consider our options and cut our losses immediately. I don't see that we have any choice but to cut our ties permanently and forever," another of the boys chimed in.

"Damn him!" another exclaimed and pounded his fist on the table, rattling silverware and glasses and drawing the attention of every eye in the restaurant their way.

"Let's not lose it," Merriweather said sternly. The place quickly went back to normal when no further outburst occurred.

"Do we call off the project?" one asked.

"Hell, no. We lose all kinds of credibility with the public if we do. Everybody in the county expects some action to be taken and they think they know who is going to take it, but fortunately, nobody knows for sure who that is. We simply need to dismiss the breaching party and there is no one with any evidence to defeat our lawsuit. I'll talk to our man and see how that can be arranged," Merriweather answered. "In the meantime, we proceed accordingly and with all due diligence."

They all agreed.

@ @ @ @ @ @ @

Paul was on the phone in his office trying to get in touch with Ralph West so he could check that task off his "to do" list and get back to cleaning bigger fish. He hoped that the equipment they had found over in Sunflower County would be Mr. West's lost electronics because, though the man was somewhat of a pest, he was extremely likable. Maybe for once good things would happen to good people. He got him on the phone, told him what he had learned last night from the Sunflower County SO and gave him the name and number of Deputy Sharpe so he could contact him and make arrangements for him to look at the equipment to see if it could be his. West thanked him profusely and Paul asked him to let him know if it worked out. They would proceed from there and see if they could pin the burglary on someone at that point, said their goodbyes and they both hung up.

Immediately after his conversation with West, the intercom buzzed.

"Lonnie Braid would like to speak to you on line 1," his secretary said.

"Thanks," Paul said and picked up the phone, pushing the button for line 1.

"Mr. Braid, this is Paul Lane, thank you so much for calling me. I hope this is not an inconvenient time for you," Paul said.

"No, sir, not at all. I'm in my niece's hospital room visiting," Lonnie returned.

"I'm sorry to hear she's ill," Paul said, momentarily forgetting that the deputy in Sunflower County had told him she was in a serious accident.

"She was in a terrible accident a week or so ago and has still not regained consciousness," Lonnie said solemnly. "Thank you for your concern."

"Any other time I would suggest that we talk later, but I have a matter that is very urgent and very important. Is there any way I could meet you and talk with you?" Paul asked. "I do apologize for the inconvenience."

"I see no reason why not. Could you possibly meet me at the hospital? Perhaps the ICU waiting room?" Lonnie inquired.

"Absolutely, I'll be there in about ten minutes," Paul answered.

"Very well, I'll see you there," Lonnie said.

Paul grabbed his blazer from the coat rack in his office and headed out. He drove the short distance from the courthouse square to the hospital and parked in the front parking lot. He looked at the directory at the receptionist's desk and found what floor the ICU waiting room was located. He took the elevator and walked in. No one was there at the time, so he took a seat and waited. A few minutes later, a large black man dressed in business clothes without a tie or coat walked in and approached him.

"I'm Lonnie Braid, you must be Paul," he said as he extended his hand.

"Yes, sir. Very good to meet you. I've heard many good things about you," Paul said.

"Only believe the good things," Lonnie said with a laugh.

The two sat in chairs at the far end of the waiting room.

"Mr. Braid, I hate to be the bearer of bad news, but I am afraid I will have to be," Paul started. He leaned back in his chair and began telling the story of the GalBerry murders and the facts and circumstances leading to the sheriff's belief in Tyrone's involvement in them. He was straight and to the point about everything that had transpired; the trip to Chicago, Tyrone's escaping them there, his car being found, towed and searched, and how he had purposely kept Tyrone's name from being disclosed to the general public for fear of vigilante justice. Then he told him the story that Dewitt Strawberry had told him the day before. As that part of Paul's story unfolded, Lonnie slumped into his chair, his eyes fixed on Paul in disbelief.

"You know I have lived in the Delta all my life and I've seen some racial prejudice exhibited before, but very rarely toward me or my family," Lonnie said. "I had hoped we had moved past that."

"I understand, and I hope you don't get the impression that all white people are like that. They are a few, and they exist to the detriment of the majority," Paul said.

"No, sir. I know too many good and decent white people to believe that they are all like that. Just like among the black people, there a few who are bad and they seem to taint the rest," he observed. "Let me ask you this, though, do you believe Tyrone murdered these girls?" Lonnie asked.

"Mr. Braid, I don't deal in beliefs. I deal in proof. If I can't prove it, it didn't happen. At this time, honestly, I have a lot of circumstantial proof that tends to lean toward Tyrone as a viable suspect, but I do not have sufficient proof to charge him at this time," Paul admitted.

"My nephew is a lot of things, some not so good, but I would find it hard to believe he could kill someone, let alone be a multiple murderer. But that's for another day. What do we need to do now to help him?" Lonnie responded.

"I need to get in touch with him some kind of way and let him know what is going on. I could bring him in to custody for his own protection for a period of time, talk to him and if I can see that he clearly is not involved, then we can issue a press release to that effect. Once the general public hears he has been cleared unequivocally by the DA's office and perhaps the sheriff's office, there will be nothing to be gained by the hit and it will be called off," Paul said.

Lonnie shifted in his seat and crossed his legs. He had just heard an incredible tale of multiple murder, rape and murder for hire with terms like protective custody, press releases and incarceration used, and for the first time in his life, it was all related to his family. It was a lot to take in in a short period of time.

"I have a number for my nephew in Chicago, for his apartment," Lonnie said. "I believe it better if I call him and explain the situation to him. I doubt he would talk to you or believe you if he did," he added.

"I agree completely. He would think it nothing more than a ploy to get him down here so we could charge him, anyway," Paul said.

"I will have to go back to the house to get the number and call him. I'll do that just as soon as I get my wife and her things together," Lonnie said.

"I hate to ask you this, but would it be possible not to tell your wife what is happening? I'm certainly not concerned with her telling anyone, but the less anyone knows, the better. I would not want these people pressuring her for information. Do you understand what I am telling you?" Paul asked.

"I think I do, and I believe you may be right," Lonnie answered.

"Thank you so much for your help, Mr. Braid," Paul said. "Please call me once you have talked to him and let me know something," he added.

"I certainly will, and thank you. I hope we can meet sometimes under better circumstances."

The two men got up, shook hands and Paul left the hospital, with Lonnie heading down the hall back to Darcel's room.

CHAPTER 32

Wayne was like a captured animal in a cage, standing in his yard out near the road. Every now and then he would walk to the other side of his front yard and stand, then retreat back to the opposite side for a while. His mother felt sorry for him as she watched him from the front porch, but not sorry enough to let him go free. She was still shaken from his confession and had no definitive word from his counselor that what he had told her was not reality. She looked forward to his appointment with the counselor in the morning, maybe she would gain a little peace of mind then. She had heard him crying in his bedroom last night before he fell asleep, but she didn't know if it was his guilt in what he had done, or his grounding at home that had made him weep.

Pastor Kirksey contacted Norma Leonard by phone later that day in anticipation of Wayne's appointment the following day.

"Do you think you are going to be able to make a determination as to whether your patient is telling the truth about his involvement this time?" he asked her.

"I have no idea. If he keeps telling these facts that we know are not consistent with what happened, I would have to conclude he is lying about his involvement in the killings for some reason. Consistency in what a person says, whether a lie or the truth, is usually the key," she said, hoping that was correct. "Why are you so interested anyway?"

"Because half this county knows I pointed an accusing finger at him after he confessed in my office. All of my church members do. I need it for credibility," he responded.

"Believe me, I'd love to be the one who helps crack the murders of those two girls, but if it ain't there, it ain't there. I have some credibility I'd like to keep too," she said. "We'll see tomorrow," she added.

@ @ @ @ @ @

Dewitt Strawberry had done exactly as he had been instructed by Paul to do. He kept his mouth shut and went about his usual daily activities as normally as he could manage. He wasn't particularly concerned with retaliation from the boys since they knew nothing about his revelations to the DA's office. He was more concerned with the safety of Tyrone Braid, not so much because he cared that much for the bastard that killed his little girl, but because he didn't want Tyrone's blood on his hands. Besides, he had a tremendous amount of work to be done on the farm and the busier he was, the less he thought about the issues before him.

What Dewitt did not know, was that a man had been tailing him and spying on him since earlier in the afternoon that day. He was a member of the Citizen's Council and his sole job was to keep up with Dewitt and take advantage of any unfortunate position he might find him in. He had been quickly hired by the boys with an endorsement from Edker, but only Merriweather knew of that endorsement because only Merriweather had ever dealt with Edker or even knew his name. In a black 1965 Ford pickup, he had tailed him throughout the day, keeping at least one vehicle between him and his subject. When Dewitt stopped, so had he, and watched from a distance with binoculars that he normally used for deer hunting. He carefully watched him across the fields of cotton as he delivered tools to some of his workers, carried others to other places on the farm and worked on equipment that needed to be repaired at his tractor shed. It was there that the man saw the opportunity he had looked for all day.

Dewitt was attempting to replace a faulty starter on an old farm truck that he had parked under the equipment shed. When the man realized what Dewitt was attempting, he got out of his truck and moved through the field of tall cotton stalks toward the shed. Dewitt had jacked up the truck from the front so that he could crawl under it in order to better remove the old starter and replace it with the new, something a lot of people did in order to better reach the part, but one that was dangerous for fear of the vehicle falling on them. When the man arrived at the shed, Dewitt was completely under the truck on his back while lying on a creeper, a raised platform that allowed him to avoid getting any dirtier than necessary and increased his mobility, but made the jacking up of the truck more necessary. His feet were sticking out from the front of the truck, his upper body located perilously under the engine. Slowly, and almost casually, the man walked up to Dewitt and the jack, said nothing to him, and casually pushed the jack to one side. The truck shifted with the push, caused the jack to topple and the truck, with its immense weight, fell squarely onto the upper body of Dewitt, caving his upper chest.

Dewitt gasped for breath as the weight of the vehicle pressed down upon him, cutting off his ability to inhale the needed oxygen. The harder he tried to inhale air, the heavier the force came down on him. His face turned blue from the lack of oxygen and he tried to cry out for help to no avail. Internally, he had begun to bleed from the tissue damage caused by sharp broken ribs, the blood flooding his lungs. He was dead in minutes.

The man, seeing that his work was done, turned around, jogged down the road to his parked vehicle, climbed inside and sped away. He was soaked in sweat from the time he had been out in the hot sun away from the comfortable air conditioner in his truck and he wiped his brow with the sleeve of his shirt. He looked at his watch. It had been 2:41 when he got out of the truck. It was now just after three o'clock. His mind did the math in his head. Ten thousand dollars for about twenty minutes work, that came to five hundred dollars per minute. Not bad for what he had just done. Not bad timing either, he thought. It had been just over 24 hours since Dewitt had gone to Paul Lane's office. The boys should be satisfied.

@ @ @ @ @ @ @

Lonnie Braid and his wife had left the hospital shortly after Lonnie's conversation with Paul Lane with Lonnie telling his wife that, yes, the

DA's office wanted to talk to Tyrone, but did not elaborate on the extent or nature of the conversation. They left John at the hospital with Darcel and headed back home so that Lonnie could attempt to contact Tyrone in Chicago. When they got home, Lonnie retrieved Tyrone's number from the back pages of one of his ledgers where he had placed it earlier, memorized it, and once sure he had it committed to memory, returned it to the ledger. He went into his bedroom and dialed the number but hung up after seven rings with no one answering. It was the middle of the day and Tyrone had hopefully returned to his job, he thought, so he decided to try later in the day. That was no problem for Lonnie, because the staying at the hospital all day while trying to keep a business running, coupled with the stress of trying to keep his nephew out of jail, had left him fatigued. He laid down on his bed, called to his wife and told her he was going to take a nap, but to wake him for lunch.

Try as he might, sleep would not come to Lonnie. He turned to his side, lay flat on his back and then turned to the other side, but couldn't get comfortable. He had indigestion, probably from the donuts he had eaten at the hospital, so he took an antacid tablet and tried to nap again. He felt the pain of indigestion grow within him despite the tablet he took to the point that it not only affected his ability to fall asleep, but he found himself having difficulty breathing. When he felt a pain in his left arm, he knew he was in trouble. He tried to get up, but the pressure on his chest that he had once believed was indigestion, had now intensified as if someone was sitting on him, making breathing almost impossible. He cried out for his wife to come, but she had stepped outside to gather some tomatoes from their garden for lunch and never heard him.

Lonnie grabbed his chest and rolled off the bed onto the floor, tried to get up, but couldn't. Suddenly, he felt the last gasp of air that he would ever have, draw into his lungs, but it was not enough to keep him from losing consciousness. He saw the room begin to grow dark and if he had been able to look in the mirror, he would have seen that his face had become discolored from the lack of oxygen. Finally, he lost complete consciousness and was never revived. He was dead. Later, after his wife found him and called the ambulance, doctors in the emergency room told his wife that they probably could not have saved him even if he had been on the emergency room table when such a heart attack occurred. He had no chance.

@ @ @ @ @ @ @

Paul Lane wondered why he had not received the promised call from Lonnie Braid. It was almost five o'clock and he had assumed Lonnie had called and explained the situation to Tyrone and was hoping Tyrone would believe his uncle and come in to talk and to be protected. He had no way of knowing if the failure to call him by Lonnie meant he had not reached him or if Tyrone was going to play hard to find. Likewise, he had also assumed that Dewitt Strawberry would have called him sometime that day just to report that nothing out of the ordinary had transpired in his life. Oh, well, Paul thought, everyone has their own time lines and they rarely coincided with his, anyway. He would hear from them soon. He just had to be patient. He was torn between leaving the office and in so doing, leaving the telephone, thereby missing an important call, or just hanging around the office and waiting. He elected to wait a while longer. He had plenty he could do around the office if he was really interested in working, but his mind was fixated on GalBerry and the issues surrounding that case.

Shortly after 6:30 that evening, the office phone rang. Paul, with his feet up on the desk and very relaxed, had dozed off with the quietness of the room. He dropped his feet to the floor and grabbed the phone.

"Hello," he said.

"Paul, I'm afraid I have some very bad news." It was Landon Fall and he sounded as serious as Paul had ever heard him. "Lonnie Braid dropped dead earlier this afternoon at his home from a massive heart attack. They transported him to East Bolivar, but he was DOA. I was told by one of my assistants about an hour ago and just got confirmation from the coroner. Were you able to speak with him earlier?" he asked.

"Yes, sir, ironically at the hospital where he was visiting his niece. He was going to call his nephew and tell him to come in or at least contact us. I'm sure that's why he was home, to get his nephew's number. Wonder if he was able to call him before he died?" Paul wondered aloud. "That's a shame, Landon. Lonnie Braid was as good a man as you could find. Helluva guy."

"Never heard a bad word about him from anybody, but never met him," replied Landon. "Not to sound callous, but do you know anyone else that can get in touch with his nephew?"

"Not a soul. But I'll find somebody in that family, surely. Maybe his wife or someone. If he gets word of Lonnie's death, he'll surely come home for the funeral, don't you think?" Paul asked.

"I'm sure he would. But you know how black folks are, that could be a week from now. Better than nothing, I suppose," Landon agreed.

"Problem is, if we have this thought, the boys looking for him are thinking the same thing and they will be looking for him at the same time. We need to get to him first or all we may find is a dead body," Paul speculated.

"Why are you wasting time talking to me, then. See what you can find. I'd start with whoever you can find in the family at the funeral home. Probably going to be in Indianola," Landon advised.

"I probably need to wait until tomorrow to give the family time to catch their breath, but I'm on it," Paul agreed.

CHAPTER 33

Norma Leonard was late getting to her office, having had to make a home visit for a child that was reportedly abused and neglected, and consequently she arrived some twenty minutes late for the Mullen's appointment, leaving the elderly couple frustrated to no end, but not seeming to bother their son at all. She came in, made her apologies to the Mullens, which seemed to pacify them for the time being, and as before, asked them to leave Wayne with her for a while and return in an hour or so. They left and she immediately ushered Wayne to her office in the back of the building.

"How have you been, Wayne?" she asked.

"Pretty good, you?" he responded.

"I'm fine. Do you remember what we talked about the other day when you were here?" she asked.

"Yes'm," he said. "I need to tell you something, though," he added.

"What is that?"

"I didn't tell you right the other day. I'm sorry," he said.

"What did you tell me that was wrong?" she asked. He had her full and complete attention. This was the breakthrough she expected from the beginning, the time when he would open up and tell her what she wanted to know--the truth.

"I didn't stab them," he cried, tears running down his face all of a sudden, "It wasn't like I said."

"Tell the truth, Wayne. Only you know what the truth is. God wants you to tell the truth, you know. You'll feel so much better when you do," she pressed, sounding for all the world like the pastor.

"I didn't stab them. I'm sorry I said that. I shot both of them!" he wailed. He put his face in both of his hands and cried into them as he bent over in the chair in front of her. He wiped his eyes on his short-sleeved khaki shirt that left a dark spot on it from the moisture. He slumped in the chair and leaned his head back in it, looking at the ceiling, trying to stop crying.

The look on Norma Leonard's face resembled someone who had just been fired from her job when she expected a raise. She was stunned. She picked up a legal pad and pretended to write something on it while she regained her composure to proceed with her questioning. Her shock turned to frustration at the old boy and then moved to anger.

"Are you sure this time that you aren't lying, Wayne. How do you expect me to trust you? Are you through playing games, now?" she snapped. She had lost all sense of professionalism, what little she had to begin with.

"Yes'm, that's the truth," he plead.

"I'm not sure you know the truth. Tell me how you shot them, Wayne. Where did you get a gun? What kind of gun was it?" she fired at him with compound questions.

"I don't know, I don't know," he responded.

You're lying to me again, aren't you, Wayne?"

"No ma'am."

"You didn't shoot those girls did you, Wayne? You didn't have anything to do with at it all, did you? Why would you say that? You know why I know you're lying to me Wayne, because they weren't shot. That's not how they were killed. Do you even know how they were killed, Wayne? Tell me, Wayne," she continued with her barrage.

"I don't know, ma'am. What do you want me to say?" he asked, his frustration showing as well.

Norma dropped her pad and pen on her desk. With that seven-word sentence, he had said it all. "What do you want me to say" is exactly what he was trying to do. He was trying to figure out what it was that he was supposed to say, just like a child would do when pressed by someone in authority over them. The truth didn't matter if it pleased the interrogator, be it her, his mother or the pastor. She had been a fool to think that she could coax anything from the retarded man before her.

"I think we have talked enough for today, don't you think so, too, Wayne?"

"Yes'm," he agreed.

"Why don't you go back out to the waiting room and I'll bring you a coke to drink," she promised. "You okay now?"

"Yes'm."

He headed out to the waiting room as she opened the office door for him and then retrieved him a canned coke from her office's refrigerator, pulled the tab and handed it to him.

"You sure you okay?" she asked.

"Yes'm," he said.

Shortly thereafter the Mullens returned for their son and were met by Norma in the waiting room.

"He got a little upset in our session, but he says he's okay now," Norma announced to his parents. Why don't you run on out to the car, Wayne and let me talk to your Momma and Daddy for just a second."

Wayne got up and went out the door without any more instructions, leaving the three other adults in the office building. Norma began explaining what she believed the session had revealed.

"Wayne is doing exceptionally well, I believe. He is beginning to open up with me more and more. We had to have a discussion about the truth and I believe he understands better now than before. I believe with a little bit of work we can have him dealing better with his self-esteem issues he has been experiencing which has caused him to have mood changes in the past. He seems to really, really like sharing with me," she lied. "Let's make him an appointment for the first of next week and continue our progress."

The Mullens had no idea what on earth she was talking about, but they did understand the terms "doing well," "better" as well as "really,

really likes." Accordingly, despite the cost for the sessions with Norma, they were willing to do whatever it took if it meant getting their child back to normal and determine his role, if any in the killings. Apparently, he had not said anything about that to her or she would have surely have mentioned it to them, they were sure. They made the additional appointment, thanked Norma and returned to the car. They were so proud of his progress as indicated by his counselor, they didn't bother to pick him for information. The longer the confession was not mentioned by him or anyone else, the more likely it was that he had imagined it. Out of sight and out of mind. Wayne broke the silence between them in the car.

"Momma, do I have to stay in the yard, now," he asked hopefully.

"Yes, son you do, but I don't think it will be much longer. Do you remember what you told us the other night last week? About the girls? That's what we are concerned with," she said.

Wayne's look of disappointment was obvious, but he said nothing. He just watched out the window as the rows and rows of white cotton passed by him as they got closer to home. When they arrived, he got out without a word, went into his bedroom and closed the door behind him. He remained there the rest of the day and night.

@ @ @ @ @ @

It wasn't unusual for Dewitt to work until 8 o'clock on any given day, so when he hadn't come in for supper by then, his wife wasn't concerned. She decided, however, that because he hadn't been in, she would send Carolyn, their daughter, to see about when he thought he might be home so she could plan to warm his dinner up for him.

"He is probably at the tractor shed fiddlin' with something," she told Carolyn. Take my car and see what he says."

Carolyn left, going down the long drive to the tractor shed no more than a half mile away at the most. As she turned on the road to it, she saw his truck parked there and knew for certain that he was there. Her mother had been right, but that was no secret. She knew him like a memorized poem. She pulled up behind his pickup, got out of the car and looked around. She sensed the familiar smell of diesel fuel on dirt, saw the various pieces of equipment stored under that shed, including the old farm truck, but didn't immediately see her father. She walked to the front of the old truck to look for him further back into the enormous shed and stumbled over his feet that protruded from under the front of the truck.

"I was looking for you. Momma wants to know when you think you'll be through," she said. "Did you hear me, Daddy? Momma wants to know when you're coming home."

She dropped to her knees to look up under the truck to see what he was doing and why he didn't hear her. Her subsequent scream could be heard all the way to her house.

CHAPTER 34

Paul wore a tie with his blazer this morning, something he did only out of necessity. He was going to Byas Funeral Home in Indianola to talk with Mrs. Braid if he could find her and if not, would go by the house and the store. He hated to bother her in her time of mourning, but he satisfied himself with the thought that if he didn't, she may well be attending yet another funeral in the days to come if he couldn't bring Tyrone in. He only hoped Lonnie had been able to contact him and if not, that she would know how. He lamented his telling Lonnie not to inform his wife of the problem, now.

He went the backroads that morning to Indianola, the same way he had returned a couple of nights ago. This time, no matter how fast he was able to navigate the curvy road that paralleled Jones Bayou and the other backroads toward the town, it seemed to take forever, much unlike the trip the previous two nights ago that seemed to take only minutes in comparison. When he got there, he looked at his note that he had made himself when he looked up the funeral home in the phone book: 407 Front Street, Extended. Shouldn't be that hard to find in a town the size of Indianola, and it wasn't.

He parked on the street, put his blazer on, straightened his tie and proceeded in the front door. The smell of flowers, that sickening sweet smell that always seems to infect any funeral home, hit him in the face as he entered. The cold blast of air from the room that greeted him was more than welcome, however. He was met by a smartly dressed black gentleman almost immediately who looked at him with some suspicion, but extended his hand to him, nonetheless.

"I'm Nathan Byas, may I help you?" he asked.

"Yes, sir, I'm Paul Lane, a friend of Lonnie Braid. I was looking for Mrs. Braid," Paul responded.

"The family is not scheduled to be here until 10:30 this morning to make arrangements," he said. "May I give them a message for you or tell them what it is regarding?"

The man spoke professionally and seemed educated. His manner of talk did not reflect the local slang or laziness of speech that seemed to pollute most Southerners, black or white. He also gave the impression that he could not imagine a white man in a black funeral home, friend of the deceased or not. The funeral homes were as segregated as the churches ever thought about being, on both sides for both races.

"No, sir, that will be fine. I'll talk to her later. Thank you very much, though."

They shook hands again, said their goodbyes and Paul left. He climbed back into his car and was on the way out of town when he thought of Deputy Sharpe, the regimented greenhorn that was all business for the Sunflower County Sheriff's Office that he had met in his earlier visit here. He thought he might check on whether Ralph West was able to retrieve any of his property or if the theft had been from some other residence. That would be easier than calling Mr. West and finding out in the negative and have to listen to another lecture on the unfairness shown to crime victims.

He wheeled around in the middle of the road, an illegal U-turn, and went back into town toward the sheriff's office. He walked in, asked the dispatcher for "Supercop" and was told with disappointment that he was not on shift, but would be in at six that evening.

"I really thought after talking with him that he never went off duty," Paul laughed.

"Honey, he's probably dreaming about catching crooks even as we speak," the dispatcher, a rather large woman who showed the major stress points of her uniform even while sitting, replied. "I'll tell him to call you when he gets on duty," she said.

"Only if he has time. No big hurry," Paul responded.

He left the sheriff's office and headed out toward the Braid home and Braid's Grocery in an attempt to locate Mrs. Braid. He carried a sense of guilt with him about bothering her at this time, but again, he thought it for the best. Some things simply can't wait. He had not gone far when his car radio squawked.

"DA-3, Bolivar SO," the dispatcher said.

Paul picked up the microphone and pressed the push to talk button. "DA-3," he responded.

"DA-3, please call SO-1 from a landline the first opportunity you have," the dispatcher said.

"Will do. Tell him I should be at a pay phone in about 10. I'm in the sticks right now," he told her.

"10-4, DA-3. Will relay the message," she said and ended the transmission.

Wonder what that is about, Paul thought. Could be he got the word on Lonnie Braid and wanting to make sure Paul knew, he reasoned in his mind. That wouldn't explain the secrecy, though. He saw no reason why L.B. couldn't tell him that over the radio. The curiosity caused him to drive faster as he sped toward Braid's Grocery and a pay telephone.

Less than ten minutes from receiving the call, Paul was on the pay phone that hung from a pole outside of Braid's Grocery under an awning that shielded it from the weather. When it was answered by the sheriff's office in Cleveland, Paul began the conversation.

"Louise, this is Paul. I'm returning the sheriff's call," he told her.

"Hang on, he's looking for your call," she said and placed him on hold. Seconds later the sheriff picked up.

"Paul, I just came from Landon's office. I wanted to let him know that Linda Strawberry's father, Dewitt was killed last night or yesterday evening when a truck he was working on fell off of a jack and crushed him. He came clean with me about Dewitt and what you told him day before yesterday. Why the hell didn't you brief me?"

Paul was absolutely stunned at this revelation, his mind trying to go in three different directions. He was speechless about the news.

"Dammit, Paul, I'm the chief law enforcement officer in this county and I have a right to know these things, not have some burned out lawyer hide it from me because he doesn't think I need to know. I've already chewed out Landon's ass about it after he told me. What the hell is going on here? Are you still there? Are you listening to me, boy?" he asked after the outburst he had just finished.

"I don't know what to say, L.B., I uh, I uh…." he stammered, more in shock over the death of Dewitt than the chewing out he was receiving from the sheriff. "What the hell happened?" he asked in frustration.

"Just like I told you, he was working on a truck and had it jacked up and under it when the jack fell and the truck crushed him. At least that was what was apparent then, before I found out what he had done with you. "Now I wonder if it *was* an accident," the sheriff returned.

"Who worked the scene, what deputy?" Paul inquired.

"Nobody worked the scene. It wasn't a crime scene to anybody, just an accident scene. The ambulance crew called the coroner, he pronounced him dead and they brought him to the hospital and then to Thweat-King Funeral Home. No pictures, no search for fingerprints, footprints, nothing. Them ambulance boys and the coroner as well as God knows who else at the scene have tainted it to the extent it won't do no good to check it out, now. All because you and Landon want to play Batman and Robin."

"That's not what happened, L.B. We had no intention of keeping it from you. I tried to get ahold of you the night he left my office telling me his story. For supper at Brock's as a matter of fact," he added.

"And that was the last you thought of telling the sheriff of the county about a hit on a suspect in a twin murder, is that right?" L.B. asked with sarcasm.

"I have been snowed under with this thing, L.B, trying to keep a man from being snuffed," he said.

"Again, you're more concerned with a damn thug nigger than somebody like me. I want to see you and Landon together on this one, Paul. This ain't ever gonna happen again, my friend, never again," he said and slammed down the phone.

Jesus Christ, thought Landon. Was the man killed or was it just a coincidental tragedy? His gut told him yes, he had been killed by somebody and it was no accident, but he remembered what he had told Lonnie Braid, just yesterday. He didn't deal in beliefs, just proof. If he couldn't prove it, it didn't happen. He now knew he was wrong to say that. It had happened, he couldn't prove it, but Dewitt Strawberry was still dead. All because he decided what he was doing was wrong and wanted to make it right. The boys had gotten away with murder and there was absolutely nothing he or anyone else could do about it. He realized he was still holding the phone in his hand and had never hung it up. He hung up the receiver, walked into the store and bought an RC Cola from the lady inside, who charged him 35 cents and gave him back change from a dollar. He pulled the tab and placed it on a pinball machine in the corner of the store that he leaned against while he downed his soda. His mind was racing in several directions and he was thinking about several people. Dewitt and his family who had suffered tremendously in the last month. Lonnie Braid and his family. Tyrone, who may be a killer, but still deserved to be protected until a jury said so. He was certain and non-equivocating on that principle of law. Then he thought of the victims, Linda Strawberry and Janice Galtelli. They deserved justice and he had not provided it to them, so far, leaving him depressed.

He chugged the RC and walked out the door of the store into the heat, made the short walk across the parking lot into the yard of the house adjoining the store property and knocked on the door. A middle-aged black woman answered the door.

"I need to see Mrs. Lonnie Braid if I could, ma'am. I'm Paul Lane from Cleveland and I'm with the District Attorney's Office there," he recited.

"She not here right now. She over at her sisters in Shaw. She won't be back here until this afternoon, I believe. Her husband died yesterday and she got to make his arrangements in Indianola at the funeral home this morning," she volunteered.

Frustrated, Paul told her, "Would you give her my card and ask her to call me when she's able, please?" It is very important. Tell her I'm the one that talked to Lonnie yesterday morning at the hospital."

"I'll give it to her, yes, sir," she told him and then shut the door.

Paul had at least got her word that he needed to talk to her. She would give Mrs. Braid the card and tell her and perhaps the funeral home owner would do likewise. He tried not to think of the possibility that she would think he only wanted to arrest and charge her nephew with murder and accordingly put him off and try to avoid him. Oh well, no use worrying about something until it happens.

CHAPTER 35

Word of Dewitt's death spread through the community with usual speed and reached and touched every household in some way. Most couldn't imagine the grief that befell the remaining family members of the Strawberry family in their community. Few people were so unfortunate as to suffer the kind of loss they had suffered in the last month, but perhaps the Biblical Job, and everyone's heart was breaking for them. The Mullen family was no different. As a church member and neighbor, regardless of the distance between their homes, they knew Dewitt and his family all too well. Wayne was particularly upset when his mother brought him the news, withdrawing further into his personal shell and speaking even less. He crossed back and forth from one side of his home's front yard even more than before, pacing like a dog on a tie-out stake from one end to the other and then returning. Inside the home, Mrs. Milton prepared skillet fried chicken and fresh yeast rolls for the family, fulfilling the Southern obligation of feeding the mourning. Wayne could smell the aroma of the baking bread from out in the yard, but didn't bother to check it out, not being hungry in the least. That should have been the first sign of trouble to come, but it went unnoticed.

In Cleveland, Paul and Landon were sitting down to a meeting about the Strawberry situation. They met at Landon's office in his conference room, just the two, and Landon had sandwiches and chips brought in from The Varsity Grill over near Delta State. Paul selected the roast beef and cheese and began eating.

"You don't believe for a minute that Dewitt's death was accidental do you, Paul?" Landon asked. He unwrapped the BLT which was the last sandwich available and took a bite.

"Not in a million years. My only hesitation in remotely thinking it was an accident, is wondering how did word get out that Dewitt had turned on the boys so fast," Paul replied.

"That's the only thing that makes me question it," Landon said. "Less than 24 hours from his confession to you, and the man is knocked off? That's fast for a planned hit. Maybe it was just a coincidence. Then I think, well, they already had a hit in place, just changed the target of the hit and go with it."

"You know what my daddy always said about coincidences? He didn't believe in them," Landon said. "And I already thought about how word got out so quickly and I agree with you. Somebody, either you or me have a mole in our offices," Landon conceded. He was halfway through the sandwich and showed no signs of letting up on it.

"Did you speak to Karen about it in your office?" Landon asked.

"Did not, but she saw him there and knew who he was, I'm sure," replied Paul. "What about you? Anyone in your office know about him coming to mine?"

"No one. By the time you left and talked to me everyone had left for the day," Landon said. "You know, we said that day that we may have a mole, but we thought it may be L.B. shooting off his mouth that leaked Tyrone Braid's name to the boys, but we know for certain that is not the case here, because we both just took an ass chewing from L.B. for not saying anything to him about Dewitt. Your girl may be the key."

Paul did his best to remember anything he might have said to his receptionist and secretary, Karen Collins that day when Dewitt left his office. He scarfed down the last bite of sandwich, washed it down with a coke and thought harder.

"Oh crap!" he exclaimed. "I remember telling Karen to see if she could set up a meeting with me and L.B. for supper at Brock's that night so I could brief him on a hit on Tyrone Braid. Son of a bitch," he bemoaned.

"Got to be it," Landon agreed. "She could have called or gone to one of them, told 'em that Dewitt had been there talking to you all afternoon, even knew what he said to you was being recorded so it had to be very important. After Dewitt had talked to Merriweather earlier, it didn't take a rocket scientist to put it all together. She's our mole."

"Son of a bitch!" Paul said again in frustration. "She's got to go."

"Wait a minute, Paul, don't go off half-cocked. We have absolutely nothing to take these boys down right now. We'd have a hard time proving this death was anything but an accident unless we can show someone had a motive to kill him. The only way to get that is to roll the dice on your girl and have her believe we have the evidence to put her in jail for a long, long time. If she snaps up the bait, we might can pull in the whole wad of them, Merriweather especially. It all depends on how convincing we are when we question her. It's not much, but it's all we have to go on."

"I agree. What's the plan?" Paul asked.

"Business as usual in your office. The only mention of the death of Dewitt Strawberry will be you mentioning what a tragic accident that was. Maybe you can dog-cuss L.B. for not working the scene of the accident as a crime scene and getting no prints, statement or photos, leaving us with no way to prosecute anyone if it wasn't an accident. Hopefully she'll report that to the boys and they will feel comfortable enough to let their guard down. Then, in a few days, we confront her with the "statement" we have from one of the boys about her involvement. Hopefully, she'll roll on them to save herself. If she does, we do the same to all the boys, except this time, it won't be a gamble like it will be with her because we will already have her statement incriminating each one of the bastards," Landon articulated.

"Sounds like a plan. I just hope I can conceal my anger at her," he responded.

"As I said, business as usual. Stay on the Braid kid. We don't need another death by accident," Landon observed. "Just keep Karen out of the loop from now on."

"Got it. Will do, Boss."

They gathered their trash from the meal that had spread across the conference table, disposed of it and Paul left. He needed to make contact with Mrs. Braid soon for Tyrone's sake. His life depended on it.

@ @ @ @ @ @ @

Norma Leonard had called Kirksey shortly after the Mullens left her office but he did not answer her call. Subsequently, she forgot about calling him until the next morning. A deeply perturbed and aggravated preacher answered when she called again.

"Reverend, I want to report to you about my session with Wayne Milton yesterday," she said. Apparently, though she longed to be a professional, the ethics of disclosing a patient's communications didn't apply or concern her in this case.

"I would hope so. Nothing like being put off for a day," he snapped.

"Look, I called yesterday and you didn't answer," she shot back.

"I'd think for a person making good money off of my referral you would try again before now," he declared.

"Let's get past the pettiness, shall we? I just wanted to let you know that in my professional (and she apparently used the word loosely) opinion from talking with Wayne, there is zero chance that he had anything to do with those murders, regardless of what he has said or confessed to in the past. He has no concept of the manner of death, the locations, the physical surroundings at the time of the murder—nothing. Just that "I killed them." He's like a child that wants to please whoever is questioning him by giving them the answer he thinks they want to hear. Somewhere he got the impression that somebody questioning him wanted him to say that and he has stuck with it. I don't know if that was the sheriff's office when he was questioned there or what. You didn't lead him in that direction when you talked to him and he confessed did you?" she stated and asked.

"Of course, I did not!" he exclaimed. If she could have seen his face at the time, the lie would have been apparent even to a novice such as she. "James Weeks is the only one that has been raving about a killer on our roads out here, not me!" he lied.

"Well, either way, I'm going to counsel him some more, at least 'til the money dries up from his folks, but as far as his involvement in any murder, that case is closed as far as he is concerned," she admitted.

"It was always about what was best for Wayne as far as I am concerned," the preacher lied again. "I'm really glad to hear it."

"Sure, you are, pastor, sure you are. Send me some more patients sometimes, will ya? I need all the help I can get with what the state pays me," she told him, and hung up the phone.

@ @ @ @ @ @

Lunch at Brock's that day was much more relaxed and jovial than breakfast the day before had been. Though some of the boys were not present, those that were there showed signs of relief as if a burden had been lifted from them, despite the fact that a man was dead at their hands, not directly of course, but his blood was on their hands nonetheless.

"Everyone here knows we had to do what we had to do, and though it was distasteful, I think we all are resting a little easier knowing that nobody that weak will stop us from our work," Merriweather declared, wanting desperately not to speak in code, but doing so anyway out of an abundance of caution.

"I just hate he cost us what he did, the bastard!" one of the boys said shoveling vegetables from the blue-plate special in his mouth.

"Well, sometimes business ventures exceed their projected costs. I think in the long run we will all be happy with our investment," Merriweather advised. "Now we need to focus on closing the project for good. I think the party of the second part will soon be in town from Chicago for the funeral of his uncle, whenever that may be. I am hoping we can consummate the deal when he arrives without any further delay."

"Is our foreman ready when he gets here?" one questioned.

"Oh yes, indeed. He tells me he will be waiting at the station for him when he arrives if he can. If not, he will meet up with him shortly afterwards. He's as eager to close this deal as anyone of us, perhaps more so," Merriweather announced.

"Does anyone feel like we need another meeting afterward, to discuss how things went?" one of the others inquired.

"I don't. We can get back to our regular meetings when this is concluded," another chimed in.

"Absolutely," said Merriweather. "Let's look forward to a little normalcy."

@ @ @ @ @ @ @

L.B. sat in his office pondering the phone call he had just had with Paul. Things had gotten out of hand now and were spinning more out of control daily. There was little doubt in his own mind that the death of Dewitt Strawberry was no accident. Knowing now that Merriweather and his goons planned to take care of the murderer of Dewitt's daughter, they would not let anyone interfere, not even the grieving father. He was well aware of Stanton Merriweather and frankly, was a little intimidated by him. Hell, he wasn't even sure he supported him in the last election. Either way, if these guys wanted to play judge and jury, he decided then and there he wanted no part of it. Spending his retirement years in Parchman wasn't his idea of golden years at all. The boys and Merriweather would want him as sheriff to cover for them. Elected office holder or not, future election wins be damned, he was out.

CHAPTER 36

Paul walked into his office and greeted his receptionist as he always did when he came in, but he was concerned that she could read his thoughts. She was pleasant as always but he was so paranoid that he probably overreacted in any communication to her.

"Any calls, Karen?" he asked. "I mean, did you receive any calls from me, I mean *for* me?" What a dumbass he was. If he kept this up, there would be no doubt he was on to her little scheme.

"Only from Sheriff Williams, but he said he would try to get you on the radio. Did he ever talk to you this morning?"

"He did, thanks," he was trying to cut the conversation about the sheriff's call short, remembering that it was about Dewitt's death and he hoped it didn't sound like he was doing that.

"Oh, there's one more, from Ralph West," she added. "I forgot this one because he said he would probably call you back, anyway," she said.

"Great. I bet that means the equipment he went to look at over in Indianola didn't belong to him. It was a shot in the dark anyway," lamented Paul. "I'll call him."

Paul went into his office, took off his blazer and tie and hung them both on the coat rack. He sat behind the desk and opened one of the large drawers on it and used it for a footrest. He picked up the phone and settled in for what he hoped would be a long, but fruitful conversation with Mrs. Braid. He dialed her home number and listened intently while it rang, three, four, five times. After the seventh ring, he hung it up. If he was going to talk to her it apparently would have to be face-to-face either at her home or the funeral home. If he knew her sister's address in Shaw, he'd try that for God's sake, but the lady at her house didn't offer that information and he thought better than to ask.

Without changing positions, he looked at the phone memo that Karen had given him and dialed the number of Ralph West. Might as well get this one over with, he thought. This little peckerwood would worry the hell out of him until he talked to him anyway. Mr. West answered after the first ring.

"Mr. West, this is Paul Lane returning your call," he said into the phone.

"Thank you for calling me back, Mr. Lane. I just wanted to call and thank you for finding my stuff they stole from me," he told him quite cheerfully.

"Oh, it *was* your stuff taken from you, was it? I had hoped it was, but I didn't think you or I were that lucky," Paul responded with a laugh.

"Yes sir, I got everything they took and it wasn't damaged or anything," he said.

"Well I'm happy for you. Sometimes we get lucky, most times we don't."

"That deputy over in Indianola was a good guy, too. A little intense, but a good guy," Mr. West added.

"Intense may not adequately describe him," Paul said. "I'll need to get with him, and you as well, and see what we can do about prosecuting a suspect. Maybe he has some leads now that the stuff has been recovered. I know he said they lifted some prints from the equipment, did he bother to take yours for comparison? We took them you may remember."

"He did, but I thought the man used gloves so we didn't get any prints at my house," West stated.

"That's true, but usually they take them off eventually and then handle the equipment with their bare hands. You usually get prints from the goods when you recover the goods from the pawn shop. Even if they used a fake name when they pawned them but have a record where they have been fingerprinted before, we are sometimes able to nail them. Understand what I'm saying?" Paul inquired.

"I do. I hope they find something. It still burns me up that somebody would just come into my house and help themselves to my things," he answered. "Anyway, just wanted to say thanks for a good job."

"You are most welcome and hopefully we will find someone. I'll be in touch," Paul told him.

That was a rare conversation, thought Paul after they hung up. Most people never say thanks, but to be fair, he really had done nothing that was helpful. It was all Supercop over in Sunflower County. Thinking about Sunflower County made him remember he needed to get over there and talk to Mrs. Braid, so he got up and walked back into his receptionist's office.

"Karen, I've got to go out again and probably won't be back until in the morning," he said. "By the way, you remember Dewitt Strawberry coming in here a couple afternoons ago? He got killed in a farming accident yesterday. Can you imagine one family losing two members in a month's time? They are lucky people, but it's all bad luck."

"I heard that, too and thought the same thing," she said without making any eye contact with him. It seemed to him that she purposely looked away when he broached the subject.

"We need to implement some protocols about accidents or events that appear as accidents in order to make certain there is no foul play involved. We need to be notified by L.B. or whoever arrives on the scene so we can process it for evidence. There was nothing suspicious about this one, just a tragic accident, but if it had been, we couldn't prosecute it now if we wanted. Ambulance personnel and the coroner worked it and never called for anyone in law enforcement to come out. See if you can get with L.B. and set up a meeting sometime next week to check on implementing some protocols by agreement. Check with the coroner as well, he needs to be there and you might as well see about the manager of Delta Ambulance, too. We all need to be on the same page," Paul dictated.

"I'll do it. Any particular day next week?" she asked.

"Try to avoid Monday or Friday," he said. He thought about his tie and blazer and went back into his office momentarily to retrieve them. He put them on in front of the mirror hanging in the reception area, said goodbye and left. "I thought that was convincing enough," he said to himself with a smile as he got into his car.

@ @ @ @ @ @ @

Mrs. Mullen had worked in the kitchen making food for the Strawberry family most of the afternoon. As soon as one dish was ready, she thought of something else she might fix for them. When she was finished, she had prepared fried chicken, yeast rolls, sliced tomatoes and cucumbers and made a peach cobbler for them. They might grieve themselves to death, but they would never starve. Wayne had not been in the house all day but had remained outside the entire time except to eat a tomato sandwich his mother made for him in the midst of her cooking. As soon as he finished, he went right back out to the yard and stood or paced by the road, never saying more than a handful of words.

It had been over an hour since she had seen her son and she and her husband were ready to load the car with the food to take over to the Strawberry house. She looked for him around the yard, but didn't see him and he couldn't have come into the house without her knowing. Apparently, he had struck out walking despite her restrictions, something he had never done. When she told him to do something, he did it. She expressed her fear of his leaving the yard to her husband who thought they might run into him on the way to deliver the food and pick him up then. Accordingly, they left and headed to the Strawberry place, food in tow and looking for the now AWOL Wayne. They failed to see him on that stretch of road going or coming from the food delivery and got back to the house about thirty minutes from the time they left.

Not having seen him on the road in one direction, they thought they should drive north toward Cleveland in their efforts to locate him and bring him back. Mrs. Mullen was more perturbed about his disobedience than his well-being because it was a rarity for the family, a situation where Wayne had openly and purposely defied his parents. It had simply never happened before. They traveled along the road looking for him all the way to the city limits of Cleveland and saw nothing of him. They still weren't overly concerned for his whereabouts but were anxious to get him home where he was supposed to be. The fact that they didn't find him was of little concern, because he always managed to catch a ride with someone. He would have been in Cleveland in no time and from there he could go anywhere in the town and he would be hard to run down. In frustration, they turned around and headed back home.

It had begun to get late in the afternoon, perhaps an hour before dark, when Mrs. Mullen took some scraps out in the yard to feed the mixed breed dog that they had raised from a puppy after Wayne had found him abandoned between their house and Shaw. She called for him, but he didn't come running as he usually did, especially this time of day when he knew he was likely to be fed. She looked and saw him stretched out in the pasture next to the yard in front of their old barn. He was looking at her and wagging his tail as he lay there, but refused to come to her. She watched him and called to him several times but he would not come to her. Fearing that he may be hurt, she asked her husband to go into the pasture and check on him. He begrudgingly did so. He went through the old gate and proceeded toward the dog who continued to look at him, wag his tail but continued to refuse to come to him. When he got close to him, the dog got up and ran toward the barn and stopped, looking back. Mr. Mullen walked up to him and was about to pet him when out of the corner of his eye he saw a pile of clothes—Wayne's clothes. He went into the barn and could never have been prepared for what he found.

Apparently, Wayne had taken several strands of seagrass rope, the type used to hold bales of hay together, twisted them into a strong single cord and looped it over the rafter of the old barn. He had stripped all of his clothes off and thrown them into a pile, beginning with his new straw hat, climbed onto one of the stalls, placed the strong cord around his neck tightly and jumped from the stall. His nude body hung there grotesquely, having defecated on himself as he slowly strangled to death. Chollie Mullen dropped to his knees in disbelief, horror and sorrow, screaming for his wife to call an ambulance. He rose to his feet and rushed toward Wayne, doing his best to free him from the rope, he was too heavy. Back on his knees again, Chollie sobbed into his hands. He knew an ambulance wasn't really needed, but wanted one anyway. Wayne's body continued to hang, his arms limp at his side, his eyes grotesquely opened. He no longer had to worry about what to say in order to please anyone.

CHAPTER 37

Tyrone was at his place of employment at the shipping company bright and early in the morning. The early September weather in Chicago was cool, but by no means crisp. The wind from the lake helped the temperature fall to the mid to low seventies most of the time, but it was not uncommon to see it in the mid-eighties at times during the day. Today it seemed as mild as it had all summer long. He was settled back in his job after his trip down south, but he still harbored concerns for Darcel, and had never quit looking over his shoulder for the law. He had heard nothing from his uncle or anyone else since he had returned but, how could he? Only Lonnie had his number unless he had shared it with John or someone else and he doubted that. When he took his lunch break, he would go to a pay phone and check on things back home.

When he got through with his lunch, he walked down the street to a pay phone located on the corner by a drugstore. He called Darcel's hospital room, but got no answer when the receptionist put him through. Maybe that was good news, he thought. Maybe she had come around, gotten better and was discharged, but the front desk did not confirm any of this. He dialed his Uncle Lonnie's home number and again, there was no answer. When he got no answer at the house where he, John and Darcel had lived, the panic began to set in. Finally, in a last-ditch effort to reach someone, anyone, he called Braid's Grocery. When someone finally picked up the phone, he was relieved.

"I'm looking for Uncle Lonnie. Is he there?" Tyrone asked without any introduction or pleasantries.

"He isn't, honey. I uh, he uh, you need to call your Aunt Victoria," she told him.

"I did, but she wasn't home. Do you know where she is?" Tyrone asked, anxiousness showing in his voice.

"I really don't right now, child. I don't," she replied, desperately trying not to tell him the truth.

"Is something wrong down there, I'm out of town and my name is Tyrone. What's going on down there?" he asked in a panic.

"Tyrone, you really need to talk to Victoria. Is there a number she can call you back?" she pleaded with him.

"Tell her to call me tonight. It's urgent. My number is 708-469-8374," he said.

"I'll try to get the message to her," she responded, glad to get the conversation over so she wasn't pressed into delivering the tragic news.

Tyrone hung up the phone and went back to work, but he was unable to think about anything else the rest of the day. He feared that Darcel had passed away and that was the reason for the coyness of the worker at the store, but not knowing exactly what the problem was, was worse than knowing the truth. He had no other option but to be patient until later that night when he could call again if he didn't receive a call from home first. The remainder of the work day was the longest he could ever remember.

After work, he picked up a foot-long sandwich at a local sandwich shop that he intended to eat at his apartment so he could wait by the phone for a call from home. He stuck it in the refrigerator on arrival and tried the numbers for the hospital, Lonnie's house and John's place, all without anyone answering. This solidified his thought that there was a terrible problem somewhere back home that he was not privy to at the moment and sent his paranoia into overdrive. He waited another hour and tried them again with the same result. It was as if everyone he knew back home had vanished and left him behind without warning.

After another failed attempt to reach someone and his fear factor raging, he thought of the worse possible scenario, and that would be the death of Darcel. He knew from past experience that his family had always used the services of Byas Funeral Home in Indianola when there was a death in the family, so he decided to roll the dice and contact the funeral home there. If he was wrong, and no one there knew anything about a death in the Braid family, at least he would have some sense of relief come to him and pacify him for a little while. If they responded in the affirmative, well, he would just have to deal with whatever it was.

He called directory assistance and got the number of the funeral home, was informed of it and dialed it. It was answered by a receptionist.

"Ma'am, I'm trying to get in touch with any member of the Braid family and I'm calling from Chicago. Is anyone there that I can talk to?" he inquired.

"Yes, I think Victoria Braid is here, let me get her for you," the lady replied.

Tyrone's heart sank. He had been right about someone dying, probably Darcel. He waited for someone to answer and in the meantime heard steps and shuffling as the secretary retrieved Victoria for him. Then, he heard her pick up the receiver and thank the lady for coming to get her.

"This is Victoria," she said into the phone.

"Auntie Victoria, this is Tyrone! What happened?" he said excitedly.

"Your uncle had a massive heart attack and died, Tyrone. I wanted to call you, but I had no idea what your number was. Lonnie was trying to call you shortly before he died, but he was the only one that had your number. I'm so sorry, Tyrone," she apologetically told him.

"Oh, God!" Tyrone cried. He couldn't believe it. He was primed to accept the news of Darcel's death, not Uncle Lonnie and the shock effect was jarring to him.

"He loved you, Tyrone. You know he did," she said as she broke down and started crying.

"What happened?" he asked rhetorically, already aware of the fact that his uncle had died of a heart attack. "Why was he trying to call me?"

"He had met with some cop earlier at the hospital who was trying to locate you. I don't know why he was looking for you, but he was.

Lonnie was going to call you and let you know, to see if you wanted to talk to him. That's all I know about it," she replied.

"Probably the same one who tried to get me up here," he said. "I ain't talkin' to nobody."

"You better lay as low as you can, Tyrone. I don't know what you are supposed to have done, but somebody down here is doing their best to catch up with you."

"I got to come home, Auntie," he announced. "When is the funeral?"

"Funeral is this Sunday at two in the afternoon, four days from now," she responded. "You sure you need to come here?" she asked.

"I have to. If they catch me while I'm there, they just gone have to catch me, but I ain't missin' Uncle Lonnie's service."

"Call me back with your bus schedule and I'll have John pick you up," she offered.

"I will," he said.

Tyrone gave her his apartment phone number and even his work number. Victoria told him the best time to call and then gave him her sister's number where she was staying. They shouldn't have trouble getting in touch with each other any longer. Tyrone hung up the phone and buried his face in a pillow and cried. He could not believe that Lonnie was gone.

@ @ @ @ @ @

Paul got a call from the sheriff's office in Cleveland by radio advising him to contact Sunflower SO-19, Deputy Sharpe, by phone when he got the chance. He was almost to Indianola anyway, desperately trying to find Victoria Braid, so he disregarded the message and drove straight to the sheriff's office to meet him instead of calling. He found him at the office having just returned from working a domestic dispute in town where he had been able to negotiate a truce with the couple, at least temporarily. Paul was certain he was about to hear some crowing by Supercop about how the Sunflower Sheriff's office had helped retrieve goods from a Bolivar burglary and he would surely offer to come over and instruct the boys over there how to do it if they would ask nicely.

"Didn't know you were in the area or I would have met you on patrol," Sharpe told Paul.

"Still over here looking for some of the Braid family," Paul returned.

"That's actually what I was calling you about. I got a hit on some prints from the equipment taken in your burglary that we recovered from the grain bin. Didn't take long to match them up once we began looking, mainly because the guy has a felony record. Prints on the equipment, and that's each piece of the electronic equipment, belong to a Tyrone Leroy Braid who shows an address on Highway 442, Shaw, Mississippi. That's one of those addresses that shows a Bolivar County town, but in reality, is actually in Sunflower County. I know where it is if you need help finding it. Just thought you might want a face to go with the crime," Sharpe informed him.

"Good Lord, what are the chances?" Paul exclaimed. "I'm trying to catch up with him right now on another possible charge and he pops up again!"

"Same old, same old," Sharpe added. "Repeat offenders fascinate me because they're so stupid," Sharpe said.

"If you'll send me a report with your findings, I'll add it to the to do list with this guy," Paul told him.

"Got it in a file for you right here," Sharpe said as he handed the file to Paul. "Knew that was what you would want. Glad to get it off my desk since it happened in Bolivar County and we have no jurisdiction to prosecute."

"Appreciate the help," Paul told him and returned to his car.

He sat in the car after cranking it and getting the air conditioning going and flipped through the file. The date of occurrence of the offense was listed as the night of August 4, 1969. Paul remembered that Sharpe had told him the farmer had been cleaning out the grain bin that Monday until late and then discovered the goods stored there the next morning. Something about August 4th sounded familiar, but he couldn't place it. He put the file back together, tossed it onto the seat beside him and left the sheriff's parking lot. He was heading toward Byas Funeral Home and was almost there when it hit him like a sledge hammer. August 4, 1969 was the date of the Strawberry murder! The chances of Tyrone committing both crimes, the Strawberry murder and the West burglary in one night was somewhere between zero and none! Tyrone had managed to concoct the best alibi around for murder by committing another felony. Though he was almost certainly a thief, he could not be a murderer. Despite that, he was about to pay for someone else's crime with his life—unless Paul could stop it.

CHAPTER 38

The funeral home was crowded and became more crowded as time moved forward. Paul entered through the front door and stopped for a minute to let his eyes adjust to the dimly lit foyer where a line of people had formed behind the guest register. Again, that sweet smell of flowers that he often associated with death, permeated the air throughout the room. He walked across the room, avoiding the line of people and followed the plush shag carpet under his feet to the office. There, he saw Mr. Nathan Byas who he had met earlier on his first trip there, sitting behind a desk and casually talking on the phone in a hushed tone. Though Paul hated to intrude on his business and conversation, it was better than waiting in the hall with the others, as his presence could not have been more noticeable, mainly because he was the only white person in the building. He had managed to draw the attention of every black person in the foyer and beyond, when he walked through the door, causing many to whisper among themselves, no doubt about his presence. He thought for a second that he knew how some black people felt almost any time they entered a business, event or school. It was no fun being in the minority.

Mr. Byas looked up at him from his desk, smiled and held up a finger indicating he would be with him shortly. Momentarily, he hung up the phone and greeted Paul as an old friend.

"Good evening, Mr. Lane, so good to see you, again. How may I help you?" he asked.

"I'm still trying to locate Mrs. Braid. Victoria Braid. Do you know if she is still here?" Paul inquired.

"I'm certain that she is, let me see if I can find her. Would you like to come with me or should I bring her here to meet with you?" he asked, sensing that Paul needed to talk with her away from family or friends.

"If you could ask her to meet me right here, that would be great," Paul replied.

Mr. Byas left and went around the corner to find Victoria, leaving Paul alone in his office. He admired the furnishings which were not to his individual taste, but appropriate nonetheless. All of the light fixtures on the walls were upturned so that the light shown up on the wall instead of flooding the room. The furniture was upholstered in bright colors of red and purple and the wood on all of it was brash and ornate. The pictures on the wall were of different religious scenes of Jesus in the garden of Gethsemane as well as angels among clouds. It caused him to remember that Elvis Presley was heavily influenced in his music and his personal taste in clothes by the black people of Tupelo, Mississippi and it all made sense to him. The bright colors, the gaudy and ornate furnishings for which he was famous, all of it was inspired by the black people of Tupelo and Memphis with which he came into contact. His thoughts were interrupted by Mr. Byas who immediately introduced him to Victoria Braid whom he had sought for what seemed like forever. Mr. Byas excused himself and the two exchanged pleasantries with Paul extending his condolences and remarking how pleasant her husband had been when they met earlier in the week. Then Paul got right to the point.

"Mrs. Braid, what I am about to tell you is extremely unpleasant, but I would ask that it not be told to anyone after I tell you. My investigation has revealed that a group of people have singled out your nephew, Tyrone, and have blamed him for the death of two women over in Bolivar County this past month. Frankly, it appears that they do not intend to wait for him to be arrested and tried, but have planned to take him out by their own means. Now, I know…" Paul was saying when she interrupted him.

"What do you mean, take him out by their own means?' she asked

"They intend to kill him," Paul returned with no hesitation.

"How do you know this?" she asked.

"Because one of the men involved in the plot voluntarily turned himself in and advised us," Paul replied. "Anyway, I know that Tyrone is, or at least was recently, in Chicago and I desperately need to get him back here and place him in protective custody for his safety. I tried to talk to him earlier in Chicago, but he eluded me. I can't press on you how important it is that he come in."

"Excuse me, Mr. Lane, but what reasonable assurances do I have that he is being taken into custody for his own safety and that this is not just some plot by the authorities to arrest him for whatever crimes you wish to charge him?" she asked.

"Ma'am, you have my word that there are no charges pending against him at this time. I cannot assure you that future evidence will not be found to indicate his guilt that may result in a charge, however. I want to be perfectly honest with you about that. Either way, his chances with us are better than his chances on the street, I can promise you," Paul told her. He did not want to mislead her about the burglary charge, but he wasn't prepared to tell her about it either. He was also trying to read her eyes and facial expressions to see if she believed him, but she had a poker face that he would not want on the other side of the table from him in a game.

She fidgeted and turned her head for a second and said, "I'll make you this promise. I will call him and let him know what you have told me. I'll do that tonight as soon as this visitation is over at the funeral home if I can reach him, and I'll let him make his own decision about what to do. To be honest, if he stays up north, it would appear he would be safe. I mean, you haven't been able to get to him, how would the others?"

"I don't know how elaborate their operating plan is. They are only concerned with finding one person, whereas I have a hundred more cases that occupy my time. I would have to ask myself, is it worth the risk of staying in Chicago? Please press on him all the variables, Mrs. Braid," Paul added.

"I will do that, I promise," she said. She extended her hand to him and he shook it as he walked into the hall to leave. "One other thing, Mr. Lane. Do you believe my nephew is a murderer?" she asked in parting.

"Absolutely not, ma'am," he responded and walked away. Frankly, that was not the answer she thought she would get from him.

@ @ @ @ @ @ @

Edker Bentley sat in a bar in Cleveland at the Holiday Inn and sipped his Jack Daniels on the rocks. Around him, the five o'clock crowd had begun to filter in after getting off work for the day. The rednecks that could only afford draft beer and the businessmen with expense accounts, wanting to take the edge off with hard liquor, filed in one by one, some with a woman on their arm, others in search mode. For the time being a sound system with recordings supplied the music, but a little later, a four-piece band would strike up and encourage every drunk fool to show off their moves on the dance floor. Edker had not come for any of that, just the booze and a place to think. No one spoke to him because he exuded an air of hostility without ever hearing him speak. He was pissed off, mostly at himself for letting the damn nigger get the best of him in the truck that day. He was also pissed off because his buddy, who Edker had recommended for the job, had accomplished his mission of taking out Dewitt in a single day and earned the same amount of money that Edker had failed to make over the last two weeks. That, in his mind, made him look foolish and certainly wasn't good for business. If only he had gone ahead and shot the black bastard when he had drawn his gun instead of trying to hold him at bay until they could get out into the country and finish him off, leaving the body there, he would be through with this job and better yet, he would be paid in full.

Edker had originally thought that he would follow Tyrone's brother, John, around until he linked up with his target again and then take him out. When he learned of Lonnie Braid's death yesterday, he knew every nigger in the family, including his man, would be flocking to Indianola for the services. He thought about watching the bus station in Cleveland as he had before, but he was in no hurry. Niggers always waited until Sunday for a funeral so all of 'em from up north could get down here, he assured himself. Sure enough, that is when Lonnie's service was taking place. He would start his surveillance just shortly before then and take him out when he found him, even if that meant taking out one or two more that happened to be with him. That was the plan. He turned up his last drink, threw a dollar on the bar for a tip and headed out the door.

@ @ @ @ @ @ @

By this time Tyrone had memorized the Chicago to Mississippi bus schedule and knew that the bus left Chicago at 9:15, having ridden it before on his first return home. He purchased a one-way ticket, stuck it into the back pocket of his jeans and went back to his apartment. He had not been there any amount of time before the phone rang. It was his Aunt Victoria. He listened in wide-eyed amazement as she laid out the plot to take his life just as Paul had explained it to her. He never interrupted her the entire time she talked to ask a question and when she was through, she had to ask if he was still on the line.

"I'm here Auntie Victoria, I just don't believe what I'm hearing," he finally replied. "How can they pin a murder on me? I ain't never in my life done nothing to hurt nobody, much less kill 'em!" he exclaimed.

"The man told me he doesn't believe it either, Sweetie," she told him. "But it doesn't matter what the law believes, these people are not the law. They are the Klan, child. They may not go by the name, but they are the Klan," she said with conviction.

"What should I do, Auntie? What would you do?" he asked her.

"I just don't know, Tyrone. I don't."

"I ain't goin' to let 'em keep me from coming to Uncle Lonnie's service or seeing Darcel," he announced. "I already got the ticket and I'll be there day after tomorrow at 9:15 in Cleveland," he added. She knew he was serious and didn't bother to try to convince him otherwise.

"Maybe you should ride the bus on in to Shaw, instead. Or maybe even get off at Clarksdale up the road so nobody will know when you get here. I can get John to pick you up in Clarksdale if you want to," she offered.

"I can do that, he said. I won't have to change my ticket, I'll just get off in Clarksdale before I ever get to Cleveland," he agreed. I'll look and see when the bus gets to Clarksdale and let you know."

"Don't worry. We can check here and I'll have John meet you there day after tomorrow," she told him. "You think about what I told you and you can decide what to do when you get here," she advised him.

"Okay, Auntie. Thanks."

He hung up the phone and fell back on the bed, shocked and in disbelief. It wasn't every day that somebody told you there was a hitman looking for you. His paranoia had now risen to a whole new level, and he didn't know what to do and really didn't want to think about it, but there was no way he could not. Every time he heard footsteps in the hall of his apartment building or voices outside his door, he recoiled in fear at the possibility that he had been found by a killer, intent on putting an end to his life for something he had not done and worse still, knew absolutely nothing about.

CHAPTER 39

Paul drove back in the twilight of the day from Indianola to his home in Bolivar County. It had been a fruitful trip to say the least. He had secured evidence that Tyrone Braid had nothing to do with the GalBerry murders and had finally talked with Victoria Braid about Tyrone's predicament. It was the latter accomplishment that bothered him, however. He couldn't help but feel that Victoria did not trust him and was suspicious of his motives in wanting to bring Tyrone in, much unlike the feeling he got after talking with her husband on the day of his death. He and Lonnie had connected and he believed Lonnie trusted him completely. Had he not died that day, Tyrone may very well be in protective custody at this time. There was nothing else he could do to make Tyrone come in. Only time would tell if he would choose the route he had suggested to his aunt. What he had to do now, was press his receptionist for information about the hit and hopefully find out who the bastards were that thought they were the law of the land. That wouldn't be easy and he would need help. First thing in the morning, he would start putting that together.

@ @ @ @ @ @

The boys at Brock's Café were not happy as they ate their ritual breakfast that morning. They had put an end to the threat of exposure by snuffing Dewitt, but it had cost them dearly in money. At the same time, their man assigned to Tyrone had failed in his attempt and had done nothing but take half the fee from them and produced nothing. Dissension among the group was growing and Stanton Merriweather felt it his obligation to stem the tide of discourse.

"Look gentlemen, you are beginning to sound like a client that has his lawyer file a collection case one day for him and then wonders why he hasn't gotten any money for it the next week. We all know that these things take time and we need to be patient," he told them.

"I'm thinking we need to hire the second man to take over for the first. He didn't waste much time," one observed.

"That's certainly a possibility. Would you like to be the first to pony up the additional five thousand for him with another five thousand due and payable upon completion?" Merriweather asked. The boys grew quiet and that seemed to take the air out of the discussion. They were all still on board, just ready for some finality. It wasn't far from becoming reality.

Paul saw them at their usual table when he came in to Brock's to pick up a to-go order of cinnamon rolls and donuts. They saw him likewise and pretended to ignore him, prompting Paul to speak to Merriweather from nearly across the room.

"Good to see you, Stanton. I keep waiting for you to plead your man to the marijuana charge any plea day, now. I thought we made you a reasonable offer," Paul said as cheerfully as he knew how under the circumstances.

"Only if he was guilty, Paul. It would be a good deal if he was guilty. Tell Landon to get ready for a trial, my boy," Merriweather returned as cheerfully as Paul, some of the guys laughing along with him.

Paul paid for his order, bundled up the sacks and left for Landon's office. This would be a working breakfast and one he couldn't wait to start, especially after seeing the boys conspiring at their table.

He walked into Landon's office, spoke to his receptionist and went on back to Landon's office. He laid the pastries on his desk, took out a donut and started to eat it when Landon emerged from the bathroom adjoining his office.

"Thanks for waiting," he said sarcastically to Paul.

"I was afraid you would want the only chocolate covered one they had," Paul confessed. Landon dug into the sack, retrieved a cinnamon roll and bit into it.

"Coffee's over here if you want any," Landon offered.

"I'm more interested in cornering my receptionist," Paul admitted. "Are we going to attempt that today?"

"I see no reason to wait," Landon said. "Do we involve L.B. or not?"

"I've thought about that and I'd just as soon keep him in the dark for now. He could tip off the boys if he wanted to," Paul observed. He stretched his legs out in front of Landon's desk.

"You don't trust him, either, huh?" Landon laughed.

"Not completely, no. I still think back to that stunt he pulled at the press conference. He was doing his best to tip everyone off that his suspect was black. He never denied it," Paul added. "I don't have anything concrete on him, but I just don't trust him."

"No problem, you and I can do it," Landon decided.

"When?" Paul asked.

"Soon as we finish here."

They finished their breakfast, planned how to approach his employee and then Paul and Landon walked together to his office. The butterflies in Paul's stomach had already started. They had one shot to get the old girl to squeal and that was it—one shot at it that had better be good. If they failed, she would probably tip off the boys and any shot they had to bring the whole bunch to justice would be gone.

When they got to his office, both of them spoke to Karen and told her to hold any calls for Paul while he and Landon met in his office. Paul got out the reel to reel tape recorder and placed it on his desk in plain view. He threaded a new roll of tape on it and had it ready to go. He sat behind his desk while Landon sat in a chair on the far side of the room. Paul then dictated an opening of the recording stating who he was, that Landon was present, the date and time, and that the following would be the questioning of Karen Collins, a suspect in a conspiracy for murder case involving Tyrone Braid and Dewitt Strawberry. After a few minutes, Paul called her in and asked her politely to sit down. He reached down and turned the tape recorder back on, causing the two reels to slowly start turning with the red light indicating "record" flashing.

"Karen, before we begin this discussion, I want to advise you of your rights. You have the right to remain silent and anything you say, can and will be used against you in a court of law. You have the right to an attorney and to have one here with you while being questioned. If you cannot afford an attorney, one will be appointed for you by the court. Do you understand these rights?" he inquired.

"Is this a joke," she asked, trying to laugh, but the look on her face showed she was petrified with fear. "Are you serious?"

"Absolutely," Landon answered from his position across the room.

"Do you understand the rights that I have explained to you?" Paul asked again.

"I guess so," Karen answered. "I just don't understand what this is about."

"Karen, we have information from two sources that you have been involved in a conspiracy to commit murder," Paul said. "On several occasions, you have provided information from this office to certain individuals who plotted the death of Dewitt Strawberry and are plotting the death of Tyrone Braid. Now, one of the individuals has already rolled over on several others, including you, so we believe we have more than enough information for an indictment as well as a conviction against you, in particular. Because you worked for me, I have asked Landon to give me an opportunity to have you talk on the record in an order to help yourself. Your cooperation will be taken into consideration by the district attorney in deciding what charges you should face and our recommendation will be considered by the court at the time of sentencing. Plainly put, Karen, this is your one shot to help yourself. There won't be any others. Your testimony now is not required, but is optional, I want you to understand that right now. However, if you do not cooperate with us about the extent of the conspiracy, we will not be back asking again, we won't give you another opportunity and we will give you no more consideration than Merriweather or any others. Do you understand what I'm saying?"

From the use of the word "conspiracy", Karen had begun to sob. Paul had intentionally worked that in to his soliloquy from the outset for the shock value it would have. He also used Merriweather's name to let her know that he knew what he was talking about, though he had no idea if she even knew Merriweather was involved. It was a big gamble, but it appeared to be working. Paul tossed a box of tissues from a drawer in his desk over to her chair which she failed to catch and had to pick up from the floor.

"What kind of deal can I expect if I help you," she asked. "I suppose I can't keep my job, can I?"

The ignorance of some people never ceased to amaze and amuse Paul. Here she was facing life in prison or even death by gas for conspiracy to commit murder and she was concerned with a $11,000 per year job. Good grief!

"No Karen, your life as you knew it when you came in this morning is over. You are discharged at this time and we are not prepared to offer you any plea deal at this point, but I assure you we will be fair in our consideration, depending upon your cooperation," Paul told her. "I can tell you that the maximum you are looking at this time is death in the gas chamber if we seek the death penalty or life in prison at the women's camp in Parchman, and we will be seeking the maximum," he added. He was as stern with her or as he ever was with the worse repeat violent defendant in his career, and it was beginning to pay off for him.

She fell into her hands crying louder then and said, "I cannot believe this. I am so sorry."

"Sorry you became involved or sorry you were caught?" Paul asked sarcastically. Now was not the time to stop with her and go soft.

"What do you want me to do?" she asked through the tears.

Landon entered the fray then. "We want a statement from you incriminating each and every one of the boys from beginning to end. We want to know what they ate for their meals when you talked to them, where they were and who else was present. Then we may want you to meet in secrecy with them, but that's for another day. Our concern now is for the remaining suspect that you *did not* help kill," Landon said.

"One more thing, Karen. One lie, no matter how small or insignificant it may be, and our session today or any other day will be over and we will proceed as if you never cooperated," he said. "Do you understand that?"

"I do," she cried. "When do we start?"

Both Paul and Landon felt a heavy burden lift from them when she said that. They had gambled and won. Their approach, as it had been many times before, was spot on. Landon began the questioning and Paul chimed in when necessary.

"You made a call to the Bank of Cleveland at 4:53 right after Dewitt Strawberry left this office the day before he was killed. Who was it to and what was the substance of the conversation?" Landon asked. Paul had checked the phone records from his office earlier and discovered that call, so he knew it was the call that informed the boys about Dewitt's change of heart.

She shifted in her seat and pulled her skirt down. "That was to Sam Baker. He and I have been having an affair for the last year and a half and he is the one that approached me first about giving them information through this office. He's supported me along with this job during the time and I felt I had to help him," she cried. Just like every other person who is cornered, Paul thought, do your best to blame someone else for "forcing" you to do it.

She continued to spin her tale and roll over on the boys one by one: Sam Baker, Sr. Vice-President of the Bank of Cleveland; Morgan Tollison, Owner of Tollison Ford out on Highway 61; James Baker, no relation to Sam, CPA; Reeves Spencer, owner of Delta Materials; Steve Davidson, M.D.; and of course, Stanton Merriweather, attorney at law, but she said that was strictly hearsay from her boyfriend. All of the rest she had heard discuss the matter at one time or the other as they drank whiskey at her boyfriend's house and played poker while his wife was out of town at various times. The drunker they got, the more loose lipped they had become, one night laughing that Baker had better keep sleeping with her or she could burn all their asses.

Unfortunately, she had no idea who was hired by the group to do the hit. She knew how much he was paid, how he got his money, what each's share was and who delivered it, but had no idea as to the identity of the man. Merriweather had been in charge of that and he was extremely cautious and did not drink, a habit that he did not need or want. She was certain they had used a second hit man for the Strawberry hit, but again, had no idea who he was.

When it was all over, they had talked with her through lunch, a span of about four hours, and were delighted with the information they had received from her. When they concluded and the recorder put away, with its multiple reels that had been changed over that span, Paul told her to clean out her desk and go home. They agreed that she would be reflected as resigning in her personnel file, supposedly having gotten mad at Paul over some petty office matter and walked out, never to return. If word got out that she was fired and what the reason of her dismissal was actually about, her life may well be in danger, too. She accepted that reason, signed a letter of resignation noted the time and date and left, still crying as she went. They would be in touch shortly, both Paul and Landon assured her.

Now the hard part began. Round up each suspect and make them roll over against the rest, and do it before Tyrone Braid got himself killed.

CHAPTER 40

The bus ride was every bit as bad as Tyrone remembered from a week or so ago: Hot, bumpy and with multiple stops along the way. He had boarded it that morning only minutes before departure, having tarried too long in a pastry shop. As usual, he did not check any baggage, just carried what little he had with him in a small duffel bag he had purchased at the Salvation Army store. Presently, he was using them for a pillow as he tried to catch some sleep aboard the rumbling bus as it headed south toward Mississippi.

Paul was alone in his office and it felt strange to him without Karen there to shield him from unsolicited visitors and calls. He would replace her soon, but in the meantime, he would look for someone part-time or temporary to help him out in the office. Landon had suggested that he would allow his calls to be taken by one of the girls in his office, but had never followed up with the name of one that he was willing to depart with, so that had not worked out just yet.

Despite his missing employee, he had to continue to churn out the work, be it from the GalBerry case that Landon had restricted him to, or any of the others that might need his attention at any time. For the moment, he had planned a conference with Sheriff Williams in an effort to calm the waters of discourse that had been stirred up by their failure to inform him of the hit on Dewitt Strawberry. Since the information they had now recovered came from within Paul's office through his former employee, even the sensitive sheriff would understand that they had to move quickly and without his knowledge, provided they didn't delay too long in informing him. Paul had scheduled the meeting in his own office so he could answer the phone should someone attempt to reach him. To have met anywhere else would have left the office unattended. He was particularly hopeful that Mrs. Braid or even Tyrone might call him about possibly coming in, but he knew that was a long shot at best. His meeting with L.B. would be huge. Would L.B. jump in with Landon and himself or would he feel any allegiance toward the boys and try to diffuse the situation. There was no way for Paul to know.

When L.B. arrived at the appointed time, Paul had him come back to his office and make himself comfortable. He offered him coffee or a soda, but the sheriff declined both. It was obvious, at least to Paul, that the sheriff was suspicious of the purpose of the meeting by his actions, but that was to be understood after the last fiasco which resulted from their failing to keep him informed of the latest developments in the case. Perhaps he had a right to be a little suspicious.

Paul began the discussion by breaking the news to the sheriff that Tyrone was excluded as a possible suspect in GalBerry because of his alibi derived from robbing a house in another part of the county at the time of the murder. The sheriff could not contain his disappointment that he exhibited by shaking his head in disgust and drumming his fingers nervously on the arm of his chair. However, when he realized that at least he had him nailed on the burglary charge, his mood lightened a little.

"Black bastard will go back to Parchman for a stretch one way or the other," L.B. announced as if Paul had not considered that.

Paul then began a lengthy briefing about the planned hit, not only on Tyrone, but on Dewitt Strawberry as well, being careful not to leave out any vital information. Since he was the sheriff of the county, they would have to trust him to do his job lawfully and not hide any evidence from him, a decision Paul and Landon had come to after a long discussion the night before. Neither of them had been perfectly fine with that conclusion, but that was the situation in which they found themselves. L.B. listened in silent astonishment, his facial expressions showing new surprise with each name and revelation that Paul gave him. He never interrupted Paul until he was finished and that was the first time Paul ever remembered that occurring since he had known the sheriff. Paul was well aware that some of the named conspirators were very good friends and supporters of L.B. from way back and it had to hurt him to hear the adverse news. Paul watched his face as he spoke to him, looking for any indication that the sheriff didn't believe him or was hesitant to accept the truth. He saw nothing. When he finished, Paul asked him what he thought.

For the first time in his life as far as Paul knew, the sheriff was stunned and shocked at what he had just heard, so much so that he didn't respond to the question from Paul immediately, just looked down at his feet that were flat on the floor in front of his chair.

"God, almighty," L.B. said. The moment was so awkward that Paul wasn't sure if the sheriff was flabbergasted and commenting accordingly, or he was beginning a prayer. "How in the hell did it come to this?" he added.

"What do you mean, L.B.?" Paul wanted to know. He was so desperately trying to gauge his reaction.

"All of us have always talked about how much we hated niggers for years, but in my wildest dreams, I never thought of trying to kill one off vigilante-style," he confessed. "I knew that was the way things had been done in the past, but I thought that was back then and this was now. Never dreamed that kind of thing went on now, not to that extent, anyway. Always been a lot of bold talk, but no action by some. Can't believe some of the players here either."

"You understand the Emmitt Till case was just fourteen years ago and happened within less than an hour's drive of here, right? Also, it hasn't been but five years since they buried those civil rights workers in a dam over in Philadelphia, and two of the three of them were white. The past is not so distant, now is it?" Paul asked.

"I guess not. I just can't believe that *these* guys would plan something like that," L.B. responded.

"I know," Paul conceded. "You would think they had better things to do than get balled up into something like this. But look at Dewitt Strawberry. He was just a family man who scratched out a living from farming and he got caught up into it," Paul pointed out.

"Question is, what do we do now?" L.B. asked. He knew his political career was over as soon as he turned on his friends and past supporters, but the thought of entering Parchman Farm by trying to help these guys overtook any fear of being unemployed.

"We bust them," Paul said with a smile. "You in or not?" Paul knew for L.B. this had to be a tough decision, but he figured where his own posterior was concerned, L.B. would fold like a napkin. If he didn't join in, despite the political and social ramifications, Paul might go to the Hoover Boys up in D.C., and Stanton and the rest, maybe even including L.B., would go down anyway with the evidence he had.

"Oh, I'm in. I hate it, but I'm in," he said. "Where do you want to start?" He had thrown the boys under the bus with little thought.

"Bring Sam Baker in for questioning from the bank," Paul said.

Within the hour, Sam Baker had been brought to Paul's office, voluntarily for the time being, but he had no idea what they wanted to talk to him about. When they played part of the tape of his mistress spilling her guts about the affair and his role in the hits, he asked for water because of his mouth had become so dry. He took off his suitcoat and asked the sheriff to hang it up for him, revealing that he was sweating profusely to the extent that his white shirt underneath it had become soaked and was sticking to him despite the fact that the air conditioning was working perfectly. He had been read his rights under *Miranda* at the beginning of the interview and had said at that point he had nothing to fear and they may ask him any questions, but the tape had changed his attitude. Now he was scared, depressed and worried. He had no idea what else she might have told them, but he had to assume it was everything. Paul assured him it was.

"What are my options here?" he asked in desperation. Paul wasn't sure if he feared the prosecution or his wife more, but he told him that his life in the free world was over and if he had to guess, so was his marriage. In fact, under Mississippi law he was a principal in a murder for hire scheme that came with the death penalty if so sought and proven by the prosecutor.

"You tell me, Mr. Baker. Are you willing to risk the death penalty in this prosecution, or do you want to help yourself at this juncture?" Paul had him by the balls and he knew it, but now was the time to twist them tightly, not ease up.

"The only promise I can make you at this time is that the DA has authorized me to take the death penalty off the table if you cooperate in the prosecution of the remaining conspirators. Now, before you answer, don't think I am stupid and promise to do that today. You will be indicted and charged with capital murder and your actions in cooperating with us will determine if we seek the death penalty," he advised. Paul had come from behind his desk and was standing over the man who was nothing more than a basket of nerves at this point. The day was not working out as he thought when he got up this morning, obviously.

"Do I have to tell you right this minute?" Baker asked.

"Oh, no sir," Paul responded. "But my offer is good for the next five minutes only, so take your time."

"What do I have to do?" Baker asked sheepishly, knowing he was beaten.

Paul replaced the tape on the tape recorder and threaded it onto a reel. He hit the record button which started the reels turning and the record button flashing. He stepped away and dictated the same type of opening he had done with Karen, announcing who was in the room, the date and time and that this was a statement given freely after having been advised of his right to remain silent and his right to counsel.

"All you have to do now, Mr. Baker, is acknowledge that what I have just dictated is true and correct and then tell me in detail about your involvement in a murder for hire plot involving Tyrone Braid and Dewitt Strawberry," Paul told him. "Your cooperation will be most appreciated by me and you as well in the long run."

Unlike with Karen, when the man had finished his statement and answered all questions put to him by Paul and the sheriff, he was placed in handcuffs and held in custody at the Bolivar County jail. He was formally charged later that day and his bond was set at one hundred thousand dollars, an enormous amount but certainly understandable by all. Likewise, a warrant was issued for Karen Collins who was promptly picked up, placed in jail and a similar bond was set.

In order to keep the others from planning their testimony among themselves or leaving town on the run, individual warrants were issued for Morgan Tollison, James Baker, Reeves Spencer, Dr. Steve Davidson and of course, Stanton Merriweather. All of them were ordered to be held without bond pending further orders of the court. Each and every one, except Stanton Merriweather, would later request an opportunity to speak with the DA and cooperate in the investigation. Merriweather never asked, just simply retained his own attorney and waited for further proceedings.

The day had been a busy one for Paul and the sheriff and they both heaved a sigh of relief when it was over. They laughed about their success in the case, and then lamented the fact that they had to perform such a distasteful duty. Although it was impressive that they had infiltrated and broken a vicious murder for hire conspiracy, it was sad to think of the many families that would be adversely affected by the prosecution. It certainly was no one's fault but the conspirators, but the ripple effect would have far and everlasting effects on many in the county who had nothing to do with it.

"What say we go for a beer out at The Thicket?" Paul asked the sheriff. "That old gal out there makes a mean ham and cheese and great BLT as well," he added to entice the sheriff.

L.B. pulled his hat off, ran his fingers through his hair and replaced it. "Sounds like a winner," he said. "You owe me, anyway."

Both the men got up, put away the files that lay strewn across Paul's desk and exited the room. They climbed into Paul's car and headed out to the bar, leaving the sheriff's car in the parking space in front of the office. They had really done well, they thought.

CHAPTER 41

The Thicket was jumping on a Friday night, with its assortment of blue-collar workers and a smattering of professionals like Paul and the sheriff filling up the tables of the joint and the seats at the old bar as well. Credence Clearwater Revival blasted over the juke box and the smoke from cigarettes hung like a light fog over the room. This was relaxation Southern style at its very best. The waitresses couldn't keep up with the plates of sandwiches, burgers and sides and keep the pitchers of draft beer full at the same time. Paul and the sheriff had caused a little uneasiness when they walked into the place as law enforcement officers almost always did. Those who weren't eighteen yet found other places to party and those who had been there too long and consumed too much alcohol tried to steady themselves and not appear as drunk as they really were. Of course, there were those who could give a damn about the sheriff and an investigator with the DA's office seeing them in whatever inebriated state they may have been in at the time, and kept right on with their business. Finally, there was the steady string of yahoos that wanted to speak to the sheriff and remind him they supported him in the last election and pledged their eternal support thenceforth if he decided to run again. The sheriff was happy to see them all.

Paul grabbed a table while the sheriff spoke to his fans and ordered two Miller High Life beers for starters. He told the waitress that they would want some food as well, but she could take that order when they got their beers from her. Her shorts could not have been any shorter and still cover the subject Paul thought, and there was clearly more cotton in the top of an aspirin bottle than there was in them. When she returned, the sheriff was still with his posse of fans, so Paul took the liberty of ordering them both BLTs with a side of fries. It was the first time in a long while that Paul felt relieved enough to enjoy a beer. He pulled the tab on the can and flipped it onto the floor. He turned up the beer and chugged half of it before putting it back down. His highness, the sheriff was there at the table by then and started in on his beer as well.

Though the mood of the two was incredibly relaxed compared to what they had been in the last few weeks, the success of nailing the conspiracy boys was overshadowed by the knowledge that somewhere out there, a hit man was looking for his target, a target who was innocent of the charges for which he had been accused. With the boys in jail and all of it happening as quickly as it had, there was little way that the hit man could have been called off by Merriweather or any of the rest who may have known who he was or how he could be contacted. The *Bolivar Commercial* would come out tomorrow afternoon and the staff would surely be aware of the story of Bolivar's finest being busted for conspiracy to commit murder, and murder for hire, two counts each. It would probably scream across the front page, advising the world, but until then, there was a distinct possibility that the man was going to carry out his mission as he had been hired to do if he could find his target.

"We've still got a hit man on the loose, L.B.," Paul said.

"Yeah, but he's not going to get paid if his financiers have been put away. If he knows that, he'll keep the money they gave him and that will be it. Funny how when the money dries up, nobody does anything ain't it?" L.B. almost laughingly asked.

"You aren't concerned about the hit at all, now?" Paul asked him, finishing off his first beer.

"Not really. Soon as he finds out the boys are in jail and won't be giving him a payday, that's the end of it. The man ain't in it for his health. He'll find out about it sometime tomorrow and the rest will be history. He'll slink back into his hole and wait for another opportunity from somebody else maybe, glad he got paid for doing nothing, but mad he didn't get all that was coming to him," the sheriff speculated as he shook hands with another voter who walked past the table.

"I hope you're right," Paul added. The sandwiches had arrived and the sheriff did his best to drown the fries in ketchup before eating the first one.

"Relax, boy. Besides that, the Braid kid is in Chicago. Now, if he was here now, I'd be a little worried."

Paul nodded his agreement, his mouth full of sandwich. They ordered another round of beers and continued to eat.

@ @ @ @ @ @ @

The Greyhound Bus continued its very interrupted journey to the Delta and would be in Clarksdale, some 36 miles north of Cleveland on Highway 61, with a scheduled arrival of 7:50 a.m. Tyrone rested easy or at least as best he could with the frequent stops, the changing of passengers and the unloading and loading of luggage at almost every stop. He was already tired of the ride and had a way to go before he could get off the thing and go with John who he knew would be there waiting for him.

Back in Cleveland, a beige Plymouth driven by Edker Bentley zoomed down highway 61 toward Shaw and eventually over to Indianola in the darkness. He knew it was time for the whole Braid clan to get together in anticipation of the service Sunday afternoon and it was time to start some surveillance. He planned to ride over to the funeral home, take up a position where he could clearly see that large group of blacks coming and going and see if his man was among them. He was well prepared with his binoculars and a half pint of Jack Daniels that he sipped from the bottle as he drove. The skies that night could not have been clearer, with a new moon rising and casting a glow over the land that mimicked the daytime. The stars of the Milky Way were brightly lit against a dark canvas that added to the beauty of the night.

Edker found the funeral home and parked across the street in the lot of a closed clothing store, his car facing the funeral home so he would have the best point of view. The street lights, coupled with the light of that gorgeous moon, enabled him to view the face of each patron who entered or left the funeral home. He sat there for a period of at least three hours until he was sure anyone who had come had been viewed and that anyone who was going to visit that night had already arrived. His man was clearly not there, so he must not have arrived from Chicago. Perhaps if he had, he had stopped by the hospital to check on his sister, but that was unlikely. In all probability, he would make a beeline for the funeral home to see the entire family and then check on her later. His money was clearly on Tyrone not arriving yet from his hideout in Chicago.

As he was about to pull away from his point of observation, he saw a familiar vehicle that had pulled from around the building. He took a quick sip of the sour mash whiskey, set it down and picked up his binoculars. He scanned the face of the driver and recognized him. It was John Braid, still driving his deceased uncle's car. He cranked the Plymouth and after the brown Caddy was far enough away so as to not allow John to notice he was being followed, pulled out of the store lot and followed it. His original thought in attempting to find Tyrone was to follow John who appeared to chauffeur his brother, something he had learned from his hospital surveillance. John would eventually lead him to Tyrone, he thought. However, when his uncle had died, he had abandoned that theory and decided to look for his subject at the family gathering in honor of his uncle's life. Now, he was second guessing himself.

He followed the car, intermittently changing between sipping on the whiskey or smoking a cigarette as he did so. John went right where he thought he would, right back to his house on Highway 442 near Braid's Grocery. When John pulled into his drive, Edker slowed to see if anyone else was in the car, possibly laying down, but John was the only person to exit the vehicle. Knowing now that Tyrone was not with him, Edker picked up his speed and headed back to Cleveland. He would start in the morning fresh by watching the bus station in Cleveland and would get there early enough to see if any of his family, particularly John, would be there to meet him.

Paul had gotten home somewhere around 10:00 from the Thicket. He and L.B. had eaten, visited and had drunk a total of four beers each during that time, not nearly enough to impair their ability to drive, but enough to satisfy them that they had celebrated sufficiently from the previous day's accomplishments. He walked inside the house and began to strip down for bed. He had not heard from Mrs. Braid concerning Tyrone and that irked him. He decided he would call her one more time to impress on her the importance of his catching up with Tyrone, though he knew that his coming in would be a long shot. He tried her home number, her sister's number and was about to try to contact her through the funeral home, but thought better of it and hung up the phone. He walked into the kitchen and took a beer from the fridge, pulled the tab and tossed it into the wastebasket. He turned it up and took a drink, then turned it up again and took a chug of it. He had not thought of it before, but John may be able to assist him, if Victoria would not. He had John's number that he had gotten from Darcel of all people when he went to the house originally to interview Tyrone that time that seemed like months ago. In their conversation at the hospital, Lonnie had indicated that John and Tyrone were close.

He put his beer down on the lamp table, picked the phone back up and dialed the number he had stuck in his wallet. It was answered on the second ring and Paul could hear the television playing in the background.

"My name is Paul Lane and I am trying to get in touch with Victoria, would she be at this number?" he asked the person who answered.

"No, she is not," the man answered rather coolly.

"Am I speaking to John?" Paul asked.

"Yes." His tone had not changed.

"John, I haven't met you, but I work . . . "

"I know who you are and who you work for," John said, again rather shortly. "You don't need to be callin' here harassin' my auntie," he added.

"John, I don't know what you have been told, but I am not trying to harass anyone, I promise. I have information that your brother's life may be in danger and I at least need you to warn him if nothing else. I talked to your uncle Lonnie before he died and explained it to him and you evidently know I have talked to your aunt about this. I understand you have no reason to trust me, but you need to believe me, this is no trick, there is someone out there trying to kill him. Several people have been arrested today for their attempt to hire this hit man. You'll probably see it in the newspaper tomorrow, but it could be too late by then," Paul told him. He was encouraged that John had not hung up on him or at least not interrupted him while he was trying to explain.

John reached over and turned the television down so he could hear better, another good sign for Paul.

"How do you know about this?" John asked. Paul took the time to go through what they had discovered over the last few days. He told him about their suspicions about Tyrone and any connection he may have to the GalBerry case, but how they knew now he was not involved, though he didn't elaborate on how he had been excluded as a suspect. He even went so far as to tell him that they had Tyrone's car and where they had found it, making it suspicious that he would be in that area the night of the Strawberry murder.

"I'm the one who ran it in a ditch, man. Tyrone had nothing to do with it!" John interjected excitedly.

"It doesn't matter now, John. We know Tyrone had nothing to do with the murder, but the people who hired a killer to take him out believe it. I just want to make sure he doesn't get hurt," John pleaded. "Can you help me out?"

"What can I do, anyway?" John asked him.

"See if you can get him to come in and talk to me. I can guarantee his safety by taking him in to protective custody. If he won't do that, at least tell him to watch his backside all the time. There is no telling where this man may try to strike, but I feel confident that he will do so when Tyrone comes for his uncle's funeral," Paul replied.

"How did you know he was coming back for that?" John asked, puzzled that he knew.

"You just told me, John, you just confirmed it for me. And if I know it, you can bet the hired man knows it. Tyrone has got to be careful. Can you talk to him and at least warn him?" John pleaded again.

"I'll do what I can," John promised, and hung up the phone.

Paul sat there a few minutes with the phone in his hand listening to the silence. He had done all he could do at this stage of the game. He had pleaded with everyone he knew that was close to Tyrone Braid to convince him to come in to protective custody to no avail. He had interrogated the conspirators, but nobody in the group except for Merriweather knew the identity of the hit man so that he may be called off, and Merriweather wasn't talking. He had nothing to deal in order to make Merriweather talk, even if he would. Merriweather knew what he was facing if convicted. Might as well die in the gas chamber or spend life without parole for the death of Tyrone if you were going to do so anyway for the death of Dewitt. Paul had run out of options and there was absolutely nothing more he could do except let events run their course and hope for the best. He hung up the phone, downed his beer and went to the fridge for another one.

CHAPTER 42

Edker arose very early the next morning. He didn't sleep that much the night before because he had the pending job on his mind. He would have slept even less if he had not had the assistance of the whiskey. He was slightly hungover and in a foul mood consequently, to start the day. He showered, poured himself a cup of coffee and began the first of many, many cigarettes that he inhaled on a daily basis. When he finished his cup of coffee, he climbed into the beige Plymouth, forsaking the old pickup that he had because Tyrone might recognize it, and prepared to head to the bus station in Cleveland to watch for his target to arrive. Today was the day, he had convinced himself, that the boy would come home to his family. He hadn't been there yet and he wouldn't chance waiting until the day of the service to arrive because any slip-up in bus schedules would cause him to miss the whole affair. Today had to be the day. He reached behind the seat of the car and retrieved a double barreled twelve-gauge shotgun from the back seat. He breeched it open and made sure it was loaded, which it was, with two rounds of double-aught buckshot shells. In the glove compartment, was a half empty box of more shells, so he grabbed four more and stuffed them into the front pocket of his blue jeans. He cranked the old car and pulled out of his drive toward Cleveland. It was only 6 a.m.

John Braid was looking forward to the drive to Clarksdale to pick up his brother. It would give them time to talk and he could explain that he now knew where Tyrone's car was, but doubted seriously if Tyrone would go to the sheriff's office to retrieve it. He wondered if that crazy white man he had talked to on the phone the night before was real and knew what he was talking about, or if he was just scamming him to get Tyrone arrested. He would bet it was a scam, but in the back of his mind, he wondered why someone would concoct such an elaborate story to catch somebody like that. Usually, once they find out where a man was staying, they just found a way to get to him without asking him or trying to scam him by warning him like that. What was the deal here, anyway? The more he thought about it, the stranger it got and it made John a little paranoid, to the extent that he watched every car behind him or that passed him going the same direction on the highway with suspicions, as if it could have evil intentions.

Like Edker, John had arisen early, dressed and was on his way to Clarksdale by six that morning, and had gotten to Cleveland a short time afterwards when he got behind a beige Plymouth at a red light on the highway. Edker recognized him in his rearview mirror and slowly pulled away from the light after it changed, causing the impatient black man to pass him shortly thereafter. Edker would follow him to the bus station, certain that was his destination and collect his prize shortly thereafter. When John pulled into a gas station for fuel, Edker did likewise, just to make sure that wasn't a rendezvous point for his brother. He pulled to the service area of the station, got out and pretended to check the air in the tires of the old car and waited—and listened. John asked the attendant for three dollars-worth of gas and got out of the Cadillac to get a drink from the soda machine. Another car pulled up to the opposite side of the pump that John was occupying and a young black man got out after asking the attendant for a fill-up. He and John obviously knew each other and carried on a raucous conversation after exchanging soul shakes.

"Come on and go with me, man, we'll be back by this afternoon," the man told John.

"Can't do it, dude. Gotta lot to do today. My uncle died and his service is tomorrow. Lotsa family in town. Goin' to pick up my brother, now," John told him. Edker smiled as he replaced the cap on the valve stem of one of the tires of his car.

"Sorry man, didn't know. Yo brother live in Cleveland?" the man asked.

"Naw, he been up in Chicago. Gotta go to Clarksdale to pick him up at the bus stop there," John answered.

Bingo, thought Edker, again unable to control a smile. Niggers can never keep their mouth shut, he thought and he had just learned more in a matter of minutes than his surveillance had produced over the last couple of weeks. He replaced another cap and started back to his car. When he pulled out of the gas station, John was still talking to his buddy and Edker drove away to another business about a half a mile away and pulled over again. He would just wait and follow the Caddy and his motor-mouthed driver all the way to Clarksdale and the bus station. Edker didn't know where the station was located in Clarksdale, but he would be happy to allow John to show him. No more than five minutes later, the brown Caddy with John at the wheel passed him on his way north, oblivious to the fact that he was now being tailed. What a dumbass, Edker thought, again.

@ @ @ @ @ @

Paul received a call early that morning from *The Bolivar Commercial* reporter, Jed Burns, seeking information and a quote on the arrest of the distinguished men yesterday. The jackals are up early, I see, and they are hungry, he thought. As bad as he would have liked to tell the paper what he thought of the whole bunch and very meticulously lay out their sins, he refrained and referred all questions to either Landon Fall, the District Attorney or Sheriff L.B. Williams. They needed their time in the sun anyway, especially considering the fact that they were prosecuting Bolivar County's finest while attempting to save a black man for Christ's sake! He fumbled around the kitchen for cereal and orange juice, ate and plopped down in front of the television to watch Saturday morning cartoons, a passion of his, the knowledge of which he shared with no one, but immensely enjoyed. The phone would ring again and again during the morning from media outlets in the area and he would send them to Landon and L.B each time until they finally ended somewhere close to ten o'clock.

@ @ @ @ @ @

John Braid pulled into the parking lot of the bus station in Clarksdale, sometime shortly after seven o'clock that morning, well ahead of the expected 7:50 arrival of the bus. He parked and got out to stretch his legs, went to the restroom and then purchased another soda from a machine out front. He knew he was early, but better to be early than late and have to listen to Tyrone chastise him all the way back to the house. He did not notice, nor did he have any reason to notice, a beige Plymouth pass the station, head down the street and then stop and turn around, heading back toward him. It pulled over to the right-side curb and parked, a hundred yards or so from where John had parked his uncle's Cadillac. John got back in his car, switched on the radio and laid back in the front seat, patiently waiting for Tyrone to arrive. Edker, just up the street, watched his every move through his binoculars.

At 7:40, ahead of schedule for a change, the big gray bus turned the corner at the station and rumbled into the parking lot. A crowd of passengers began filing off, one by one, some waiting there for the driver to deliver their luggage from the underneath compartment of the bus, while others either entered the station or met friends and relatives waiting for them. As usual, Tyrone was one of the last to get off, luggage in hand and looked around for a familiar face. John never got out of the car, merely honked the horn of the Cadillac and waved out the driver's side window at his brother. Tyrone saw him, waved back and headed to the car, climbing in on the passenger side of the front seat. Moments later, John cranked the car and pulled out on the street heading for Highway 61 and all points south. The Plymouth waited a minute, like a snake waiting to strike, and then followed a safe distance behind. Edker was in no hurry. There was nothing he could do until they got out into the country, away from any witnesses.

Approximately 17 miles out of town and some twenty minutes later, the two cars, John and Tyrone in the brown Cadillac and Edker in the beige Plymouth a quarter mile or so behind, passed the small Bolivar County town of Duncan, nothing more than a store and what was left of an old plantation. From there for a distance of miles was nothing more than cotton fields on either side of the highway, the only roads intersecting 61 being small, lightly traveled, gravel farm roads.

Though John didn't notice until the car was almost alongside him, the Plymouth had increased speed from its position behind him and had caught up with him and proceeded to pass. When he was perfectly alongside, Edker held the wheel with one hand and pointed the double barrel shotgun toward the Cadillac and its occupants with the other. A deafening boom shattered the driver's side window and the Cadillac careened off the highway onto the embankment of the ditch, bounded up the other side and came to rest on the opposite side of the ditch surrounded by high stalks of cotton. There was no movement from either of the occupants in the car, just the cloud of dust from the abrupt stop in the cotton field and the sound emitting from the idling engine.

Edker slammed to a stop after whipping over onto the shoulder of the highway and burst out of the Plymouth, breaching the double barrel as he did and reloading with two new shells as the empty hulls from the first blast ejected onto the ground. He had yet to see movement from within the Caddy and when he approached it, he snatched open the door and leveled the shotgun at the two bodies lying across the front seat. There was an instant blast and everything fell quiet.

Edker backed away, bending over as he did and then falling backwards onto the grass and dirt of the bank of the ditch. He was dead before he hit the ground, the shot from a .38 caliber pistol splitting his aorta as it penetrated his chest from near point-blank range. Inside the Cadillac, Tyrone and John scrambled from both doors, both of them bleeding profusely from shattered glass and lead pellets that had found their mark, but were not life threatening.

Tyrone's left arm dangled helplessly at his side, the bone of the upper arm splintered by buckshot. His entire left side seemed to be bleeding and his shirt was soaked in minutes. His face was covered in blood from the flying glass from the window that had been fragmented by the shotgun blast. John, though alive, was in worse condition than was Tyrone, his body taking the brunt of the simultaneous double blast from the shotgun. His shoulder and left arm were mangled, and the injury to his left side made it painful to breathe, indicating some ribs had been demolished. Like Tyrone, his face was bleeding profusely from the flying glass and lead. Both stumbled across the ditch and onto the highway's shoulder, each in tremendous pain but happy to be alive. They avoided the body of Edker that lay prostrate on the ground, only feet from their car.

It seemed that from out of nowhere, cars began stacking up and causing a traffic jam along the side of the highway, some stopping to help believing there had been an automobile accident, the others slowing down just to gawk at the scene. Someone called an ambulance for the two injured ones as well as the Coroner and Sheriff's Department for Edker. The Sheriff's deputy was the first to arrive and roped off the scene so it would not become tainted by anyone. Another did his best to keep traffic moving to eliminate the traffic jam. The ambulance arrived next and both Tyrone and John were loaded onto stretchers and placed inside where they were transported back to the all too familiar East Bolivar County Hospital for treatment. After a second ambulance arrived Edker was transported to the hospital as well, for safekeeping in the morgue after the coroner had pronounced him dead. From the outset, the deputies began to process the scene by taking photographs with instant cameras and noting the location of potential evidence. The shotgun, still loaded, two spent 12-gauge hulls, a .38 caliber revolver, loaded with five rounds, one of them fired, were all picked up at the scene, bagged and placed into a box in the back of one of the patrol cars. Wreckers came and towed both cars for processing later and were towed to the impound lot of the sheriff's office, and each was covered with a tarp. Ironically, the two were stored next to the '62 Ford belonging to Tyrone.

CHAPTER 43

Paul had just sat down to eat his lunch consisting of a frozen pizza that he had cooked along with a large glass of sweet iced tea when his phone rang for no less than the tenth time that morning. Everyone from *The Clarion Ledger* in Jackson, to the *Commercial Appeal* in Memphis, and all newspapers in between wanted to find out the details of the conspiracy gang. He referred them as he had all morning, to the DA and the sheriff for any comment. This probably was just another media source wanting more, he thought to himself. He was surprised when the familiar voice of the sheriff sounded in the receiver.

"Paul, it looks like we have a shooting up on Highway 61 near Duncan this morning. Sounds like the hit we were afraid of. I understand there's one dead and two injured, but don't know much more than that. I'm walking out of the office and headin' to the scene. I want you to meet me there if you can," the sheriff told him.

Paul's heart was in his throat. "I'm on my way," he said.

He pulled on some jeans and cowboy boots, buttoned up a shirt over the t-shirt he had slept in the night before and went to his car. Dammit, he thought, what else could I have done? He peeled out of his drive, hit the blacktop road and was on Highway 61 speeding north from Cleveland in a matter of minutes. When he arrived on the scene, the deputy who had first arrived gave him a rundown of what he had found when he got there: A dead white man, and two bloody black guys.

"Them nigger boys told me the white guy tried to kill 'em and they ended up in the ditch. He tried again and one of 'em shot him. Least that's what they sayin'," he told Paul. "The dead man is identified as

Edker Bentley from over in Leflore County according to his driver's license. He's been transported to the morgue at East Bolivar. Them two niggers are identified as Tyrone Braid and John Braid, both with a Shaw address, but they told me they lived in Sunflower County. They been transported to East Bolivar. Both of 'em bloody as stuck hogs and hurt bad, but they goin' to be all right, I think."

"What about weapons?" Paul asked the deputy.

"Picked up a double barrel 12 gauge, still loaded with two rounds in it right beside the dead man. Got a .38 caliber revolver, four live rounds and one fired round in it from the front seat of the Cadillac on the driver's side. Lotsa blood in there, too. Don't know if the lead shot or the glass eat 'em up so bad, but they was cut up pretty good," he advised Paul.

Paul and the sheriff talked to each other on the side of the highway and both agreed this was the scenario they had both feared for a while now. It didn't take a professional to figure out exactly what had happened. The boys in the Caddy had been ambushed from the driver's side by the man in the Plymouth who had fired on them causing them to crash. He could have just run them off the road, but according to the deputy on the scene, there was no damage to the fender of either vehicle. They wouldn't be sure until they questioned the Braid boys, but in all probability, knowing what they knew about the case before, John was probably driving, with Tyrone on the passenger side. The biggest question right now, other than for them to corroborate what Paul suspected had happened, was who fired the shot that killed Edker Bentley and how did he get the chance.

The sheriff had more pictures taken of the scene even though it duplicated those taken earlier. Tire tracks and skid marks were particularly photographed since the vehicles were no longer there. That was about all there was left to do. Paul wanted to talk to the Braid brothers but he assumed they were sedated and being treated for injuries at the hospital. He would go up tomorrow afternoon and see what they had to say. Looks like Tyrone is not going to make his uncle's service after all, Paul thought.

The following day after church and a Sunday meal of a hamburger and fries from The Keene Freeze, a hamburger joint in Cleveland, Paul headed over to the hospital. When he got off the elevator on the third floor, he was surprised to see Victoria Braid there, assuming she would be at the church for the funeral of her husband. There was a small crowd gathered there with her, all black, of course. As he neared the group, Victoria recognized him and came over and gave him a hug, surprising him even further.

"I want to thank you for what you did," she expressed to him

I'm not sure I did anything ma'am. Everything I tried to do failed," he returned.

"That's not true. We all know you tried to save my nephew and we just didn't believe you. Furthermore, without your warning us of what might happen, I would have never given Lonnie's gun to John to carry with him for protection in case you were telling the truth," she told him. "We thank you, Mr. Lane."

"Call me, Paul," he said with a smile. The others around her wanted to shake his hand and introduce themselves to Paul, almost all of which were family members of Lonnie.

"You know, Paul, it's funny really. Lonnie has taken care of those two boys almost all of their lives, whenever he could. Now it looks like he's still taking care of them, even though he's gone, by letting them use his gun. Neither of them ever had a father and neither one of them even owns a gun," Victoria told him as she began to cry.

Paul talked to those in the group for a few minutes and then asked about Darcel and the brothers. Darcel had shown movement toward consciousness and the family was elated. The doctor had confirmed that was a good sign and was cautiously optimistic for her recovery for the first time. As for the brothers, they were as fine as could be expected, but they had some serious mending to do. He asked if they were well enough to talk with him and Victoria said they were. As soon as a couple came out of the room dressed in their Sunday best from visiting with them, Paul went in alone.

He introduced himself to both of them, reminding both that they had either talked with him before or seen him. Tyrone had the privilege of running from him in Chicago, while John had talked to him just a couple nights ago on the phone. When they realized Paul harbored no hard feelings, the mood in the room became lighter. They even laughed about Tyrone fleeing and John being an ass on the phone. Paul said he understood.

He took a chair and dragged it between the two beds that the brothers occupied. From his briefcase, he withdrew a legal pad and ink pen. He scribbled the date time and place for the moment and proceeded to question the men. Paul got right down to the interview, and each one told his story as they remembered it. They had been surprised by Edker on the highway and he had gotten the drop on them, fortunately doing no more damage than he did with the first blast. They were hurt bad after they crashed into the field, but John had convinced Tyrone to stay down in the seat in the hope that Edker would go away thinking they were dead. When they heard him stop his vehicle, get out and come toward them, John had drawn the .38 he had stuck in his pants with his right hand, the only one he had that he was still able to use. If Edker had shot them again through the open window, they would be dead now, but when he opened the door to the car and John saw the shotgun, he pointed the gun and fired. He could not have been more accurate and lethal if he had held the gun squarely against Edker's chest.

"Based upon what I knew about the hit and what I saw at the scene, you have told me exactly what I thought had happened," Paul announced.

"So, we not in trouble?" John asked.

"No sir, not at all," Paul confirmed. "However, there's a little problem Tyrone and I are going to have to work on stemming from a burglary in Shaw on August 4. Do you remember that, Tyrone?"

Tyrone looked down from his position up on his pillow and nodded his head, obviously embarrassed. The demons from his earlier days at Parchman flooded his thoughts and he felt nauseated.

"I'll tell you what, though, you get better and we'll talk about that then. It's not going away, but there's nothing to be gained by doing anything right this minute," Paul told him. Unfortunately, your parole officer has already placed a hold on you for violating your parole by leaving the state and going to Chicago. When they discharge you from the hospital, they'll just transport you to the jail until you deal with that as well. Sorry, but that's out of my hands," Paul added almost apologetically. "By the way, what about Lonnie's service?"

"They moved it to Wednesday because of all this," Tyrone said. "We supposed to get out of here by then. I guess they won't let me go there because of the hold, will they?"

"No sir, you have to remain in custody. But I'll tell you what, I admired your uncle very much, what little I was around him, and I plan to attend. I'll take you with me so you'll still be in custody. You mind going with a honky?" Paul asked him with a laugh.

"No sir, I don't, if you don't mind goin' with a nigger," he laughed back.

"Done deal, then," Paul said to him. "I'll get back with you before Wednesday." He gathered his legal pad and pen and stuffed it into his briefcase and headed out the door. He spoke to Victoria one more time before he left and caught the elevator as it let another person off on the floor.

CHAPTER 44

By the end of that week, Lonnie Braid had been buried, Tyrone was being held for a parole violation, and the news of the murder for hire plots had just about died down completely. The boys were all locked up and would remain that way for a long, long time, unless Landon backed off the death penalty after talking to the family members of Dewitt Strawberry. Paul, had hired a new receptionist, a lady old enough to be his mother who had applied for the job and had more secretarial experience than all the other applicants combined. The sheriff accused him of hiring her so he didn't have to worry about her sleeping with someone and telling his secrets like the last one. Though that was certainly not the case, Paul had no doubt that he need not worry about her sleeping around.

Landon and Paul met just after lunch on Friday afternoon so that Paul could brief Landon on the cases that he had under investigation, something they routinely did, but not necessarily every week. They would normally meet over sandwiches brought in, but Friday happened to be the day that Rotary Club met in Cleveland at noon and Landon was as faithful in those meetings as most people are about church on Easter, his job permitting.

Paul gathered up some files from his desk, stuffed them into his briefcase, and told his receptionist that he would be out for a couple hours. He ambled across the courthouse lawn, past the Confederate statue and across to Landon's office. The crowd at Brock's across the street didn't seem as large as it had when the boys met there, seemingly at every meal, but it was busy nonetheless. He entered Landon's office, spoke to his receptionist and helped himself to a coke from the refrigerator in the hall on the way back to Landon's private office. Landon was already there and waiting. They went through the files, Landon commenting on each from his swivel chair behind the big mahogany desk that dominated the furniture in his office. Landon sat across from him shuffling papers and giving Landon the play by play on each case he had in his office that was still open.

When they had finished, Paul began putting the files back into his briefcase and collecting his legal pads in readiness to leave.

"What's on your mind, Paul? I sense some disgruntlement," Landon asked as he watched Paul packing up.

"No big deal. I didn't bring up GalBerry and you didn't ask about it," Paul replied, zipping his briefcase and finishing off the coke that was hot by now. "Are you as frustrated by it as I am?"

"Probably not, but then I've been in the business longer than you and understand the realities of prosecuting cases better, I believe," he told Paul. He had reared back in his leather chair with his hands behind his head.

"I mean, we have gotten absolutely nowhere on it. L.B. thought he had a suspect in Tyrone and frankly, so did I at one point. Then Wayne Milton confesses and that's a bust as well, since I don't believe he had anything to do with it. We've had the father of one of the victims killed over it, an ambush of two totally innocent people in connection with it, and we still haven't gotten off first base. It's like a bad dream that we can't stop. You're telling me that doesn't bother you?" Paul asked, standing at the door with his briefcase in tow, ready to leave.

"Didn't say it doesn't bother me. It does, but probably not as much as it apparently bothers you," Landon replied. "You see Paul, you have to learn to recognize the victories when they come so that they offset the losses. Yes, we still have a killer out there somewhere, unless Wayne Milton really did it, which after his suicide, a lot of the people believe he did. Neither you or I know the truth there, and probably never will. But in the process of investigating those murders, we busted one of the most heinous group of thugs that ever marred the reputation of this county. Seven people altogether sit in jail because of what we managed from our investigation of GalBerry. Sure, one of the victim's father was killed, but whose fault is that? Neither you or anybody else can blame us for that. Okay, two people were seriously hurt by a hit man, but if not for your relentless warnings and efforts to protect one of them, both of them would probably be dead now. A killer who had no qualms about taking a human life or two for cash is dead and we don't have to worry about him anymore. I say good riddance. So, ask yourself Paul, all in all, is the investigation a complete waste of time? Would you rather have these people free, Dewitt Strawberry alive and the Braid brothers dead in exchange for solving the case and convicting the culprit? I don't know about you, but short of no crime happening at all in the first place, I'll take what we have," he said, leaning forward in his chair and looking right into Paul's eyes.

"Do we keep looking for a suspect, then?" Paul asked.

"Damn right we do. We never quit, but sometimes the leads run out. We'll keep our eyes open and see what develops," Landon responded.

"I hear you, boss, I hear you. We'll get him one day," Paul said, with a smile. He turned and walked out the door, helping himself to yet another coke as he passed the fridge in the hall.

@ @ @ @ @ @ @

September in Mississippi was every bit as hot and humid as August, until the final days of the month at least. In the minds of the citizenry, it didn't appear so because of the nearness of fall, that welcome time when the north wind blew from time to time, bringing changes in the temperature and the color of the hardwood trees at the same time. September also meant football time in Mississippi and the Rebels of Ole Miss were expected to have a banner year with a red-headed quarterback named Archie Manning, a product of the Delta himself from over in Drew. It was hard to think about football without thinking of cooler temperatures. All of that influenced everyone's perception of the weather and it made a stunning difference.

At the Interstate Baptist Church, the pastor was meeting with the chairman of the Harvest Festival, an event that coincided with the Thanksgiving holiday and featured a true smorgasbord of delicacies from the many church members who had all seemingly been raised in the kitchen. It was a big event for the church and behind only Christmas or Easter in importance to the flock. It required months of preparation because of its importance and popularity to the members.

W.D. Kirksey sat behind his desk talking to the lady who had the burden of her small world on her shoulders at the present time. As chairman, if the festival was a failure, she would bear the shame of it, something no one wanted in a small church or community like Interstate, where the trivial sometimes took on immense proportions. They talked for a good hour, setting the proposed date, the budget and all the other things that seem so important when you are engaged in such an activity. When they finished their skull session, he thanked the church member for her dedication, promised that she had his total support and walked her out of his office, talking to her as they walked. They were met at the door by the woman's daughter, a girl of 18 who had just enrolled and begun the fall semester at Delta State College, having recently finished formal rush and pledging Phi Mu. She had dropped by to see her mother before returning to the dorm, having seen her car parked at the church.

The pastor smiled and the three spoke briefly before the mother and daughter headed out to their cars. The pastor continued to watch as the two walked away, enjoying the view of the young girl's backside in her cutoff shorts and the dark tan that she sported, a byproduct of a summer at the private community pool where her family was a member. Interestingly, the pool had been previously owned and operated by the City of Shaw but was sold for one dollar to a group of whites, allowing the pool to remain open, but disallowing entry to any blacks because it was then private and not public.

When they had gone, he returned to his office and sat behind his desk again. He reached into the middle drawer of his desk, retrieved a plastic sandwich bag and took out the items contained in it. He rolled the items around in his hand for a few minutes, toying with them, and at one point held them close to his face and under his nose so he could sense any smell that they may have had. After a few minutes, he placed the items back in the bag, folded it closed and returned it to the drawer. There were two items in the bag, a small opal ring and second ring with a small diamond cluster setting.